What Others Are Saying

The contents of this book captured my attention from start to end so much so that I could not stop reading it. The book is about the immeasurable love from God; and there is no doubt that the creative and agile mind of the writer is able to make the reader feel that even though the principal character suffered tragic abandonment, God changed his story and destiny and provided a surprising resolution. This story will fill the reader with faith and hope.

—Beatriz De Granados
Associate pastor of Jesus is King and
Lord Church of El Salvador

This is by far one of the best spiritual novels I have ever read! It reads like a biography and keeps you on the edge of your seat, rooting for Eduardito to find stability and happiness. This book deserves to be made into a movie and translated to several other languages. Kudos to Ana Lillian for her brilliance in describing the tragic but not hopeless lives of all the Eddys out there!

—Federico Hirlemann, SPHR, CHP, CPP, MBA
Chief Financial Officer/HR Director

Totally sad that I had no more pages to read! This book touched my heart! I encourage you to read it. It is spectacular because it has not been written by a spectacular woman but because God used her to bring this story to touch many hearts! Only God restores, transforms, and changes the old man to a new one.

When God has chosen you, even if you reject Him, thousands of his alerts. And even if you do the wrong things, cry, whine, or try to hide, there is nothing that will stop God's purpose from being realized!

—Ivania De Safie
Businesswoman, wife, and mother

A very moving book which makes you think deeply. You can identify with the main character, Eduardo, in so many ways. It is so moving that it will make you cry with all the ups and downs in Eduardo's life. So good that you do not want to stop reading it until you know what happens all the way to the end (like I did in one night)! I recommend it to strengthen your faith. I am waiting for more novels like this one, for it has been a blessing to me! I love reading, and this is a treasure! The Holy Spirit was definitely present in the making of this book.

—Dr. Alejandra Mira Rosas
Physcian, Wife and mother

There is no doubt that the writer was inspired by the Holy Spirit. Believer or nonbeliever, this story will make an impact on your heart! It describes the hard reality of the country El Salvador during the war and that faced by the characters who lived through it. On the contrary, it illustrates faithfully without getting to a traumatic drama for the reader all the issues involved during the war. It creates the big desire to continue reading to learn about the outcome of the story. Very proud of this literary and spiritual work written by a Salvadoran writer.

—Lula Lubiere
Businesswoman, wife, and mother

I loved the excellent narrative of the book. I laughed and cried and did not want to stop reading it! I feel that my faith has become stronger. Thank you, AnaLillianMunguia, a proud Salvadoran writer. God bless you.

—Gloria De Lopez
Housewife and mother

My friend, I finished reading your book at 3:00 a.m.! I couldn't stop reading! I loved it! What a testimony! Then I couldn't sleep thinking of all the Eduardos out there. You made me cry and also meditate on the day I met Christ and helped me change my life. With Christ in my heart, I see everything so differently, and I have joy even in the hard times. I was able to identify myself with several characters in many parts of the novel, and I enjoyed it a lot! Thanks, my friend, for such a great story. May God bless you and give you success but, mostly, help you deliver this novel to many people who feel lost and haven't learned about how wonderful it is to know Jesus and find their paths through Him.

—Andie Rossell
Mother and grandmother

A VERDICT

CHANGED BY GOD

ANA MUNGUIA

A VERDICT
CHANGED BY GOD

YorkshirePublishing
www.yorkshirepublishing.com
Write Now.

ISBN: 978-1-946977-59-5

A Verdict Changed By God—English Version

Copyright © 2016 by Ana Munguia

Yorkshire Publishing
3207 South Norwood Avenue
Tulsa, Oklahoma 74135
www.YorkshirePublishing.com
918.394.2665

I dedicate this book to Yahweh Almighty; to Yeshua, my personal Savior; and to the Ruaj HaKodesh, who inspired this novel.

I also dedicate this to my beloved husband, Hans, and to my three children, Anna Andrea, Xavier Eduardo, and Anna Rebecca, my fellow dreamers, first readers and first fans.

Acknowledgments

I am grateful to my cyber tutors, Steve Harrison and Jack Canfield, for their Bestseller Blueprint Internet course. It is where I learned that when I finish a book, I should give it to a few people for them to read and to get feedback, comments, suggestions, and constructive criticism from them to improve it. Therefore, I am grateful for the people who believed in this project and were kind enough to read a rough draft, taking time from their busy schedules. Thank you for helping me to produce the final output.

I am mostly grateful with my beloved husband, Hans, and my three children: Anna Andrea, Xavier Eduardo, and Anna Rebecca, who became my fellow dreamers and let me have the periods of time away from them to focus on fulfilling this dream, which my Heavenly Father implanted in my heart.

A million thanks to all my Spanish fans and readers, who have encouraged me to continue with the translation of this novel in English and have motivated me in the promotion to making the movie.

I cannot adequately describe my gratitude to Pastor Philemon Samuels of the Fresh Bread Ministries International in Jamaica. He has given me the courage and enthusiasm to write this novel, plus the gift of being a great role model as a leader, pastor, and missionary. Pastor Philemon had the kindness to acknowledge this novel and write the foreword. I really appreciate his wisdom and his friendship and that of his staff and all the people who have been going on missions to El Salvador since 2005.

A very special thank-you to Pastor Eduvigis Nerio and his wife, Marty, for all their feedback, corrections, and help in putting together this novel and making my dream a reality.

Thank you very much to everyone for having given me the strength and the encouragement to continue this project and for believing that this novel will reach millions of people around the world, giving them peace and directing them to God, who is waiting for us to surrender ourselves to him. Thank you for believing that this novel can become a best seller and a Hollywood hit.

Contents

Foreword

Proverbs 21:19 (NIV) declares that "Many are the plans in a person's heart, but it is the LORD's purpose that prevails." This means that God has a way of interweaving the negative experiences of life caused many times by our bad decisions into His purpose for our lives when we eventually surrender to Him.

The grace and love of God is truly shown in a remarkable way in this story. It shows that no one is beyond the reach of these amazing virtues. This story brings encouragement and hope to all who have seen and experienced the obstacles that life throws. However, in the midst of despair, God shows up and divinely orchestrates the people, circumstances, and events that would radically impact our lives so that we may discover the purpose for our existence.

For indeed no one is beyond the scope of God's redemptive love. He specializes in changing people's stories. He has the final word on our destiny. This story is intriguing and compelling because it speaks of a journey that started with so much pain and so many mishaps complicated by bad decisions and uncontrollable deaths; yet God's power, grace, and love have brought on such a great outcome.

This story truly mirrors the lives of thousands of people around the world. If you are one of those persons described in this book, I pray that you will find hope, encouragement, faith, and purpose, to achieve by God's grace a similar outcome in your life.

—Pastor Philemon Samuels
Senior Pastor, Fresh Bread Ministries International (Jamaica)

Preface

Upon my meditation and deciding on my goals for 2011, God put it in my heart to write a novel about a Salvadoran. (I chose a man, not a woman, to make it more dramatic.)

El Salvador is a beautiful country, the smallest in Central America, (The Little Thumb of America as it was known). It is approximately the size of Israel or Rhode Island to put you in perspective and it has a population of 6 million It is a country that during the '70s was considered "the land of the smile." It even hosted the 1975 Miss Universe pageant in those gracious years of peace and prosperity.

Everything changed when in the late'70s and early 80s, a group of displeased citizens rose against the affluent and the working class, arming themselves with communist ideals. They were the guerrillas. The soldiers defended the state of liberty, but the guerrillas wanted what the rich had to this date.

The Salvadorans suffered from the war in different degrees—depending on the family one grew up in. Many events of political unrest happened in those days—including a coup d'état to overthrow the last military president in the history of El Salvador, General Carlos Humberto Romero, who was a fine man.

A governing body was formed. Later on, a new presidential elections without having a Colonel or General as president (which was a requisite before the coup d'état for the governing party). Then that was followed by: new political parties, agrarian reform, bank nationalization, extremely high taxes on imported goods (including refrigerators, stoves, cars, etc.), strikes and demonstrations, graffiti, tires on fire, bridges blown up, blackouts, government-imposed curfews, etc. All that destruction became the norm in people's daily life. In those days, many young people, complete families, and successful businessmen left the country—

as a consequence, also they left behind other relatives, businesses, homes, and priceless possessions.

With the *Chapultepec Peace Accords signed, the end of the war came upon the country.* It was signed in January 1993 and in the mid-90s. prosperity came back to the country, more political parties were formed, and the guerrillas became a formal political party (an opposing party for the right wing who started to govern the country, and did so for 20 years). Prosperity began as the successful entrepreneurs returned to this beloved country and invested on reconstruction.

Nowadays, the guerrillas, who started the war, are the actual governors—even the actual president (2014–2019) one of the highest guerrilla thinkers in the '80s who is only a high school graduate with specialty as a teacher, is the one that govern our country. They won the war 25 years later by getting into power. We do not know what the outcome of our country will be by having the guerrilla party governing us for the second presidential term in a row; but what we remember is the suffering that we Salvadorans have lived through in those days of war. Now-a-days, we have another type of suffering with the gangs who have invaded our country (just like the guerrillas did more than thirty years ago): again, the country has a lack of investors, and many people are leaving out of fear from gang violence and that the country will go bankrupt with the new Socialist thinking in government. We have a war with no soldiers out there to defend us. The gangs kill twenty to thirty people daily and saldly, no one is stopping them. Many of the gang members started with the deported people from the U.S.A. who did not find jobs, but this is another story.

I grew up exactly in those days—in the '70s and '80s. I lived part of this drama in a different way than the one featured in this novel. I was part of the drama and one of the people who migrated in 1980 but in my case to go to college in USA. I saw the demonstrations of U.S. OUT OF EL SALVADOR that went around the Federal Building near my university. Having believed in my country, I came back in 1983, after graduation, when the new presidential elections took place. To this day, I still ask myself if I did the right thing by coming back!

I talked with people who suffered from the war, investigating the different paths that people took in the '60s to the '90s and even up to 2014. I found the stories to be with dramatic differences—some of great successes and others of great failures. As I said, the decisions we made, the paths we followed, and the means of survival we used during the years of the civil war affected our future, which is our present.

This story represents, in some way or another, part of the lives of so many Salvadorans around the world—the ones who migrated and also the brave ones who stayed and the ones that returned voluntarily or deported. With this story, God has launched me into the world as a writer. There is no doubt that the Holy Spirit has inspired it since I am the first one who is surprised with the result. There are many emotions captured in this story, including many of my own during those years.

But the real meaning of and reward from the process and experience of writing this novel is the discovery of my real passion. I love writing and I aim to write novels to inspire people to have faith and hope and to encourage them to look for God and His purpose for them in their life! It is also my dream to make this story a Hollywood movie, so after reading it, please write to me telling your experience upon reading it. Recommend this book, and help me to help many people around the world to find hope, plus help to make it a bestseller and a movie. Dream with me.

1

Eddy's Stormy Beginning

It was a sunny day filled with people around me. I could feel the breeze against my face. Everyone was dressed in either black or white. The people's facial expressions ranged from sad to somber. There were some who cried. And then there were some people who looked at me with a "Poor boy" expression, like they pitied me. Some carried me in their arms, hugged me, cried, and told me "Everything will be okay, Eddie"; then afterward, they put me down.

At that time, I didn't understand their sorrow, their hurt. I was going to be four years old in a month. I did not understand what was going on. There was a coffin in the middle of the room, and I could not even see what's inside. People walked up to see the person inside and said, "Poor thing." But I did not figure out that they were talking about me. The people whispered, "Poor thing. Now she rests in peace," referring to the person in the coffin.

I was playing with a stick while staying close to the coffin. Suddenly, I hit the coffin to get my mother's attention because I didn't see her and I missed her. I didn't know where she was. I thought that by doing that, she would come looking for me and scold me.

There were other kids around that I played with for a while, but then I would go back instinctively. I tried to distract myself because I didn't understand (or maybe didn't want to understand). *And Mother?* I thought. *Why doesn't Mom hug me yet other people do?... Where is my dad?*

My dad was suffering and I didn't even see it. He greeted many people. They went up to him and hugged him. Some had tears in their eyes (at least from what I've seen from afar). Then I saw my father trying to get a good view of where I was. Most of the time, I was hitting the coffin with the long stick. I hit it and hit it and hit it once again, trying to get someone's attention. Then I got bored and went back to playing with the other kids and repeated the cycle.

After a while, I went back to my spot under the coffin with the stick. I was only trying to get my mother's attention, but she never came to me. Suddenly, my father reacted: with all the sorrow in his heart, he came for me and got me from under the coffin. He carried me and hugged me tight, and I hugged him back. I felt loved, but I still did not understand why my mother wasn't there for me.

After all the people left that night, we went home, and Dad put me to bed. It was the first time he did this, so I thought it was weird. But I liked it very much. I remember he stayed by my side until I fell asleep. Around midnight, I woke up to the sound of my father crying . That was the first time that I heard my father crying. He bawled like a child. I still didn't understand what was happening.

I remember that the following day, we went to a place with many crosses and statues. I learned that the place was called the Mejicanos Cemetery. The coffin was buried there. I still couldn't figure it out; no one explained anything to me then. But I felt an overwhelming feeling of loneliness and sorrow inside me. Nobody thought it was important to tell me what was going on.

Before that tragic day, I remember that we used to sit at the dining table. My brothers, Guillermo (Billy) and Hector, and my dad and I waited while Mom served us the food. We had very happy times during dinner, talking and laughing. I sat around and mostly listened to them talk because I was so young and had not much to say. I do not remember much of those conversations, but I have a very vivid memory of a particular scene I'm sure I will never forget.

One day we were at the dinner table as usual, and Mom was serving us a plate with beans and eggs. My brother Hector (sixteen years older than me) stood up from the chair took the plate, threw it to the table at Mom, and yelled, "I am sick of this food! Can't you give us something else to eat? Only beans and beans and more beans every night! I am tired of that!" Then he got up and left the table. He went to his room furious.

I only noticed that Dad got up from the table, screamed who knows what, took off his belt, and hit him on the back for being so mean to Mom. After scolding him, Dad grounded him for a week, during that time he wasn't permitted to go out.

Hector was already a man and started dating women. I supposed that maybe he ate other things with them outside, and that was why he reacted in that way. He already had a job, and we were poor though I didn't know we were—I thought it was normal to eat beans every night, and I didn't ask for anything else. I felt my mom's and dad's love for me. Since I was the youngest, they all spoiled me every possible way.

The following days after the funeral, I started to notice my mother's absence at home. I knew that I hadn't been told the truth, so I had to figure it out all by myself. We started going to eat breakfast very early to the market of Mejicanos. The family was reduced to me, my two brothers, and my dad. I felt emptiness in my heart and in our home. She died at fifty-two and I never knew why—at least not until much later.

Nobody explained anything to me. I was so young that they thought that it wasn't necessary to explain my own mother's death to me. And without thinking about that issue, my beloved family marked my heart profoundly: they marked it with a void and a sense of abandonment that followed me for a very long time crying—my adolescent years.

I never saw my Mom really sick. She didn't say good-bye, and no one explained to me that she was really sick—let alone that she was dying. Maybe it was because no one expected her to die so young. I was born when she was forty-eight, so I didn't get to enjoy her company for too long. I hardly remember her.

After my mom's death, we started frequently visiting a house in Venezuela Boulevard, where a woman lived with her daughter, Estela. The woman's name was Margarita. She was older than my mother, but her daughter was more or less the same age as Hector. At some point, I learned that Margarita and my mom were pregnant at the same time and later on discovered that Margarita had been my dad's mistress. So Estela was my half sister, and her mother, let's say was my stepmother. In my innocence, that news made me happy because I didn't have a mother to love. Suddenly, I had a woman to see and love as my new mom.

They both were nice to me and earned my heart very quickly, especially my sister, Estela, because she had no other brothers or sisters and she loved to play with me (and I loved it too). My dad decided that since my mother wasn't around anymore, it was good for me and my brothers to know them. We visited their house pretty often, but we always went back to our home in Mejicanos to sleep. Dad respected my mom's memory albeit not by much.

Another scene ingrained into my young memory was a Friday night event:

I was playing with Dad with a ball made of old socks when a neighbor came over to tell my dad that my brothers were playing pool in a pub near our home. The place was for older men, drunks, smokers, and just bad men in general (according to my father).

Even though my parents were poor, they had taught us to be honest and well educated, and they also warned us of the consequences of bad habits. My father was a very strict, serious man and was also a shouter. When he knew that my brothers were there, he grabbed my hand; and we went right away, walking real fast, almost running. When we got there, Dad was furious and yelled in front of everyone, "Billy, Hector, come on out!"

My brother Guillermo came out with a ball rack around his neck, and my brother Hector with a big stick (I learned later on that's a pool cue) in his hand. They looked funny to me! They had scared faces, and I just giggled and tried to hold in my laughter! Dad was clearly very upset. There was a police officer next to my dad, and my dad just told my brothers, "You have two options. One, you go with the police officer, and he will take you to jail for being in an illegal place for kids. Two, go home with me. If you go with the police, you know you go to jail, and I will make sure you are in it until you learn your lesson. If you come with me, you know the consequences that wait for you…Decide right now!"

Both came home with us really upset, mad, and frustrated. They said that they did not drink or smoke, that they were just having fun with some friends. Still, it was an illegal place for them (well, actually only for Guillermo). It was around four or five blocks away from home. We walked home in utter silence. I felt the tension in the air.

When we got home, Dad told them, "Take off your shirts, and face the wall." He then went to look for a rope with knots that he had with his tools. He hit them with that rope on the back for about four or five times. Guillermo cried because it hurt him and because he was mad. Hector was in total silence. When Dad finished hitting them, Hector said in a sarcastic tone, "Finished?"

"I think it's enough for today."

"You did not win, Dad," Hector said between his teeth. "You will never beat me again. No one will ever make me do anything against my will!"

He then went to his room mad, resentful, and hurt but said nothing. That was the last time I saw Hector in my childhood. He disappeared the following day.

Hector was about sixteen years older than me. (If I was four and Hector was about sixteen years older, he must have already been around twenty.) He was an adult already, but for my dad, he was his boy and didn't want him to be in those places. He wanted to have good kids and not troubled ones. I, however, thought he was old enough. After all, he had already had girlfriends.

That episode, plus Mom's death, made a big mark in my brother's life. Later on, I learned that he had a relationship with a woman named Esmeralda. Esmeralda was a nurse, but she was also a madam and a bad woman. She was in her forties and managed a brothel. I learned that Hector visited her very often, not to be with the prostitutes but with the owner of the place. Dad was never going to approve of their relationship; but Esmeralda accepted my brother for his youth, strength, good looks, and she was going to give him the love he did not find at home. (I think that Hector went to her place when he left home, but that is just my guess.)

So my family was reduced to Guillermo, Dad, and me. My dad was really affected by Hector's disappearance. It was a bad fight, and emotionally he got too affected. I think Hector was also very affected as he never came back to see Dad. He disappeared from my life at that early age.

From then on, I observed my dad. He always seemed to be very distracted and sad. I didn't know for sure if it was because of Mom or Hector or both. I was afraid to ask because I did not want to upset him or make him sadder. But the good part out of all this is that Dad and I became inseparable! Maybe because I was so young, I gave him a reason to live, so he kept going. Where he went, I went too.

As time went by, we started to stay over at Margarita's house once in a while, especially since Hector disappeared from our lives. Our family shrunk and grew: I lost a brother in Hector but gained a sister in Estela. Estela loved me. That love took away the loneliness from my heart due to my mother's death and my brother Hector's disappearance.

Guillermo, who was fourteen, helped with the expenses at home. He worked as a bus assistant. He was in charge of collecting the bus fare from the passengers. (All buses had a bus driver and an assistant.) He was also one of the youngest with this type of job. I admired him very much. Plus, he bought me candies and other things with his earnings. Sometimes he gave me some coins, and it made me feel like the richest kid in the world!

Guillermo spent a lot of time away from home since he stopped studying as he worked from sunrise to sunset. He felt happy and fulfilled that he worked and was able to contribute to the living expenses.

One day when we were at Margarita's home, before Guillermo went out to work, he and I played with some bottles that we pretended were toy cars. He was starting work late that day, so he had time to play with me. He went on to peel some oranges and hit me with the peelings. Then I started crying to get Dad's attention. Dad scolded him, and I cried more because I liked to get all the attention. Then Guillermo cut the orange in half, gave me the first half, and ate the second one. And just like that, he left for his job.

I stayed put and played with Dad. About fifteen minutes later, we heard a crash from around the corner of our block, but we didn't pay attention to it. I continued playing alone because Dad got up, curious to see what happened. He saw nothing. An hour later, however, someone came over to our house to let my dad know that Guillermo was in the hospital. Dad left in a hurry to see him, but when he got there, he found out that Guillermo had died. Inconsolable, Dad cried and shouted, "Another death! I can't believe it! My son! My son! Where are you, Guillermo! Billyyyyyy!" That night, he cried and cried and cried. For the second time, I saw him crying uncontrollably. It was too much for my old man.

Guillermo used to dangle outside the bus to get more passengers, just like every other assistant does. He enjoyed that part of his job. But on that fateful day, he did so at the last minute when the bus started to move. But this time, the driver thought that Billy was holding on so he made an abrupt turn. Guillermo tried to grab on, but he missed. The driver closed the door, Guillermo fell to the street, and the driver unknowingly drove over him. My brother was killed almost instantly.

Coincidently, a Red Cross ambulance was driving by. The volunteers picked him up immediately (this is why Dad didn't see anything when he stood up to check the commotion). When the ambulance arrived at the hospital, my brother was already dead; nothing could be done for him. This took place on August 28, 1968. I was only five years old.

Between the death of Mom and Guillermo and Hector's disappearance, Dad went into a deep depression. Everything was really too much for him to handle. He was always sad, and it clearly reflected on his face. Dad was already over sixty years old, and the only happiness he had was me—his youngest son, young enough to practically be his grandson! I felt responsible for his happiness, so I tried to make him laugh. But his burden was too much.

Dad married Mom when he was thirty-four, Mom only twenty. Mrs. Chayito, a neighbor, told me that Mom was a pale blonde originally from Chalatenango (a city that is located more than seventy miles north of the capital of El Salvador and was first conquered by the Spaniards). In that city, one can find many fair, blonde blue-eyed people who look like foreigners (Mom was one of them).

Mrs. Chayito described her as a beautiful thin, tall blue-eyed girl who stole my father's heart. When Mom was almost twenty, Dad convinced her to run away with him, against my grandfather's will. They ran away, got married at twenty, and built a home. Contrary to everyone's expectations, Mom was not pregnant; she and Dad got married for love. Back then my grandfather and father were about the same age, and that is why my grandfather was opposed to their relationship. He had taken good care of her and had intended for her to marry a man her age, not someone too old. But Dad had stolen her heart, and they were really in love.

Mom was a housekeeper, and Dad was a carpenter. Some years later, Hector was born; and almost three years later, Guillermo followed. Twenty-six years later, I was born. Mom was forty-eight years old then. She thought she was having the menopause, but as it turned out, it was me forming in her womb.

Because of her age, she had a high-risk pregnancy with me. There were no ultrasounds to monitor how I was (unlike nowadays). I was premature. I was told that I spent almost two months in the hospital—mostly in the incubator, at the brink of death—but God wanted me to be alive to tell my story. I also think that if I hadn't survived, Dad would have been very alone in that stage of his life. Because I survived, Dad tried to be strong, healthy, and happy to go on living.

I was told that Dad was a hard-hearted man and rude in the way he treated Mom—he was offensive and yelled at her all the time. He liked to dominate her. He was a macho man. He always told her that he was the man of the house and that he brought the money to feed us all, so she always stayed quiet and ignored his comments.

He liked to feel in control and never entertained the idea that Mom would die first. He always thought that she was going to take care of him when he became old. Neither had he thought that he was going to lose his two older sons the way he did. He had buried Hector in his heart to stifle the pain, but now, he was going to have to bury Guillermo (aged fourteen) for real.

2

Margarita and Estela

Even though we stayed more often at Margarita's place, every weekend, we went to our home at Mejicanos. By then I already considered Margarita my stepmom even though Dad never married her. But I didn't care because she was nice to me. Estela was too. Estela was a great company for me, and she played with me very often. She played that she was my mother because she was much older and I had no more siblings left just her and me.

With all the tragedies happening in Dad's life, he ended up frequenting Esmeralda's brothel to relieve his feelings of anguish. He always liked women and was a big flirt with them, so I was not surprised whenever he went there to visit the prostitutes. I do not know exactly how, when, and why my dad got involved with Esmeralda since she was my brother's woman (well, maybe Dad never knew). The point is that other than having a brothel, Esmeralda also lent money at high interest rates. I believe that sometime after my brother's death, Dad asked for a loan; and she asked as collateral the title of our house, which he gave to her.

Unknown to me, my dad's health was deteriorating. I just knew that he tried to be happy and playful with me to hide his mourning and sorrow. He took me to every place with him and gave me instructions. For example, he would say, "Look, the bus route 4. You can find it in such and such place, and that one will take you to the west terminal. Margarita lives three blocks to your right."

He constantly showed me how to get from one place to another, saying, "If you take bus route 8, you will be two blocks away from your godmother." I did not know why he taught me those things as I was young and really small, but I am very grateful he did. He was everything to me.

In my young mind, with time, I accepted as fact that Margarita was my dad's woman and that Estela was his daughter too, even though I did not understand my dad's relationship with them when we started going to their place. Estela always made me feel loved, and she was very kind to me. She entertained me and played with me, and I felt happy being around her every time Dad and I went to their place. I loved Estela. In my young heart, what I had for Margarita and Estela was true love. As far as what I knew in my heart, they were part of my family now. I just accepted them as so and I simply loved them.

My dad was a man I admired very much. We played together when we were at home. I loved to play with him, to have him chase me around the house because he was never able to catch me since he was already old. I laughed so much. He was so clumsy whenever he chased me! I also liked playing hide-and-seek around the house with him.

Dad and I also played ball. I remember one day when Mom scolded us because we broke the only piece of decoration we had in the house. She sent us out on the street to play. We spent so much time together that we had many good memories. I felt happy with him, and he made my burden from not having a mom and brothers more bearable.

Dad used to be a carpenter, and he worked on the railroad when he met Mom. He had many friends—he even mentioned some of them, but I never paid attention. After Mom died, we stayed alone at home since he never remarried, even though he and Margarita seemed to be serious. I hardly remember Mom as

I was only four when she died. So Dad made it a point to care for me. We were happy together despite the emptiness in my heart and the sadness we both felt.

As time went on, Dad and I had practically moved in to Margarita's home; but most weekends, we went back to our house in Mejicanos. On bright, sunny days very early, we would get dressed to go to eat breakfast at the local market. There was a hill we had to walk down to get there and back up to return home. I always went down jumping and playing. However, one Saturday, early in the morning, we were on our way to the local market…

"Aughhh," said Dad.

My dad suddenly fell down!

"Dad!" I shouted "Dad! What's wrong with you, Dad?"

He said, "Take my wallet and run, Son! Run to your godmother."

I looked at him and tried to lift him up. Then I screamed in panic, "Help, help!" I asked for help, but when people started coming over, he said to me again, "Run, Son! Run and leave me here. Go get help!"

So I took his wallet and started running, not looking back. I ran faster than I had ever run before. I ran in a panic, trying to get to my godmother's place as soon as possible. I was hysterical—running and crying and yelling. I went up the hill really fast. My head was spinning, and I was running like a crazy kid pumped up with adrenaline.

My godmother was the only older lady I knew (other than Margarita), and she lived near our house. I got there really nervous, crying and shouting and hitting the door as hard as I could. It was only 6:30 a.m., so everyone was asleep; no one answered for a while. When, finally, a guy opens the door, I start shouting to him about what happened to my dad. He turned out to be my godmother's older son. He was a tall man with brown complexion, but he was deaf and dumb. When he saw the look on my face, he couldn't understand me. But then he saw my dad's wallet; he took it to his mother.

"My dad fell down the hill going to the market! He fell! My dad fell! And he told me to come here to ask for help! Please help me!" I sobbed. "Please help him, Godmother. Please help!" My heart was destroyed.

My godmother took his wallet, and she went running to find him. She knew we went to the market every weekend because she was the owner of the cafeteria we frequented. When she got down the hill, she did not find him. Apparently, he was already taken to the Rosales National Hospital, which was the closest hospital.

The deaf guy picked me up and hugged me. I was crying my heart out, and he held me as I cried. I was heartbroken. *Another death? Can it be possible?* My head was spinning. Then it went blank for a moment. The deaf guy consoled me and bought me an ice cream. I stopped crying for a moment, and my hunger was satisfied. I just remembered that after finishing the ice cream, he picked me up and hugged me until I fell asleep. I was so exhausted physically and emotionally that I woke up in the afternoon. By then, I was really hungry.

After eating, my godmother asked me again what had happened.

"I don't know. I was going very happy down the hill with Dad—like every weekend—when he fell, and he just told me to take his wallet and run to you, and here I am." I cried hysterically. "I do not know what happened, Godmother, but please help him! Help him! I do not have anyone else in this world, Godmother! Help him to be alive please!"

"Don't worry, Son. You are going to be okay here. I will go to the hospital to look for him, and I will talk to him to know what happened. You will stay here while we find out what is going on."

That was the last thing I remembered about Dad and I have never again heard anything about him. After a few days, no one said anything to me. I tried asking to my godmother, but she always changed the subject. No one wanted to talk about it, and all I heard one day was that he was in a very delicate condition. No one took me to see him at the hospital. Then a few days later, they took me to the cemetery—to the same place where my mom was buried. My little head turned around to look at them and to ask them if that was my dad in the casket. I wanted to see him for the last time. To hug him and to tell him how much I loved him.

That sunny day, it wasn't just any other day—it was the day that my dad was buried. When I finally understood that the casket held my dad, I started crying again, not knowing what was next up for me! I cried like I never had before, and everyone there looked at me with sorrowful expressions. He died on the fifteenth of April 1969, and my birthday was in November. I was almost six and a half years old, and I was alone in the world.

What else is going to happen to me? It was the worst tragedy I had lived. All the bad things had already happened to me: I lost Mom before I was four, my brother Hector disappeared before I was five, my brother Guillermo died before I was six, and now Dad's gone before I turn seven! What will I do now that I'm alone? I was an orphan now, and I didn't know what I would do to survive. My dad left me, and I couldn't even say good-bye to him. *Where am I going to live? What will I do? What will happen to my life?*

No one offered to take care of me. The people all looked at me with compassionate eyes, but no one offered to take me in. No one. I didn't know what I was going to do. I was too young to make decisions. I just didn't want to think about anything right then. When Mom died, Dad was there for me, but now…*Who is going to be there for me? Should I stay with my godmother or my stepmother? Will they take me to an orphanage? Will someone adopt me?* All those things went around my head.

3

Esmeralda

Finally, that same afternoon, Margarita and Estela took me home with them. I went on to live with them for a few days or maybe weeks, I do not remember. I do not how and why it happened; but one afternoon, Esmeralda, my brother's ex—the one who had the title of my family home and was also my dad's mistress—went to Margarita's house to take me away from them. They argued and fought over me, but knowing that she was a wicked woman and fearing what she was capable of, Margarita had no choice but to let me go with her.

I did not know her at this point. I had seen her only from faraway, but when she got there, I wasn't afraid of going; I just thought she was my dad's friend or an aunt or something. I thought she was a good woman.

Her house was beautiful. It was very big and had a huge dining table (I counted the places on the table and found that there were twelve. I counted them because I was really impressed with the size!). It had some beautiful paintings that I have never seen before. It looked like a rich person's house, so I thought that things weren't so bad after all. Later on, I learned that she was a nurse and that one of her daughters also was one. So I concluded that someone who had gone to the university must be rich. *It will be all right*, I thought.

Esmeralda did not have a husband. The one she did have left her. Apparently her daughters were from different men (some were even married). Whatever the case was, I thought she had a very nice house, but I did not expect what was coming next.

A couple of weeks later, I went to her place of business, the brothel on the street called La Avenida. That was a famous place among men as it was where they found girls. That was the place my brother used to go to. He had been one of Esmeralda's lovers (maybe the youngest). Just a few days after showing me the nice house, she took me over to that horrible place to live there. It turned out that she only showed me the nice house so that I would not suspect what she planned for me.

When one of her girls became pregnant because of some failure with the birth control, she allowed her to keep the baby. She loved babies, but it was not because she loved them for real—it was just her way of keeping the girls working for her and part of her plan to have someone take care of her when she became old.

The babies had grown already, and she was looking for someone to help her with them. I was the oldest of them and just the helper she was looking for. I was their "big brother" now. One kid had Down syndrome, and there was a baby of around eight months old. There were also two "normal" kids: a four-year-old and a five-year-old. The one that was called Hector (people said that my brother was the father though they did not look alike at all) and the other one was Walter. Now I had two friends/ brothers to play and pull pranks with.

Of all the kids, I was the only one who was orphaned. Each one had their mother working there in exchange for food, shelter, and clothing, plus a few more dollars to take care of themselves and their children. Esmeralda always made sure her girls were clean, so that the customers who visited them would return and hopefully often. They generally worked five to six men daily. She had a good reputation because she always made sure her workers were healthy. A sick worker meant no money, so she made sure they were clean and healthy, doing doctor's check-ups every 3 months.

I didn't like that place too much since it was not too pretty and I felt the heaviness in the air from the people's way of living. When I first arrived in that place, Esmeralda took me upstairs to a bedroom and locked me up in a closet for who knows how long. She apparently wanted to make a point that she was the boss and that what she says goes. For instance, every time I was naughty with my "brothers" or misbehaved, she locked me up. I did not like to be locked up, and as far as I remembered, my parents never did that to me. I grew up free in my house, and I went out with Dad all the time. Needless to say, this was something new for me.

Esmeralda was sometimes very affectionate, but I got to understand that when she was like that, her real intention was to abuse me. When she started to touch me in a way, I intuitively felt that it was wrong. Fortunately, I always managed to escape from her: I would push her away, kick her, do anything I could to get away from her. When she finally caught up with me, she always locked me up in a closet. (That was her favorite punishment.)

I didn't like being locked up, but I preferred that over being abused. I do not know how I knew that, but I did. I just felt like she wasn't touching me like Margarita or Estela did, and my heart felt that it was different. She didn't like that she could not dominate me, but I would rather be locked up than touched in a way I didn't like. No woman, man, or kid had ever touched me the way she tried to. It felt so wrong and bad, and I didn't like it.

Looking back now, I can see that God took care of me in all senses though at the time, I did not understand it yet. The Holy Spirit was protecting me, but of course, I knew nothing about God or the Holy Spirit then—not even Jesus.

Whenever I was locked up in the closet, I stayed there for many hours. When that happened, I had time to think and plan that one day, I was going to escape from this witch! I was sure that she was not someone my dad would have sent me to live with.

When I was free around the house, I went to every corner and sought out every window, door, entrance and learned the schedule of everyone in the house. I knew the time when people came in and when they went out. I memorized everything. The place was like a prison to me. My friends/siblings were still too young, so I didn't tell them anything. I kept everything to myself.

One day, after a few months, I made my escape. I had all my belongings in a plastic bag (I did not have much, but they were mine). That day, I ran, ran, and ran really fast—the fastest I could go until I could find the bus stop that would take me to my sister, Estela. Children did not have to pay a fare. I learned that from Dad, so I just hopped in as if I knew what I was doing. But the bus driver looked intently into my eyes and asked, "Are you alone?"

"Yes."

"And where are you going?"

"To my sister's house," I said, sure of myself, and I held on tightly to my belongings. The bus driver got suspicious as I was only seven at that time, so when he saw a policeman, he stopped and talked to him about me. The policeman sat beside me, in the first row, and asked me the same questions again. After that, he asked, "Where does your sister live?"

"Where there is a picture of a *big* ice cream!" I said with a big smile, trying to look very mature actually. I still wasn't taught how to read or write then, so I did not know it was an AD for Foremost Ice Cream. Anyway, I think he thought I looked sure enough and believed me, but he went with me all the same. We got down at the right place, and as he followed me, I recognized the place immediately. I knocked on the door. Margarita opened it. With her eyes wide open and with utter surprise, she said, "My boy! How are you? How great to see you! What are you doing here?…Come on in. Come inside." And without any more encouragement from her, I went in.

The policeman talked to her, but I did not hear their conversation clearly. He did not seem to be suspicious about me escaping from that horrible place though. He was happy that I was telling the truth, and he left without any further questioning. Quickly, I started to play with Estela's daughter. I felt loved, well received welcome and, most importantly, safe. My heart was full of happiness! My perfect plan had come out excellent, and I was safe now; I had nothing to worry about, or so I thought.

Not too much time had passed (maybe just a few days) when someone abruptly and furiously knocked on the door. When Margarita opened it, Esmeralda burst right through. I had no time to hide. They argued and yelled at each other, fighting over me. Then Esmeralda looked at me with an evil glare that she normally had when she was furious and said, "Ed, you have to come with me *right now!*" in a commanding tone. Surprisingly, I had the guts to shout, "I do not want to go with you! I want to stay here! I do not want to go!" I cried and looked to Margarita for help. "Please help me, Margarita!"

But Esmeralda pulled me by my hair and took me away without my consent. Margarita did nothing; she just looked on and did not try to stop her. Estela wasn't there and didn't see anything. Margarita had a friend visiting at the time, and both just stood there helpless and petrified. I do not know if Margarita did not look after me because she was afraid or because she did not feel like fighting for me. The point is that Esmeralda pulled me and pushed me into a taxi cab with all her strength. She couldn't care less if I screamed and cried and didn't want to go with her.

I regretted so, so much not telling the police about that wicked woman and why I had escaped (since I thought I was already saved). I was really sad that there was not a single policeman near me then to see me crying and yelling, to have someone there to look after me.

That day became a turning point in my life: Hatred was born in me. I became mad, upset; and all I had inside me was hatred toward Esmeralda, Margarita, Estela, and the world. Loneliness and despair also became my companions. That day, I was forced to live with someone I did not want to live with, and there was no one to rescue me. *Everyone in my family was dead, and my big brother ran away, and now this witch says I have to live with her? What a horror movie I am in! I want to grow up!* I thought, wanting to shout it out to the world. *One day, when I grow up, I will get my revenge on her...Just wait,* I said to myself.

That day was clearly the day that negativity came into my life. It made an indelible mark on my soul. That day, a new boy—the troublemaker—was born. The happy, obedient, and timid boy died; the angry, rebellious boy came to life. I became a snob and someone who would fight anyone who tried to bully me or a friend. I new boy was born.

I did not care about life; I couldn't care less if I died since everyone I cared about was either dead or missing anyway no one cared for me. For the first time, I thought about death. I thought that dying could end my sorrow, my sadness, and my loneliness. But since I didn't plan to kill myself as I had no idea how, I promised myself that until death came, I was not going to be manipulated by anyone *ever*. No one was going to force me to do anything against my will.

Never again did I try to escape to go look for Estela and Margarita as I felt abandoned by them—by everyone really. I felt totally on my own, and a deep loneliness settled within me. I became really angry with Estela and Margarita because they had not defended or protected me. Sure, Margarita was not my relative, but I hated her because she was my stepmother as far as I was concerned and did not do anything to help me. I hated Estela, I hated Margarita, and I hated Esmeralda. That hatred inside me made me a big fighter—so much so that I would fight even with the dogs. I would fight with anyone who did not look at me nicely. I became greatly aggressive and relentlessly naughty. Life didn't matter to me anymore.

I did not look for Estela anymore, but every time, I ran away from Esmeralda's place to nowhere in particular. I went around the streets dreaming that someone would pick me up, that I would find my lost family, or that someone could adopt me and take me somewhere. I also dreamed that I could take care of myself and that I would go out thinking that I would never go back to that hell but I was not old enough (as I was only seven years old), and when I was hungry, I had no other choice but to search trash cans to look for something decent to eat. I hardly ever found anything safe to eat, just rotten food. It was yucky, but with the hunger that I felt, I didn't mind—I would eat at least a bad tortilla or dirty bread.

I went around the streets aimlessly. Not only did I suffer from hunger, but I also suffered cold and rainy days outside in the streets. Sometimes my whole body was drenched all night, and there was no one looking after me. Sometimes I disappeared for a couple of days—some other times, three or four days—and when I couldn't handle my life outside and I had hardly eaten, I returned to the hellhole I had escaped from: Esmeralda's brothel. At least in that place, I had a roof over my head and clean food to eat every day; and she always took me back in, no matter what. She scolded me and imposed a curfew but also said that I could come back.

Sometimes, when I wandered the streets and got very hungry, I visited Mrs. Chayito, my dad's neighbor. When I was dirty, smelly, wet, and hungry, she let me into her home. She didn't care how dirty or smelly I was—which was a big deal as sometimes I've gone many days without washing myself. She always gave me something to eat and then sent me to take a shower. When I was clean, I stuck around to watch TV. My favorite cartoon show was *The Flintstones*. I loved watching that cartoon, and Mrs. Chayito loved having me there. She liked talking to me. She advised me to look for my sister and then told me stories about my mother.

She told me one day that dad went to pick up my mother from Chalatenango. She said that Mom often went to the central market in San Salvador with her father (my grandfather) to sell the vegetables that they'd harvested. That was where they met, and he fell in love immediately. Mom was a strong woman who put up with dad's bad temper. She was beautiful, tall, thin, and blonde. I wished to see a picture of her, but no one ever showed me one, so I just imagined her as beautiful as fairy tale character.

Mrs. Chayito often told me about the time Mom was pregnant with me.

"Chayito, I think I'm already in menopause."

"And why do you say that, Mary?"

"Because my period had stopped, but what I think it's weird is that I also have a lot of nausea. Do you think this is normal?"

"If I was you, I would go to the doctor to know what is wrong with you because I do not think that is normal.

"And the menopause was you, Eddy!"

"Hahahahahahaha!"

I practically laughed to death every time she told me that story. I just loved it. She told me other stories, but that was my favorite.

Oh, how I missed my mother! Every night that I wandered in the streets, I thought that my mother sent angels to take care of me and look after me. Every day that I suffered from cold weather, hunger, and thirst, I was sure that there definitely were angels looking after me. Mrs. Chayito always welcomed me with a big smile. She became my beacon of hope! Now that I think about it, she must have been an angel—my biggest angel actually.

Mrs. Chayito was the only person who had a television in her neighborhood, which meant that being able to watch TV in her house was a great privilege. In my fantasy, I dreamed that she was one day going to tell me to stay there for good. But she never offered. Maybe it was because she did not have a room or a bed for me, or maybe it was because she didn't want to get into trouble with the witch. I do not know. But I dreamed about it, and that made me want to visit her every time I could.

4

First Time in School

Whenever I had no better options, I went back to the witch. I tried to come back thinking I was going to behave until I planned my next escape, dreaming that the next time, I was going to be successful in finding a family that would adopt me or have a better life in general. But one day, when I came back from a three-day adventure, the witch gave me the big news that I was to start school. She didn't ask if I wanted to go to school, she simply told me, "Soon you will start going to school." I was intrigued because I didn't know what that meant.

And just like that, I started school in January, at age seven. (The school year started in January and ended in November I learned later on.) I started in first grade and learned to read and write. I had never seen a school before (or perhaps I had not noticed that they existed), so everything was new to me.

The school wasn't that big, but the classrooms were (or at least that was my impression). The one I attended was a public school and had a basketball court in the middle of the building. All rooms were around the court. Each classroom had four windows and no fan. It was really hot during the last part of the morning when all students were together in the room. The desks were old and worn from all the kids who had previously used them. I felt important and enthusiastic about the idea of learning to read. I felt that, that was going to change everything in my life.

Well, at first, I went every morning at 7:00 a.m. sharp to learn. I was ready in line when the bell rang. I liked being with other kids of my age. However, as time went by, I got used to the kids, the teacher, the routine, so I started misbehaving: I started skipping school when I got bored because I didn't feel free—the routine was that I came in at seven and left at noon, went to classes from one subject to the next, in the same classroom kept up with a strict schedule; and it was all too much for me, who had never been disciplined.

I felt like I was in prison, really, so I escaped every time I could. There was no one to supervise me, and I had no parents, for whom the school could inform about my misconduct. So I just skipped school and didn't care about what the teacher told me whenever I went back to class.

Esmeralda must have put me through school thinking that that structure would keep me busy and out of trouble and off the streets... *for a while*. There were many kids in each classroom (maybe about thirty to thirty-five). The teacher was an older woman, a little overweight, and maybe around forty-five. She was serious and strict; and she taught us Spanish grammar, reading, mathematics, language, and social studies. Yep. All these subjects were taught by the same teacher. We also had physical education and recess. My favorites were these last two.

Esmeralda gave me some pencils and notebooks for school. I was the only one of the brothel kids who went to school since I was the oldest, so I felt important. The rest were not old enough to go to school. There was no kindergarten at that time, so all kids, aged seven, started school at first grade. It was in this school where I met my first actual set of friends, other than my "brothers," that is. All my classmates had a mother and a father or at least one or the other or even a grandmother who took care of them. I was the only orphan, as far as I knew.

Our classroom was a big one, but it was still very hot inside. It only had a few midsize windows and I felt trapped. It was like I was in the closet but with many kids. I liked playing during recess with the other kids my age. Since the school year went from January to November, the end of the school year was announced in October, with what we call the Winds of October. It was a time when it got chilly and windy, perfect to go out to raise comets. So I used to escape in those days the most.

I also skipped school when I didn't finish my homework but mostly whenever I didn't feel like going. When I skipped school, I went around the streets near the hills of San Ramon in Mejicanos and in the surrounding area. Nobody could order me around: I had no boss and no parents. I was the owner of my life. Like a lamb without a shepherd. I was on my own, and since I was mad at life, whenever anyone tried to tease or bother me, I started a fight and hit hard; if someone tried to scold me, I yelled at them. I think my classmates were afraid of me.

I was the bully of the class. Charlie was the clown, and Frank was the serious one. Mario was the nerd, and Angela and Oscar were the ones who stood up for me when someone started picking on me. Then there were Lissette and Lucy, two friends who always gave me a piece of their bread with beans or a cookie because I never brought lunch (there was no one to prepare it for me). Jaime, Alfredo, Xenia, and Maria were the smart ones and were the ones who never got into a fight.

One day, the twins Edgardo and Alan wanted to hit me, but I hit them first and left both of them on the floor. I was a fighter. I was angry and had a lot of resentment and hatred inside me. I felt hurt, and I did not know how to handle it. I felt alone in the world, and I was. I could not even imagine myself becoming an adult, and I blamed it on the fact that I did not have a good role model to follow. All the potential ones were either dead, had abandoned me, or were cruel. I hated the adults and did not want to become one, so life no longer mattered to me.

Funny enough, whenever I tried to behave and be good to others (every time I got tired of fighting anyway), I always earned the leadership position in the discipline committee. I liked the position because I liked being the boss and telling people what to do. I loved demanding respect, which was a value I had not previously learned.

There were other committees in school that I didn't like, especially cleaning. I *hated* cleaning. What I hated the most was cleaning the toilets—this was a punishment, not a prize. There was the sales committee too, which I liked because when I was there, I ate for free. I always kept the best of everything we sold when holding fundraisers. But when I got tired of the discipline and order, I started misbehaving. Then I would skip school and forget how good it was to behave and be the boss. Everything was quickly forgotten, and I didn't care for my life again.

When I went back to Esmeralda's house and she saw me dirty from playing in school or in the streets, she sent me to the bathroom to take a cold shower. I was not allowed to get out of the shower if I was not totally cleaned. I had to smell clean and be clean. When I was all cleaned up, she came to me to touch me, be intimate with me, but her ultimate goal was to abuse me sexually. She had that in mind all the time. I hated her for that, and I never let her do anything to me.

Since I had inner madness, that feeling helped me escape, hit her or do anything I could do to get away from her grasp and her diabolical wish. Her revenge was always to lock me up inside a closet, but I didn't care. I'd rather be locked up than abused. Something inside me told me it was not right.

When I was alone, I started dreaming. I imagined myself being rescued by a family who loved me dearly. I also imagined that I was adopted by some foreign family and that I was moving to another unknown country. My imagination protected me from more internal turmoil. I had many dreams, but each of them was just that—a simple dream. I just had myself and my imagination. Period.

5

The Caregivers

It was nearing the end of the school year when one day, Esmeralda decided to go to the United States. That decision changed my life. She looked for someone to take care of us all, and the first sitter I remember was a guy named Joseph. (We stayed in Esmeralda's house.)

Joseph made fun of the six of us . He had lots of fun whenever he had us hold one end of an electric cable while the other he stuck into an electric outlet. We got little shocks, but we were always scared of them. They were not too intense, so we were not in danger of dying, but, he loved seeing our faces when we got shocked. When he was mad, he hit us for no reason, especially the kids with special needs, whom he also made fun of. Of course, we tried to defend ourselves by hitting him and fighting back the best we could for our ages; but when we did not want to play, his electrocution game, he grab us one at a time and submerged our heads in the laundry pool. He did not intend to do it to kill us but he did it to make us suffer for fifteen to twenty seconds.

He was a big adult, and we were only little kids—I was the oldest at seven—so he had power over us. He did not want to kill us, for sure, but he loved to see us suffer. He was cruel to us. One day, we were alone in the house; and for some reason, Joseph tried to not only electrocute me but also tried to sexually abuse me. I shouted as loud as I could. I threw at him everything I found near me. Fortunately, somehow, someone entered the house, and I escaped. I think Joseph had some mental problems because he did not act like a normal person. He loved being cruel to us.

When he was the only adult in the house, he was really cruel. But when Gladys, Esmeralda's granddaughter, visited, he was a real gentleman. He was even *sweet* to us. We all knew he was in love with her; but apparently, they were related, and that made it an impossible love.

I loved Gladys's visits because she always brought candy. She cared about us, bathed us, cooked for us, and even played and hugged us in a very delicate and loving way. She gave the type of love and hugs I hadn't received since my parents passed away— the type of love my heart had forgotten how to receive. Gladys was a very nice person, and we all loved her. Her hugs were pure, loving hugs, not sexually oriented ones. I felt the difference. That's why I loved her.

There were people who told me that there was a woman who went around the house with her soul suffering for me. Some said that it was my mother, who had left me so small. Joseph, however, told me that she was suffering and couldn't die in peace. Joseph often frightened me, saying that she was outside. "It is your mother!" he would say. "She can't rest in peace because you are not a good kid. You are no one good! You are a bad person and will never be anyone good in this world."

He repeated that every time he could until I couldn't hold it in anymore and I escaped, going to the streets to try to get away from him and from the "suffering woman." I couldn't take any more of his insults about my mom. When I escaped, I slept anywhere the night found me—sometimes underneath the stars, other times in the rain. And the same story began: I wanted to take care of myself or find someone who would—preferably a nice family that would give me a home. But I could never find one.

I went back to looking for food in the trash cans, and of course, all I could find was rotten food. Sometimes I would ring a doorbell, and if I was lucky, the owners gave me some leftovers. Other times, I went to Mrs. Chayito's, and she told me every time, "You should go look for your sister, Estela."

And even though I kept that in the back of my mind, I was mad at her because she did not fight for me when the witch came over and pulled me out of her house (by my hair!), and she never went out to look for me. She never tried to rescue me from the witch. Never.

Sometimes the three oldest kids—Walter, Hector, and me—went out. We went from house to house. People pitied us but did not ask any questions about us or what we were doing or anything. We were usually dirty, with ripped clothes and no shoes. We were street children. People pitied us, but no one ever offered to take care of us or help us in any way. No one offered us a home—a real home. When I was on vacation from school, the three of us spent a lot of time in the streets.

On one of those days when Gladys was visiting, after she gave us each our candy and bathed us (it was almost noontime when she finished cleaning the youngest one), she went to the kitchen to cook lunch. She was preparing eggs and beans for lunch while all the kids were outside playing. Joseph was very well behaved around Gladys, and was watching us play. Suddenly we heard a roof tile fall and break.

"Whoa! What was that?" asked Gladys.

"It might be a cat," said Joseph.

Then another roof tile fell.

"Who the hell is there? I will bring you down at once!" shouted Joseph. Another roof tile fell. Joseph then stepped outside and climbed the roof. All the kids went out to the garden to see very curiously. We saw Joseph fighting against nobody. He yelled and tried to defend himself, but we saw no one else there. It was just

Joseph fighting and going around the roof while the tiles kept falling. It was all too strange.

A few minutes later, Joseph fell from the roof. But fortunately for him, he did not break any bone. We saw him all scratched up and all his clothes in tatters. His face was as pale as snow, and his eyes were so big with a frightened expression as if he had been up against the devil in person. He left the house running as if running away from someone when no one followed him. And that was the last time I saw him. All was very strange to my young eyes.

Gladys took us inside the house and calmed us down as we were all crying and frightened. We all talked about it, trying to find out what had happened, but no one ever came up with a logical explanation. We were not hungry anymore for a while. Gladys just hugged and consoled us all.

Joseph never came back, and we never heard anything else from him. We did not know what had really happened in that house either. Had it been a ghost, a demon, or the woman whom he claimed was going around the house—the one people said he thought it was my mother? Everything was so strange, and three days later, we learned that Joseph had killed himself (hung himself from a tree in an empty lot near the house). So with that, the guy who did not treat us well disappeared from our lives. I was sure that life was going to change for us all, and I was not mistaken. That was about the time when another sitter appeared.

I suppose that it was either Gladys or Esmeralda who looked for someone to take care of us. They found a woman who had seven children. They offered her a house in Mejicanos for her to live in with her children and to take care of us six. Esmeralda was going to send money for us and for her kids as payment for her taking care of the whole gang. The name of that woman was Maria.

She accepted the deal happily because she lived in a cardboard house that was about to fall down. She lived under extremely impoverished conditions—with little to no food to feed her children—and now Esmeralda was offering a proper house made of bricks and cement, with three bedrooms, an inside bathroom and a place in the backyard to wash clothes. It was her dream come true! The house had no furniture, but then again, she didn't have any in her house either. The house had water, electricity, and a safe roof. She was also given a small electric kitchen stove instead of having to find wood to use for cooking.

For me, it was also a good deal because all that meant that I no longer had to suffer the the teasing from Joseph; neither did I have to see the witch Esmeralda. So I was really happy to live with Maria—even without getting to know her first. I was just happy at the change of situation, and I thought, *Finally, my life is going to change!* I did not care that there were no beds, no dining table, or nothing for that matter.

Gladys forgot to take into consideration (or perhaps it did not occur to her) that we needed furniture from Esmeralda's house. So for this reason, we all started to sleep on the bare floor. But it was all fine as we were under a safe roof. I never tried to escape again because I, finally, after so long, felt safe.

Maria was a short, skinny, dark-olive-skinned lady. She was of Spanish and Salvadorian Indian descent, which gave her, her brown skin color (in fact, many people in El Salvador are mixed races). She wore very worn-out clothing and had no shoes either. She was very, very poor. She sold fruits and vegetables in the market—things like mango, papaya, pineapple, and other fruits native to El Salvador. Whatever she found, she sold for a few more cents to feed her seven kids. Each kid had a different father, but none of them gave her any help—no money or food for her children. So she had to do whatever she could to feed them every day.

Each day was a new day, and each day, she had to find a way to feed them. She did the same thing over and over again—Monday through Sunday. She was alone. This is the way women lived in those days; it was totally "normal" for them to get pregnant by men who immediately disappeared to catch the next girl. So when Maria was offered a paying job and a real house, she was really excited! She felt like a millionaire! And of course, she accepted the deal. It was her dream come true!

I did not recognize the house, but it turned out to be my childhood home! It had no furniture, so it looked very different. I didn't know if the furniture was stolen or sold by Esmeralda. I was no longer in a position to care since she had the legal documents of the house; as far as I knew, she could do whatever she wanted.

A few months passed and everything went fine. Maria fed us, cared for us, cleaned the house, and washed all our clothes *by hand* (we had no idea that washing machines existed). Maria was naturally very nice, very loving, and very caring, and she treated us all the same—her kids and us, her "adopted" kids.

She always tried to care for us all the same; but Walter, Hector, and I liked to get in trouble all the time. We always gave her a hard time. She got heartbroken very often. She advised us all the time, talked to us; but never did she hit us. Never. We were just naughty by nature. Maybe it was because we were not used to feeling real love.

One day, she called us and told us, "I will not receive any more money for you guys or myself and my kids, so you will have to eat tortilla with salt and lemon most of the time. There is not much I can do. If you want to eat, Kid"—looking at me as if presenting a challenge—"you have to go out to work in the streets."

So that same week, her older son gave me the idea of selling newspapers in the streets. He said, "If you want to have your own money, you can help me sell newspapers. You can earn three to four cents per newspaper, and I will earn the rest. If you sell a hundred each day, you will have three pesos daily. Our national currency then was the colón, that we called pesos too, and that was equivalent to US $0.34 for each colón. With that, you and your five brothers can eat."

As if they are my brothers, I thought. But somehow I felt responsible for them. So I woke up really early and took the challenge as a competition and something fun to do before going to school in the mornings. I sold in the hills near the house between five and six thirty. I went every place around, trying to earn more than the other boy.

The competition was against time and against him. So I thought. But deep inside, I thought that with that business, I could move out and pay for all my things. Little did I know about how much things really cost outside. But I loved the dream of becoming independent.

I loved the streets. I went to school once in a while because I had moved on to the second grade. When I did not go to school, I went around and looked through the trash cans for something decent to eat when I went hungry. When it rained, I got wet, and the rain felt so good! I loved to get wet, especially when it was really pouring. I always felt refreshed! I was never afraid from the rain. I wasn't afraid of anything. I was not even afraid of dying or getting sick. Actually, I did not think about that. It did not occur to me that I could get a cold, the flu, or even pneumonia. I just never got sick, so I had no clue of the danger to which I exposed myself every time I got wet and stay wet. I did not have too many clothes to choose from to change into anyway. I also did not see any reason to do so.

I did not like anyone having control over me, so I looked for other ways to earn money even, more money than only selling newspapers. I learned to clean shoes to earn a few more cents. Every weekend, I went to clean the shoes of the people who walked around the central park downtown. I had no shoes that time because I had outgrown them and had no money to buy new ones. So I cleaned others shoes', all the while dreaming of having a new pair one day. So when I went to school (a public school), I went barefoot. I couldn't care less of that detail. I wasn't the only one to do that anyway.

The school I went to was the Japanese Republic Public School in Mejicanos. With school came also my cold heart and my internal rage. I got into fights with anyone who looked at me weird. If a classmate talked back to me or if I felt emotionally attacked, my anger consumed me, and I started fighting with anyone and everyone. I skipped school if I lost the fight and got hit.

In the streets, I really learned to earn a living the honest way. But when I couldn't sell enough newspapers or clean enough shoes to buy something to eat, I searched again in the trash cans for something "decent" to eat. But I also learned to steal to eat. A fruit, a piece of bread, a tortilla, a carrot, anything to fill my stomach. When you are hungry, you get forced to look for alternatives.

I learned all kinds of tricks to get something to eat. My favorite place to go to was the local market. There were plenty of fruits and veggies there, and the sellers were not always looking at their produce. Those from the market restaurants also threw away a lot of good food. I went there to get food for me and my "brothers" in the house.

In those days, I went to visit Mrs. Chayito to watch *The Flintstones.*, as often as I could. That was my safe place. It always had been. When Maria didn't let me into the house when she was mad at me, I went to Mrs. Chayito's, and she let me sleep on her patio. She always gave me a warm welcome and always took me in, even though she never offered a bed because she had none to spare.

I was always happy and thankful that she accepted me every time I went to her place. And every time, she told me, "Hey, boy, your mother wouldn't want this life for you. Behave well. You gain nothing from being aggressive and doing the wrong things. Don't fight around." Then she let me in. She fed me *always*. She sent me to the bathroom to shower *always*. And she gave me clean clothes *always* (they were usually the dirty ones I had left the last time). Even if I had eaten earlier, I always ate because I did not know when I was going to eat again.

My "brothers" and I liked to play a game called jump in. The object of the game was to try to jump into the back of a car, a truck, a pickup, anything that was moving and hold onto it until someone caught us or we were too far away from home, and then we jumped off. We got good at it. We had no fear of falling from the cars. We loved the adrenaline rush from the danger we were exposed to—the excitement from doing the wrong, the prohibited; the excitement from knowing how far we could go without paying for the ride. We loved it.

On the day before Christmas, we played jump in. Three of us jumped onto the back of a VW pickup. It was covered up. It was like a van turned into a pickup truck with bars around it to cover it with a thick cloth. The cloth was removable. We held on really well, so we laughed and celebrated that we made it. Suddenly, as we started looking around us and concentrating better on our grip, we started smelling food. *Cooked* food. *Mmmmmmm...* Raúl, Maria's youngest son, lifted the cover and discovered something marvelous.

No one was in the back part of the truck, plus the back window had a wooden piece covering it. I thought that there was no way they could discover us. So we went inside the back of the truck very quietly. We started looking around for what was smelling so good. We found some covered baskets. We checked them one by one: One had bread, another had vegetables, and another had cakebread. When we finally untied the cover of a huge pot, we saw that it was filled with one-piece chicken in a marvelous red sauce. When we saw that, it was as if our stomachs sensed it too because we felt the hunger immediately. Then we made a plan for Christmas dinner: we would take as many things as our pants could hold.

We took fruits, bread, everything we could grab, and I put my hand into the huge pot and fished out two chickens! This was the most successful round of jump in so far. As soon as we could, we jumped out of the truck. Of course, we fell on dirt. The chickens got all dirty too, but we didn't care. We could wash them anyway. With all our goods, we walked fast back home, laughing and playing. We were so happy that when we got home, we all told Maria at the same time, "Maria, today, we are eating chicken!"

"And where did this come from, kids?"

"I found them in the street. It might have fallen off someone's basket," I said, trying not to laugh.

"Well, give them to me. They are here anyway, so I will prepare them for dinner," she said in the same serious tone.

The other kids started to take out the vegetables and bread and fruits that my "brothers" and I had gotten. Maria still could not believe it. That night, we all ate delicious food! I had not eaten chicken in a long time. It was a great menu, and I felt like the richest kid on earth! It was a wonderful Christmas Eve.

My "brothers" and I kept laughing at our game—our inside joke—even when we were already trying to fall asleep on the floor. But I knew inside that what we had done was not good. After all, someone was missing the chickens we ate, and I could not imagine the reaction of the people when they found out about our petty theft. They had more chickens, but still, they were missing two. So that night, even though we ate a great deal and we had a lot of fun, my heart did not rest easy. In the morning, I talked to the other two kids involved and decided to confess everything to Maria.

"Maria, we have something to tell you," I started because I was the oldest of the bunch.

"Okay, what happened?"

And Raúl blurted out, "We want to confess that everything we brought yesterday we took from a pickup truck that we jumped onto."

"I knew it! So many good things could not be found in the streets! Well, kids, what is done is already done, and we cannot change anything. We ate good, but our good food was food missing from someone else's table. Do not do that again. We are poor, but we are honest people.

"I have not taught to any of you to go out to rob anything. We have to work to get money to buy our things. We get our food honestly. This is the first and last time this will happen. Do you understand me?"

She did not punish us or yell at us. We felt happy that she was such a nice person that we could confess our robbery to her. The confession had taken away a big burden from us.

Maria sent me and my school-age "brothers" to school, but we did not go all the time. She took care of washing our clothes and feeding us. We were thirteen in total in that house—Maria's seven children and us six (all boys and her as the only girl). We slept on the floor, over all the clothes we found because there was no bed for any of us; there was no space for hammocks either. We were too many for the small house, but we were happy even though we were very poor. It was fun to have so many brothers around. At least, I was better off than when I was in the bigger house with the witch. I did not miss her at all. (Not even the beds!)

At the end of the school year (I was eight then), we had our summer vacation from November to January and, I got a job in a firecracker factory. Cohetería Venus was the company name. The firecrackers where made of newspaper papers rolled real tight and in the middle I put the powder. They needed small fingers to put the fireworks' powder inside, and I was one of those who had such fingers. I loved working there because I was paid fifty colónes ($20.00) a month, and at the end of the job well done, I could take some firecrackers home.

Christmas season and New Year's Eve were celebrated with everyone lighting up firecrackers! I had no clue what Christmas was really all about. For me, it was just about vacation and firecrackers. I even felt really mad at families that went around together to buy firecrackers for their kids because I did not have a father or mother who could do that for me. I also felt really upset every Christmas Eve as I would see all the kids and parents with new clothes. I wondered what they did with their old ones. I remembered wishing to, at least, have the old clothes for me to use at night.

Families get together and go to church happily together. That anger and probably jealousy were my first contact with God. I had no idea God—or any superior being for that matter—existed. *How can someone like that exist?* When I first heard about God, all I remembered saying was that I hated God. There was no way that a good god can exist, especially when he took away both my parents. That was impossible. For me, if any superior being existed, it must have been a very bad god. It was impossible to think that a good god could exist. "I hate him! I hate him!" I often said.

Whenever I saw the happy families, I got so mad inside that I tried to fight with anyone who looked at me funny. I wanted to fight to let out my rage. I did not know how else to feel better.

And God sent His son to die on the cross," I heard one day from outside a Catholic church. And I thought, *I am glad his son died too because he took my mom and my dad! I hate you, God! That is, if you exist anyway!* I said that with utter hatred in my heart. I did not know at that time how irreverent it was to say that.

6

Weekends with Estela

The year that I turned eight, Estela appeared. I still deeply resented her. I was mad as I had felt rejected and abandoned by her. All those feelings rushed back in when I saw her. My face was even hot from anger. She came in really happy, with a huge smile. She looked radiant and lovely, but I did not understand her happiness as I was so furious with her. I hated her.

When I saw her from the end of the hall, I really wanted to hide, but Maria told me that she was looking for me. *I wonder what she wants*, I questioned myself.

"Hello! How are you?" she asked with a huge smile on her face.

"How am I supposed to be? I'm here. Alone. Without a family," I answered in a really mean tone.

Estela held her arms out to hug me, but I moved away from her. I just felt too much hatred for her. She felt my rejection, so she came down and sat on the floor to see me at my height and to look at me straight into my eyes.

"Eddy, Esmeralda never told you I came to look for you several times?" she said, directly looking at me.

That threw me off, and I opened my eyes wide.

"You *never* came back to look for me! You are a liar!" I responded with all the hatred from the bottom of my heart.

"No, Eddy, I swear! I came back looking for you at least four or five times, but that woman always told me you had escaped. So I went around the place for hours every time, trying to find you, but I never did."

I could not believe her words, but deep inside, I knew she was being sincere to me because she was looking at me directly into my eyes. Those few words made my heart soften a little, even though I still had my doubts.

"Are you serious?"

"I swear to you with my life, Eduardo. I started to look for you right after I got home, and Mom told me what had happened. Remember, I wasn't home. Otherwise, I would have fought with that woman!…Come give me a hug." She held her arms out again for me, encouraging me to go toward her.

I could not stand it any longer. I went toward her, and we hugged each other real tight! I felt her love. My heart fell apart and I started sobbing on her shoulder, believing every word she had said.

When I finally stopped crying, her comforting me, she said, "Look, Eduardo, you know I am your half sister, right?"

At that point, I really understood that her mother had been my dad's lover, and that made her my father's illegitimate daughter (but all that I didn't understand back then). All I heard was the word *sister*. If she was half or not, I did not understand for sure how that worked. My ears were just happy to hear that, finally, after so long, I had real family.

She continued, "Someone told me that you were at Esmeralda's house but that she was not around anymore, and this is why I started to look for you again. I wanted to know if you were all right, if you were studying, or what happened to you. And asking around, I came to this house, where you are."

I just stared at her with my eyes wide open and listened to her very closely.

"I have a proposition for you. I wanna take you to my house on the weekends. I cannot keep you there for good because it is dangerous. I have no way of proving that you are my brother, but it is safe if I take you on the weekends. Would you like that?"

My head was spinning around in confusion. All the hate that I felt when I saw her turned into love. I could not believe my ears! I was going to have a house to go to on the weekends, and I was going to have a family again!

"What you don't know is that I got married and I do not live in my old house anymore. When you got to my mom's house, my oldest daughter was there with my mother because she helps me take care of her as I already have another baby."

At this point, I couldn't care less where I was headed. I only thought about having a family again and eating good food every weekend.

"But when will this be, Estela?" I asked anxiously since it was the week right before the beginning of the new school year.

"Since this weekend, Eddy. I will take you with me to buy your notebooks, paper, pencils, a backpack, and all other stuff you need for the new school year."

I could not believe it. Luck was on my side!

"One condition. During the school days, you will return here so you go to school. I want you to behave and get good grades because if you do not get good grades, I will stop coming every weekend," she ended very serious.

"And when will you come to pick me up? Friday or Saturday?"

"This Friday when I get out from work, I will come to pick you up at around 6:00 p.m. so that you can have dinner with us."

I thought it was a great idea, and I was extremely excited— mostly because I was going to eat much better (at least on the weekends) and I was going to experience what it was like to have a family again. So I started going with her every weekend; I tagged along in every trip she and her family planned—be it to the mall, the mountains, the ice cream shop, and every other place I had never been before.

Estela was married to an Arab guy named Ali. He was an older man—like ten years older than her—but he was really kind to me. He accepted me immediately.

That very first weekend, I went for the first time to the largest mall in El Salvador called Metrocentro in San Salvador. On another day, we went to the drive-in theater in Estela's car. It was another world. To me, she was rich.

Estela started working on my feelings, and she started to earn back my love and my trust. I was starting to love her again, but deep inside, I still hated her I didn't understand these mixed feelings; I loved her and hated her.

The weekends became my reason for living. I started comparing Estela and Maria in my head: At Estela's I slept on a bed, but at Maria's, I slept on the floor. Estela fed me three times a day while Maria just fed me once or twice daily when we found food. Estela made me take a shower every day while Maria did not care if I showered or not, and when I did get to shower, it was with cold water. Estela bought me clothes and my first pair of shoes since I became an orphan, but Maria had never bought me anything since she had no means to do so.

Estela took me to out on trips and sightseeing in her car while Maria did not take me anywhere, except to go get some food somewhere. Estela made me wash my clothes so that I had clean ones to wear while Maria washed our clothes when she can and had soap to do so (otherwise, I wore dirty clothes). Estela made me clean up the house, wash dishes, help around to pick up after myself because she liked a clean house while Maria did not care to live in a dirty house (I loved living in a clean house).

Every weekend, I saw new things around the house for me—I even had my own room! It was a fairy tale every weekend, and I felt loved and accepted. Yes, she made me do things I was not used to and pushed me to my limits, but I liked that because I felt loved and cared for. I had a house, a bed, a room, and full meals. There was a table to eat at and chairs to sit on; we did not have to eat on the floor as I did at Maria's place. Estela also bought my first backpack! Ahhhhhh! I was sooooo happy! It was the first time in my whole life that I ever had my own backpack! I was the envy of my classmates!

So my little heart softened every weekend, and I learned to like the limits and discipline she imposed. And all that school year, I went back and forth between Maria's and Estela's. I started getting disgusted with living in a dirty and messy house and among dirty kids. The odor started to bother me when they did not wash themselves. I started to hate not eating three times a day.

That year, I went to school every day and became motivated to get good grades to keep my sister happy. Every time I brought in test papers with good marks, she gave me a gift. Sometimes it was a piece of candy or a bar of chocolate; and sometimes it was something bigger, like my radio and lamp. They were all earned with my good behavior and good grades. But more than that, my heart was full of happiness: I had a family again!

When the school year ended and when I turned nine, she asked, "Eduardo, would you like to come live with us for good?"

I stared at her in disbelief. "Are you serious?" I had dreamed of her asking that question all year.

"If you want to come to live with us, you will have to get here all by yourself. I will not come pick you up because I want no problems. The last thing I need is to be accused of kidnapping a kid since we do not have the same last name, and there is no way I can prove you are my half brother since our father never gave me his last name."

This information made me understand somehow why she was not my full sister, just half.

"Of course I want to go with you!" I said, excited, and hugged her real tight. I behaved with Estela because I felt loved, but with Maria, I got into trouble all the time. My heart was with Estela, and I started to see Maria with hatred. I forgot real fast all her sacrifices and all the months that she took care of us.

Mrs. Chayito's words came to my mind. *You should go look for Estela and live with her.* And she was right. With Estela, I was going to have a better life. I made up my mind, but I had to tell Maria about my decision and have her permission to do so. But if she was not going to agree, I will still go. Period.

Now I recognize that in my hard childhood years, God was always with me, by my side. He kept me safe from all those people who tried to abuse me. He delivered me from any sickness—colds, flu, bronchitis, etc. He took care of me when I slept in the rain and under the stars. Wet and cold or dry and warm, He was there. He took care of me from getting sick to my stomach when I ate food from the garbage. He cared about my health, even when I slept on the floor—I never ever got sick. Not even once.

God was there even when we stole the chickens and the other things when we jumped off the moving car. He did not approve of it, of course, but He was there to save us from being hit by another car. He has been with me ever since I was conceived in my mother's womb when I did not even see or recognize Him at that point. No one explained to me about His existence.

7

Living with Estela

I woke up real early, and when I did, all I wanted to do was to remember all those great times I had spent with my dad. In an instant, I became very emotional. I clearly remembered a time when I was around three years old, on a Saturday afternoon.

Dad announced, "Tomorrow, we are going to the beach! So I want everyone ready to go at seven." *Ahhh! The beach!*

That night, I could hardly sleep because I was too excited! I loved going to the beach! I loved going out with my family to any place really, but the beach was our favorite place. I could spend hours looking at the waves crash against the shore. I was always impressed with the huge waves.

Sometimes the adults said that the beach was full. I did not understand at that point what they meant by "full"; but when I saw the huge waves, all I could do was watch them from the shore with my family, not bothering to go into the water. Then I daydreamed that I was a fish and that I could swim around in the big waves.

Once in a while, I saw a fish jumping out the water, and I would imagine it was me—free as I could be. I dreamt that I would find a mermaid and that the mermaid was my mom. Somehow, imagining those things helped me think of her as a divine being looking after me from somewhere in heaven. And when I was at the beach, I hoped to find her as the mermaid.

Dad often told me stories before going to sleep, and my favorite was the one about beautiful mermaids in the ocean. It was because of that story that I imagined my mom as one of them. He told me that when he went to fish in the ocean, he saw dolphins, *mom*fish, monkfish, and so on. I never knew if he really went to fish in the ocean or if he made the story up, but I laughed with him and imagined every detail he told me.

My dad went to the beach with me when the tide was low, and I felt so happy! It was a dream come true! For me it was the best way to spend a family day. Those were memories I treasured.

When I stopped reminiscing about those days, I have to come to the sad conclusion that those days had long before ended. *Who will take me to the beach? Would I ever get to go again? Would Estela take me someday? Is it the right decision to go live with her? Can I trust her? Will I have to wait until I grow up to go to the beach again? Oh no, I do not want to think anymore! I do not want to feel, think, or know anything about my past or the future that awaits me!*

I got up, dressed, and went out of the house with all those thoughts spinning in my head. I ran away and cried. I cried and cried maybe for an hour or two. All those repressed feelings were surfacing. I needed to do something. I felt so much pressure from thinking about my future. I returned home when I got hungry.

All my feelings were mixed up. I had an opportunity in front of me, but I was afraid. Afraid of feeling rejected again. Afraid of loosing my family again. Afraid that Estela was only playing around with my feelings. Afraid that the witch was going to come back for me and take me away without my consent. I was afraid that it was all just a dream. Somehow I was not totally sure of her sincerity; but I had the offer I wanted, and I had to make a decision.

I went into Maria's house. Then I entered the kitchen to see if I could find something to eat. I found nothing. In that house, we hardly ever had anything extra to eat; but in Estela's house, it was only a matter of opening the fridge, a drawer, or some kitchen cabinets to find cookies, candies, bread, and anything else I'd never eaten before.

Well, be a man, I thought. *Today I will talk to Maria, and I will tell her about the offer I got. If she tells me I cannot go because the witch will be mad at her, I will escape anyway.* Maria has been a good person to me—the best so far, in fact—and she deserved respect from me. The least I could do was tell her. I could not just disappear from her life. She would get worried for sure.

That night, I waited until Maria gave us our dinner: beans and tortilla like every night. When we finished eating and everyone went to sleep, I stayed awake to talk to her. Around midnight, she saw me pacing back and forth.

"What's wrong with you, kid?" Maria asked finally.

"I need to talk with you."

"What's wrong, Son? Have you stolen something?"

"No, Miss Maria. I have not stolen anything since that night we ate chicken, and I will do it no more. It's not that. It's about a decision I have to make, and I am worried about it."

"Decision? What decision? Tell me so that I can see if I can help."

And I spit it out, "You know I had gone every weekend with my sister, Estela, all this year, right?"

"Yep, of course I know. She came to ask for permission to do so."

"Ah, I did not know that."

"And? What are you trying to tell me?"

"Estela has asked me to go to live with her, and I do not know what to do because she said that if I want to go, I have to go all by myself because she would not come to pick me up. And somehow, you are my family too, here with all these brothers." I finished, feeling an undeniable anguish in my heart, hoping that she would not get mad with me.

To my utter surprise, she said, "Okay, boy. I am happy for you. You will have a better life with her, and you will live with a real family. She has all the possibilities of dressing you and feeding you much better than I ever can. Here, we are very poor, and you see we eat once or twice a day. I just ask you that you come to visit us once in a while."

I was delighted! And my face brightened up! That was the sign I needed. I could not believe it! For the first time, I get to go from one place to another with permission and without any problems. No one was making me do anything. I was choosing my destiny, and I was so excited. I could not wait till next day to go to Estela's.

Since I knew perfectly how to go to Estela's house, the next morning, I gathered up all my belongings—which wasn't much, by the way—and said good-bye to my partners, friends, and brothers. Then I happily left. Estela had given me money to pay for the bus, if necessary. After all, I was nine years old!

I remember how happy I was in that moment: my heart was so full from all the happiness I felt. Finally, I was going to have a family that loved me, and I could hardly believe it. I no longer had to go out to work or look for food. I only had to be part of a family and behave well. I planned to be obedient and help in the house duties; and in exchange, I was going to have a family, warm food on a table, a permanent bed and room, and love from my real family. Luck was on my side, and life was good again.

Estela was fascinated with having me back for good. Her plan had been successful—a plan that at that point, I had no idea what was about. I just felt really happy and well received. I felt like I had taken the right decision without having to fight with anybody. The witch had disappeared from my life, and my sister had come to rescue me, like the prince rescues the princess but backward. We celebrated that night. We went to buy ice cream for everyone, including Estela's daughters and her husband, Ali. My stepmother was there too.

After the celebration and before going to bed, Estela presented to me her rules.

"Okay, Eddy, we are really happy you are here with us for good and not with someone else. As you know, we have rules, and now you will learn them and have to follow them to stay with us for good. Up to this point, we have not been too strict with you, but now you are part of the family. You have to follow them, or you will go back to where you came from."

What a welcome, I thought. But actually, I knew that I needed rules. Because up to that point, I had been a sheep without a shepherd, lost in the world.

"First of all, we like respect, and no one can yell here, except Ali and I if necessary to put you and the kids in order. Secondly, you have to shower every day and wash yourself fully. There is shampoo and soap in the bathroom, and when you finish it, let me know and I will give you more."

"My sister must be really rich, I thought.

"Another thing. When school starts again, you will go to learn a skill during the day so that soon, you can learn to earn your own money and we do not have to pay for all your needs."

"You will study at night, and you will learn your skill during the day. You are nine now. I had talked to some coworkers in my office, and they said that they will be happy to teach you how to use mechanical tools."

I thought that was a great idea because that sounded like a better-paying job than selling newspapers in the streets. However, I had not thought I had to work so soon. That was not in my plan. I thought I only had to behave and help around the house and study, but maybe that was a great idea and could be fun to learn so that I can have a well-paying job when I grew up.

So that school year, I went to night school; and even though I had a family, I started to learn how to use some tools so that

I can have a job soon. Learning that skill really helped me in my growing years, and I will always be grateful for that since I would have never had an opportunity like that if I had stayed with Maria.

Estela had a hidden motive, which I never imagined she had. She had started to work on it since the beginning of the year before. She had the plan of going to live in the United States with all her family, except me and her mother, that same year. She did not say anything until just before the end of May. One day, she simply got us together and announced to her mother and me that she was leaving the country with her husband and her daughters.

She's abandoning me! Again, the same story! I stay alone again? I can't believe it! This can't be true! And when I was immersed in my thoughts, she said, "Eddy, I am really sorry, but this is an emergency. We have to move to the US next month, and I *need* you to stay with my mother. You will be the man now.

"You are in charge of the house. But don't worry. You will be okay here. I had talked with my coworkers to help you learn quickly how to use those tools and become an expert so that you can have a paying job there as soon as possible, but I will be sending money for my mom and you. So you have nothing to worry about.

"You are not learning to use all those tools to have a job to pay for all the bills of the house. What I am trying to tell you is that it will be good for you to have a paying job, but what I really want is for you to stay with my mother and take care of her as she is a grown lady and is alone. This way, you are not alone, and neither is she. That makes it perfect that you had come to live with us. Otherwise, I wouldn't know what to do with my mother. You are a good kid, and I am sure you will become a great man."

She made me feel important and needed by the family, so I did not feel rejected with her explanation. It made sense to me. She was so smart; she had it all figured out. She was an only child, and she used that as an excuse so that she wouldn't feel guilty of leaving her mom behind. She made me responsible for her, and I felt important. I believed it all. But she was not thinking of me—she was only finding a solution to her problem. I never thought her offer was a plan she had in advance. It was a master plan indeed.

Although I never suspected it, I realized that it was a well-thought-out plan. She promised to come every year but never promised to come back for good or to take both me and her mother with her. I just came to the conclusion that some things in life just happen; and it just happened that she had to go, and I was to become the "man of the house." I was in charge; I felt important and needed.

Estela disappeared from my life between nine and ten years of age; and I stayed with Margarita, who was already an old lady in my eyes. Thinking back, though, she was in her sixties then and, thus, not too old. But at nine, I thought that was *really* old! Estela came to visit once a year just as she had promised. The responsibility had entered my veins during the age of ten. I saw her only two weeks each summer, but I became a very good student and a hard worker.

Since I worked with grown men (I was the only "kid learner"), they forgot I was a minor, and they often talked about women and vulgar things in front of me. They talked about drinking and smoked all day during every break they took. They swore all the time and did not hold anything back in front of me. Since I was a street kid, I was used to saying and hearing bad words, so I talked like them too.

I stayed learning my way around the job since I was nine, and when I was twelve, I grew up physically and mentally way too fast. I tried a cigarette for the first time. Then I started drinking.

Maybe I didn't try it before because I did not have the money to buy them, nor was I with people who had it. I had just decided to be good at school and at my job because I had planned to go to a tech school and then to the university to become an engineer when I graduate from ninth grade. I did not know exactly how that was going to happen, but it sounded so good to dream about becoming an engineer. I did not know where I could go to study that career, and I decided that I was not going to worry until the time came. A dream started in me then. At thirteen, I had grown as a big man, and I had learned to manage and use all the tools so that I got a paying job.

Many interesting things happened in my life in those days. I had learned to have discipline in my job and in school because the dream of going to university was in me. While I worked there, I learned to use the industrial table, to weld, and, overall, to be a good mechanic. I loved my job. I felt important; and it was a new world for me, being around men and not kids. I really enjoyed all those years and was happy to have been there.

8

Maria Elena

I attended night school, which was perfect for those of us who worked during the day and studied at night. The interesting thing about this mode of schooling was that the grade we were at did not necessarily belong to the right age, unlike the day students. I was one of the only kids who were in the right age and the right grade. For example I had a classmate that had 22 years, and yet another one that was 45 and decided to go back to school.

I was in seventh grade. There, I met girls of all ages, but since all my life I had been between other boys and men, I was afraid to talk to girls. Biologically, I was twelve, but I looked like a sixteen- or seventeen-year-old. My mind was that of a grown man because of my background.

With the help and encouragement from my coworkers, I started flirting with girls. I wanted to be like the men I worked with and be able to talk about women and those things. I felt attracted to girls for the first time, at that age, especially one girl in particular. I also started feeling weird things inside me when I was close to her. We started talking, but the closeness did not develop into a relationship. She got scared of me because of my background and started to turn away from me. I just did not know what to talk about or how to behave around her. I just understood that I was too young and she was not for me.

When I turned thirteen and had a paying job, I earned 300 colones (which, with the exchange rate those days, equaled $120 US dollars). I grew up real fast, and since I had my own money, I started to dress much better. I looked eighteen and had money that was a lot for someone my age, so I started to feel like a grown man. Having money gave me the liberty of not asking for money from my stepmother. I had enough money to invite a girl out to eat without having to ask anyone for some money or seeking permission to go out.

I was thirteen when for the first time I became interested in a young girl and I started to observe her. Because I was tall, I played basketball and got in on the team, and I noticed that she stayed for the practices most of the time and definitely to *all* the games. She was a really serious person, like I was. She was shy, like I was. Sometimes we ran into each other in the halls, and we just looked at each other without saying a word. I had noticed that she often looked at me, and we even caught ourselves staring at each other. But neither she nor I had the courage to start talking to the other. I was afraid to talk to her and get rejected again.

I also observed that she was very dedicated with her studies and that she went to school , wasting no time. She was a very responsible girl (by the way, she was in the ninth grade and I was in the eighth). She was so beautiful. I loved her long, straight hair. She was as tall as me, thin and very attractive. She did not use any makeup—and didn't need to because she had a natural beauty. What I liked the most about her was that she was just as timid as me.

Another member of the basketball team noticed that we stared at each other, and he said, "Haven't you noticed that Maria Elena follows you with her eyes everywhere you go? Talk to her. Don't be a fool!"

Maria Elena studied at night because her family had a bakery, and at 2:00 a.m., she had to wake up to help put bread into the oven to have them ready at 5:00 a.m. for the bicycle sellers. Then, she helped sell all morning in the bakery store until midday.

She worked up to two o'clock then rested a little or finished up homework. Then at five thirty, she went to school while the rest of the employees and her family prepared all the ingredients for the following day. She had no time to waste, so she went to school to learn. I had never seen her flirt with anyone, and I learned that she had to be responsible at an early age too. We had that in common. We both worked and had paying jobs. We both paid our way through school. That I liked very much.

One fine day, I got the courage to get close to her and started talking to her. The excuse was to ask her if she played basketball or wanted to start. Because of her height, she was a good candidate. But that was just to break the ice between us. When we started getting to know each other, I learned about her work schedule; and little by little, we started knowing more about each other's difficult lives.

We started talking about everything, and I told her about my background and that I was an orphan I told her how I lost my mom when I was a small kid; how I lost my brother, who worked as a bus collector, and how I did not want to be like him; and how grateful I was for my sister, who had shown me a way to learn a valuable skill. Another day, I finally told her how I had lost my father. I shared with her how my brother Hector had run furiously away from home too and that I heard nothing from him since.

When I finally told her about the death of my father, I did not tell her I had gone to live in a brothel. Neither had I told her that I had escaped many times from being sexually abused because there was no point in telling her about that part of my life. But I did tell her about Maria and all the brothers I had when I lived with her. She laughed so hard when I told her about all the adventures and things we used to do with them. She especially enjoyed the one about the day we jumped into the VW panel and robbed the veggies, bread, and chicken. She never judged me for that episode. On the contrary, she just saw it as a childhood adventure. I loved seeing her smile (she had such an angelic smile) and more so when she laughed hard. I was falling in love really fast, but this time, I felt like my feelings were returned.

I was a very vibrant boy, a street boy; I was explosive, a fighter, a person angry at life itself. Yes, I was from the streets, but I had never gotten encounters with girls. For some reason, life had only made me meet boys and men. The only girls I had known were my sister, her daughters, my stepmother, and my schoolmates from when I went to school from first to third grade.

Maria Elena turned me into the most sensitive guy on earth. I was soft and happy with her. I felt so different with her, around her. I admired and respected her. And I was falling in love with her more and more every day. I felt butterflies in my stomach. I felt like I had found my partner for life! Yes, I was thirteen, but I had fallen in love. I felt that this was a true love.

Maria Elena told me about her own struggles too, and even though she had a home and both parents and she never had to work for food and everything else she needed, she felt bad about her parents fighting all the time. Her father had been a man that had been unfaithful to his wife many times. He was a macho man, a person who liked to drink alcohol until he got heavily drunk. He was controlling and mad (probably just like my dad and many men of his generation). Her mother couldn't stand that lifestyle anymore, and one day when they had a really serious fight, she said that she was going to leave him. Then she took Maria Elena and her other two daughters in that precise moment, put some things in a bag, and left for her mother's.

Since that day, Maria Elena went on to live at her grandma's. Her dad never came for them, asked for forgiveness from her mother, or anything. That day, their relationship ended abruptly. Since she was too small to understand, she got no explanation of what happened with her father. She was old enough to help around in the bakery but too young to learn about adult problems. Her father used to work in the bakery too; but with that fight, he had no job, no wife, and no daughters. He disappeared from their lives.

So she would tell me how she had started working in the bakery doing Dad's job (or actually, her mom took his job and she took her mom's job). She helped her mother and grandmother and made plans to study business administration to help manage the bakery in a better way. She also felt that feeling of loss in her life. She had no father figure since her mother never remarried and her dad never came back.

She always brought to school delicious, sweet bread, so me and my stomach were falling more in love. And even though I worked as a mechanic, I always went home to take a good shower to go to school real clean and shaved. I kept myself well dressed—clothes ironed and clean (I had my stepmother iron all my clothes real well as I had no time to do so). I was a very responsible person in my job and in school because I had decided to be someone important in life, more so after having fallen in love with Maria Elena. I had a good reason to become someone important. I was going to be a good professional and an owner of a successful business.

Going to night school helped us have time to get to know more about each other. And even though I was really frightened to get close to a girl, with Maria Elena, I felt so comfortable. I could not explain it myself. We were just so compatible: we were two hardworking people with dreams of success, and we both worked and studied hard. At one point, we discovered that we lived only five blocks away from each other. This discovery made everything more exciting. I mean, what a coincidence! We talked about anything and everything about our lives. We built castles in the air and dreamed of both becoming professionals. Up to this point, I had not even tried to hold her hand. We just talked and talked all the time. We laughed and dreamed together.

One day, there was a dance, and a common friend invited us separately to go. But for some reason, we had not told each other about it. Apparently, it was a secret arrangement that my friend had made to have us there together as a surprise to both of us. When we saw each other, we immediately started dancing together. It was our first time dancing.

When I saw her, my heart almost jumped out of my chest. She looked so beautiful. I could wait no longer, so while we were dancing to a slow song, I sought her lips and gave her my first kiss. It was a very soft kiss. A sweet, delicate kiss on her lips. It was my first kiss ever! I was so afraid that she would turn around or reject me, and I was trembling all over. My heart was pounding really fast. I did not know if she had kissed someone else before, and I did not want to know at that point.

I never asked her if she had had a boyfriend before. All I knew was that in that moment, it was only her and me. Together. Dancing. I did not know if she would like the kiss. But she accepted me, and that first kiss was the beginning of a great romance. That night we became steady, and from that day on, we were boyfriend and girlfriend. I could not believe it!

Pretty soon, we started going out on weekends. I invited her to go to Metrocentro, the largest mall in El Salvador. We went window-shopping all day, going up and down, looking at all the stores around there. Her mother had only taken her there when they had to buy something specific but never to just go around the whole mall. It took us several visits to check out all of it. We loved to go window-shopping and daydreaming about a life together. We planned all the things we wanted to buy when we finished school and already had good jobs. Metrocentro was so big and so well stocked that we found all types of stores, clothing, furniture, banks, and restaurants; anything and everything was found there. We also dreamed of settling down together, having a family, and living happily ever after.

One day, we planned a trip to the beach with other classmates instead of going to Metrocentro. Since it was my favorite place as a child, this was the beginning to several trips to the Majahual Beach at La Libertad, forty minutes away from the capital city.

As the year went by, we found new ways to pass the time: I took her dancing to a disco on Fridays. We went dancing or walking in the park just to see the stars in the sky after 6 p.m., daydream, and make more castles in the air. I learned to be a romantic boy because I discovered Maria Elena loved that. I wrote some poems once in a while, and that made her really happy. Little by little, we fell madly in love with each other. We did not want to be apart from each other because we seemed to be two halves of a whole. The kissing started to become more frequent. My body shook, but I wanted to be how my friends at work were when they talked about women, adventures, and romance.

I started to get home later than what my stepmother was used to before I had a girlfriend. We stayed outside of her house talking and kissing here and there. My stepmother started questioning me about my late arrivals, but I always told her I had stayed out late to study with a friend. I also started lying. When I went dancing on the weekends, I told her I went out with some friends from school or work. I never mentioned my relationship with Maria Elena because I was afraid that she was going to be mad at me. After all, I was only thirteen (which Maria Elena had no clue about). That was one secret I wanted to keep because she could reject me and be afraid to fall more in love with me as I was four years younger than her.

One day, Margarita saw me holding hands with Maria Elena as we were walking toward the bakery. So she discovered that day that I had a girlfriend. She got really upset with me and started forbidding me from going out. She started questioning me every time I went out. She asked me where I had met her, and I innocently told her that I met her at school. So she forbade me from going to school to continue studying and I had to break up with my girlfriend. She started yelling at me; she verbally abused me, and I was not used to that.

I became a rebel with her. I disobeyed her totally since she did not look after my best interests. When she told me I had an early curfew, I returned home really late at night. Margarita threatened me that she would tell Estela, but I couldn't care less because she was gone from my life. She had abandoned me again, so I did not care what Estela had to say. (I kind of hated her really deep inside.)

A couple of months after Margarita discovered my relationship, Estela made a trip home just to scold me really hard. She said that she was going to take me out of school so that I can concentrate on my job and because I was not of proper age to have a girlfriend. My duty was to take care of her mother, and I was giving her such a hard time that she was not feeling too good. She was getting sick, and it was all my fault—all the anguish she had suffered.

She made me feel bad and guilty, and as always, she had control over me. She convinced me that she was right about this craziness of being in love at thirteen. Since I was that young, I should not have been thinking about having such a serious relationship with a girl. My friends at work told me the same thing, and they were right. But I knew Maria Elena was different. They did not know her.

Suddenly I stopped going to school, and all my dreams of becoming a professional engineer were put aside for the moment. I even stopped going to the places she and I went together so that I could not run into her. I stopped the relationship without telling her anything. I simply disappeared. Almost in the same way my beloved parents had disappeared from my life when they died (of course, except I was alive). I had no clue of how to do it otherwise. I was commanded by my sister to do so, and I just obeyed like a robot. She controlled me, and I did not even recognize that she did. So I just disappeared from Maria Elena's life.

I went back to being that aggressive young man I was. The little monster I had inside governed me now. That was something I knew I could become very easily—the mad, aggressive kid. I continued to work because I really liked my job (plus, I liked having my own money). Maria Elena was just scratched out from my life. I analyzed my sister's command and came to the conclusion that she was right: even though I was in love, I sacrificed my feelings and my dreams. *My sister's right*, said my weak, dominated mind.

Maria Elena knew exactly where I lived, but she was a very decent girl—she was a lady—so she never went out to look for me. Never. Girls don't go looking for the boys; they wait for the boys to look for them. Maria Elena was a very proper girl. I knew that she would never come looking for me. So I just stop going to the places we could meet.

A couple months later, Maria Elena's cousin Pedro came looking for me at my job. He said that since I disappeared, Maria Elena had become totally depressed, and all she had been doing was crying. She had even stopped eating and working, and she didn't want to go to school anymore. She had a severe depression because I had disappeared without warning.

She had changed too much and was in really bad health, so her mother had sent Pedro out to look for me. She was worried about her daughter's health and state of mind. He asked me to go look for her and talk to her, explain my decision. Her mother was very worried because Maria Elena had told her mother that she was really in love with me and that she herself could not explain what could have happened when I disappeared without a word. We had not had a fight or anything, so she felt abandoned and confused. She wanted to die, and that was why she had stopped eating. Maria Elena's mother did not like that. She said that she'd rather have me back than have her daughter dead.

When I heard all that, my heart sank, and I felt so bad for leaving her just like that. I felt so guilty because I had not stopped thinking about her. I just obeyed my sister and followed her instructions like a robot because she controlled me. She had a way of doing so. I felt bad about the health of my stepmother because Estela had made me responsible for her. But Maria Elena's depression was undeniably my fault, and if she was going to die, I would never forgive myself. I did not want her to die. I was still in love with her.

I loved Maria Elena, and she was too important to me. So I went to look for her against my family's will. I did not share anything to Margarita because I knew that she would scold me for that. I felt like a young man and that I was in no position to be scolded when I was a person who worked and had been very responsible and earned my own money. Besides, I was already fourteen, but I felt as if I was nineteen or twenty (at least Maria Elena thought that was my age, anyway).

The encounter with Maria Elena was full of excitement. My heart was filled with happiness. I felt butterflies in my stomach once again, and I am sure she did too. We realized that we were really in love and that we could not live without each other. I asked her for forgiveness for leaving her alone and just disappearing from her life; and I explained to her that I got in trouble with my stepmother, that she got sick, that everything was blamed on me for having been disobedient and having stayed out too late, and that she had even prohibited me from going to school (just as long as I was away from her). But I could not stop thinking about her, so I came back.

Ours was a true, pure love. Neither of us had been in love before, so we could not compare it to any other relationship. But what I knew was that my heart melted when I was beside her. However, since I was a man (a macho man), I could not express all my feelings to her. I just enjoyed being mellow with her. Maybe it was because I had grown up without a mother. I do not know. I just enjoyed it. My heart felt full when I was next to her.

Our secret love was growing, and so was our touch. Meeting in secret made everything more exciting because I had to pretend with Margarita that nothing was going on and had to make up stories to go out. What was prohibited was, of course, more exciting. Maybe that was what made our hearts beat rapidly every time we were together. But we had a secret love only from my side because her mother had given us permission to see each other and go out. She was just happy to see her daughter happy, and her eyes were also full of love toward me. With that, my girlfriend became herself again.

Her mother let me stay in the living room with her till 10:00 p.m. and, sometimes, later. I always went back home happy from visiting my beloved one. We started going out (with permission) to the beach and to other places alone, and we enjoyed it so much. Being alone changed everything between us and our relationship: it became intense. And the day came when she gave me the exciting but hard news.

"My love, I have some news for you."

"Tell me, my love. What news? You are accepted to the university?" I asked innocently (she had continued her studies and had already graduated from high school a couple of months before).

"No, no. It's not that," she said. "But it is about the university… of parents…I am pregnant," she said seriously, waiting for my reaction.

I became pale and lightheaded. I almost fainted right there and then, but I managed to say, "Seriously, my love? How exciting! I am going to be a father! I can't believe it!"

I do not know how I managed to say those words because I was in total shock. I added immediately without thinking, "Then I will talk to your mother so that we can get married as soon as possible. Do you want to get married?"

She was really excited by my words because she was afraid that I would reject her (as many men do after getting their girlfriends pregnant). But I was in love, and I knew that baby was mine. So that same afternoon, as we got back from the beach, I went directly to talk to her mother. I just told her that we had talked all afternoon and that we had decided that we wanted to get married.

"What is your plan with my daughter?"

"Ma'am, I love her, and I want to marry her. I am serious about it."

"And what can you offer her? You are young and you are a student."

"I have had a job for the past four years, and I earn 300 colones a month [$120]. I think we can live with my salary without any problem."

Luckily, she saw that I really was a responsible person, so she had no problem and even felt happy about our decision. She was happy I had a job and had a way to provide for her daughter]. She never asked if Maria Elena was pregnant, but I suppose she suspected that could be the reason for the quick marriage proposal. She accepted me immediately and said to talk about a date for the wedding to help us plan it soon.

I was soooo happy! I was happier than I'd ever been in my life. I was going to have my own family, and no one can deny that or get in between us. *I am going to be a father! I could not believe it! Wow, I am only fourteen, and I do not even know how long a pregnancy lasts. I will have to ask my coworkers to help me plan so that I can get married before the due date.* I was excited though I was also afraid at the same time.

Now, I had to tell my stepmother, and that was another story: she went hysterical, screaming and yelling at me, telling me how stupid I had been. She even told me to get an abortion so I would not ruin my life! How stupid of her! I had never seen her like that before. Immediately she got on the phone and called Estela, but I couldn't care less at that point. I was decided: I was going to marry Maria Elena and go live at her place. I did not care what Margarita was going to do with her life. After all, she was not my real relative, and I need not to be responsible for her. She didn't even fight for me when I was a kid anyway!

I felt grown up enough to be able to raise my own family, so I shouted back, "I can't care less what my sister says, or what you think or say. This is *my* life and my decision, and I will be responsible for my acts. Her mother is happy, so like it or not, I will marry my girlfriend! There is nothing you or Estela can do about it!" Then I slammed the bedroom door in her face, and just when I did that, I got her out of my heart and mind. There was a new life that had my blood, and that was my baby. My baby was going to be my first priority, and I will never abandon him or her. No matter what.

On Monday morning, I told to one of my coworkers, the one I trusted most, that my girlfriend was pregnant.

"Good boy! You became a man real fast! Congratulations!" he said. Then and there, I learned that a pregnancy typically lasted nine months, so I immediately started counting down the months and realized that I was going to be fifteen when the baby was going to be delivered.

We started planning the wedding and set a date with my girlfriend, thinking that everything was going to be so easy. In my childish mind, I thought we only had to get a lawyer and a priest and tell them that we wanted to get married and that's all! But things were very different.

Maria Elena was four years older than me; so she was an adult, at eighteen years old. But the father of the baby was underage. I told my future mother-in-law that I would go get my birth certificate from the mayor's office so that we can get married. It was there that I learned that I could not marry without my parents' permission, who no longer existed. My only other option was to wait to be an adult. I told the lady that I was an orphan and that it was impossible to get my parents' permission as they had died when I was a child, and I added that I was responsible for my own decisions.

"You are still a child, Eduardo! You are too young to make those types of decisions," she said. "The requisite is that you turn eighteen or have the written consent of your parents and bring them here to say it in person."

"But I am an orphan!" I answered desperately.

"That is what all the kids your age say to us when they want to marry, and it's not true. Stop thinking about getting married. You are only *fourteen*! Continue studying and then fall in love again. Leave that girl alone!"

"I will *not* leave her. I am in love with her, and she is expecting my baby."

The lady just looked at me without believing a word I had said. She then turned back to her typewriter and continued with the next person in line. So that was that. For me to be able to marry my girlfriend, I had to be wait until I turned eighteen. I also had to present my ID to prove that I was old enough. Obviously, I could not prove that, and this was when I had to confess my age to Maria Elena. She could not believe it and got really mad at me because I never mentioned it before.

"You never asked!" was my excuse, and since I really looked older, she never ever imagined I was four years younger.

"But it is important to be honest and transparent in everything," she said to me.

"My love, sweetheart, (touching her kindly) would you have accepted me if I told you I was thirteen when we started going out?"

"No, I don't think so."

"Do you love me less because I am younger than you?"

"No, darling, I do not love you less," she said after having calmed down and having thought it through.

I was a young man and not a child anymore. So with the consent of my future mother-in-law after Maria Elena and I explained my situation, she gave us permission to start living together as of that same day. Maria Elena was in shock for a while, thinking that she had slept with a fourteen-year-old because I looked and sounded older.

Of course, Margarita and Estela did not approve of our relationship. They did not know me well enough and did not even attempt to get to know Maria Elena (even though Margarita knew I was in love with one of the daughters of the bakery owners and she knew exactly where to find us). So I forgot about them completely.

After I turned fifteen, my beautiful daughter, Guadalupe, was born. It was mid-1978 (June 22 to be exact), and I was so excited! Becoming a father changed my life completely. I could not believe that I had a little human being that shared my blood. I fell in love with another woman: my little baby. Now I had two loves in my life, and I planned to give them the best possible life.

My future mother-in-law and my love were also very happy to have another member in the family. I had a family again, a *real* family of my own. She was conceived from a true love, from dreams in the air, and now she was here. By then, I had gotten a raise in my job because I had finished ninth grade since I had gone back to school. I had a real good reason to work hard and study hard: I had someone to be responsible for. In fact, I was already considered an expert mechanic. Life looked good after all.

Margarita and Estela had rejected my relationship with Maria Elena and didn't even take the time to meet her or my new baby, I took the hard decision to resign from my job to cut all ties with my sister and stepmother (they always knew everything about me through my coworkers since Estela had taken me there in the first place, and she kept tabs on me through them).

Because of my knowledge and talent as a mechanic and welder, I thought it was going to be easy to get a new job, but that was not so. It was a very bad decision quitting my old job. Because of my age, no one wanted to hire me. All positions required applicants to be eighteen or older. So I started working whatever job I could find: mason, plumber, laborer, welder, whatever I could find to provide for my wife and child.

Around that time, Mrs. Chayito had told me that the house I left in Mejicanos a few years back was my father's and that it supposedly belonged to me as I was the only heir alive. But then she told me that the person who had the title was Esmeralda, the witch. So when I found out that she was back in the country, I went to look for her. After all, I had grown up and was already a father, so that property had to be mine again.

Esmeralda was an older woman now (over sixty-five), so I felt confident that she could do nothing to me as I had grown tall and strong. When I saw her, however, I noticed that somehow something had changed in her. She looked different. I sensed that her heart seemed softer than that from my childhood memories. She was happy to see me, and yes, she had the legal document of the house intact. She gave it back to me without further discussion. She was happy to learn about my new baby and wished me well.

Her heart was transformed, from what I perceived. I had no clue what had happened to her and wasn't ready to ask since I did not have good memories of her. All I knew was that I now had the title to the house and Esmeralda and I made peace with each other. My hatred for her disappeared with this good act.

With those papers with me, I had the power to make all the people who "lived" in that house leave, to get ahold of it and rent it to someone who could pay for it. Those people were not Maria and her kids anymore because she already had grown-up kids and they moved out to their own place a couple of years after I left. The squatters were strangers who had noticed that no one occupied that house, and all they did was pay the electricity and water bills. So after kicking them out, I rented it out, and that helped to improve our financial situation since I did not have a fixed job yet. I decided that was better than moving ourselves to that house. Besides, in my future mother-in-law's home, there were many people who could help out with Guadalupe in case Maria Elena and I had to go out.

Before I knew it, Guadalupe started taking her first steps! So I went rapidly to buy her, her first pair of shoes because I did not want her to be shoeless as I had been when I was growing up. She deserved the best, and she will never have to go into the garbage to get something to eat. Never. For as long as I was alive! *That would never happen to her*, I promised myself.

I never found a job as an industrial mechanic, which was what I had learned to be an expert in. Even though I had experience, the companies wanted applicants of ages eighteen or over. I could not get married, and I couldn't get a job either. This was a backward world I was living in: I wanted to be a good human being, earn my money in an honest way, but no one gave me the opportunity. I had no idea how hard it was going to be to get a job when I left the secure one I had.

Because of these circumstances, I became a little distant from everything and was most of the time out in the streets. I went to the discos at night alone, without Maria Elena because she stayed at home to take care of the baby. I started getting angry at life and easily got into fights again. My painful childhood memories came back to me, and I was totally frustrated.

As the owner of a disco called Black Christ saw me, finding me big and a fighter, he offered me a job as security there. My job was to get out the drunk people or the ones who would start a riot or a fight inside. I happily accepted as I was going to earn some money to be out of my house in my favorite place. I could drink and smoke free too as part of my pay. I would drink and smoke behind Maria Elena's back. She didn't have to know about it because she didn't like to go out to discos any more, since she got pregnant.

My anger at life made me the perfect candidate to fight with anybody and everybody. I felt trapped by my age and all the responsibility I had acquired. There was a time that I worked in the bakery store with my future mother-in-law, but I could never get used to that daily routine: get up at 2:00 a.m., prepare the bread mix, put the dough into the oven, wait for it to be ready, send it to the bike sellers at 5:00 a.m., sell all day in the store, and do it again and again and again on the following days. That was not a life I was used to or wanted to have. It was nothing I had dreamed about. I wanted to become an engineer.

So the truth was that working at the disco as a security guard was fun, and I enjoyed it more so than any other job. El Salvador is mainly Catholic and in every city they have Catholic celebrations to celebrate their local saint. In San Salvador, the capital, the first week of August is in honor of the Savior (Jesus). I had no clue how to honor a saint, so for me, those celebrations meant going to the fair, the rides, drinking out, going to the beach, or getting an extra job. It is such a big celebration that all private and government offices are closed at least three days and the whole country is practically paralyzed. Many companies give annual vacations to the employees for the whole week. Even the banks close.

This particular year, the disco I worked with put together an extra disco in the middle of the International Fair complex in one of the buildings. Rides, food, a lot of stands with different products, some of them to be introduced to the country for the first time, shows, firecrackers, etc. This is the fun that goes on in the International Fair Complex, and the disco was one of the attractions. We always had to deal with a lot of drunks, and I enjoyed how I had to fight with them out of the place. I met a lot of people, and several girls flirted with me. That feeling made me feel alive again. I kept that security job for several months.

After Guadalupe's first steps, time just flew by, and we celebrated her turning two years old. She was a real doll that made me want to kiss her all day long. My heart was growing from utter happiness.

It was mid-1979, and we started hearing reports about a civil war. New organizations had been formed: "Las Fuerzas Populares de Liberación 'Farabundo Martí'"(Liberation Forces of Popularity "Farabundo Martí"), (FPL) "Ejército Revolucionario del Pueblo" (Revolutionary Army of the Town), (ERP) "Resistencia Nacional" (National Resistence), (RN) "Partido Revolucionario de los Trabajadores Centroamericanos" (Revolutionary Party of the Central American Workers), (PRTC) and "Partido Comunista Salvadoreño" (Salvadoran Communist Party) (PCS). They merged together on October 10, 1980, forming the FMLN ("Frente Farabundo Martí de Liberación Nacional"). (Our actual governors).

During the formation of those parties, there was a coup d'état when General Carlos Humberto Romero was the President for the National Conciliation Party (PCN) . After the coup d'état, a revolutionary government group was formed. There was a lot of chaos in the streets and all over the place, downtown, and in other main cities in the country. The most important businessmen started leaving the country and left behind their businesses, trying to protect them from the US. Kidnapping rich people was very common because the guerrilla raised money for their cause this way.

Because I was curious and did not like to be home, I went to the protests that were held downtown. And since I worked only at night in the disco, during the day, I did not like to be home because I got bored. So I got distracted by going to the protests. They were pacific most of the time, but once in a while, they turned into riots! I enjoyed seeing how the policemen started to discuss and fight against the protestors. Some of the protestors decided to make graffiti on the walls of the businesses downtown.

The business people just locked their doors and waited for the anarchy to be over. At the beginning, it was just the police, but soon the military forces got involved. The leftists were getting organized and recruiting more and more people to join them in their protest against the oligarchy.

"In the name of God, in the name of this suffered people, whose crying has gone up to heaven, more and more repressed people, I beg you, I order you to stop repression of the people." Monsignor Romero finished his sermon that morning in the downtown main cathedral. It was March 24, 1980. A few minutes after his sermon, Monsignor Oscar Arnulfo Romero was assassinated with a sniper's single shot. I do not recall why there was a lot of people in the downtown cathedral that day.

A huge riot broke out after the priest was shot. People started shouting and running for their lives, and when they fell down in the chaos, other people just ran over them. A lot of people died, and most lost their shoes and purses and several other personal belongings.

I was one of the people who ran as fast as they could. In that moment, I didn't know why people were running. Afterward I learned that Monsignor Romero had been assassinated. The war had officially started—the rich against the poor, the oppressed for whom Monsignor stood up against the businessmen. He was against the rich, and I did not understand this: if there were no rich people to start businesses, there'd be no jobs, and there'd be no opportunity to work.

What I did know, though, was that I was soon turning eighteen and able to marry my beloved, Maria Elena. I was also going to be able to go find a decent job to earn better for my family although there was already a lot of uncertainty if the businesses were going to close up because of the war and what was happening in our country.

A couple of months after Guadalupe turned three, I was going to turn eighteen. *Finally, we will be able to get married!* So as soon as my birthday came up, I went to get my legal ID and took it very proudly to my wife-to-be. I saw her happy face again (a huge smile!). We set our wedding date for the twenty-second of December that same year, 1980.

9

Estela's Return

At the beginning of 1981, a friend from my previous job went looking for me to let me know that Estela was coming to El Salvador and that she wanted to meet with me. She had already learned that I was married and had become a father a few years back. I couldn't care less that she knew about it because I was extremely happy, and I had finally married the love of my life.

When Estela came, I met up with her without saying anything to Maria Elena since she knew about her rejection. But deep inside, I still felt bad about leaving Margarita alone since Estela had pointed it out; Margarita was doing somewhat bad health-wise, and I thought it was partly my fault because Estela had managed to let me feel that way. Somehow, deep inside I was happy to see my sister and Margarita again. After all, they had rescued me from the streets, and I owed Estela my life and that opportunity to work in a good place (which I had left). So I loved them anyway, and my heart was divided between them and my wife and child.

My meeting with Estela was significant; it was a turning point in my life. She asked me if I was happy with the decision I had taken of becoming a father and a husband. She was so smart. She did not scold me or give me a sermon about my decisions. Even though she didn't have any interest in meeting them, I talked to her about my wife and daughter completely happy, and I really wanted her to approve of them and have them all together. But she had another plan in mind.

Suddenly, she asked me, "Eddy, where do you see yourself in five years?"

"Oh, Sis. I see myself working hard to give my family a good life, of course. I have responsibilities now. And a beautiful daughter, whom you should meet."

She just looked at me and said, "Look, Eddy. Here, things are not going well. War has started already, and the situation in our country does not look good. It will not get any better. I think you should come to the United States with me. Ali and I have a good life over there.

"I will pay the coyote so that you can cross the border illegally—since getting you a visa will be impossible. When you get to the US and get established, then you can take your family too. And only then will I meet your wife and daughter. Right now it is not a good time to do so. Besides, I have no time to socialize."

I did not expect to have this proposition, and she got me perplexed.

"You really think that that is the best thing to do?"

"Of course, Eddy. What future do you have here? Look around!"

Immediately, she changed the subject and started talking about Ali, how he was becoming prosperous over there in the US, and how happy she was to have left a few years back. She also said that the girls were growing fast and they were happy, but they always asked about their Uncle Eddy.

Before we parted ways, she said, "Look, Brother, I love you very much. You know that. I only want the best for you, and this is why I offer my help to take you illegally. But there is one condition. A *very* important condition…You have to keep everything in a secret. You shall not say anything to anyone. You cannot tell your wife, your child, or any friend. No one. Nobody. If you tell someone, our plan will fail. Only my mother knows about this plan because here at my house is where I will send the money.

"From here, you will get together with the coyote. I will contact him and will send you specific instructions when I get the money to you. I leave in three days. The day after tomorrow, I expect your answer, to know if you want to leave this troubled country. Come over for breakfast, and tell me your decision."

My jaw fell right open. My head was going crazy with this information. I had not thought about leaving my wife and child, much less my country. Again, I had to make a drastic decision that will change my life forever.

During the next two days, I analyzed everything, all scenarios and possibilities. My job was not a stable job. War had begun, and there was no stopping the guerrillas against the army. I heard bombs every night. It seemed like things were getting worse through time: three years ago, I could not get a job as an industrial mechanic as easily as I had thought; and now that I was turning eighteen, we were starting a war.

We had military-imposed curfews—from 6:00 p.m. to 6:00 a.m. Because of this, the discos started opening from 2:00 p.m. to 5:00 p.m. for the students, but because they were underage, they could not buy alcoholic drinks. They opened from 5:30 p.m. to 6:00 a.m. for the adults to sell alcohol, but very few went all night because it was very risky to be away from home. So very soon the discos went bankrupt and were forced to close.

Electricity started to be rationed, and establishments had no proper lighting, just candles. Most of us employees were unemployed now. Things didn't go good around and my sister was right. She had given me a very good offer and a good opportunity. The best thing I could do for my wife and child was to leave the country first and then bring them with me. There was nothing else to think about. Once more, Estela was rescuing me, and I was very glad she had done it again.

Two days later, I met with her and said, "Thanks again, Estela, for thinking about me and my future and for giving me this opportunity. You are right about the whole thing. The war will not get any better, and because of the love I have for my daughter and my wife, I have to go. It would be very irresponsible for me not to do anything for them and leave them here, in a risky situation. Definitely, I accept your offer to go first, and then I will send for them."

Estela smiled, happy that she had won. She was happy that her plan had worked exactly as she had envision it. She was happy that she had influenced in my decisions again and had controlled my very weak heart. Her plan to separate me from my real family had worked. But I didn't see it that way; I just saw the perfect plan that gave me an opportunity to give my family a better life. It never occured to me that this was a very evil plan of hers.

"Good. On the date I will let you know, around six months from now, I will send the money you need. In those six months, you have to go to the Mexican Embassy after getting your passport, and get a visa to go to Mexico. You will fly to Mexico. So you have to go to get your passport and then the visa. You will say you are going to Mexico to visit some relatives who live in DF, city of Mexico."

She gave detailed instructions, and I tried to remember everything she said. Then she added, "You have to promise that you will not say a word to your wife or daughter. Not even a clue about our plan because if they discover us, all the plans with the coyote will get ruined. Swear to me, Eddy."

"Yes, of course. I swear, Sis."

"You have six months to start getting your clothes out of your closet. Take them out little by little. On one trip to my mom's house, you put on two socks then two shirts or two pants and so on so that your wife doesn't discover about the clothes that are missing from your closet. You have to go to work as always, as if nothing else is going on. If you have a job, if not, go out to find one or make believe you do."

"Okay, Sister," I said hooked on to her plan.

"Whenever the time comes for you to leave, it will only take two weeks to get to my house in New York. When you get there, you can call your wife and tell her where you are and your plans for her and your kid. This way, you will avoid any discussions with her before time. It is better to ask for forgiveness than to get permission as she will probably will not give it to you in the first place anyway." (She was right.)

Everything made total sense to me. I became blinded and just obeyed everything she said, dreaming about the American dream. I dreamt about my daughter getting her education over there and having a great life, one much better than her mother's and mine. She was going to have much better opportunities. Her life was going to be different, and my wife's will be too. She will not have to wake up at 2:00 a.m. to help in the bakery anymore. She will be able to work in normal hours, if necessary. The war did not let me think differently.

The National University of El Salvador was taken over by the students helping the guerrilla, and classes where suspended. So Maria Elena had to stop her studies, and so did I. We could not continue with our university education furthermore. I had to be grateful that I was given that opportunity to get a better future. With the abilities I had as a mechanic, I knew I was going to have success over in America. It was just a matter of time.

My sister, Estela, was there to rescue me from another risky situation, and I only had love for her. I admired her deeply and was very, very grateful toward her—even though she had left me when I was nine, but that was nine years ago (just a few months after I started living with her). She was the one who helped me with my life and my future. I ignored that Estela was furious deep inside her heart because she was an illegitimate child as my father never married her mother and never gave her his last name. (He died before he got to do so anyway.) So she felt less of a person for being a daughter outside of marriage. She felt rejected but did not make it known to anyone.

She saw me as her instrument for revenge in a horrible way for everything she had suffered from when she was a child, not having her father there with her all the time. She had no one else but me to get her revenge on, and she knew that I had a weak heart. She created every situation in such a way that I thought I was deciding for myself, but I was really being manipulated by her; and every time, I did what she had in mind, letting her manipulate my decisions. She controlled my heart and feelings with her beautiful words and false sweetness that I could not tell that she hated my father and that she was really seeking revenge against him. I was a reflection of him, and she hated me by extension but made me believe in the contrary.

She was so smart, and I ignored everything. Besides, I was very determined to go after the dream she had implanted in my heart—the famed American dream. So I just followed her instructions as they were given to me. First, I found out that I needed to get a passport (which I got). Then I found out how to get a visa to Mexico. Since I had the legal ownership of my house , the officials did not suspect anything from me. I got the Mexican visa without any problem. Everything went perfectly. Margarita had already bought a suitcase and a backpack to put all my clothes in. I took them from my house one by one as I had been instructed six months before. Everything was going perfectly, according to the plan. It was just a matter of time.

Even though I knew nothing of Estela's plan then and I did not know anything about God, looking back on it now I realize that God was there for me, taking care of me in each adventure I got into, even when I did not make the right choices. God is good and looks for the lost, the sinners, the ones who do not know Him. I had not met Him yet, and I certainly felt like I was the worst sinner of all, but He protected me anyway.

10

The Decision

My relationship with Maria Elena became affected—I felt distant emotionally—as I no longer saw any reason to stay in this country: It got difficult to find a job, and since I could not find anything, I started working at the bakery again to help my wife. But very soon, I got tired and bored with that schedule. I quit almost immediately as I hated that schedule starting at two in the morning.

I loved coming home at two in the morning from the discos, but getting up at that time to start my job was something I could not deal with. I felt like a slave, and my mind always drifted toward the American dream more and more every day. Most of the time, the civil war was taken place away from the capital city of San Salvador, and every day, it was getting closer and closer to the capital city. There was no sense of belonging to any of the groups that had been formed. It was either joining the guerrillas and going to war against the military forces or becoming a soldier to fight against the guerrillas. Neither was my dream.

Both involved risking my life, and I was not of a mindset to risk myself for the ideals of others. I had my own ideals and goals, and the main one was to go to the United States before I was forced to become part of one or the other group in the war. And in the midst of all these thoughts and waking up early and hating it, I started secretly preparing my trip to liberty.

It did not take six months but, like, seven or eight for me to get the money and the instructions, but I was totally reserved about it. It was a perfect plan, and not even my shadow knew about it. I was confident that no one was going to know about it.

There was a problem in those days, however: Before I started working at the bakery, when I worked at night in the disco before it went bankrupt, I started flirting around and liked a girl who visited the disco very often. My mind and heart were getting far away from each other. I tried not to feel guilty and hurt with what I was about to do.

I put up an emotional wall between my family and me. I loved Maria Elena and Guadalupe, but I did not recall when or how I started to like another girl. Maybe my subconscious did it in self-defense so that I would not feel the hurt. I started talking more and more with this girl, and I started liking her more and more every day too. My mind kept telling me that I did not have the liberty to entertain other girls as I had just married the love of my life. Besides, my heart told me that it was not proper to do so.

Even though I was a street boy, a bad boy (and even a wicked boy), my heart was a good one. I think my father taught me the basics of honesty. I never saw him with other women—except for my godmother and stepmother, Margarita. That was why even though my body was trying to be unfaithful and cheat on Maria Elena because I had lost interest in her, my heart could never do it for real. I did not even get to the point of kissing the other girl, much less anything else. It was only flirting for me. That was the closest I got to cheating on my wife.

But one day, Maria Elena followed me to know if I really went to work at the disco. She saw from afar that I was with that girl. Maria Elena immediately thought of the worst, but I could not blame her as I had grown distant from her and I had not told her in the last few months how much I loved her.

When I saw her the following day, when the curfew was over, we had a big argument. She accused me of being unfaithful to her, that I was lying to her and cheating on her and everything else that wives tell husbands in this scenario. She bombarded me with questions like "Since when have you been dating her?" and "Do you not love me anymore?" and "Why did you marry me?" All the other repressed thoughts she had came out right there and then. I swore and promised that nothing had happened, but of course, even though it was true, all cheaters said the same thing.

I could not blame her at all. I could not defend myself even being clean about it, so to prove her that she was more important, I went to the disco that night to quit and to tell the other girl that I was a married guy. Of course, she got upset too because she had no idea, but she disappeared from my life once and for all, and that was when I started working once more at the bakery.

So I had to convince Maria Elena that I had nothing to do with anyone else, and I started becoming more mellow with her. I worked on it deliberately, but my heart was set on my trip to the US. By this time, I already had my passport, and then I went to get my Mexican visa. I was really happy inside because my dream was getting closer and closer to becoming a reality...Going to the United States and then in less than a year, sending money for my wife and my daughter. Over there, we will be very close, and I will make things up to them for leaving without saying anything. I was sure that she would understand and that she will forgive me for leaving her. Over there, we will create a bigger family and have many kids, but first, I would have to get her out of the war.

I visited my stepmother often to take clothes to her house, and one day when I least expected it, she told me that Estela had sent the money for my trip. I had to go to buy the airplane ticket to go to Mexico. Having the Mexican visa with me, I went straight to a travel agency to buy my ticket for the date given to me.

At that point, I already had my suitcase filled with clothes at my stepmother's house. I had taken one at a time as I was instructed and waited for the right date to leave. Maria Elena did not notice the clothes, disappearing one day at a time.

The night before I was to leave, I was very loving and mellow with her and my daughter. We made love as we used to every Friday night, and I waited until she was sleeping soundly. I could not sleep, thinking about everything that was coming up, and I was having an internal turmoil.

I had to go early to the appointed place the next morning. My excuse was that I was going to go to pick up the rent of the house and then to an interview. When she was deeply asleep, I got up and wrote a note. It read:

> Maria Elena, I love you with all my heart. I want you to know that what I am doing is because I love you dearly, and I love my daughter too. Don't worry about me because nothing wrong has happened to me. Soon you will hear from me. I love you.
>
> Ed

The note was folded up well, and I put it inside the sock drawer. I hoped that she was going to find it when I was already on the other side of the border (which was at least a week or two afterward). I thought, *That will calm her nerves, and everything would be fine when I call her in a couple of weeks.*

The next day, I woke up really early and got ready as if I was headed to the fake interview. So at 6:00 a.m., I gave her a kiss before leaving. I hugged and kissed Guadalupe, and without looking back, I started to walk fast. My heart was beating so quickly that I thought it was going to beat out of my chest! Nervously I walked toward my destiny. Suddenly I had the thought that I did not know if I was doing the right thing by just disappearing. I knew it was wrong, but I repeatedly told myself that it was the best decision for everyone.

I did collect the rent of the house, actually, but I did not bring it back to my wife. Instead, I took it with me as extra money. Then

I went to my stepmother's place to pick up my suitcase. During the trip to those two places, I kept up my internal monologue. "You are doing the right thing. You will have a better life in the United States for yourself and your family. Hurry up, Eduardo! Don't change your mind. Everything is planned." Again and again, I repeated that to myself. When I got to Margarita's place, I only said hello to her, got my suitcase, and said good-bye.

When I said good-bye, she said to me, "Remember, Eduardo, you have to follow all the instructions that are written on this paper. I will be here in case you need me. Besides, I will tell another bilingual person to help you with your interaction with others. I will be expecting your call in a couple of weeks. Then, you will call your wife when your are safe in the States. Go with God."

Go with God? I am a man now, not a child. I know everything will go fine. My sister wants the best for me, and that is why she is helping me. I am sure about it. And I need no god to help me.

"Bye and thanks for everything."

I turned away and got out the paper given to me to read. The instructions were clear: it said that I had to go to an office downtown.

When I got there, I realized that I was not the only one in this adventure. All this time, I thought that I was alone in this meeting with the coyote. Now I see that the coyote works with a group of people and not only with one person. It probably would have been too expensive for one person. The system is very structured. We got specific instructions right there and then and we had to go to the airport in the date of the ticket, which I had with me already.

The group was traveling to Mexico by plane within three to four days. We would travel in different dates so we wouldn't be detected. We were all headed to the United States but to different destinations. They partnered me with an older lady who was supposed to be my stepmother. Some younger kids were partnered with older ones to pretend to be a family. We had to check in in the groups assigned, even having different last names. We had to look natural and experienced travelers. There was all types of ages: children, teens, young adults, adults in their thirties, forties, and even up to fifties. We all had the American dream, and all of us had someone waiting for us in the U.S.

During the flight we had to go in the groups assigned. There were groups of two, three, four, and five people. I had to take care of my "mother" and help her with her luggage. When arriving to the airport in Mexico DF, which was a hundred times larger, we were told specifically to follow the crowd. We should not look as foreigners or tourists so we shall not create any alerts.

When getting to Mexico, each group would take a different taxi. My "mom" and I shall take a cab and go to the same address as the rest, as the instructions where given.

The date in my ticket was for that same afternoon, so I had no time to waste. I was in the first group. Very confident and without showing any fear, I went to the El Salvador International Airport, that was no longer in Ilopango because they had relocated it around forty minutes from the capital city in the department of La Paz. We got into a taxi to go faster to our destination. That new airport was inaugurated a few months before the coup d'état and the original airport in Ilopango was converted into the air force airport, just on time for the war. Like if everything had been planned for this historical situation in my country.

Thanks to my street days, I could not be easily mocked. I had already decided that I was not going to be intimidated by the coyote or anyone else in this trip and adventure toward a new life. All the members of the first group got into different taxis to go to the airport. We checked in as we were told and when the boarding time came we got into the plane. All of this was totally new to me.

It was fascinating to be inside an airport. However, I had to act like it was not a big deal so I did not look too much like a tourist, and much less to suspect I was going to go "wetback" to the United States. I have no clue why the ones who wanted to cross the border are called wetbacks nor why the guys that help us cross the border are called coyotes, but that is the vocabulary used for this procedure, which I quickly learned in all this adventure.

In the airplane we sat in designated sits given at the time to check in. My seat was next to the window, which I was grateful for because I was dying to know how the world looked from up in the sky. I had seen the planes go up in the sky, but couldn't imagine how it looked from up there. I was fascinated. We went up above the clouds and the houses looked like little toy houses, and the cars looked like ants. I was so impressed. *This is the first time, but it's not going to be the last that I would get on a plane*, I promised myself.

The clouds made me think that maybe one day I can go to the moon. But at this point, I was only going to Mexico. My mind was thinking of all the possibilities that I had in front of me. It may sound really bad, but up to this point, I had not thought once about my wife or baby. My mind was too busy thinking of all the things that were about to happen in the next two weeks.

In those two weeks, I was going to be with my sister and I was going to be able to communicate with my wife. I would rather ask for forgiveness than permission in this situation because I am sure my wife would not have agree to it. It is only two weeks, I constantly repeated to myself. Two weeks for liberty! In two weeks, I will discover a whole new world, a better world. No doubt about it!

Absorbed by my thoughts, I did not feel the time and soon, the stewardess came over to offer food and drinks. I did not know food was included in the trip, but I was grateful it did because I was starving. It was not beans and tortillas, which I was used to, but I devoured it at once. Since I am a big guy, it was not enough to feel full, but it was plenty to not be so hungry any more. My "mother" was sound asleep, maybe because she was nervous, but I was too excited to fall asleep. I wanted to see it all, experience it all.

During the trip, I wanted to go to the bathroom but I did not know if there were bathrooms in the planes. After all it was like an elegant bus and in the buses there are no bathrooms. I did not want to look as a fool if I asked about it, I wanted to look like an experienced traveler. So singing in my mind distracted my organs, but suddenly, the passenger in the aisle got up and went to the back of the plane. Curious, when he came back, I asked where had he gone, whispering, so my "mother" wouldn't wake up, since she was in the middle seat.

"Went to the bathroom. Ya wanna go too?" He asked, maybe because my face said it clearly. I had to wake up my neighbor, my "mother" to be able to pass to the hall. I told her I was going to the bathroom. The man told me it was at the end of the hall and there was a line of people waiting, which was good so I could observe what others did.

"Thank goodness you asked about the bathroom," said Miss Conny. "I had fallen asleep because I had the urge to go to the bathroom but was afraid to ask if there was one in the plane."

"You go ahead first and I follow you."

So the other traveler moved so we both could go to the back of the plane. It was the smoking side of the plane. Half was smoking and half was non-smoking. As we were walking down the aisle, it felt as if a bus went through a bump. The plane had gone through a turbulent zone and it moved weirdly. Miss Conny yelled "Ahhhh!" but saw that no one else yelled, so quickly she got quiet.

When we got to the end of the plane, there were a couple of people in line. I observed every detail. I saw that they pushed the door, which looked like an accordion, and went inside, and then a signed that said "busy" was shown. I wondered how that happened. When I got inside, I was fascinated with how small the bathroom was. I stared to the door behind where it said Busy, and I moved that knob to the side. It was a big awe for me when I saw the light turn on as I slid the knob. Awesome! I was exactly wondering were to turn on the light! Ha!

How ingenious are these bathrooms, I thought.

I stayed there observing every detail. Because of my height I had no other choice but to sit down to pee. Everything was in that little space. There was a mini sink, a mirror, toilet paper, Kleenex, liquid soap, paper towels and even a trash can! It was so complete. Then, as I got up, was looking for the knob to flush the toilet, but could not find it. Finally I observed a circle that said Push, and since I do not speak English, I could not understand it but seemed that it was talking to me to push it, so I did, and to my surprise, that was the right thing to do.

"I am so happy I passed this test!" I thought, very thankful that I had learned to go to the bathroom in a plane!

I lost track of time, but I think I stayed too long because when I got out, I did not see Miss Conny, so I went fast to look for her in her seat and she was not there.

"Did she jump out of the plane?" I asked myself in my mind.

But then, thinking about it, that was impossible as it was a closed apparatus. So I went back to the end of the plane and to my surprise, she came out from the front door, the one I had not noticed for some reason. She came out with such a satisfaction face! I just smiled seen her smile. When "Mom" and I were together again, I knew she had been inside a long time, just like me, observing everything inside. It was her first time in a plane too.

The man in the aisle seat got up again to let us in. Like twenty minutes later, the plane started to descend, and a voice came out from somewhere that said to fasten our seat belts as we would soon arrive in Mexico DF. It was said in Spanish and English, so we understood everything. I closed my eyes and imagined myself arriving to New York!

Out the window there was a huge city. Maybe the size of El Salvador itself! I could see how little by little we were getting close to the airport. There were houses and buildings all over the place. The airport is in the middle of the city. When we landed, people clapped and I did the same. I do not know if people applauded to the captain because we had arrived without any problem or to celebrate we were close to our destiny. I clapped anyway! For me was a victory applause.

When the airplane landed, people started to get up, just like in the buses, but the voice appeared again saying that we had to seat down until the plane gets to the terminal. We had to fasten our seat belts. My heart has excited. The first part of my goal was fulfilled, and only a few hours had gone by.

Finally the plane got to the terminal, and we got up in order without people yelling or pushing like in the buses. Frankly, I thought that a plane was like a bus, except it goes up in the air, and people are more educated, clean and decent. No bad odors, no pushing, no swearing. We went out properly, following the people ahead of us as we were instructed to go through customs, and to pick up our luggage. We walked until we found a big line of people and we learned that was customs. Observing people would get out their passports, we did the same thing. There were uniformed guys that looked like policemen, but they were not.

Miss Conny and I went together, and when asked if we were relatives, we said yes—she was my stepmother, and that was why we had different last names—and they believed us! We showed our passport and the paper we filled out on the plane. Then we went to the luggage claim area, following the signs saying Baggage Claim. We got our baggage and going toward the exit, they checked our luggage inside. We carried nothing but clothes. No food as indicated before leaving El Salvador, but I wished I could have brought some beans and tortillas.

We got to the door that said *Salida* (exit) and went out to the street. I told Mrs Conny to take care of the luggage while I went to look for a cab. In the plane we did not talk to any one else of the group, neither in the airport. We would all go to the same address, but all in separate taxi cabs and with their own groups. They had told us to use an official taxi cab so we would not be swindled. There were so many taxis; it was unreal! Miss Conny had to go in at my same pace, and even though she was much older, she had to hurry, and I could not leave her behind, so I went to get her to go into the taxi with me and immediately the taxi driver took us to the hotel we were assigned.

We arrived to the hotel, and I was really happy, but for some reason, I stopped thinking about Maria Elena and my daughter because my mind was really busy worrying about taking care of myself. My two loves I took them out of my heart, selfishly, I defended my own feelings and my own decisions.

When we checked in the hotel, we were given a set of keys according to the groups. But after a while, they went to knock in our doors and took our keys back and put us all together in two rooms: one for girls and one for boys. We were like twenty-six to twenty-eight people. And we only had two rooms to share.

When we were all together, some men came in telling us that they were from immigration services and that they were going to help us go to the border, but we had to give them all the money we had, all the cash we were carrying with us to proceed to our destination. The next day some people would come to pick us up. All the men in my room believed them, but for some reason I did not. I had a hunch they were not real. I suppose the women believed them too.

My sister had told me to put money in between my underpants and pants, in my socks, in the belt, in all parts of my body, and keep only a few bills in my pocket. In the black market in El Salvador, we had exchanged our colones to dollars. The exchange rate in the black market was 5.00 colones for a dollar and the official exchange rate was 2.50 colones to 1. We all had changed dollars before going to the airport. I learned that those men were burglars and I do not know if the owner of the hotel had told them or how they knew about us. Everyone gave everything except me.

I kept around $600 within all my body. The guys were supposed to be from immigration services and they were bad men, they were burglars. All twenty-six to twenty-eight people were ripped off! But within all the men that were together I observed an older guy than me, maybe in his early thirties or late twenties that looked smarter than the rest. I think he did not believed them either and I presumed he had hidden some money within himself too, but I wasn't sure. I did not trust anyone, so I was not going to share my secret.

We started talking at the end of the night after those men left and he told me he was an evangelical pastor. At that moment I could not understand what he meant for evangelical pastor, since I saw him as a regular guy and saw nothing special on him, except he seemed smarter.

While we stayed in Mexico, I saw him drinking beer and saying bad words and cursing here and there. I do not know if he did so just to protect himself from others or because he was exactly like that. I didn't ask. He never talked to me about Jesus or what his faith meant to him, but it was the first time I ever heard that evangelical pastors existed. What is an evangelical pastor? I wondered. I thought only priests and Jews existed in the churches, so I had no clue what he meant.

I did not understand that God was taking care of me since I was an infant, and the encounter with this guy was like an encounter with an angel sent from heaven. Even though he did not share his faith or say how to get saved through getting born again, I could tell that he was different and that he was the only one I could maybe trust a little. Even though he acted like everyone else with his bad words and drinking habits, my heart told me that he was different and that his life was going to impact mine somehow, somewhere along this trip. Without thinking too much about it, I became close to him. Subconsciously, I knew I had to do it.

After they got all the money from us, and back to our own two rooms, we, the pastor and I, were the only ones who had talked back to them and even discussed with the men about our giving them the money. Finally they won and got what they wanted, but in that event, we became the clear leaders of the group. Everyone was afraid and without planning it, we were silently assigned their leaders.

We both had hidden money within ourselves, and we ourselves were sincere about it, apart from the rest. He also carried around $600 and only had in his pocket $30, just like me who had $20. Luckily, they did not register us physically.

We had all been robbed and of course, next day no one appeared to pick us up. Simply, no one came back to give us instructions and just as we had feared, it was a hoax. Money was lost and people did not want to move, not even to eat, hoping that someone was going to appear. We all had the number from the guy in San Salvador to contact him in case it was necessary, but no one did so they had given away all their money. The contact in El Salvador was an ex military guy who refused to go to war and he was the one who coordinated with the coyotes to take us across the border. Most of the people kept a few dollars somewhere else than their pockets and wallets, but that was the least money since they gave the larger amount to them.

After been robbed, they had told us not to move from the rooms because someone was coming for us. No one came and when finally we realized that all was a big trick and we had been robbed, after noon that everyone was really hungry, we got all of them together. We told the people what we had perceived, but they still did not believe us. They wanted to wait in the rooms, believing the words of the thieves.

We waited a couple of hours, and at the end of the afternoon, people started to cry, getting mad, and angry and far beyond their nerves. They cried because they were disappointed and they were desperate and we were all hungry. Finally, pastor and I told them to join forces and combine their money to send someone for food and to call to the ex military contact we had. Neither pastor or I said we had enough money because everyone would want to use it and we were going to use it later on in our trip.

So after putting together one-, five-, and ten-dollar bills, we had enough to get something to eat and to call back to El Salvador. I decided to make the call myself, so that made me automatically the principal leader of the group, and take in the risk which also made me their hero. Pastor went to get the food, so he was the second leader. I did not know all these people, but my strong desire to get to my sister's made me act and do something about it instead of just staying there whining and complaining about it.

Life had made me bold, thoughtful, a problem solver, and here was the biggest one to solve. Since we did not know what the next step was going to be as the person that was supposed to come never showed up; pastor and I went out to the streets and found fried chicken for everyone to eat, and after we found the food I stayed behind and made the phone call. When I communicated to the ex military guy and told him what had happened, he confirmed we had been robbed since the guys that were to pick us up, would not ask for money until we were close to the border. We had been victims of an assault and fell in the trap.

He simply said he knew nothing about those men and apparently we had missed the train that was going to take us to Ciudad Juárez, without knowing or not understanding the clear instructions given. We were supposed to stay only overnight and then go to the train station, but we all thought someone was going to pick us up and take us. So when the men appeared, we thought they had been sent for us to arrange the train station tickets and so on.

Ciudad Juárez is the city that is closest to the border between México and United States, close to where we would cross the border. It was so close that there were a lot of people who lived in Ciudad Juarez but worked in Texas crossing the border daily. Everything had changed now and we had to call our relatives to send us more money to continue with the trip.

Putting together money to buy food was one thing, but putting together money to buy a train ticket was a different thing. We needed to call to our relatives for more money and tell them our stories, even if they get upset. The ex-military man told me we could all call "collect" from Mexico to El Salvador, without any money. That was good news! He would get in touch with the coyotes again to tell them our story to rearrange our travelling route, as soon as we got more money to proceed, or else, go back home with the round ticket bought to come to Mexico.

The trip to the border was to take us a maximum of six to ten days and six days more to finally get to my destination, but it was not like that what happened. It took around ten days for all of us to receive money again, after we made our calls. Our relatives were very upset and mad with us, but also worried, so all agreed to send more money for us to continue our trip. Now they had to send money to pay the hotel plus the train and for the new coyotes.

We had to move to a half-star hotel, with hard beds but with clean sheets and clean bathrooms. We stayed six to a room to pay a cheaper rate for the room. The owner was not too happy, but felt pity for us and accepted us without paying anything until getting the money from our relatives, as we had promised.

Of course, pastor and I had no problem paying, but we did as everyone else: we called for more money. Something inside me told me I was going to need it anyway. Ten long days passed by, hardly eating.

Somewhere along the line during that time, I thought that pastor and I could continue alone in this trip, but my responsibility instinct made me not to leave all these people behind. In those ten days, I had a profound sense of loneliness in my heart and for the first time I stopped and thought about going back home. I meditated it. I cried like a child, far from everyone and asked myself if I was doing the right thing. I was getting desperate and even thought about calling Maria Elena.

I had not called her yet, and two weeks had already gone by. I thought about calling her but deep inside I knew all I was going to hear was shouting, moaning, whining and rejection for my decision of leaving. Even though I was getting desperate to hear her voice, emotionally I was not ready to hear all her whining for my decision. I could get desperate and drop my dream for a better life, but I decided not to call her and postponed it until I was safe over the boarder.

I analyzed that there is no sense in going back to a country in war. There was no point in going through everything that I had gone through in Mexico and then give up so easily. Instead of calling Maria Elena, I called my sister when I got the money. She encouraged me and told me to go on. She advised me not to call home until I get to her place. I obeyed since she confirmed exactly what I had thought about inside my heart.

"You will only get scolded by her," she said. "And your goal is to get here to give them a better life. Don't stop now, Bro. We are waiting for you."

Those words comforted me and again made me focus on my goal to cross the border and get to my sister's place.

"I'm doing this because I love them," I told myself. "It is not the time to call yet. I will have plenty of time to do that later."

11

New Beginnings

The ex-military guy had communicated with new people to plan new logistics. Finally, eleven days after my call to him, a new person appeared with new precise instructions. He looked very self confident and we believed him. He did not ask for any money upfront, and told us we would pay him when we get close to the border. We felt safe with him, but by this time, since almost two months had gone by, the group of twenty-six to twenty-eight people had grown to about a hundred dreamers.

He told us we had to go to Ciudad Juárez in different groups and different times, going through small cities and towns through Mexico. The object was to get to the closest city to the border, but since the group had grown, we had to go in different times and date and that took us like three weeks. The situation was getting tense. We were not sure when we would be able to cross the border.

The two weeks initially offered had been converted in almost seven weeks. I don't think I was the only one that was feeling desperate, but no one said anything. We saw our lost faces, but we all wanted to get to our destination. So no one complained to anyone else. I suppose everyone else cried as I did, but we all kept it to ourselves. I cried in silence may times. I missed my family, the one I promised I was never going to leave. At the same time,

I was afraid of her rejection, her whining about my decisions, but most of all, I did not want to be a failure and go back at this point without anything.

I did not want to disappoint my wife and thought that by not calling her, I was protecting myself and protecting her too from disappointment. I never thought that she was going to be worried about me and think me dead, or recruited by the guerrilla in that horrible war. Never thought about her anguish, I just thought about mine. I was a totally selfish person with my feelings, my objectives, my goals. I should have shared them with her, but at this point I could do nothing else but to take care of my heart from failure.

My group went through several towns and one of them was Jalisco. I remember this one the most because I liked it very much. We also went through other beautiful towns, different than the ones I had seen in my country. In those five weeks or so I had learned the Mexican accent, which saved me in several occasions. I had gotten a fake ID in Mexico D.F. as a student I was supposed to be a Chiapas Student. I remember that we where offered those ID's for US $40, which luckily I had with me and I bought it. Most of the people did not have money when they offered it, so I made a good use of the forty bucks.

Finally we got into a train that was going directly to Ciudad Juárez. On our way there were stops and in one of them, the real people from immigration got into the cart where I was. They would ask us where we were from and some other things to investigate if we were telling the truth. They were looking for people with the goal of crossing the border. Two guys that were going with me did not pass the interrogation. They got nervous and got deported. My "mother" was in another group, and I did not know if I was going to see her again. I showed my fake student ID and tried to look confident, but inside I was dying if I would get caught.

"Qué andás haciendo por estos lado huey?" (What are you doing around here, man?)

"Pos voy donde mis primos en Ciudad Juárez." (I'm going to my cousin's in Ciudad Juárez.")

"Órale, pues, ve con cuidado, huey." (All right. Be careful, man.)

Talking as a Mexican, they believed me and they went to the next person. Besides, my dark skin complexion helped me pass for a local. I was thankful for the first time I did not look like mother: white and blonde!

I am alone without my trip buddies. All was in my hands. I felt all alone without the rest of the group and that is when I knew it was all in my hands. The rest of the group were in other wagons and in other trains so it was impossible to know what was going on with them. I was going to know if they made it when I get to my destination.

When I got to Juárez, I was starving. Instinctively, I went to look for food in the places that looked economical, so I went looking for the market in the downtown area of Juárez. Over there, I met other Salvadorans that I recognized and others I had not met before. I knew they were Salvadorans by their accent.

I was extremely happy when I saw a guy we called Chino (Chinese). I had met him in the company where I learned industrial mechanic. He was headed north too, but I hadn't seen him before. Chino told me he was hiding in the house of a Mexican couple who helped Salvadorans before they cross the border. This couple gave them a place to eat and sleep, and in exchange, they worked at their car wash for a low fare to save to continue their trip. Chino had been working for them for months.

"How long have you been here?" I asked.

"Eight months," he said in a matter-of-fact tone of voice.

He is not worried for being here so long. I shivered just to think I might have to stay so long to cross the border, but he is comfortable here in Mexico. I was getting desperate to go over, and to get to my sister's. The sooner the better. Chino got me into the couple's house and I stayed with them and worked for about two weeks, while I could find everyone else. This calmed my stress on how to pay my stay before moving on.

I lost the guy who had contacted us in the hotel in Mexico DF, so I met a coyote that offered to take me to New Mexico for $300 dollars to take me to the border and $300 when I get to the U.S. I had that kind of money so I forgot about the other guy and made business with this new one. He took me to the border to pass it but we got caught on the other side and they sent me back to Mexico instead of El Salvador. I think it was because I was very good at talking in Mexican accent and when I showed the U.S. border police people my Mexican ID, they thought I was a local but I lost those first three hundred bucks.

The war rumors and the "peace demonstrations" in the streets continued in the capital city of San Salvador while the war is being fought in the country. Formal war had exploded between the guerrilla made up of unhappy people who were against the military forces—who defend the whole country. The guerrillas are backed up by the Jesuits, Cuba, and Russia and they get more and more adepts and armament to fight against military forces being formed all their lives. There is a big discontent with the oligarchy and the people, mostly the people who worked with the land. The working people of the city, who want to continue with their jobs, under the bullets, without public buses running, they still get to their working places, even if they have to walk long distances. They are admirable people. I don't really understand what is the dynamics behind the war because if there is no rich people, there is no businesses and there is no jobs. Where are the people going to work if they all close down? I heard many businessmen had left the country. I couldn't get any decent job before the war exploded as it is now.... Everyone is going to have to emigrate?

Luckily, I was not there any more and I just kept my mind away from all those things happening in El Salvador. I was only worried about crossing the border since I was still in Mexico. Around three months had gone by, and I still haven't called my wife. Maria Elena knew nothing about me and the more time goes by, the more afraid I am to call to explain everything that is happening to me and telling her I had not crossed the border.

I am afraid of rejection and I keep trying to survive all this problems by myself. This is the story of my life. No father, no mother, no brothers, I have no one else to help me but my half sister in the United States. I call her more or less every month to let her know I am alright, and alive and everything that is happening around our mutual goal to get together.

In my desperation and not having any plan set to cross the border, I start recalling my childhood days: having to survive in those sad days. Living in the streets running away from "home" was what I applied to live in Mexico, in Ciudad Juárez. I would sell fruits and vegetables; I would wash cars and even gamble to try to multiply the Mexican pesos I earned. The exchange rate of Mexican pesos with dollars where much higher than Salvadoran colones to dollars. Mexican pesos were ten pesos for a dollar and Salvadoran colones were in the black market 5.00 to a dollar. Legal exchange rate was only 2.50 colones for a dollar. Of course, we could only get dollars in the black market.

Ciudad Juárez, far from been a land that I was going to be at for a short period, it became my home for six long months. It became a very cold place in all senses. It was literally cold in weather, but also for the loneliness I felt around that place. It was a real hardship living there without seen a way out. My ego did not let me give up and go back with my empty hands.

Like in most cities, Juárez had some very dangerous districts and very nice and secure places. I was not afraid of those dangerous places since I had to survive the streets and I had gone to similar places in my country. Arid streets, not too welcoming either, but

I entered those places to try to make extra money to save as much as I could to try again to find the solution to cross the border.

It was never enough to pay another coyote, and I did not have the guts to travel alone. I could die all by myself trying alone. I had heard horror stories about it, people dying in the desert and in the river. I was trapped. I felt trapped. I did not know what to do. I had no one to call….and in that moment I remembered I still have the contact of the ex military guy. In trying to figure this out on my own, I had forgotten about him and his contacts in Mexico.

In those six months, I met other Salvadorans who were exactly like me: trapped in their way toward the US. We all got together trying to cross the border by ourselves becoming brave and going together, helping each other, but it was impossible. We always got trapped and back to the beginning: Ciudad Juárez.

Finally I got the courage to call the ex military contact I had from the beginning of my adventure. I begged him to please help me cross the border. He had mercy of me and he gave me some contacts to call and their address, but he advised:

"If you do not bring money with you, don't even try to look for them because they do not work without any money in between."

"How much do I need?" I asked. "Everything you can get, the more the better, and the more you can get, the faster you will cross."

I had saved many Mexican pesos, but when changing them to dollars, it was not much, so I had no other choice but to call my half sister to ask for more money. She was really upset and was skeptical to help me one more time, but she made sure I knew this was my last opportunity.

"The third time I ask for more money is the last one sister," I told her. "If I cannot pass the border this last time, I will go back home. Even if I have to go with nothing in my hands and beg for forgiveness from my wife. I will never ask for anything else the rest of my life. I promise."

Angrily she shouted, "How do you even think about giving up at this point?? You are too close to give up. You have to cross the border. Yes or yes, Eddy. Go for it. You will soon be here. You will see."

She encouraged me again to follow my dream, even though she was not happy I was asking for more money. She sent enough to get to my final destination in New York. When I was ready with the money, I said good bye to Chino and the family who had given me a home and I asked Chino to come with me but he said he was not ready yet.

"Let me know when you get to your sister's place. Maybe when I decide to come, you can help me over," said Chino.

We hugged and I said, "Of course, I will help you, Chino. We are friends! Friends help each other, so count on me for that!"

So I left to look for the phone company to call one of the numbers I have gotten from the ex military man."

I was sad that he didn't come with me because he had become my only friend in Mexico. We had cried and laughed together, and we had shared dreams and also deceptions in our own lives. My goal was Manhattan, and I couldn't stop until I got there. I think Chino is never going to try and he would stay in Mexico, but my heart could not settle with less than the American dream even with all these obstacles that stood in the way of my goal.

I found the place to call with no problem, but stayed outside staring at the phone company door. *This is it. My last chance.* When I called a very nice person answered. I explained my case and we made business over the phone. He gave me an address I had to go that same afternoon. The deal we made was good for me because I had more money to keep after paying to them and to have after crossing the border. The deal included crossing the border and taking me to New Mexico, also a hotel for the first night. However, it did not include the plane ticket to get to Manhattan. Still it was a great deal because I was going to pay when I was on the other side of the border. These people were serious about it. They were pros.

I asked myself why that state was called New Mexico and I just imagined that it had belonged to Mexico before being part of the United States, maybe as a result of a war long time ago. *Could the United States buy El Salvador to become another state?* I wondered in my mind, thinking about New Mexico.

Would New Mexico be similar to Mexico? Would they have many Mexicans speaking Spanish? I asked myself. Up to that point, it did not occur to me that when crossing the border, everyone would speak English and I spoke nothing else but Spanish. I did not know how I would communicate with people over there. Maybe in New Mexico I would have no problem because they must have Mexicans but in Manhattan, I don't know. It was a thought I had not have before. The language barrier was not part of my analysis to go after the American Dream. Since my object was to meet my sister and obviously she speaks Spanish, I had not even weighted the possibility of not being able to work in any place because I could not communicate. All I thought about was my abilities and nothing more.

Immediately I thought that not knowing English could not be an obstacle because I was smart enough to learn a new language. Besides, I already knew some words, important words to communicate with others. Some of them were: *bathroom* (bazrum), *toilet (toylet)*, *train* (trein), *bus* (bas), *ticket* (tiquet), *how much* (jau mash), *food* (fud), *taxi* was taxi, *hotel* (jotel), *address* (adres). That was all I needed to start with if I would meet someone who did not know any Spanish. Ah! I also knew how to say, "My name is" (mai neim is). Everything I had learned in Juárez.

When I got to the address given I learned that they were several Mexican families from Juárez that also helped other Central American people who wanted to cross the border. They had helped many Salvadorans going after the American Dream in the last six months. What I did not know till then, was that we had to wait a few days until the whole group would get together. I was the first of the group. Immigration services in the US border was alerted about many Salvadorans escaping the war trying to go after the American Dream, so we could not cross alone. Too dangerous. During those days, I only went out to buy food for the new group I had.

Again, I was the best person to do it because of my Mexican accent and my leadership skills. To my surprise, I met again the evangelical pastor. We both were really happy to see each other again, since we knew nothing of the rest of the original group. We were familiar faces and the rest were new faces. We made a really good friendship and we promised not to separate ourselves any more until we could cross the border and each of us get on our way to our final destination. We didn't know if afterward we would see each other again, but in this phase, we would not separate ourselves and both were surprised we were still in Mexico.

Again, he never talked to me about his relationship with Jesus and again did not explain to me what meant to be an evangelical pastor. I just never touched the subject, and he didn't either. We were so happy to find ourselves that we only talked about our adventures up to this point since we left home, not being able to cross the border. We had such a great connection that I could not explain, maybe because we had been away from home for so long and seeing a familiar face was the best that could happen to us.

We talked about everything that had happened during all those months in Mexico. We both ignored what had happened to the rest of the original group. He had called home several times to tell his parents every time he had tried to cross and that he didn't want to give up. After all, he was single and he had to call his parents to keep them at ease. I confessed to him I had not had the courage to call my wife. I told him I felt so lonely, but I was more afraid of her reaction and rejection and did not think of the anguish she could feel in my silence. His situation was so different. He was a son, and I was a husband. Very different, and I was afraid.

We were ten people in the group to cross the border. I was the risk taker to go out for food. Besides, I looked like a Mexican and nobody could be suspicious of me. I knew my way around since I had been in Juárez several months now. I liked going out because I felt free, plus I bought what I wanted to eat with everyone else's money because I was the risk taker. That was the deal. That was my pay to risk myself, and of course I did not feel I was at risk, but everyone agreed on it because they were new in the area, except pastor. This made me save a lot of money while we waited.

Every morning, we did not know if that was the day or if we had to keep waiting. Those days felt an eternity because we had no set date. The contacts on the other side of the border had to give the green light about it and we had to wait. Every day felt like a month. After the first week went by, we felt we had been there a whole year. Emotionally speaking, a year went by for each day and each day I grew a year older. I observed that pastor went away every night and came back with a peaceful face and I saw him so calm.

Secretly, I envied him. I was agonizing and he was calm, but I did not get the courage to ask and he didn't tell me his secret either. Maybe that would have saved me so many bad choices, but he kept his peace to himself. I just imagined that he had called home and his parents were happy he had called and that made him be calmed. It never occurred to me that maybe he had gone to pray and to be in the presence of God. I guess he was selfish about sharing his beliefs with me. Or maybe too shy. Who knows?

After two long weeks that felt like two years, the day came. That afternoon, they told us to get ready and to go at night to a pub. This pub was about ten blocks away. We could only bring with us a backpack and we had to choose the correct clothes to bring. We needed to bring black or dark blue or dark brown shirt and pants. All white clothes must be left behind unless it was underwear. We had to go to the pub asking for a drink. The backpacks were the sign for the pub owner to give us the next instruction.

So we got in and we asked for a beer. It felt so good, since I had months of not drinking trying to save every cent that came to my hands. This was an excellent excuse to drink a beer or two. It felt great after drinking! With the bill, we got the instructions. These people were professionals in what they did. This were not any coyotes. These were very structured people helping us all in a very professional way, without getting to be suspicious. In the back of the pub, there was a building that looked like private apartments, but there were rooms for rent. We would spend the night there.

We had to go out of the pub and walk out to the right one block, then go around the corner and go to the rooms by the back part of the building. We had the room number and the key was going to be under the carpet. We had to wait inside until someone came to knock our doors around 2:00 a.m. We rested a little while we waited, but we were too anxious and nervous to fall asleep, not deeply anyway. We lay down anyway trying to rest.

It was around 11 p.m. when we where in our rooms. They sent us food—a big meal so that we could eat well that night. It was our last meal in the Mexican side and we did not know at what time we would be able to eat again. At 2 a.m. sharp, someone knocked on the door, and we jumped out of our beds! I think we had fallen asleep but we got up immediately, went to the bathroom, washed our faces and out the door in less than five minutes. Our guide was there. We had to go into a van, the ten of us at the same time. Inside the van, the guide talked to us and told us who he was, and another guy was waiting for us outside.

Our guide was a man dressed up all in black. We all dressed up in black, dark blue or dark brown as indicated before. We must follow him without saying a word. We had to go in total silence.

This was crucial because it could make a difference between living or dying for the whole group, that matter. If someone talked and woke up the guards in our way to the border, the guide was going to disappear and we were on our own. No questions asked, no talking, total silence. We had to follow him at his pace and not stay behind either. Whoever fell behind, it was his or her problem. We shall not stop for anything—not even bathroom stops or water breaks, much less to rest. We were going to walk a long distance, so we had to have comfortable shoes. We had no time to waste if we wanted to be on the other side before dawn. It was going to be a long walk, a *very* long walk.

They never said how long, so I thought it was going to be for an hour or two. Whoever was not ready at this point before getting to our destination, could stay in the van and will go back to Juárez. No problem with that, and they did not have to pay anything. Those were the instructions. We were riding in the van for about forty-five minutes going into the countryside of Juárez. It was a very lonely place there. Finally the van stopped, and we had to go down. Everyone who was willing to walk the long distance, will come out. We all went down, so no one stayed behind. The group was formed by six men and four women with no children.

The guide was there, and the van guide just pointed him. We could not separate ourselves, but we had to walk about eight feet behind him. No lamps were aloud. He set the pace of the walk. One by one we started walking leaving the space we were instructed. My heart was beating hard, nervously, excited, and I couldn't believe I was finally close to the border. We walked from 2:45 a.m. to 5:00 a.m., at a fast pace. We had to walk fast if we wanted to be at the border while it was still dark. We could hardly see our way, but we kept ourselves quiet with our own thoughts, walking and walking.

The adrenaline was at its max, and that helped us not get tired. When we least expected it, we got to the border. The border was a metallic fence more than eight feet tall. But the fence was cut in a very professional way that nobody could tell at a glance. The guide knew exactly where it was cut. The ten of us passed the other side to close it back again. The guide said good-bye in sign language and said to wait until someone else comes for us. We had to go down slowly so that we did not fall into the river. We got to the other side and waited down closer to the water, waiting for a sign. We were nervous waiting. Every minute counted.

On the other side of the fence, we found a border like a canal, like the one Olivia Newton John of the movie Grease, sat on while watching the race, except the one she was at was empty and this was full of water. Now I understand why they call the people who cross the border wetbacks. Most likely we were going to get all wet on our intent to cross that river. But to my surprise, there is a man under the river, actually many men that helped us cross the border.

They tell each of us to take the shoes off and keep them in our hands, and to raise our feet while we put ourselves on their shoulders to help us cross the river to the other side. The water is low now and it is up to their chest, and we must not get wet so we do not become suspicious to the people on the other side. Impressive! This people are really pro! A huge smile brightened my face! I was amazed!

We all made it to the other side without getting wet, and a Lincoln car and other cars await us on there I just recognized the Lincoln because that is were we got in, the pastor and another guy and me. When we were inside, the men in the Lincoln told us, "Our job is finished when we get you to the hotel. You have to pay us now."

They continued with the instructions.

"Here are some vodka bottles. You have to drink as much as you need to get drunk."

Pastor and I looked at each other as we did not understand. When they saw our confused faces, a guy continued, "You have to be drunk on our way to the hotel because it is a few hours from here and the police can stop us."

And another guy continued, "If they stop us, we will say we are coming from a party and that we had our friends that got drunk and that is why you are asleep. This will avoid further questioning by having an assigned sober driver. The other cars are going in different routes so we are not suspicious. So drink up as much as you need to feel drunk, even if you had never drank vodka before."

So we started to drink vodka with artificial orange juice to soften the drink. We felt the vodka was somewhat light. Pastor told me he had never drank vodka before, so with a couple of drinks he had enough and got drunk. I had drank beer before, but I had never tried vodka, so I did feel it a little strong, but it tasted good with the orange juice. I put more orange juice than vodka , so it took me about five or six glasses to become drunk. The other partner did the same, five or six, and he was knocked down. They drove who knows for how long until we reached a Super 8 motel.

I woke up very hungry and it was around noon already. The other seven people had arrived already, and were starving too. I do not know if they had gotten drunk too, but we were extremely hungry. The guys that had driven us, went to buy some hamburgers at a fast food restaurant that was near the motel. They felt sorry for us and they used part of our payment to feed us. It was our first meal in the United States.

New Mexico is totally different than Ciudad Juárez. I could see progress even in this hotel, even though this type of motels are considered one of the cheapest, it was way better than the little hotel we stayed at in México D.F. The roads were clean, many lanes and there were many fast food restaurants I had never seen before. I could feel the liberty sensation. I felt free! I am finally on the other side, in the United States side! There were restaurants pretty close to us. Even the environment felt different. The liberty environment is what we can feel! I feel free! I am finally in the other side of the border. My heart is about to blow up of the excitement I feel!

"I am free! I am free!" I shout in my mind and would like to yell it to the world, but I don't thinking that immigration could come for me.

Everyone has a different destination from there. Some will go to Los Angeles, others to Chicago, others to Washington and some to Brooklyn. The pastor was headed to New Jersey, so we said good-bye to all our fellow wetbacks (that did not get wet)! We shared the contact information of our relatives to get in touch in the future. Each of us got instructions according to our final destination. I was on my way to Manhattan, and a woman in her midforties was also going that way. So everyone got on their way; but to this lady, Ana Maria and me, they gave a book that said Bible on it.

They tell us to walk toward a Baptist church that was three blocks away. We had to walk toward the church pretending she was my mother. It was Sunday, so there was a meeting with lots of people there. I had never had a Bible before, and I had no idea what they were for, or what was inside. I just knew it was a Bible because the book cover said The Bible. Mrs. Ana Maria was surprised when I told her that I didn't know what that was about because she said she read it constantly and she thought that everyone had one. She shared with me that she had met Jesus through the Bible and He had changed her life. I did not understand what she meant.

I can see how God took care of me throughout that process. He sent me angels to protect me from evil. He sent me the best and greatest tool I could get my hands on—His Word—though I did not appreciate it or know that it was a great treasure. I just saw it as a book, a tool toward my final destination. So as soon as I could, I left it behind. Even though I am sure God sent it to my hands at the right time because He knew how much I was going to need it, I did not see the same. I despised it.

12

Finally Manhattan

In the church parking lot, there was a van and a man next to it. They put us inside the van and inside was a lady from Santa Ana, a department from El Salvador. She was my sister's friend and said, "Your sister sent money to buy the ticket to Manhattan. When you are ready to board, we will call her and tell her to be waiting for you. This is the address you must go when you get to Manhattan. When you get out of the airport, you will find many taxis, but look for a driver that speaks Spanish so you do not get lost."

And she added, "We are on our way to the airport and we will buy her ticket too so you travel together. You must pretend she is your mother or stepmother so everything goes smoothly"

On our way to the Albuquerque airport, they gave us the instructions of what to do in each airport and especially in La Guardia Airport which was the closest to Manhattan, and was as big or bigger than the one in Mexico DF, so we had to do the same: follow the crowd.

"Since it is a domestic flight within the US, they will not ask for any ID or passport or anything, but you have to behave self-confident because if you look nervous, they will detect you as suspicious and in an investigation they will discover you as wetbacks and they will deport you immediately," said the man at the van.

When we got to the airport, I told Miss Ana Maria not to talk because I was going to do all the talking since she did look too nervous already. When I got to the counter, I tried to look as calmed as possible and told the lady:

"I am traveling with my stepmother and she is afraid of planes, that's the reason she looks so nervous. Can she get something to calm her down?"

She thought nothing of it and just checked our boarding passes and told us to wait until the boarding time was announced. It was a medium size plane, smaller than the one from San Salvador to Mexico DF but comfortable enough. It was a domestic airline, that did not have international flights, so it was a cheaper airline plus no documents were needed to fly.

The flight was a good experience and it took more time to get from Albuquerque to La Guardia, than from San Salvador to Mexico. We were also given food and drinks, but had to pay for them at a reasonable price. As we were told, we arrived to a huge airport. As in Mexico, we followed the crowd since all the signs were in English and could not understand anything. Arriving in Manhattan I already felt a winner, I had finished my first goal:

Finally! I am successful getting to my destination! Good things await me out there, I thought with a huge smile on my face.

Unbelievably, it had taken me more than seven months to get to Manhattan instead of two weeks, and the only thing I regretted and felt ashamed of was that I had not called Maria Elena yet. And as time went by, I was even more scared to call.

I had not thought too much about my wife and my daughter in all this time because I was trying to survive and fulfill my goal and my mind was programmed to call as soon as I got to my goal place: my sister's home. It was blocked to do it before as I had nothing to say. It didn't occur to me that she would be worried, with anguish looking for me within all the dead bodies of the war.

I was so selfish, totally selfish because I only thought of getting to my goal to give them a better future, but ignored all her feelings, her anguish, her searching for me, her imagination of what had happened when I left without saying a word, just the same as when we were just girlfriend and boyfriend, with the big difference that now we are husband and wife and have a child in between. Never thought about all her feelings nor the possibility that she would think I was dead and find another man that would love her and protect her and be by her side instead of me. After all, almost a year had gone by already and I continue without communication. How selfish of me.

When I got out of the airport, I looked for a taxi driver that looked Latin to me. I came close to the window and asked, "Hablas español?" (You speak Spanish?)

"Sí . Entra, entra." (Yes. Come in, come in.)

"Cuánto me cobrás por llevarnos a esta dirección?" ("How much do you charge to take us to this address?") showing him the paper with the address. Back home, you show the address or say the address first to the cab driver to know how much they will charge before hand.

"Pasa y te explico, no te preocupes, es dependiendo de la distancia." (Come on in, and I will explain to you. Don't worry. It is depending on the distance.)

I didn't get it.

We grabbed our backpacks and got into the taxi. I gave the address to him in a paper. I had it written in two parts: one for the driver and one in my little notebook. The taxi driver sees the address and we leave. Seeing him so confident, we relaxed and started to see all the buildings around.

The taxis in United States have a small machine in front of the car where it marks the miles traveled and they charge for the distance accordingly. It starts at $2.00 and I asked what that meant. He explained that was the entry fee for the service, and from there on, the distance will be measured and that was what we will pay. They do not make up the fee, like in my country. *They are organized and fair*, I thought.

For both of us everything was all new, so we happily looked around, enjoying everything that was out there. We got distracted about where we were heading trying to see everything we could. We passed by all those huge buildings, they were so tall, and we had never seen one like them in our country. We saw malls too, similar to Metrocentro, but some were vertical, not horizontal like Metrocentro. We saw many fast food restaurants around us. *Manhattan is an extraordinary place*, I thought.

My thoughts were going around how well I was going to do, in the success I was going to have, in the freedom I experienced here away from the war. Suddenly, I looked back to the taxi driver's machine and it marked much more than we were expecting to pay between us both, and then I started noticing that we were going in circles around the same places, trying to get more money from us, tourist faces! Maybe our happy and amazing faces made us look too much like tourists, and I perceived he was trying to charge more, since the more he drives the more he charges because it is charged by distance.

So I asked, "Oye, qué pasa que nunca llegamos? Sé que nuestro destino no es muy lejos del aeropuerto y llevamos varios minutos afuera y no veo que nos acerquemos. Tú estas dando vueltas sobre el mismo lugar," ("Hey, what's wrong with you? I know our place is not far from the airport, and you are going around and around and not getting close to the place.") I tried to sound sure of myself and in Mexican accent because I thought he was Mexican.

And the taxi driver answered, "Disculpe hermano, pero realmente me he perdido, preguntaré en una gasolinera porque no encuentro la dirección." (Sorry, my brother, I am lost. We will ask in the gas station because I can't find the address.)

My life in the streets had taught me this was not right and he was trying to rip us off.

When we got to the gas station and he got out of the cab asking for directions, Miss Ana Maria and I got out with our backpacks and ran to a Peruvian restaurant next door. Fortunately for us, we asked for help, and they called the head waiter who was Mexican and we told him our story and asked for help. We were afraid and that is why we ran for help. The owner was from Peru, and the head waiter thought I was Mexican. So he told the owner to help us, and he did. The head waiter was given permission to take us to the address we were looking for, as it was about seven minutes away, not so far away.

The owner of the restaurant, a tall and tough guy, went to talk to the taxi driver and told him to leave or he was going to report him with the police for trying to cheat some tourists. The taxi driver left without our payment. The man of the restaurant offered us food, which we happily accepted since we still had the money that we would have paid for the taxi. He lent me the phone to call my sister and he also explained where we were, to my sister. She said she would come for us when her husband Ali got home and he offered to take Miss Ana Maria to her place as it was very close too. They were all too kind to us. I felt happy. People in this part of the world seemed nicer than back home or Ciudad Juarez.

Rescuing us and being as good as the restaurant owner was, he did not even charge us for the meal. *He was a real angel put by God in our way. That is for sure*, I can think now. But in the moment, I just thought that I was very lucky and that everything that would happen to me in that part of the world was going to be simply good. I had made the right decision to go to the US, after all.

Estela called the restaurant to let us know that Ali was home and were on their way to pick us up. The restaurant owner was so nice to us that I promised we were going to come back to eat to his restaurant as often as possible. He just smiled and was happy to help. He had a hard start in the States too, so he related to us.

To my surprise, Ali picked us up without my sister and we went to drop off Miss Ana Maria. She felt happy to finally arrive at her destination. and after saying good by to her, we promised to visit often as we were very close to each other. You tend to make a relationship with the people who become your family in this type of adventures.

Finally, we get to my final destination: meet with my sister. I was happy! It was a mixture of feelings never experienced before. It was a mixture of feelings of success, happiness, expectation, relief, emotion, and thankfulness.

When we were finally in Estela's house, I started telling them part of my adventure, and things I had gone through. I told her I was really happy I was finally with them. We talked so happily that I did not noticed the silence in the house. The baby was asleep and the boy was playing alone in his room and they had told him not to get out until they called him. Estela and Ali said that they already had a lot of good plans for me, so soon I was going to start working.

"When you start working, you will communicate with your wife and tell her all about you," she said subtly.

With that phrase, I did not ask for the phone to call Maria Elena. It was clear that she was not going to give it to me at that time. She continued manipulating my destiny, but I thought, innocently, that she was right because up to this point, I had nothing good to tell her, but when I get a job, I will have something good to say and a clear view of the time needed to save money to bring them to the US with me. I wanted to give her the biggest surprise of her life. She deserved that.

Suddenly I noticed that her kids were not around us.

"And your kids, where are they? With some friends or neighbors?" I asked and her facial expression changed to a sad one in seconds.

And she said, "The boy and the baby girl are in their rooms quietly playing, as we asked them not to come out until we told them, but Xenia…That is something I need to resolve, Eduardo. The oldest, Xenia, she is gone to live with some friends and I need your help on this Eduardo. Do you remember how much she loved you? How she loved to play with you when we were together?"

"Of course I remember! I love her to death and loved to play with her too."

"She always asked for you when we came here, and I think you are the right person that can help us convince her to come back home now that you are here with us," she said. "Now it would be you, Ali, and I as responsible adults in her life."

"And I? How can *I* help? She has a lot of years of not seeing me, and she will not recognize me. Why did she leave in the first place?"

But she insisted to me to help her and never got to the point of why she left. Of course she manipulated me again and convinced me to go to look for her the next day which was Monday.

During the night, when I finally went to bed, in my loneliness with my own thoughts, after all the excitement of the day, I started crying. I cried for all the internal feelings I had. It was a mixture of relief, happiness, but at the same time I felt frustrated. I felt happy to finally be in my destiny place, but unhappy that I could not fulfill my own promise to call my wife as soon as I got to my sister's place.

That night, for the first time, I thought carefully how I had met Maria Elena. The day I had seen her for the first time very dedicated with her books and studies, apart from everyone. How I got the guts to start talking to her and how we started to know each other. How we started to fall in love with each other and how romanticism was born within us. Every date, every talk, those looks, how we stared at each other, before talking for the first time. All was new to us since I had never had a girlfriend and she hadn't had a boyfriend either.

Suddenly I remembered that first kiss. It was such a special kiss, for both of us, the first. I remember shaking inside and outside. I did not know if she was going to reject me or accept me, and luckily was the second. She accepted me without hesitating. I learned to kiss her softly and tenderly because I felt tender and lovely next to her. I loved her soft lips next to mine, and I kissed her every time I could.

My feelings for her were pure, totally pure. I did not know what else to do with her, or where to put my arms every time we kissed. So I started to touch her in other parts of her body other than her face. When I least expected, our touching went further than we should. She would take my arms away but every day we became closer and closer and our love flourished rapidly.

We were inseparable, twin souls. I could not stop thinking about her all day long. Our trips to the beach, to the park, to the discos, all evolved into more closeness and more touch between us. Suddenly, the day least expected, and don't know at what time our kisses became more. We could not resist ourselves and we couldn't stop our passion that had grown within us. I thought for the first time that we should have not lost our senses, but we did and now we were parents of a baby girl.

I was a fourteen-year-old, a kid by then, but I certainly did not feel like a kid, of course. I felt a man, a macho man by then. Very adult, just because I was working since a kid, and could earn money. *What was I thinking?* I did not measure myself and did not see the future. I could not care at the moment because I had a job. I was a good man and all I wanted to do is to foresee for my wife and family.

In that moment, everything was pure instinct because I had no idea how babies were made or born. I was naïve in a lot of ways. Even a very innocent boy. The passion took us up to that point were we made a baby. I can never regret that as it was a great happiness and love that was in between the baby and us. The consequence is that I became a father and after all, I had come to the U.S. for them, thinking on their future. My baby has my blood and she deserves the best.

Suddenly I come back into reality. I realized that Guadalupe had turned three already and I was not there with her. And now she was about to turn four, and that was the age I lost my mother. But in Guadalupe's case, she had lost her father. I realize what I had done to my daughter, abandonment to her as I had, except I am alive and my mother is dead.

I will look for my daughter and wife in less than a year, and I will have them with me right here, I promised myself again.

I have feelings of profound loneliness, profound sadness, even though I am at my destiny, the one I had worked so hard for up to this point. I cannot start imagining, or think the profound hurt I had caused to Maria Elena for disappearing without a word, much less I can imagine the feeling of abandonment I had caused my daughter, the same I had felt all my life after my mom and dad died.

I cried for a long time thinking for the first time of all that hurt caused and I feel shame for what I had done, and I feel ashamed of myself. It is the first time I think that instead of giving her a great surprise, I will give her a bad surprise and probably she will feel happy I am not dead, but most likely she will be very upset with me. I do not know yet, but I do not think she will be too happy. But I had learned that the war is getting worse and the guerrilla is kidnapping rich people to finance the war and they are putting bombs on the electric posts and in important bridges. The Martial Law with curfew has continued from 6:00 p.m. to 6:00 a.m. Suddenly I thought for the first time that maybe Maria Elena has thought I am dead.

But that night I decide I will call her when I get the offered job and do the math of how much I would have to save to bring her with me.

"If I work hard and save as much as possible, I can bring her with me in less than six months." Living with my sister, I can save faster, assuming I do not have to pay for my stay. *I will talk to her about it tomorrow*, I thought. *Maybe she'll charge me a low fare or maybe nothing.*

I plan to buy just basic clothes to work—nothing fancy because I had only rescued a few things, other than what I am wearing: a pair of slacks, a couple of shirts, three pairs of socks and underwear. I need to buy some clothes with my first salary, but that will be it. I will save everything else. "I will send some money for my family and save the rest" I said to myself. I want them with me soon."

Monday morning we went to visit some of Ali's friends to introduce me to them and to ask for a job for me. They liked all the work experience I had and my desire to work hard. They spoke Spanish so we could easily communicate and they told me to come back Wednesday to talk about what type of job they could offer to me. They were really nice and kind to me and I felt very comfortable with them. There was no need to go any other place, I already had an offer there. We did not talk about how much they would pay because that was the Wednesday meeting for. I was happy! Wednesday morning I will have defined my destiny and at night I will call Maria Elena to tell her all my story and my plan to get her out of a war country.

That same afternoon, we had lunch together and happy with the job offer, we had a very delightful lunch time. Estela had asked me to go in the afternoon with her to look for her daughter Xenia so I could talk with her. Estela drove me to the school where she studied and she stayed inside the car about a hundred yards away. She showed me who was Xenia as soon as she came out and she observed me getting close to the school from the car. I did not know why she did not come closer and introduced me to her. I ignored what was going on in that house. She did not say anything to me. Not a word about the real reason she had left home.

We arrived at the school area at the time school was over for the day. I had never seen such a beautiful school before in my life. It was a huge, beautiful, clean, nice horizontal building and was well constructed, well painted. There was no graffiti on the walls either. Actually all the surrounding was totally clean, no garbage on the floors, streets or around it. Kids where coming out of the building and the outside was full of them, but there was no garbage on the floor. Amazing! That was different for me. When I saw Xenia, I observed she had turned into a beautiful teen girl. I felt happy to see her, and in seconds, I imagined my daughter growing up in a place like this one. Xenia was walking down with some friends, happy and laughing, all the contrary of what I had imagined. I shouted, "Xenia!" She turned around with a surprised yet scared face.

When she saw me, she started running fast. I was right behind her. Some of her friends, went inside the school to alert the principal about it in case something could happen to her, while others saw me chasing her. The ones that observed the whole scene thought I was going to do something wrong to her. She ran rapidly, but because of my height, and my long legs, I ran faster and I could reach her and as I grabbed her I said:

"Xenia, I am your Uncle Eddy. I just want to talk to you. Probably you did not recognize me with this beard."

She kicked and tried to get loose while I hugged her strongly so that she could not escape.

"Let me go, Uncle! Let me go!" she said in an anguished voice, shouting at me, and I couldn't understand.

Her friends went running toward us too, trying to help her, and everyone heard.

Your mother has sent me to talk to you.

"My mother!"

"Let me go, let me go! I am not going anywhere with you!" she shouted with all her heart.

By her body language, I knew she did not want to be with me, but I continued.

"I have not come to take you with me. I have come to talk to you."

I assured her slowly and in a calming way so she stopped being afraid of me, she breathed deeply and said.

"Seriously, Uncle? Ahh, Uncle, you had frightened me so badly!"

"I thought you wanted to kidnap me and force me to go to my mother's. What are you doing here, Uncle Ed?"

"Looking for you, darling."

"You have come from El Salvador just to look for me?"

"No, sweetie. I came from El Salvador getting away from the war, and your mother helped me come over. But I will tell you about it another day. I have not come to talk about me but to talk about you. Your mom said you are not living with her, that you are with some friends. What happened?"

"She has not told you anything?"

"Nope."

"Well, yes, Uncle Ed. I left home six months ago, and sincerely I never want to go back."

She continued.

"I am sure my mother sent you thinking you can convince me, but you have no idea who she is. You do not know her. She is a witch."

Imagining the witch of Esmeralda, I asked, "Why do you say so?"

"Oh, Uncle, you have no idea what we had gone through after we got here. I do not understand my mother. She keeps fighting all the time with my dad. She shouts and she hits him, and it becomes a huge fight all the time. It is always a big fuss that she makes, and my dad is so stupid. He stays quiet, and later in a soft voice, he verbally abuses her but without hitting her or yelling back. That makes her more furious, and she becomes the devil in person! When Dad tells her, her truths, she jumps on him hitting him, abusing him physically, but he only defends himself.

I have never seen him hit her back. Sometimes he screams back but never hits her because he is afraid of going to jail. And then, when she cannot win the fight, she shouts on us kids and tell us horrible things, and if we want to tell her to calm down to shut up or try to defend ourselves from what she tell us, she hits us until she gets tired. All her anger is against us, her children. Since I am the oldest, she hits me more—especially because when she tries to hit my smaller siblings, I get in between them and preferred to get them myself. Look, Uncle…This is not what I want for my life. I do not know if she continues to hit my siblings, but I could not live like that anymore. I was planning to escape one day."

"But, sweetheart, the best you can do is talk to your parents about it and go back home. You do not need to escape from home. No one will love you more than your parents. Let's go to the restaurant over there to continue talking. I want to know everything that has happened."

"Okay, let's go and I will tell you all about it."

"Uncle, I discovered that this is a free country where we have rights as children. The government protects us. I did not run away. I discovered this because one day, I came to school with my blue-and-purple arm, full of bruises after my mother had hit me all over. She always hit me on the body so that I could cover it with my clothes, but this time, she got so angry that she forgot and couldn't care less when I put my arm up to defend myself. I could not come to school with long sleeves since it was summer. I was taking some summer classes to reinforce my math skills just before going to high school because I got a low grade."

My teacher saw the bruises on my arm and did not say anything to me, but she reported it to the superintendent of the school. She told the psychologist, and she sent for me for a meeting the following day.

"She asked me how I had done it, and I told her I had fallen and put my arm during the fall, and that is how I did it. I was afraid to tell the truth. She said to show her my knees to see the scrapes from the fall. I had none. I was really scared because my mom always threatened that if we would tell anyone about it, she would hit us to death! And I believed her. She would say, 'What happens in the house stays in the house,' and I thought that was right. No one had to know about her mistreatment."

"I have years of suffering the same abuse over me and my siblings. I thought all families were the same. I didn't know any different. But the psychologist opened my eyes about it and told me that I was a victim of child abuse, and that was not right.

"The psychologist looked into my eyes and said, 'You are lying to me. Who hit you? You had not fallen. Your dad or your mom? Who is hitting you? You have the obligation to tell me because this is a crime, and he or she should go to jail.' And she added, 'As a psychologist, I am required by law to report it to the authorities because the law tells me so. To me and all psychologists and counselors, when a client is in danger, we have to tell the authorities to break confidentiality, and they make an investigation in your home. So tell me…Your mom or your dad?' So I had to talk and told her all about it, but I begged and cried not to report her as I did not want her in jail either. I told her I had no one else in this country, and I had no one to go to, and that is why I was waiting to turn eighteen to go away from home. But she explained to me that there were nice families that accept children in risk and give room and board until they turn eighteen. That totally changed my situation. It gave me hope."

"But you're only fifteen. What will you do for three years?"

"My new parents encourage me to dream. I dream about turning eighteen. To be independent, to start working formally, and to live in peace. Have my siblings come to live with me, and I will take care of them, and we will take care of ourselves."

"Are your serious?"

"Yep, my mother can go to hell herself!"

She said that with a lot of anger in her face and a profound look looking directly into my eyes.

"She deserves to go to hell! I am sick and tired of her, and I will never come back home to her!"

Then she continued.

"In my new home, I do not see fights between my new parents. In my real family, all I see are fights, and Dad is so stupid that he does not defend himself or defend us kids. I am resentful with him, and I think he is stupid. I am tired of that environment, and to me it is nothing else but hell. I am much better in my foster home."

"Foster Home?"

"Yep, the substitute homes are called foster homes, and my new family is so different. They are very lovely people. They say they are Christians, and even though I do not understand what that means because they have still not taught me about it or pressure me to learn with them, I can see that it is a family that gets along very well, and I do not hear any screaming or yelling. I live in peace. They pray before every meal, and I like that. They give thanksgiving for all their things, their day, and for me. They give thanksgiving to God for me. Totally the opposite of what I hear at home. All I hear is complaining to God, and I really do not understand too well where God is in my mother's life, and I think all that exists in her life is hell and the devil. My new mother has God all around her mouth. And all I know is that ever since I live in a peaceful place, my grades are going up when before, I was almost failing. My new parents encourage me to dream of getting a scholarship to go to the university when I graduate and become someone."

"University?"

"Yes, Uncle Ed, I want to get a scholarship to go to the university and work at the same time to earn money soon so that I can live on my own and bring my siblings, Idalia and Alcides, far away from my real parents. If we go to France, a whole ocean will be between us! That would be perfect!"

I was listening closely when she proceeded.

"I dream of been someone in my life, Uncle, and I cannot go back to them and go back to that hell world of my family. I would not be able to fulfill my dreams. Please be with me. Support my dreams, Uncle. If I don't get a scholarship in this state, I will apply for a scholarship in another state far away from home. You just do not know my mother. She is the devil in person!"

"Maybe we talked for an hour or so, how well she was doing away from my sister. I could not understand everything she was telling me. It was too much bad information about my sister. I did not understand since I felt loved and well received and I felt in peace and grateful with my sister and her husband, but my niece was telling me the contrary. I could not believe that my sister hits my brother-in-law much less that she hit my nieces. For me, she had been an angel rescuing me every time I had needed it most."

Am I missing something here? I asked myself.

"Don't worry about me, Uncle. I will be fine. Now you are an extra family member here, but there is nothing that will convince me to go back to my parents. I'd rather continue my journey away from that crazy family."

Changing the subject, she asked, "And tell me about you. What are you planning to do?"

"Well, as we talked at the beginning, there is war in El Salvador. And I came here running away from it, thanks to your mother's help. This is why I cannot understand you. For me, your mother has been an angel, and you say she is the devil herself. But anyway, maybe later I will understand, and hopefully I will not have to be in between any fights. What I want to do is work hard to bring my wife and daughter here as soon as possible."

"Wife? Daughter? How can that be so? You got married so young?"

"Yep, I have a daughter, who is almost four now, but I will tell you all about her some other day. I think your mother must be worried that I do not go back to the car, and your substitute parents must be wondering why you are not home. I hope to see you again and continue talking. You can count on me, and maybe when I have my family together, you can come to live with us too."

"Well, I doubt it, Uncle. I would have to think about it because you are too close to Mom, and I don't think that would be the best for me, but I appreciate your offer. We will see when you are established."

"Well, sweetheart, hope to see ya soon."

"Okay, Uncle. It has been good to see you, and I am happy for you that you are here, but I assure you that going back to my house is not an option."

She repeated again and gave me a kiss on the cheek, and I hugged her as I used to do it when she was a little girl and she went her way walking calmly.

So I observed her very thoughtfully and I did not know what to think about all this information. I was confused. What was waiting for me in this country? Will I have a great future or more problems? Was it worth all this effort? Was it worth leaving my wife and child? All this questions surrounded my head and I was totally confused about my sister and her household and me in between them. I did not understand anything.

We went back to my sister's home without her daughter. We were riding back in total silence. I did not want to talk. Finally Estela asked, "What did my daughter say?" I did not want to tell her all that I had learned about her. Everything was too strange for me. So I just said, "Your daughter told me she is not ready to come back home and she said that you used to hit her and she did not like that, but she will think about coming back some other time. But not now."

I did not want to tell her about all the horrible things she had told me about her parents going on in that house. After all, I had just gotten there and I had not seen any sign of abuse. That night we had dinner and the environment felt kind of uncomfortable. No one touched the subject at the dinner table. I had a good concept of my sister that had helped me so many times in my life, even though she had left me after all. If she had not existed in my life, I would be in the middle of the war in my country without a job. She helped me go away from my "brothers" when I used to live with Maria, she helped me learn to work and get a job. She helped me learn to keep myself clean and to behave. She has helped me to come to Manhattan. So she has helped me in so many ways. I did not know what to say about all the things her daughter had confessed to me. That night, we had dinner and went to our bedrooms without further talking.

It was before 7:00 a.m. when the doorbell rang. It was the county sheriff.

"Go inside," said Ali.

I got really scared because I thought the taxi driver had given my address and told immigration services about my existence in this part of the world. That is all I could think of.

Estela told Ali in Spanish, "Amor, vienen por Eddy, ya lo descubrieron." (My love, they are coming for Eddy. They had discovered him.)

She also thought they came for me because I was an illegal immigrant.

Ali grabbed me toward the back door and we went into the garage and got into his van and we left running away. So now, two days after finally fulfilling my dream of coming to the United States, I am running away from justice. Ali was my accomplice, and he didn't mind. Without thinking about it, he risked his life with me and we ran away..

Ali, as a good Arab, was a merchant. He sold all type of things. He bought things to re-sell. He would buy things like slacks, blouses, T-shirts and shirts, belts, socks, anything useful that he thought he could sell, he had it. He knew his way very well and knew where to buy cheap to resell at a good price. He loved to sell to the illegal aliens, in the plantations and factories, and brought everything they needed.

They lived in a place with lots of produce like strawberry, cauliflower, grapes, artichoke, lettuce, etc. It was a very nice place, and Ali had discovered that the people who worked as illegal aliens did not like to go to the malls because they did not feel safe, so every time Ali would come to them, they fell happy and of course they bought everything from him. He was their savior. They even asked him for specific things and he would bring it to them. All was a cash deal. No taxes, no formalities.

When we finished with the people nearby, we went to other places. I observed he drove south looking for other plantations, looking for opportunities. We would stop where we saw people working in little towns and big towns. We would stop just to put gas, eat and sell. And when the night came, we would look for a cheap place to stay, a Bed and Breakfast place and sometimes we would sleep in the van. After going south, just before getting into Florida, we headed west toward California.

In that time I met the real Ali for the first time. He was a very smart well educated man, from a good Arab family who had fallen in love with my sister. He did not care she was not Arab, he admired her beauty and her strong character. He did not care either that she was a daughter outside of marriage. What he never knew was that his wife was going to hit him again and again every time she was angry and frustrated. He confessed that he also get real mad with her, but because he was a family man, he did not want to expose himself to go to prison and leave his children without a father, and this was the reason he did not hit her back.

"Besides," he said, "I was taught that man never hits a woman. We must respect them, love them, and find a way to make a living until death separates us. For an Arab man, his biggest treasure is his wife, and we must cultivate her and the relationship. Your sister has a very bad temper, but you know what? She has a very good heart most of the time. It is only when she gets mad or frustrated that she goes wild. It is like a demon gets into her. She converts herself into another person. I hope someday she outgrows from it because in my family, there are no divorces, and this is why I do not plan to leave her ever. A divorce is a sign of failure, and I do not plan to be the first failure in the family. And all in all, I continue loving her, hoping she will change someday."

I felt compassion for this man, and I could understand why my sister was with him and why she did not worry about him leaving. It was him that had to put up with her, and she was the one that took advantage of having a very responsible man by her side. I started to see my sister as a woman with many issues and a problem person. I started to not trust her too much in my heart.

We shared like two men, and told him my real story, and how grateful I was that he had accepted me in his house when I was a child. I told him that I also loved my sister very much, but did not understand why she got so crazy to the point of pushing away her own daughter. I told him everything I had gone through for seven months to get here since I left San Salvador. The complete story. How I missed my wife and daughter. Sometimes we would laugh and sometimes we would cry from nostalgia.

"I can't believe I am running away, we are fugitives," I said. "And what is going to happen now? Will I stop running away some day, Ali?" I asked intrigued of the situation.

"I do not know my brother," he said. "but now, you are safe with me, and we are together. Money is not a problem in this country, you see? We are doing fine, don't worry about the future. We will take one day at a time."

He was right and his calmness made me not to worry. I could not be thinking of tomorrow, when I should be grateful I was well and alive, within considering our situation.

When we least expected it, we arrived at Los Ángeles coming from Manhattan. We had gone across the whole country and we didn't even feel the time going. The streets, the highways, the sightseeing were all exceptional. We would go through highways of four and five lanes in each side, and outside the cities we had roads more like ours but in a better shape, one or two lanes each side. I can not even imagine having a highway in my country. That was impossible to my eyes.

Oh my country! I left you behind! I thought.

We learned that after the coup d'état, a governing board took over our country. It was made of several men but that didn't last too long, so another one was formed. They cannot come to an agreement to have new elections. A new party has born of a man of last name D'Abuisson, who named the party ARENA (Alianza Republicana Nacionalista or the Nationalist Republican Alience). We had always had only two parties: The PCN (Partido de Conciliación Nacional or the National Conciliation Party) and PDC (Partido Demócrata Cristiano or the Christian Democratic Party). The PCN has governed for ever, since I have memory and to become a president, they had to be either General or Colonel. Military party always won. The PDC was civil people. This was one of the issues of unhappiness in the country. The military had all the power and they (the civils) had to get them out of power. This was one of the big statements for the guerrilla to be formed.

I cannot even imagine how my wife and child are doing.

"Ali, I have to work to get my family here as soon as possible," I tell him out of the blue.

"As soon as we get back to Manhattan, we will look for my friends again and this way you can plan when to bring them," he calmed my anxiety.

"And why are we going from one place to the other and not stay in one same place?" I ask.

"Because we are running away from immigration services that came to arrest you in our house, that is why we cannot come back too soon. This is why we are running away. As soon as my wife tells me that everything is okay around our house, without vigilance, we go back. Don't worry, we will take care of you. You are family," he assured me.

Sharing with Ali, I felt sorry for him. I felt sorry for him as a man and his life with my sister. I could see Ali had it all, but did not have a happy life. On the other side, I had nothing but dreamed of having it all to become happy. I thought that was happiness about. I felt my dream was incomplete. I wanted so bad to start working and earn my own money to be able to bring my family with me.

Running away within the United States, I do not need anything to live since Ali pays for everything with the sales we make in every stop. He pays for food, clothing and the hotels we sleep at. But I have nothing to send my wife and I still do not have the guts to call her. What will I tell her? I am running away and I do not know why I ran away except probably because I am illegal? It makes no sense to call her. Seriously, I have nothing to say.

Finally, after five or six months of running away, my sister tells her husband we can come back. The police officers are gone from the surroundings. Happy with the good news, we start driving back, stopping the least possible. We always stayed at least two nights in each hotel and Ali would call home every time he could and give our information so that my sister knew where to contact us.

When we finally arrived, they were really happy to be together again and I was glad they looked happy with the reencounter. Estela was rarely calmed and I must say, even happy and mellow with her husband. She had prepared a very good welcome dinner and then we went around to the mall close to their house.

Finally. Back to step one, I thought. *Now it's just a matter of a few months to bring my family together.*

13

The Arrest

The following day, before 6:00 a.m., they were knocking the door and ringing the door bell. Again, the county sheriff was there, very nicely dressed with his typical sheriff hat. He came over with several patrol cars surrounding the house, in the front and the back were covered. There was no way out. They had to turn me in. I felt like an offender, a thief, or who knows what for the first time in my life. I had never been arrested as I have never had any problems with the law. Yes, I had stolen to eat, but that was it. What a welcome to the country of opportunities!

They put the handcuffs on me and put me into one of the police patrol cars. I did not resist, I had been running away for too long. All my thoughts were around throwing away all my dreams and I had no other choice but to go back home to a country in war, empty handed. I had been captured after all the suffering I had gone through to get to the United States. This is not fair and all this troubles had been for nothing.

I let my wife and daughter suffer for nothing, leaving without a word, in vein. One more time I have to postpone my call as I do not know what would happen to me in the next weeks. More than a year has gone by since I left: around seven months to cross the border and more than five running away. Now I am going to jail because I am a wetback? And illegal alien? I had seen so many illegals in my travels running away, I just could not think that I could go to jail for being illegal. Is that so?

In jail, they tell me to take off my clothes, with body language signs and they give me a white uniform with a number. They take pictures of my front and side face for my record, just like I had seen in the movies. I felt like a real prisoner, being not guilty, and my only sin was to try to go after the American Dream all this time. A whole year wasted. This has been a nightmare instead of a dream.

This was a county jail, a small one. It was divided in three sections. I could observe that one was for the drunks, other for the girls that looked like prostitutes (I could recognized them well), and the other, where I was, for "minor infractions" waiting for court. It was a jail of about five by six meters or around twelve by fifteen feet. It was a clean place as we were forced to keep it clean ourselves. There was a toilet and we had to take turns cleaning it. The showers were outside without curtains, so there was no privacy. The new one would go first. I got caught on a Friday and on Monday I was supposed to have an audience with the Judge, or at least that is what I thought. Monday nothing happened for me, only my other jail mates were called. I felt in total abandonment. The other members of my jail would try to talk to me, but I understood nothing. They all spoke English and I could not understand. They were all Americans and no Latino was there or someone who spoke Spanish. I only observed them.

Of course, no one came to see me as nobody knew I was there, except my sister and brother in law. I assume they got afraid to come visit me. I excused them like that. I had no one to call. I got a full sense of loneliness in my heart. I thought about the pastor and Mrs Ana Maria, but I didn't call them because I felt ashamed of this situation, but wondered if they had a problem like I had. I even thought about letting them know the are arresting illegals so they could be careful, but I just didn't call. It was me and myself only.

I seriously thought and meditated on the fact that I should have never gone away from my wife and child. What a fool. I will make full circle and after all, will go back with nothing but the agony of this adventure.

I have been such a fool! I thought. *I fought for the American dream but ended up with nothing good. Trying hard to come to be a good person, a savior for my family, and now I am in jail for the sole reason that I am an illegal alien? This cannot be happening to me. I do not understand all those people working in the fields and nothing happens to them. Why me? What price am I paying?*

Immediately, the scene when we stole the chicken from the VW truck comes to my mind, leaving some families without a complete dinner. Is that what I am paying for? Or the times I stole in the market because I was hungry? I would ask these questions again and again around in my mind. I was defeated. I felt like a failure. I felt lonely and abandoned, the same way I felt when I became an orphan. The witch would lock me into a closet, but this is a real locked in. I do not like anything that is happening to me. At this point I knew I must go back and go beg Maria Elena to forgive me for trying to come after a dream that is a nightmare, hoping for her forgiveness and that she would let me go back with her.

At least I have free food. It was not a restaurant, but I ate better in jail than when I was in the streets back home; especially when I ran away from the witch when I was a child. It was definitely only a matter of time until I was sent back home. I felt totally defeated as I would go back with nothing in my hands, no money, no clothes, no nothing after a year away. What a waste.

I really hoped my wife would receive me back after more than a year of silence.

I have not been unfaithful in any way, so she must forgive my stupidity. I hope she believes me all that I have gone through because it is hard to believe, I thought.

I probably should have never left El Salvador, I kept thinking. *But now it is too late to say that. I can only think about asking for Maria Elena's forgiveness for abandoning her as I did.*

Maria Elena, my beautiful wife with splendid figure, tall as a model, lovely at all times…I tried imagining myself in the encounter with her ; she would have a huge smile on her face, happy for my return and that she couldn't stop kissing me, happy to see me alive and back to her side. I was ready to go home. Even if it was totally the opposite. If that was my destiny, to go back, so be it! It was the best I can do: be by her side and my daughter's side.

I had made up my mind to tell the truth. I was going to say that I had crossed illegally after the American dream, running away from a war in my country. And if possible, and if they let me stay, I will ask for a special permission to bring my family here. Ali had told me about a law when someone would ask for an amnesty, that the person could stay with a special permission. I did not totally understand how that worked, but we had planned to say that if I was caught, I was going to ask for amnesty.

Each Monday I would wait to be called for my audience with the Judge, but nothing happened. I did not understand what was going on and why I wasn't called. Is it so bad to be an illegal person? In those days, for the first time I asked myself if God really existed. I had seen some American prisoners kneel down, cry their hearts out, maybe in repentance, and the next thing I knew was that they were called and never came back. Maybe I looked depressed and very lonely, I had seen everyone leave except me. The white guards would call me with signs to go close to them to the bars, and sometimes they would offer me a cigarette and some coffee so I could be at ease. I felt gratitude to them, and

I thought I was lucky for that treatment, and also grateful that it was a clean jail.

One day, finally, I kneel myself in front of everyone around me and asked, "God, do you exist? Can you exist for me?"

Then I added, "I do not know you or if You really exist or if there is an existence of a superior being, but if You exist, I need a signal from You, since everything I have ever lived, all my life is abandonment, and loneliness, I am an orphan and no one had ever taught me if You exist or not, so I do not know if you really exist; but if you do, please get me out of here."

I do not know if He listened to me showing me His existence or if it was pure coincidence, but my audience with the Judge happened the following Monday. Five weeks had gone by. I did not understand this culture, its language, or its laws. I knew nothing about this country and I had not spoken to anyone in those five weeks. I had had total loneliness inside my heart.

When I went out to my audience that Monday, to my surprise I saw Estela, Ali and their two younger kids with them. Xenia was not there. I was happy they had come to pick me up. My face got a great smile when I saw them, but their faces were very serious. I did not understand.

I came out in my white uniform and handcuffed. They made me swear with my hand over a Bible that I would say nothing but the truth. I didn't understand why over a Bible and not over the law book. I had an interpreter for the first time, and he introduced himself. Finally, someone that spoke Spanish was with me. I asked him:

" ¿Qué va a pasar conmigo?" (What is going to happen to me?)

"No lo sé, yo solo soy tu intérprete y todo lo que sé es que te acusan de un crimen que ahora mismo escucharás." (I do not know. I am just your interpreter, and all I know is that you are accused of a crime that you will hear about right now.)

"¿Cómo? ¿Qué crimen? Yo no he cometido ningún crimen. Recién llego a Estados Unidos." (What? What crime? I have not committed any crime. I just got to the United States.)

"Cállate y te traduciré todo lo que dicen, yo no soy abogado, no puedo decirte nada." (Shut up and I will translate everything they say. I am not the lawyer and can't tell you anything)

With that, they told me to sit down and to be quiet. I got a state lawyer for my case. I had never seen him.

In the court I got a document in English that I do not understand, but I learned that the county is the one accusing me. I looked around and I saw all these police men surrounding me as if I am a dangerous criminal, plus there is, a judge, a secretary that types in a weird looking black machine, my lawyer and the interpreter. In the seats in the back of the courtroom behind of where I was seated, was my family that up to this point, I think they are here to see the court releasing me to go home with them or saying good bye to go back home to El Salvador. Everything is the same as in the movies. I feel in a movie.

The judge says, "Eduardo Antonio Jiménez, you are accused of coming to the United States of America specifically to kidnap Xenia Salume, daughter of Estela and Ali Salume, to take her with you back to your country." (The interpreter translates to me)

It totally blew my mind, and I got scared and upset at the same time. Out of my mind, I shouted, looking directly at my sister, "Quéééé? Yo secuestrar a Xenia? Sería incapaz de hacer eso! Defendéme Estela, tú sabés que no es así! de qué hablan Estela! Están locos!" (Whaaaaaat? Me kidnap Xenia? I am incapable of doing so! Estela, what are they talking about? You know this is not true! That's crazy!)

And I continued shouting, "Alí, diles que no es cierto!" (Ali, tell them that's not true!)

I desperately shouted, but none of them said anything. A big fuss is formed by my shouting and the Judge does not understand

what is going on and he hits the stage and says, "Order please."
They translate to me, "Orden por favor."

The interpreter translates to the lawyer and to the Judge close
to the Judge's stand as he called them up. For the first time I
learned why I am in jail and the accusation I have. The defendant
lawyer, has only looked over the case without putting too much
attention to it, thinking that the accusation was true, and we had
not talked before the hearing. When he sees my reaction, and
the face of my family, cold as if they do not know me, he asks
to reschedule the audience for more investigation. I can't believe
my sister is doing this to me! I start to understand Xenia for the
first time.

I was so wrong about my sister she could do anything she
wants to do and manipulate everyone she proposes to. I learned
that the policemen came after me, not for being illegal, but
because my niece had accused me of trying to kidnap her the
day I went to see her and my sister had agreed on that. I imagine
that the people at the school saw her running away and I was
behind her trying to reach her and the school authorities made
the accusation knowing she did not live with her parents.

So this happened in the first Monday I was in the United
States—only one day after arriving to my destination, my sister
used me, manipulated me and I fell right in her trap. The police
had a very serious accusation against me. Ali felt guilty, I could
see it in his face, but my sister had no regrets on her face. She
was happy to use me because in her mind, I was a proof that her
daughter was in danger away from home. For Xenia it was a proof
that she could not live with her mother because she was in danger
there. Either way, I was in between in a very horrible crime issue
I had not done.

Again, the idea of calling my wife disappeared from my mind.
I had to burry my feelings and to swallow my stupidity for going
along with my sister's plan to bring me to the United States. She

put the dream in my head and it was just that: A dream. A dream
that had become a nightmare. When will this end?

I will never be able to bring my wife and daughter to this place.

Now I will be on file in this country and the next thing I
will know is that I will be deported to my country in war with
nothing, and accused of a crime I had not done. And I sincerely
do not want to go back yet. How can I go back after a little more
than a year lost? What story will I tell my wife? That the guerrilla
kidnapped me and I had escaped? Or should I tell her that the
army got me? Telling her the truth will be too fantastic for her,
and she will not believe me anyway. She will be too furious to
forgive me. Whatever I say, it will be the same: She will kick me
out anyway. Truth or lie, I will go back empty handed and exposed
to start a life without her. I will probably end up in the house I
have rented in Mejicanos as I doubt she will take me back.

I was totally confused. Alone again. I am without a destiny
or a plan again. In difficulties again. What is in the future for
me? I couldn't understand why anything good could happen
to me in this life. I did not know why I was even born. I was
a complete disaster. I am not meant to be happy. For the first
time, I questioned my parents for conceiving me so old. Without
having my half sister to trust, with my disappeared brother, and
my dead parents and brother, I will just adapt to live here in jail
as long as necessary. At least I have shelter and food every day.
I decided to see the good part of all this mess, at least for now,
because this can not be the end of my days.

The jail I was in was not that bad. I had gone to visit some
friends in the Mariona Prison in El Salvador and that prison is
horrible. It is overpopulated, dark and dirty. This jail is on the
contrary, is clean, it has a toilet inside each section, and it has
light. Natural light and lamps. There was no door to go to the
bathroom, but we had a clean bathroom. We had to clean it daily.
We took turns. There was a sink with soap to clean our hands
too. There were common showers so men used them at a certain

hour and the women at another hour. Food was not luxurious, but it was not bad. It was not a hotel, but we had a bed with clean sheets every Monday and they did not mistreat us.

After a while, I calmed down my feelings and started weighing my options. That same week I decided to prove my innocence. To prove it, I had to tell them I had come into the country illegally. I had no other choice but to say the truth. I am a good man, trying to be an honest man. Yes, I grew up in the streets, and yes, I did some wrong things like stealing to eat, but that was out of pure necessity. I have had a very hard life, but I do not consider myself a bad man.

I cannot stay forever in jail. I have all the intention of working honestly. I can't give up at this time, and accept a crime I had not done. I am not a burglar, I am not a criminal, much less a kidnapper!. I am innocent. The only illegal thing I have done is to come as a wetback. My sister had used me. I finally understand that every time she had rescued me was under her proper plan, not to give me a better life, she just made me think so. I fell in her trap every time.

I started to remember about all that had happened around her: When she went to look for me when I was eight to take me to her home over the weekends is when she started to plan her malicious plan of taking me "rescued" when I turned nine. At that point, she must have known that she was going to come to the United States and that is why she needed me for me to take care of her mother so she would not stay alone. She needed me, and I thought she was being kind to me.

The only thing she did not think of was that I was going to fall in love with a great woman—the love of my life—and that I would marry soon, much less have a child so early in my life. She never met my wife or my child, Guadalupe, and that should have given me the sign about it, a warning sign in my life. I just did not see that the detail of becoming a father was a problem to her and she wanted to destroy my marriage and family as soon as possible, my only real family. But no, I thought she was rescuing me for a better opportunity. The worst part is that I had sworn to my daughter that I would never, never leave her, and that is exactly what I did, at exactly the same age my mother died on me. How dumb I had been, falling in her traps every time she has looked for me.

Now I am in jail because of my sister. That was not the plan. This is not my destiny. I will prove my innocence and go with the consequences. If I get deported, so be it. At least I will be able to say that I was sent to jail wrongly. What I still do not know, even if I prove my innocence, is if my wife will ever forgive me. She must be so upset with me by now. Upset and worried, but probably more upset for disappearing.

More than ever, I felt profoundly lonely. No one would visit me. I did not have a lawyer to defend me and to be my friend, and I had no right to ask for one either because I did not pay taxes. I could not afford to hire one either as I had no money and no one would pay it for me. The people that had offered me a job, will probably not help me any more as now I have a police record. *This is not fair! After all I had gone through*, I thought.

My head went around and around. I do not understand how my niece had said I tried to kidnap her, especially after we talked for more than an hour, very nicely, and her telling me so many things about my sister that now I believe them all. I do not know if I should reveal that information at the trial… if I even have a trial, that is! I went through the whole incident in my mind, trying to remember every detail and it did really look bad that I was chasing after Xenia that afternoon. I did it innocently, that's for sure, but still looked bad.

How will I convince the Judge that I was only trying to talk to my niece trying to convince her to go back home, ignoring why she had left ?"

Of course, the last time I saw her, she was like five or six. And now she's a teenager.

I really have bad luck, I thought. *My sister promised that in only two weeks, I was going to be on the other side of the border, but it took me seven months. And when I finally make it, I stay at her house two nights, and then I have to run away with Ali for more than five months. Then we come back, and only one day later, I go to jail. This is a complete nightmare!*

I came to the conclusion that again, I cannot call Maria Elena or the pastor or Miss Ana Maria, which are the only phones numbers I have.

I kept thinking, *I feel like a total failure, and I can care less about life. Once again, I have no family. I am alone in this world—now more so than ever before. In El Salvador, at least I had a wife, a child, and a mother-in-law. Now I have nothing…I have been a fool.*

The jail makes me recall all those days I stayed locked in the closets in Esmeralda's Brothel. Being in jail is like being in a closet. There was nothing else to do but think and analyze all the situation around me. I had no one to talk to in Spanish, so all I did was think. The big difference is that I could not plan to run away, since this was jail and not a house, and I have nowhere to go. Suddenly, I think, *When they let me go free, where will I go?*

"I wished that my parents would be alive and that Maria Elena understand everything I am going through and that she would receive me with her open arms."

I started to daydream and imagined that the pastor would come to rescue me, or even my lost brother, Hector, who ran away when I was young. I had no one to ask help from. *What a messy life! Why did I not die instead of one of my parents or my brother? Why was I born? To come to suffer in this life? I don't want to live like that!*

For the first time, I had suicidal thoughts but I tried to put them aside because I was too young to die.

Instead, I tried thinking how to get out of jail. Finally, the following day the interpreter and the lawyer came to visit me, and the interpreter talks to me in Spanish translating at all times:

"You have to tell me all the truth."

"Lying to the state is a federal crime and five to twenty years await you in jail."

"Yes, of course. I will tell you the truth."

And he explained, "Your niece Xenia put a complaint that you had gone to look for her to school to kidnap her, and your sister said it was true. That this was your plan for coming to this country." The interpreter translates to me.

That is not true!

"That is not true! My sister had helped me to come over here. She had sent me money several times trying to cross the border. We had hired different coyotes to try to pass the border, and it took me seven months trying to do so—to come to this free country—so I can give a better life to my wife and daughter whom I left behind in a country that is in war."

"My sister helped me to come and pay all my way here. I would call her every time I needed money, but I had no idea her daughter was living with another family." (Translation done)

When the interpreter finished, the lawyer asked me, "Did you go to look for your niece at her school?"

"Yes, I did."

"Why did you do it?"

"Because my sister told me to go talk to her to convince her to go back home, but my niece explained to me that she had gone because my sister used to hit her and mistreat her even to make her bruises and become purple, and she does not want to go back home. She told me that she was rescued from my sister when she went to school full of bruises, and the government intervened and put her in a foster home."

"Did you know that your sister has a restraining order to not come closer than 130 feet from her own daughter for abusing her?"

"No I had no idea. She never said that. And she herself brought me to the school, but she did not come close—which I thought was weird—but I thought it was because she wanted me to talk alone with my niece."

I had not seen her for many years, and when she ran away, I thought it was because she did not recognized me. But when we talked, she told me her story.

And I continued.

I swear by my dead parents that I went to talk to her innocently since I had known her since she was a baby, and I loved my niece. But I never thought she would accuse me of trying to kidnap her, and much less to take her to my country since I ran away from it because we are in war. My sister has cheated me because she did not mention any of this. I thought she was a good person, actually, but I see she is vindictive and nothing stops her. My poor brother-in-law, who puts up with her.

What I want is that you help me bring my wife and daughter to this country. I am an orphan of both parents, and have no other relatives than Estela, and all I want is to work honestly in this country to follow my dreams.

The lawyer was perplexed at all he had heard since it was not what he had read in the case file. It made no sense to kidnap a child to take her to a country in a civil war. He asked for more time for more investigation and further analysis on the case. The next visit he made, he asked, "Do you have more family members in the United States?"

Not that I know of. As I told you, I am an orphan, and I had a brother who died. I had another brother who left our house when I was a child and whom I have not heard from him since, and I have no idea if he came to this country or if he is somewhere else or if he is dead. Dad never looked for him because he didn't know where to look for him and Hector, which is his name, never sent a letter or communicated with us never again since he left when I was around 5 years old. My only family was Estela, and now I am more scared than ever. And I am still in shock of what she has done to me. I do not understand why she helped me so much just to come to get me into this trouble. I ask for amnesty and a permission to stay in this country to bring my wife and daughter, I insisted.

The lawyer saw me surprised with all this information and I did not know what to think. I did not know where this was going, or how would this end. I think he perceived all my sincerity. I went back to my cell in the jail I was at, while they investigated some more, for a few more months. I was assuming that somehow, my niece will have to tell the truth and retract herself from the accusation she made. If she did that she would not have to go back to her mother, and Estela was going to have to tell the truth too, pressured by the lawyer. I did not know what was going to happen.

The one who should be in jail is Estela for mistreating her family, not me.

Again, I am called to court after five long months, the case having been studied deeply. Again, Estela and Ali are there with the kids. This time, Xenia was there too but not seated with them. Her substitute parents came with her. They called Xenia to testify.

"Xenia, do you know that man?" pointing at me.

"Yes, I do" she says.

" You felt threatened to go with this man, by force, against your will when you got out of school that afternoon of May 5, 1982? We remind you that you swore on the Bible to tell the truth and nothing but the truth, and that lying to the court is a federal crime, and that you can go to jail."

"No. I ran away when I first saw him because I did not recognize him. I had not seen him since I was six years old seeing him. But he is my uncle, and he has always been good to me."

The interpreter translates to me and I feel relief when she says that.

"That day, May the 5th , were you forced to go with him or did you go voluntarily to talk with him?"

"I went voluntarily."

"Are you afraid he could kidnap you to take you to El Salvador?"

"Of course not! Why should we go where there is war? He wouldn't do that, I don't think"

"Thank you. No more questions," said the lawyer. "Lord Judge, I find this man innocent of the accusation of trying to kidnap his own niece and his only crime is that he has crossed the border illegally running away from his country in war, and we are not judging his immigration status, so I plead you find him innocent. Everything was a misunderstanding of the school authorities and here the only responsible for all this matter is his sister Estela Salume, trying to bring her daughter back to her house, which is not the case now. So I plead again for his innocence and for him to go free of all charges."

The Judge commands a break and he comes back with the sentence: "Because there is no kidnap case, Eduardo Antonio Jiménez, has conditional liberty and has to pay a bail of $300. You can go back to your country or stay in the United States of America if and only if you have a relative that will be responsible for you and find you a place to live with him or her or somewhere were you can be alone. Do you have another relative other than Estela Salume in the United States?" the judge asks and the interpreter translates.

"Señor juez, yo no quiero regresar a mi país en guerra. Por favor. Pido amnistía pues no hay nada que pueda ir a hacer a mi país." The interpreter translates: "Lord Judge I do not want to go to my country in war. Please, I ask for amnesty because there is nothing I can go to do in my country."

And when I am about to tell him that I have no one else here, Estela interrupts and says in a simple, matter-of-fact tone:

"Excuse me, Lord Judge, he has a brother here in Brooklyn," the interpreter translates to me with wide eyes.

"Cóoooomo?" (Whaaaaat?), I shout

I turned around with a surprised look on my face.

"Hector Jiménez vive en Brooklyn, Eduardo." (Hector Jimenez lives in Brooklyn, Eduardo.) She says it like if that is not important in a matter-of-fact tone. I freeze!

I feel relieved and furious all at once.

"Who is that?" asked the judge.

"Hector Jiménez is his brother that came to the United States many years ago and now lives in Brooklyn."

"Mi hermano perdido," I said softly, and my lawyer heard me, ("My lost brother". the interpreter translated,) "Then please look for his brother to get him out and pay the bail for him," said the judge and with that the hearing was over.

When we were leaving, I yelled furiously to Estela, "Hasta aquí llega nuestra relación, ¡has arruinado mi vida! Me ocultaste que sabías de mi hermano! Nunca más te quiero ver, si te veo en la calle te mato!" Our relationship ends here. You ruined my life! You hid that you knew about my brother! I never ever want to see you again! If I see you in the streets, I swear I'll kill you!

I shouted in anger, and they took me out handcuffed.

They located Hector, and when they called, they asked, "Please. Can I talk with Hector Jiménez."

"This is me."

"Do you have a brother named Eduardo Antonio Jiménez?"

"Well, yes, I used to have a little brother with that name. But I don't know if you are talking about the same person. I have many, many years of not seeing him. Is he my brother? Is something wrong with him? Where is he? How do you know about my lost brother?" He bombarded with all these questions.

"Your brother is in the Watsonville County Jail, and he is free and innocent, but only a relative can get him out to stay in the United States of America and we found out you are his only brother. His bail is of $300 to get him out, or he will be deported immediately."

"In jail? What do you mean prisoner in Watsonville?"

"He will tell you all about it, he is innocent and he was declared free to go."

"I will be there tomorrow morning," he said somewhat scared and excited at the same time.

Hector arrived very excited, confused and scared all at once, and I was exactly the same but nervous at the same time I had mixed feelings toward him. He had left when I was around five years old, and never, never wrote to me or called me or looked for me. When dad died, he didn't care about my existence and he never appeared to console me or rescue me. I stayed completely alone, and Hector was not there at any time from my life. He disappeared of my life and I had no idea were to look for him. My life would have been so different if I would have come to the US with him when I was a kid. And now, all of a sudden, I find him? When I go to jail thanks to my other wicked sister? Is it possible that she knew all along of his existence? Why did she never mentioned him? My head was going around with all this thoughts.

On the other hand, I felt happy I was getting finally away from Estela's malevolent plans. I finally understood that her plan was to accuse me to get her daughter, but everything went wrong for her as she will never see her daughter again. She lost Xenia for ever. I was only used by her, and even though I am only a high school grad, and had also lived in the streets, and in a brothel, kidnapping my own niece? That was crazy, and could not even start thinking of the possibility to do so. Estela is malevolent and I used to have a good image of her, but it died that day.

Hector and I saw each other for the first time after fifteen years. I do not recognize him and he doesn't recognize me either. I see an obese guy (probably with more than three hundred pounds) coming into the room where I was waiting. He has more than thirty years and I saw him last when I was five. We hugged and cried in silence for finding each other. I couldn't believe my lost brother had appeared back in my life! Hector was my brother of my mom and dad, my real brother. While I was happy to finally be reconnected, I also resented that he had not been there for me.

We get into his car, and start driving to his place in silence. We did not know what to say. There was so much to talk about and to tell each other, but I did not know how to start. I did not know if I should be happy for finding him or scold him because he never looked for me. My thoughts where turning around in my head. I suppose Hector is feeling the same: happy to find me and ashamed he did not look for me, being the oldest brother, and does not know where to start all he would like to say.

To break the ice, we started talking about the weather, (which is not something common back home as we have an eternal summer climate) we talked about the landscape, how populated Manhattan was, and why he lived in the surroundings of Manhattan.

Then, suddenly he asked:

"Why were you in jail?"

"It was Estela's fault. She convinced me to leave my wife and daughter—"

"You already have a wife and a daughter?" he asked, really surprised.

"How old is the baby?"

I laugh and say, "She is four years old."

"What? At what age did you have her?" he asked me, very surprised.

"I became a father at fifteen," I said seriously.

"Wow, Brother! You really started your life fast!"

"Yeah, well…but it is the best thing that has ever happened to me, Hector," I answered coldly.

"So go on, go on. You were telling me that Estela convinced you. So you have been in touch with her all these years?"

"Yes, actually she was the only one who came to look for me. She rescued me several times in my life while I was growing up," I said in a tone of voice like you-never-came.

Hector just stayed silent, so I went on.

"So the plan was to come over here, very fast without telling my wife. Estela convinced me that it was only going to take two weeks, but everything went wrong. It took seven months to cross the border. A trip that was supposed to be only two weeks, I had one problem after another, and it took seven months to cross the border. And finally, when I crossed it, it was a Sunday and the following day that was Monday. My sister took me to look for my niece Xenia, her oldest daughter, who is living in a Foster Home. Ignoring what was going on and the reason of why she left, and I went with her to look for Xenia at her High School. I was doing her a favor to talk to the girl to convince her to return home, but everything went wrong."

"Why is she in a foster home?"

"She left home because Estela used to hit her badly, and I got into problems because they accused me of trying to kidnap her as she started running when she saw me and I chased her until I grabbed her. The next day, I had crossed the border. Can you imagine?" I told him, frustrated.

"I can't believe all you have gone through. Estela has been such a mean person. She is bad. Very bad. She is in all possible ways an evil person. How could she do that to you?"

I haven't even told Hector a year of my life and all the things I had to do to survive all those growing up years. He has no idea about all my suffering. He does not know anything, and he has not cared about me at all either!

But I kept those thoughts to myself.

"Nope, she has not been good at all. I had to learn that she is bad in a very horrible way, but at least she appeared in my life when I needed her the most" I said with a lot of pain in my heart.

I held Hector with great esteem when I was a kid. I remember I defended him every time my father reproached him for leaving and never coming back. I still had mixed feelings. The abandonment suffered from all my family was a profound feeling I had and Hector was one of them.

The only one that had looked after me with good or bad intentions was Estela, that is why I resented very much that our relationship ended so bad the way that it did. Everything was a nightmare. I only remember that Hector was much older than me when he left from home. He had had a fight with my dad after my mother's death and he ran away from home with his own suffering, and all happened too fast and ended in a bad way, and because of his own ego and his own pride he never came back. At least that is how I think it happened. Finally I get the courage to ask:

"Why did you never look for me, Hector?"

"Eduardito, I have no easy answer. In the first place, I have panic of flying, and I came here to the U.S. by road with the Mormons. I never had the courage to take a plane to go back to El Salvador. I could never find the courage, not even when dad died" he said. I did not know he had learned about my father's death. I wonder how he learned about it.

I started to understand why he hadn't gone back.

"And on the other hand, I was totally afraid of my father. I was afraid he would only shout at me and reject me, and I just did not want to expose myself to that possibility. But now I really regret it," he sincerely said.

"But Dad wanted to see you again. He always talked about you, Hector, and I tried to encourage him, telling him to look for you. But he had no idea where to start looking for you. Remember, he was an older person when I was born."

Suddenly, we got to Cap Street, the Street he lived in. We get out of the car and a woman opens the door of the apartment. His new live-in partner. Hector was divorced of an American woman that had been his wife for several years and he ran away with the maid that took care of his kids and helped around the house.

She was a brunette, short and nice looking, and she came out to greet us with a big smile on her face. She gave me a huge hug to welcome me and I even got kind of scared since I had not received a hug from no one but my wife before. Besides, I had never seen this woman before, and she was already hugging me! But I must admit I really liked her welcoming to their place, so full of love and so spontaneously. Hector got moved and he hugs me too, in front of her and tears fell through his chick. It was a very emotional moment.

"This is my little brother, Eduardito, whom I love so much," he says to introduce me with her at the doorstep.

We go into the apartment and Hector leaves me there alone with her and disappears for a moment. I think he went to cry by himself. His apartment was located in the middle of the Hispanic community of the town. Hector was very well known in the community.

All my clothes were inside a bag, which he grabbed from me and takes it inside. When he comes back, and we sit in the living room, I start bombarding him with more questions.

"How come your are alive and you never ever even at least wrote to me? I mean, you say you are afraid from flying, but you could have written a simple note a letter or something to let me know you were alive . That would have given me hope when I was a child. Knowing you were somewhere, it would have avoided many problems in my life." I tell him with some sorrow and grief, mixed with anger.

He immediately gets up. "Wait," he says. And with tears in his eyes, he goes inside his room. He comes back with a suitcase, which he throws at my feet.

"Open it," he says seriously and coldly.

Shaking, I sit on the floor and I open it slowly, looking at him. What I see, shocks me, and I get the shivers. It is a suitcase full of letters with my name on them.

"Look at all the letters that I wrote to you. I wrote to you one time after another, every week, every month, every year. I was looking for you tirelessly. When I knew you where with Estela, that is when I wrote to you most often, because I had her address, at least her mother's, but all the letters came back. Look at them." He said and then he continued:

"Estela has fooled us both Eduardo, and she has manipulated both of us all this years. She said she knew nothing of you to me, and she said the same to you about me. I would have sent for you when you were little and knew that my dad had died, but no one ever told me where you were. Estela herself told me about his death. I even called Esmeralda and she never told me where you were either."

"Esmeralda, the witch?" I asked puzzled.

"The witch?"

"Well, it is not that she was a witch literally, but she locked me in a closet and also denied me to see Estela when I was very young, when Dad died. When I became an orphan, I went to her house obligated. And she never told you I was with her? What a witch!"

"Nope, not at all. She said she knew nothing about you. I can't believe you lived with her!

"Ah. Mean witch! She always wanted to abuse me, but I always escaped from her. This is why she didn't like me too much. When I did not let her abuse me, she had me close to her, and I always ran away from her. I even escaped away from her house and was on the streets, errand living around the streets hoping someone would pick me up. When I escaped, after a few days, and when I got tired of looking into the trash cans for food and when I was too hungry, I would always go back to her."

"In the trash can?"

"Well, yeah. You have to do what you have to do to survive alone! One day, I planned escaping from her and ran to Estela's mom's house, which I knew where it was and how to get there. When I thought I was safe, she came over and grabbed me by my hair and forced me to go with her again. I hated her to death with all my heart for a long time until she left my life, leaving the country.

"Years later, she went back home, and she gave me back the legal documents of Dad's house in Mejicanos. I did not ask her why she had them, but she gave them back without asking for money or anything. We made peace that day and I felt sorry for her, even though she had made me miserable when I was a child."

"Estela neglected you with me, the same as Esmeralda neglected you with Estela. Now I can understand it was like a kind of revenge with both of us," he said, thinking about my words.

"But I never lost hope to see you again and this is why I saved every single letter I got back. I promise, I looked for you every month of my life. I looked for you every month, every year. And those days, Estela always said, she knew nothing of you."

"What a mischievous woman!"

In my heart, I could not believe everything he said, but he left me alone to read the letters. They were in order, from the oldest, to the most recent one. My heart was pounding harder and harder every time I would open a letter. I found Christmas Cards, birthday cards, letters just looking for me, cash money, bank checks, letters written with lots of love toward my father asking for his forgiveness, and letters with love to me and letters to my other brother Guillermo. I cried with many of them. I was in shock, as my life would have been so different if I would have gotten the letters. Nevertheless, my resentment was really stuck inside my heart from lack of knowledge of his search for me.

Hector cried with me as he saw me crying. I could not believe Estela's hatred toward us. She neglected us. She was taking a revenge for being the daughter outside marriage. She hated being the daughter of the mistress, the only one outside marriage. That made her the bastard daughter, as we call those children in a vulgar way. We did not see her like that, but she knew that everyone knew that her mother and my father had never married, not even when dad became a widow. She resented that so badly that all she wanted was to take revenge with us, as if we had something to do with that decision. We had no fault of being the legitimate sons of my father and mother.

I spent hours and hours reading each and every letter. It was impressive. Every letter was softening my resentment toward my brother. My brother really tried to find me, I could see that in every card, in every letter, and I had no idea until this moment. How unfair is this life. That afternoon and night was very emotional. With each letter I was forgiving my brother and I started loving him more and more. I started to respect him again internally and to hate even more Estela. I was keeping everything inside my heart. It was too much for me to digest in one day. I went to bed with all this thoughts in my head: Forgiving and hating at the same time. I could hardly sleep that night.

Next day as I woke up early, Hector said, "Well, time to start getting to know each other. It is never late to start a relationship brother, the important thing here is that we are together now, and we shall never get separated by no one ever again."

"Yes, Brother, I am really happy that I found you—even if it was not under the best circumstances, we are finally together. Sorry for questioning your lack of contact as I had absolutely no idea you had really searched for me. These letters are a real treasure for me and I will keep them safe to show them to my daughter some day so that I can tell her the story of how we found each other."

All that new information really made my heart happy and he asked me to tell him my full story and then he was going to tell me his. So I did, starting from when he left home, my father's death, the sitters, school, Estela's appearance in my life, up to the

the point where I met Maria Elena, my true love, the pregnancy, and how hard it was to get married. Hector just listened carefully every stage I had gone through impressed of all my difficulties and suddenly he interrupts me and says, "And your wife, she knows where you are?"

Ashamed I answered, "With all this I had gone through, I still do not call her since I left home" and I can hardly see him to his face.

"What?" he says with a frown face and he gets up immediately to pick up the wireless phone he had in the kitchen.

"Here. Take the phone and call her now."

"How long ago did you leave home?"

"About a year and a half."

"What? I can't believe that brother. Call her immediately. I will leave you alone so you call her, while I make some breakfast."

Maria Elena has no phone in her house, so I had to send her a telegram to schedule an appointment for her to go to ANTEL, the national telecommunication company. After giving me the instructions, I made the call and scheduled the appointment for the next day at four p.m. her time, 6:00 p.m. my time.

That night I could not sleep thinking about what I was going to tell my wife and where should I start.

14

The Phone Call

Maria Elena

One rainy afternoon in June, I got a telegram from ANTEL (National Telecommunications Association) in which I was scheduled an appointment from a relative in the United Sates. I had no idea who can that be, but my heart, deep inside, had the feeling and the desire that my relative would be Eduardo. It had been more than one year of hearing nothing from him after he left without a word.

I saw the telegram in disbelief. I took my apron off and I went slowly walking away from the bakery, toward my room in the back part of the house. I jumped into bed to cry. I cried nervously, happiness and anger, all at the same time, bringing out all my kept feelings, thinking it was him.

Eduardo is alive! I thought excited, and wanted to scream it out, but I couldn't make a fuss before time. *He is coming back soon,* I thought with hope.

But the next second, my angry feelings flourished, and I thought in anger. *And what does he think? That he can abandon me for more than a year and come back as if nothing and that I will receive him with open arms? He has no idea what I had gone through!*

All the anguish I've gone through looking for him! No way I will forgive him! My thoughts ended with resentment.

I did not know what to expect from the call. Deep inside, I had the feeling it was Eduardo. If it wasn't him, it could be my father who had also disappeared on me since I was a child. But I really hoped it was Eduardo, even with the anger I felt. Even though I was resented, I needed to hear from him. I needed to know that he was fine, that he was alive and that he still loved me. The two men I had loved the most had disappeared from my life in seconds without a word, without an explanation. Dad and Eduardo. Both of them, and that had marked my heart in distrust of men and lots of sorrow.

At 3:30 p.m., I took a taxi and went straight to ANTEL, which is located next to the Hula Hula Park in the heart of the downtown area of San Salvador. I was so nervous waiting to be called. Three minutes later, I hear in the intercom, "Miss Maria Elena, cabin 5, call from the United States.

As I heard that, my heart almost jumped out of my body. I got inside fast and closed the door of the cabin. I get the phone.

"Hello, hello?"

"Hello, Maria Elena? Hi, my love, my sweetheart."

I heard the sweet voice of my love. Immediately, my tears start coming out of my eyes while I sigh as I hear his voice. I've missed it so much!

It's him!

I internally sigh.

"WHERE ARE YOU?"

I asked him in a tough, angry voice even though I really wanted to tell him, "My love, hello! How much I missed you! Where are you, My Love? I am waiting for you, and I have missed you so much." But that is not what came out of my mouth.

"My love, Maria Elena, how much I have missed you!"

I heard from a very sweet voice on the other side. I even felt the nervousness in his voice, but my anger was much stronger than my desire to love him. Again, I asked with a very furious voice, shouting, without letting him continue talking, "WHERE ARE YOU?"

"My love, I am in the United States, in Brooklyn in New York. I found my brother Hector!"

He was excited with his discovery, but I did not want to hear his happiness. I wanted him to hear my anguish, my anger.

"IN THE UNITED STATES? WHAT DO YOU MEAN IN THE UNITED STATES? Why haven't you called before?"

"It is hard to explain to you in a phone call all the things I have gone through to finally be able to call you today."

"Hard what you had gone through? And me? What do you think? I thought you had gone with the guerrilla and that you were in the mountains fighting with them and that they had killed you! I can't believe this!"

I shouted angrily and continued.

"What are you doing in the United States, and why have you not called before? What are you doing so far away, anyway?"

I asked again, "When did you get there? It has been more than a year since you left, and I heard nothing from you. You have no idea all that I had gone through looking for you!"

Eduardo

I knew she was going to be very angry, but I had no idea how affected she was with my absence. I hear myself answering slowly and calmly to calm her down.

"Believe me, My Love, I had been through a lot too. It took me more than seven months to cross the border, and I had suffered from hunger. And I had suffered a lot to make my dream true of bringing you both to this free country. I was even in jail by mistake."

"Take us? In jail? What have you done?"

"Seriously, I had not done anything wrong. It was a misunderstanding all along. But going to jail gave me the opportunity to get reunited with Hector, as I was telling you."

I answered as sweetly as possible.

"Hector, your lost brother?"

"Yes, my lost brother. Now I found him! Can you believe it?"

I told her very excitedly, hoping her anger had already dissipated.

Maria Elena

"I had looked for you in the Red Cross, in the hospitals, between all the dead bodies, in the morgue, and even under the ground. I had seen things I wish I had not seen ever in my life! I saw dead people by bombs, shot people, without head or arms, and destroyed faces every time I was told there was a bunch of dead people trying to get identified…And you just tell me happily that you are in the United States? I can't believe you! I thought you were dead!"

I shouted more than I wanted to, my anger resurfacing.

My head was going around with my anger and all the anguish I had suffered looking for him, and he calls me all sweat and happy telling me he is in the United Sates. I really can't believe it. Who does he think I am? Someone he can play with? I reasoned in seconds.

"And what do you want?"

Eduardo

"I am calling you first to ask for your forgiveness. I am sorry, Maria Elena, for everything I have done and made you suffer."

She is furious and she is right about it, but my intention NEVER was to make anyone suffer, and she had no idea of what I have gone through and I do not have the courage to tell her anything at this point.

I continued, "I am sorry for not calling you before, for not telling you my plans, but I swear it has been impossible to call you before. Even if you do not believe me, one day I will tell you the whole story. The only thing I can assure you is that finally I am safe in my brother Hector's house, and I want to keep in touch with you as often as possible. I want to bring you girls here, and I could not tell you anything because I am sure you would not approve it and would stop me."

"Take us? Of course I would not approve for you to leave us alone! I love you, and I did not want to be separated from you ever. Going where? Are you nuts?"

I heard her telling me she loves me without hesitating.

"I love you too with all my heart, and I have never stopped doing so. I dream of bringing you and my daughter to this land.

Take me to that land? Never! You met me here, and you will find me here!"

"But, My Love, we will be fine here away from the war.

The war is far away from the city, Eduardo. Come back home if you want to see me because I will not move from my country.

Forgive me, My Love, but I do not want to go back to a country in war."

"Forgive you? And all the anguish I lived through? What? Yeah right! It sounds easy. No, Eduardo. If you want a family, it will be here. So decide yourself."

"But, My Love, there are better opportunities right here."

"Yeah right, the opportunity to be in jail."

She said that sarcastically. I do not know why I told her I had been in prison since it was not a good thing at all.

"Please understand me. I see a world full of opportunities for you and my daughter."

Maria Elena

"Look, Eduardo. You met me here, and I will stay here. Guadalupe needs a father, but I am not willing to go away from here. I cannot leave my mother alone. We have a business, and I have responsibilities. I am fine here, and my daughter will be fine too—with or without her dad. I grew up without a dad, and your daughter will grow up without one too, if you do not come. Period,"

I said seriously, hoping that would make him react to come back.

Eduardo

"I want you here with me Maria Elena," I insist. "If you do not want to follow me, it will be your decision, and our relationship will be over. I will free myself from you. Think about it. I will call you in three days."

I continued without letting her talk.

"For now, I just want to tell you that I love you, I miss you, and if I am here, it's because I want a better future for us as a family. Please forgive me for leaving without telling you anything, but I did it for us—for the three of us. For our future. This is the sacrifice I had to do to get you out of the war. I plan to start working as soon as possible."

Maria Elena

"Start working? What do you mean start working if you disappeared more than a year ago? You want me to believe you that you have done nothing so far? Where have you been? How have you lived so far? What have you done all this time?"

I bombarded him with all those questions because I did not understand it when he said that he will start to work. I was totally confused.

"It is a long story, My Love. A loooong story. And I had not been able to start working. That is the truth. This is one of the reasons I did not want to call you because I have nothing to offer at this point, but I am sure I will have pretty soon."

"Look, Eduardo, I am very happy to hear from you and know you are alive—you have no idea how much. I am happier for Lupita , but I am not joking. You met me here, and you will find me here, Eduardo. I have absolutely no interest in going away. I have a family business, and I have a business to eat from. Over there, I have nothing and you have nothing. I do not know the language, and I do not know if you do. So I am asking you to come back home if you want to see us again."

"Maria Elena, if you knew everything I have gone through, you wouldn't ask me to go back when I am just about to start my dream to work hard to be able to bring you two here to give you a better life away from the war."

"You're crazy, Eduardo. Come back home if you want to see us. No one has that dream, and I have no idea why are you talking about that dream that you never mentioned."

"My love, I have gone through anguish, hunger, cold, loneliness, sadness, and so many other things to get here that I do not plan to go back without anything. You have war over there. Here, we have peace. Where am I going to work? Are there any jobs over there?"

"Of course you can find a job. You know, in the bakery, we always need extra hands. You have a job here anytime you want it. And do not insist on me to go anywhere because I will never go over there. Guadalupe misses you, Eduardo, but I am not willing to leave something safe to go to that place I do not know at all. I do not even know the language. Not interested. I cannot leave it all and go to the uncertainty."

Eduardo

"Maria Elena, believe me. It will always be better here than over there. I have missed you so much."

I tell her and I start sobbing again. I couldn't help myself and couldn't continue talking as I could not hold back anymore all of my feelings, and I started to cry.

"I missed you so much. I miss you and I love you."

I said that several times while I cried.

Maria Elena

"I also miss you very much, Eduardo. You have no idea how much I miss you, and Lupita misses you much more."

I told him crying too, with my wall of bitterness and anger falling down. It was the highlight of our conversation, and I could not hang up. I missed his voice so much, his tenderness, his presence in my life. But my heart was very resentful, and I could not express out of my mouth all the love I have for him in my heart. I could only express all the bitterness I feel for leaving us alone. I could not accept his proposal either. I was surprised with his proposal, and I could not process it in my mind.

Eduardo

"My love, I will call you again in three days at the same time so that you have time to think about it. I really want to have you two with me, and now that I know how to cross the border, I can go pick you up without a coyote. I want to bring you two to the country of the opportunities and peace."

She had no idea how much I needed to hear her voice, even as mad as she was, and had told me whatever she had told me. This call gave me the energies I needed to continue fighting for my dream because, the truth is, I cannot imagine myself back to my country in war.

Maria Elena

"I will never go over there, Eduardo."

"Think about it, My Love. Because if you do not want to come with me, this is the end of us two."

We hung up and I was still astonished. I went out walking slowly, staring at nothing, totally lost in my thoughts. I can't believe I just talked with the love of my life and that he is alive. I can't believe he is asking me to go to a country I don't know. I can't believe I talked to him so angrily knowing I had waited for that call all this time. I am so happy he is not dead, but I have so many mixed feelings. I am really happy, but I am furious all at once. I started crying all by myself while I start walking slowly toward the park in front of the phone company.

I find a park bench, and I sit down to meditate everything we talked about. Eduardo is alive and found his lost brother, and I did not even ask him how he had found him. He said he had suffered and had starved and had been cold, but I did not understand anything he said. I just can't understand how can he has not called before. How come he had eaten, and dressed himself and could have not gotten a phone to call as he did right now? How come he did not find a way to call? I do not understand anything.

Between thoughts, I sighed and sobbed. I cried because I had no other way to process all my feelings. I wanted to vent myself before getting home. My mother will ask who had called. What should I tell her? Should I tell her the truth? I think, I will but not in front of Guadalupe. I need her advice and I do not want Lupita (Guadalupe) to know what is happening. After all I have not talked about him since I found that note in my drawer. That day that I found the note, I buried him and prohibited everyone in my house to mention his name around me.

I cannot believe that this afternoon he has risen, and I do not know what to do with all this mix feelings in my heart. I have never been in a plane and I panic just to think about it. I would have to go in a plane to Mexico and then in train and then across the border like all those wetbacks that I hear so many wicked stories of people who die or get lost. I do not think I can go to a country I do not know and leave my mother and the bakery alone. My father is not around, and my grandmother is no longer able to help around in the bakery. Simply, I cannot leave them alone even as Eduardo says that it is better over there. I have to sacrifice my love for him and stay with Mom and Grandmother to help them out. I have no other way in this one. I cannot see how I can leave them alone.

Eduardo

When Hector got home, I told him all about the call with my wife. He advised me, "If she is asking you to go back, Eduardo, you should go. The family must stay together, wherever it is."

"But is has been so hard to get to this point in my life, and I cannot throw it away!"

My desire to succeed was stronger than wanting to have my family together. Besides, who was my brother to advise me like that if he was not with his wife?

Three days later I called Maria Elena. Again we discussed about bringing them with me and her telling me that she was not interested or willing to come. It was a discussion all along. She saying no, and me begging her to come. It was one of the ugliest moments in my life. Then, in seconds after not going anywhere, my rebellious self came out, the anger, my self-sufficiency got into me, since this is not what I expected. I had so many dreams of them here, but I finally told her in anger:

"If you do not want to follow me, it is *your* decision. I want you to come over. I do not want to go back to that country in war. I have nothing to do over there. Can't you understand that I have no opportunity to become someone over there?"

Instead of being a great conversation, it was a huge fight. I could see we could not come to an understanding so I finished telling her:

"Listen to me closely what I will tell you, Maria Elena. If you do not accept my proposition to come over, it will be your decision, and I will respect it. I will not pressure you again about it. You know my position. If you decide not to get in touch, we are definitely finished, and you can do with your life whatever you want. I am out of this relationship. I expect your news in a maximum of one month. Write down my brother's address and phone number. I will wait for your answer."

I was extremely upset about the result of our conversation. It was like a mixture of frustration and anger all at the same time. I wanted to stay in the United States because I was not willing to go back to work in a bakery in that type of schedule of getting up at 2:00 a.m. until five in the afternoon, every day. That was too much for me. This was the most miserable time of my life. I felt so powerless, I felt bad, I felt upset, I felt angry all inside myself. This was too much to handle. Half of my dream was slipping out of my hands.

I was selfish, cruel, and ruthless. My manliness did not let me go back empty-handed after more than a year and a half. I was ashamed of myself from disappearing from their lives and not having anything to offer at this point, even though the circumstances where odd and not my fault. It was necessary for me to stay here to fight for our future, or should I say, my future.

After that second call, I was more frustrated than ever before. I talked with my brother and told him we could not get an agreement about our situation and that I had given her an ultimatum. If in a month I do not receive a letter, we were over.

"And why don't you want to go back with your family, Eduardito?" Hector asked.

Frustrated and angry, I answered, "You do not know me, Brother. I am an old man even though you see me young. I had suffered all my life, and in this trip, I have had hunger, loneliness...I have been cold, and I have even robbed to eat something. It has been too hard all my way here to accomplish this dream that Estela badly started, but at least I have found you, and finally I have real family with me. Of course, my wife and daughter are my family too. But sincerely, Brother, would you go back to our country in war?"

"No, I wouldn't."

"Okay, then to begin with, do not call me Eduardito. My name is Eduardo or Eddy. I am not a kid anymore for that diminutive name."

"You are right." Hector laughed giving me a pat on the shoulder, and added, "Then we have to think about how you can succeed here. The first thing we have to do is to get you enrolled in the university to learn English. Without English, it's very hard to succeed."

I did not like those words. I felt he was telling me I was a fool, and a useless person and I did not like that feeling, so I got stubborn and I did not accept any help.

"No, Hector, I am not here to live off your charity. I am capable of working hard and paying for my things and my studies. All I need is to know where I can work."

My ego was between us. My huge ego, which did not let me go back home to my family.

"And what can you do?"

"Believe it or not, I am an expert welder—a professional welder—and I know how to use many instruments because, willingly or not, Estela made me work and study at the same time since I was nine," I told him. It surprised him since he thought I had been in problems because I was a street boy and without studies. "I am a high school graduate too."

I didn't think of the huge opportunity my brother was offering me. He offered to send me to the University to learn English, also to learn music or any instrument so I could play with him, as he was a musician. My anger managed myself and my feelings and my bad decisions. My decision was taken in anger and with my macho ideas of I know-it-all attitude. I was mad and I had too many bad feelings inside me. I was happy that I have found blood of my blood but there was hatred because he did not look for me when I was little, at least that is what I thought.

I hated Estela for everything she had done to me and I had resentment for the reaction and answer of Maria Elena. Everything at the same time. And on top of that, I hated myself for all my foolishness and for feeling pride of all my bad decisions. I could not see the yellow alert signs that were everywhere around me, I simply could not see them. I was blind to my stupidity and 'independence'.

My sinful nature, the one that had followed me since very long ago, did not let me be at peace. There was absolutely no peace in my heart. I did not know God, plus I did not really knew if He existed. But when I see back to those growing years, I can now see his powerful hand protecting me since my childhood. He took care of me during my stay in Mexico, and even when I was running away with Ali. I can see that even though I had gone through many unfair circumstances, there were always angels on my way to protect me from every situation.

The problem is that at this point in my life, I could not see Him nor recognize Him. What I can see now is that I was more angry with myself than with the people who surrounded me. I could not forgive myself for every bad decision taken. I was mad with myself for my errors, my decision and with all the circumstances lived with Esmeralda, with Estela, in the streets, with life, with the war, with Maria Elena's reaction. I was mad with life that took away every member of my family. I was so frustrated with what I had accomplished but I had ruined it all. It was like trying to hold sand on my hands but it inevitably runs down out of my hands. Everything disappear.

Seriously, why was I trying so hard if nothing came out good? In my hurt heart and mind I could not see all the good things I had lived, I could only see the bad moments in my life. I have an accused heart, I accused life, accused circumstances, accused Hector for leaving us, and was not thankful for rescuing me now. I even accused my mother for dying and my father for dying too and for leaving me alone in this world. I accused Esmeralda and Estela.

I became a victim of my circumstances. Estela had been so bad to me I accused her for not defending me in court, I even accused the mayor for not being able to marry so fast. I accused the war for making me leave my country. Finally, I accused life for all my bad luck, being the full victim of circumstances instead of seen and recognizing how God had taken care of me, rescuing more than once since I do not know Him but He does know me and has never left me alone. He recognizes me since I was in my mother's womb.

Psalms 139:13:1 says:

> For You formed my inward parts;
> You covered me in my mother's womb.
> I will praise You, for I am fearfully *and* wonderfully made;[b]
> Marvelous are Your works,
> And *that* my soul knows very well.

But at this point I could not see beyond my own circumstances.

15

Family Ties

Hector was very happy to find me. I was such a small boy when he got into a fight with my father and disappeared from my life. He was so happy he arranged my room himself. He added a bed next to the bed of the son of his couple. He bought a closet just for me to put my cloth, but I only had a vest, a couple of slacks, the shirt I had on, a pair of socks and stop counting. When he saw that, he immediately took me to Walmart to buy cloth.

He perceived me so young and small, and within his happiness trying to "save" me and to be a big brother to me, we had our first discussion. He would show me a shirt and would say something like "Look at this shirt. It will look nice on you. It is long sleeve, and it looks good because it has squares." I can recognize, Hector said it with all his best intentions, as I think back, but I really felt like he was treating me as a five-year-old, and I got very angry at him.

"I hate that. I do not like it. That is good for gang people. It is horrible. I am a grown-up, Hector. You can't choose for me. If you are going to buy something for me, I want to choose it. And if not, I can wait until I can buy my things with my own money, okay?"

I was such a spoiled brat, anger was just a phrase away. Anything that would put in danger my manliness, bothered me. Anything that could be a sign of being treated as a kid, I would get mad and frustrated. That hurt my feelings and in my subconscious, I would go back to my hard childhood.

Hector had no clue of how to relate to me, and I didn't either. We were two total strangers and the only thing we had in common was that we were true brothers. He had more than thirty-five years of age and a long life lived; and I was only starting my adult life, trying to take my own decisions in this world of uncertainty.

Family Ties

Soon, I started to work with Hector and I started to show my abilities and my tenacity. Hector had an impressive recording studio with incredible instruments. I had never seen those modern instruments and I loved them. I would help him in his concerts and musical presentations in bars and bigger concerts. I would go to the fields or to the city to paint houses during the day, or wherever I would find a job. Hector tried to give me education, but my ego did not let him pay for my schooling, and that is why I did not study at that moment of my life. I was thirsty of making money anyway, and I could not continue wasting time going to study. So I thought at the time.

Some weeks later, my brother learned that there was a position in a naval company where they were looking for a person who knew how to weld and he recommended me, even though I knew no English. I learned very fast how to use the new tools. They were more sophisticated but everyone was delighted with my abilities. It was high season so it was a temporary job. I didn't care because I made good money as it was a specialized job. My brother wanted to be the big brother and wanted to have an eye on me all the time. I got suffocated by his presence, so I asked to have my schedule changed to the opposite schedule from him as soon as I could. I wasn't used to have someone caring for me, looking after me. I got the night shift and he had the day shift, because at night he had some concerts to attend. I would only help him in the concerts on the weekends or nights off.

My brother lived with his mate and her sons, who were older than me. They did not work, so my brother had to pay off their laziness. They loved to go out and flirt around with all type of women, and sleep around with them. A different one every weekend. They were exploiting my brother and his kindness. His "wife" was like twelve or fifteen years older than him too, and never got married to her. I think he never legally divorced his wife.

Before changing my schedule to work at nights, after work, we would go to eat dinner to a cafeteria and we would talk long hours about our lives. He would tell me about our mom and dad. He told me that dad was crazy in love with my mother and always respected her and helped her around the house and taking care of us kids. When I was born, he said, I was the happiness into our home.

Mom was extremely happy with me since she was not expecting me because my brothers were much older. He told me that Mom was always taking care of me and had me next to her all the time. I was always at mom's side or dad's side. Hector was jealous of me because they put more attention to me than to them. Mom liked to use her sewing machine and I would sit next to her feet and I would spend hours seen her feet going up and down with the pedal. When I got bored, I played with a plastic car she would give me to stay still next to her. I did not bother her at all, I would stay still next to her and when I got tired, I would lay on the floor just next to her. I suppose I felt safe next to her feet.

I learned that on the weekends, mom would sell chicken sandwiches in front of our house to help with the finances of our home. She would sit me on a small chair next to her, and I would help selling them. People would come over to see how cute it was that a baby boy was selling, plus to help my mother.

Hector tells me also that when mom went to the market to buy, she would always tell people around us,

"Careful with the boy." And she always overprotected me from them (my brothers) because they were big and they played with me too heavily.

"We were jealous of you because Mom was only taking care of you and ignored our needs and everything went around the baby. The baby here, the baby there, everything was your needs first and we were last." He said smiling, thoughtfully.

"Bring the little chair for the baby, bring the bottle for the baby, get the cloth for the baby, etcetera, etcetera…So everything was the baby for her. My brother and I would play together and you were a burden to us because you were too small and couldn't play ball inside the house because we could hit you. But we still loved you in our own way. Our favorite game was to push you because you always cried and mom would come over and she would scold us. That was our way of asking for her attention!" he said.

"At night, he would say, 'Don't make any noise because I am going to take the baby to sleep', and she would put you on her chest and carry you on her arms until you fell asleep and we could not play with any noise or scream or talk loud because she would get mad. Probably she also put me on her chest to put me to sleep, but I did not remember, so I was jealous all the time." Would tell me Hector.

In another occasion, he showed me pictures he had. When he showed them to me, my eyes immediately got filled with tears. I had no pictures of them, so we went to photocopy them so that I could have them too.

"Even when she got sick, she thought about you…'Take care of the baby, Hector,' she said to me.

"I could not tell how sick she was. I thought it was a normal fever that comes from a cold or the flu, so I did not put too much attention of what was going on around the house. When mom died, I took the death certificate from dad to read it and to know the cause of death. I couldn't understand how she had died so fast. It said she died from high fevers and for the lack of a doctor to check her and treat her. She had really high fevers, but we never knew exactly what caused them.

Dad had no money to pay a private doctor and the nearest public hospital was too far away to pay taxi, and a bus was not an option since she was too weak. So I saw him next to her day and night putting wet towels on her forehead and seeing her how she was going away, little by little. He would cook some vegetable soups but she ate nothing. I took care of you together with Guillermo. Dad was too busy taking care of mom, and every time we would come near, she said, 'Take good care of Eduardito. Take care of him please.' She was most likely seeing herself die and was worried about you.

I listened and my eyes were always full of tears. Then he continued.

"I never thought she was going to die, but she did. Fever never came down, and she was sick only for a few days. When she died, Dad told me to take you outside so you wouldn't see anything to protect you of all the things that followed a death. He must have called the authorities for them to send the Legal Medicine department to make sure she was dead and to make the death certificate to be able to burry her. He did not want you to see your dead mother."

As I heard him, I got very sentimental, and all the love that I stopped feeling all this time came all at once in a full wave of feelings. My eyes, filled with tears couldn't hold it any longer and I start crying silently while hearing the whole story. My tears fell over my cheeks, every minute as I listened more and more often, and couldn't stop it.

"My brother Guillermo stayed with Dad while I was with you and he told me that dad screamed and yelled and moaned in pain and he felt impotent because he could not help her. He always felt so guilty for not having the money to help her lovely wife. He regretted all the time for being too poor to help. He got emotionally destroyed and he became a very rough and tough man. He became very strict, more so than before. He would scold us and give us curfews for no reason. I think his anger from the lack of resources to help her and save her, made him get revenge on us…

"Dad was rude with us. He would talk to us roughly, strongly, in a rude manner. He suddenly became mom and dad and never thought of bringing another woman to our home, so he would cook for us or take us to the market to eat. He had a strong character, he shouted at us, he was rude, but with you, it was another story. He was soft, lovely, he was another person. He never left you alone.

"He held your hand as if he was holding Mom's hand. He was so different with you. He played with you, had patience with you, and was always aware of your needs. If you left your toys out, we had to pick them up. It didn't matter if you would make a mess in the house, we had to pick up after you. If we wouldn't do it, he would hit us with the belt, or yell at us. Guillermo had more patience with you to play. Sincerely, I was jealous too— jealous seeing the difference between us and you. Because we felt sorry for you, we just obeyed without talking back to him. We felt so sorry you would not be able to have a mother as we did. So, because of you, we would do everything he told us to do and we would put up with all his screaming."

Every time Hector shared something new, I became very sentimental. I cried as if I was going back to my childhood years, very sensitive to all this information. But I was happy to know many details I could not remember. Those great memories meant a lot to me because they were unknown to me as I could not remember anything of all this information received. Life went way too fast for me, and I lost mom and dad too early in my life. That lonely feeling was something hard to forget.

One night Hector asked for Guillermo.

"Poor Guillermo. He couldn't enjoy life," I said.

"Why?" he asked with a puzzled face.

"Don't you know that Guillermo died a few months after you left home?"

"Whaaaaaaaaaaaat?"

"Yes, Hector. Guillermo was a bus collector and he died when the same bus he worked with ran him over," I told him. Hector ignored that he had died and was so surprised that now he was the one crying our brother's death. "My poor brother, how terrible to know this long after happening."

After meditating a few minutes and trying to imagine my brother's death, he asked, "So you were totally alone in this world? No brothers and no Dad or Mom? A total orphan?"

"Yes, Hector. This is why I resented that you never appeared in my life while I was growing up. I ignored you had made many intents with the letters, but I would dream silently that you would come back for me. Of course, I had no idea if you knew about my father's death or my brother's one, which I see you didn't."

"Brother, please forgive me for not insisting more diligently to look for you." He said sincerely with tears on his eyes. "I cannot imagine all that you have to go through all this years, and how hard life was for you. I feel such a huge sorrow in my heart. I feel really sorry, bro."

My heart felt relieved and his words felt totally sincere to me. I couldn't believe I was with him, so we continued talking telling him what I could remember from childhood. My heart softened and healed with each encounter every night.

"Dad suffered very much since you left, Hector. He would sigh thinking and wishing you would come back home one day to ask his forgiveness. He talked about you constantly. I remember clearly when I saw his face like staring the wall, thinking, meditating and he would share with me that he was wondering about where were you. He knew nothing of you and was worried about your destiny. He got consoled playing with me and Guillermo. I tried to distract him when I saw him too sad.

"We went once in a while to Estela's mom's house. I never saw them too close to each other nor holding hands and much less kissing. So I really thought they were only friends and it took me a while to understand that she was the mistress, and the mother of a daughter she had with him. I kind of adopted her as my stepmother, since I had no other person to see as a mother.

"When Guillermo died in the bus accident, dad really went crazy! He yelled and screamed in front of me for all the hurt he had inside. He got totally out of himself. It was too much for him. I think he behave the same with Mom, but worse since Guillermo left home very healthy and happy, full of life."

Hector put his hand on his mouth with a totally surprised face feeling the moment. "Now that you tell me all this, I feel guilty for my dad's death," He said with red eyes.

"Life was never the same since that day," I continued. "Dad became sadder—twice as much. If with my mom's death he was sad, with you leaving home he got sadder, with Guillermo's death, he became deeply depressed. I tried to make him happy and to laugh, but it was too much for him. It was too much for an old man."

"Poor Dad," said Hector staring at the wall.

There were many nights we spent talking about everything we remembered. We cried together many nights and in the most intimate part of my heart, I could not understand all this feelings I was experimenting. I had never cried for sentimental reasons, just for anger or hurt. I could not understand myself.

My heart was a cold heart, tough, like a rock, but it had softened and had touched my inner self with all these memories of my childhood years, my family memories, my descendants. I had all this mix feelings because I was a man, a tough, rough, anger guy, and now I was all filled with tears feeling tender and soft with all this going on. It was like going back to my childhood years and becoming a kid again to live all the good and bad memories next to my lost brother. I couldn't be happier talking with him. All this was so good to know and talk about with someone that could understand me.

One day I asked, "Hector, why did you leave home?"

"I knew you were going to ask one day. There is no easy answer to that one, Eduardo."

"Really, now that you tell me all the story and talking about our time together, I did not see things the same way as you did. I just saw a very strict father, a tough one, a mean one, a dad with a hard heart for us, specially me. Remember when we went to play pool?" he asked.

"Yep, very clearly," I said. "I remember it was the day before you left."

"That night, Dad made a fool of me in front of my friends. Guillermo and I were there only learning to play pool because some friends invited us over. The condition was that we couldn't smoke or drink beer. We were in a totally clean situation, behaving healthy and properly, just trying to learn to look good in front of the girls, when we go out with someone in the future. We were having fun, laughing the hell out because we could not hit the ball right and put any ball in the bucket. We kept putting the white ball in, which is the wrong one, and they were making fun of us but in a good manner.

"My friends Pepe and Seco [the thin] were experts because their dad's showed them how to play, and we did not have the courage to ask dad if he had some friends that could teach us. So that day, we decided to go without asking for permission, that was our error, but he was too tough with us. We were afraid of his reaction. And the next thing we see is that dad gets there with a policeman, screaming at us to go out. He made such a scandal that was not necessary. He ashamed us in such a way, that I had no face to see anyone else again.

"When we got home that night, he hit us with a rope, so hard, I hated him deeply that night. I do not know if you remember, but that night, Guillermo cried, but I didn't. I couldn't drop a tear since I was too mad at him. Hatred toward him governed me ever since that night. I promised myself that no one would ever ashamed me ever again. I hated so much the old man that I promised I was going to revenge. I was destroyed inside, and all I wanted to do is to die and go with Mom. I was too ashamed to go out again. I hated him with all my heart.

"That night, I got into my room thinking what to do, what were my options. The first thing I thought was to kill myself, but mom had died just a few months before and I just couldn't do that to my dad, even as much as I hated him. Besides, believe it or not, I thought about you, more than my dad, and you had nothing to do with my anger. So I buried the idea of killing myself. I was too young anyway. You didn't even know how strict Dad was with us two.

"The other option was to leave home with no destiny at all, to see what happened day by day. And upon thinking about that, I remembered a group of Mormons that I had met two months ago that I would teach them how to play the guitar and the drums. They were nice people and they were missionaries in El Salvador for a year. They were about to leave the country because they were finishing their year of service after High School graduation. So I decided to go to look for them and tell them that Mom had died and that dad had kicked me out of the house because I wanted to be a musician."

"But Dad didn't kick you out."

"Of course not, but that is what I told them. I was so mad inside me that I begged and cried to them to take me with them. They thought it was a great idea because I could continue teaching them in the United States. I would teach them with no pay, and they would pay for all my trip and my expenses. They talked to their superiors and approved it and they adopted me immediately.

"Since I was over eighteen, I needed no permission from parents, and all they needed was for me to get my passport and my national identification. They made all the documentation and helped me get a visa to travel as if I had become a missionary like them. I did not understand their religion and they never taught me about it, but I didn't care. All I wanted was to get out of home and the farther the better. I loved playing the drums and the guitar, you know that, that is my passion since I was young, so I saw the opportunity and left to come here."

Then he continued, "When I came over to the United States, I had the difficulty that I knew no English, so they paid my tuition to learn English and then they sent me to college to study music, to get a degree on Music. They paid all my education and all I did was teach them the basics of music in return. I did not know there were universities you could attend to study music, as I had learned by ear and with friends.

"I learned to be a better musician and learned about history of music and all type of instruments I wanted to learn. It was another level of learning, professional learning, not street learning. It was another world. Of course, I had the requirement of going to church with them and I would play in the services. I learned of God, their way, but for me it was still a weird god. I liked their teachings, but I did not understand some of their teachings and privileges.

"They said things like that the highest servants of their religion could have more than one wife as long as they all had the same level. No mistresses, all wives. Also I learned that they said that Jesus had gone to Latin America to the Indians when He resurrected—which I thought was totally weird. I did not understand much about all those teachings and couldn't care much about them anyway. All I wanted was to be a musician, and the religion was against being a musician outside of its congregation. I wanted a career, to play with the famous people. Sincerely, I just used all their kindness to go to school and educate myself. I never adopted their religion. I just went as a musician in pay for all they had done with me. No one questioned me about my faith. I fooled them all, and they thought I was one of them.

"In that church, I met my wife, Diana. She was sixteen when I met her. She was white, blond, blue eyed and beautiful, just like mother, but with rich parents. Many Mormons are rich, and her parents were no exception. She was so beautiful and her dad wanted her to marry a Mormon kid, from a good family, a traditional family. We met because she sang in the chorus and I played for the group. I loved her form of being. She was humble and innocent. She was fun and had an extraordinary voice. There was immediate chemistry between us and I can say it was love at first sight. Up to that point I had never felt anything so strong for any woman, and it became a very profound love for her.

"I thought about her all the time, I went to bed thinking of her, and went to sleep thinking of her. I was crazy in love for her and couldn't help it. And she had fallen in love with me too. She had never had a boyfriend before and she could not have one until she turned eighteen. The other big problem we had was that her dad wanted her to marry a Mormon guy—a traditional Mormon guy. A blond rich boy, just like her. Her dad wanted a guy from a known, prominent Mormon family, not just anybody. I was anybody. Of course, her social status was much higher than mine as I came from a poor family that would eat beans every night. Besides I was a runaway guy, with no past, no mother, and of course, I denied my father because I hated him.

"Her father knew nothing of me and of my family, which I never mentioned. I always said I was orphan of both parents just to not go into details. He was racist and even though I was not black—I am brown skinned, Latin—he did not like that at all. He followed us everywhere, and we did not have permission to see each other. He made our lives miserable. We could not even go to the mall to eat an ice cream. The more he opposed, the more we fell in love.

"She had to escape from home to meet with me somewhere neutral every week. Her father followed me to kill me, I could sense it. But we got sick of her father making our lives miserable and his persecution so we decided to run away as soon as she turned eighteen. We left to go to Los Angeles and we lived happily many years. We were two love birds together, full of dreams and love for each other. Her father got so upset that he let her know that she was out of his will. We couldn't care less about that. We had each other.

"Since we were alone, I went to look for a job with the musical groups of the moment and I did pretty good. My musical talents were well received by the musicians, groups and singers. I was between many famous people and I even composed music for some famous people and some not so famous. I can tell you the most relevant ones were people like Dolly Parton, Kenny Rogers, Carlos Santana, and others. Life was good, and I made good money. We had three children, Emely, Elizabeth, and Hector Jr.

"As time went by, life started to get complicated and she started to demand more and more money. I got sick for a season and other musicians came by. Little by little I started to loose all the good contracts. She wanted to live with the same life style she had before running away with me, which I gave her for many years. Money started to be hard to get and she did not understand my illness. She only wanted more money. She was a very materialistic girl without any income coming from her side. She was a house wife, like her mother. All she had to do was to take care of the kids when they came from school, and many times not even that, because I hired an illegal Salvadoran lady to be our maid. I treated her like a queen. She could not be better. Marriage is of two, not of one, but she wanted all solutions from me, as she had seen from her parents.

"We got to a point where we were fighting every day, and I suddenly had no job indefinitely since I got very sick. You know, in the music industry you get into many other things. It was music for famous people and in the jet set you see all type of things like easy sex, drugs, lots of money, a very wild life. When you are there, you do not think you will not be able to get good money in the future. Money comes in big amounts. We all think it is eternal, so I did not save much.

"One day I got a heart sickness because of my overweight. I got to three hundred and thirty pounds, and my body could not hold me anymore. She did not care I was getting bigger and bigger, all that mattered to her was the money coming. I hardly had sex with her anyway, since I was away most of the time and women were constantly around me. I suppose she knew that because she did not mind I did not provoked for us to be together.

"With the sickness, money was gone really fast. I had no insurance because as I said, we always think money will always come in. With the lack of money coming and the sickness, she got fed up with all the economic situation. After a huge fight, bringing out all my inner anger, we yelled bad at each other and we said many things to each other that I regret now. That fight gave her the courage to call her dad again for the first time since running away. More than fifteen years had gone by.

"Her father was very surprised with her call, but as the prodigal son, he received her back joyfully together with his grandchildren. Of course, I was not included in the package, just my kids. She had to immediately file for divorce."

"If you want my help, Diana, I receive you gratefully. You know I love you, and I will love you forever. You had died and you resurrected today for us. Your mom and I will be more than happy to have you over and be able to enjoy our grandchildren. But you must know our condition. If you come back to us it is for ever. You have to be sure about it, because your lazy husband is not welcomed. You know that is the way it has to be.

'I never liked him, and I never will. I do not want to know your story or anything that happened between you two. You have nothing to tell us. The important thing here is that you have repented and you have resurrected for your mom and me. His name is also forbidden around here. Be sure about your decision because this is my condition and I will never change my mind about it,' her father told her. I heard all of it as she put the speaker on just for me to hear everything, to punish me more. She knew that that was going to be the condition. She knew it all along.

"She was immediately sure about her decision, and she just told me she was going back home, where she belonged. As easy as that, she packed and left me alone, sick and without money. It took her one day to get the plane tickets, paid by Daddy, of course, and packed all her important stuff. She told the kids they were going on vacation to meet Grandpa and Grandma."

"The kids were ten, almost nine, and seven."

"And your actual wife? Where did you meet her?"

"Ah, she was the maid who helped us around cleaning and taking care of the kids. Since money had gone down, she was just helping us every two weeks or whenever we needed a babysitter. We had become friends because she is from El Salvador, and we talked about my situation. She saw us get into fights more than once. She always told me to leave her and that I was going to find a job pretty soon. She encouraged me to continue fighting. So when she saw me sick, alone, and with no money, she took care of me during my whole sickness and recovery.

"I owe her my life. I started to like her, of course, and so I proposed her to come with me to Manhattan to look for a job, since in Los Angeles, I got the doors closed. She backed up my decision and even bought the tickets for both of us. She left her boys behind in LA while we could establish ourselves. She was with me in the hardest time of my life, and this is how we got together, but I do not want to marry her, really, so we are just living together.

"I have enough trying to hide from Diana to avoid giving the child support for our kids since I hardly have enough for her, and me. We lived from her savings the first three months. She is not used to a high lifestyle, and Diana does not need my money. So as soon as I started to have a steady income, I paid for the tickets for her boys to come over.

"I was thankful with her for taking care of me, so I asked her not to work anymore and just stay home as a thanksgiving, but I never thought I had to pay for her boys too. She blackmails me every time I tell her something about them, since they should go out to work because they are grown men now. She always tells me that if it wasn't for her I wouldn't be here and with that I just shut up and try to keep peace at home, since she is right about it."

"So you know nothing of your kids? You have never seen them again?"

"Sadly, no. Diana took them away without my consent, and her dad has enough money to pay for their needs. She does not need me, and she does not let me see them anyway, so what sense does it make to send them money if I cannot see them?"

I now start to understand that Hector had suffered in his life too. He suffered with the family he formed as his parents in law did not accept him, and he was now alone with a strange lady and her lazy sons. I can't believe it! Hector was not accepted by his parents in law and Maria Elena wasn't accepted either by my stepmother and sister who where something like my parents in law. We are similar in that matter. He ran away from home, I ran away from home. His wife ran away from him….Maria Elena ran away from me too when she did not accept coming with me here. We have many things in common, without planning them.

When Hector's kids grew up, they went to look for him to see him, meet him and start a new relationship with him, but he was too afraid to go to prison for not fulfilling the child support demand so he preferred to hide from them. Sadly and ironically, this woman would make him support her children who were nothing of him, just because she made him the favor of taking care of him and paid their way to NY. Life turns around in so many ways. I felt sorry for my brother.

Hector also has a bad temper, like Dad, and they were very alike and this is why they did not get along too well. They were too alike. But everything turns around sometime in our life and the woman he lived with also had a bad temper and they would constantly fight, as he did with his wife. They would shout at each other constantly. He never hit her, but shouting was part of their relationship. They would fight in any place in front of any person. They did not care who was in front of them. Her sons would always defend their mother, so they were emotionally mistreating each other. It was like a love-hate relationship all the time. It was a convenience relationship. They needed each other. She needed his money and he needed her cooking and cleaning.

My brother was still big, approximately of 280 pounds and even though he had had two heart attacks, he had not learned about it and had not changed his lifestyle or his eating habits. He loved eating, it was a joy for him. He would eat anything and everything he might want to eat. No restrains. Maybe he had lost any love for living and could care less if he died. He had lost the love of his life anyway and his children probably hated him for not wanting to see them. So the truth was, that Hector was also alone. I was not the only one.

One night I went out with the sons of my brother's mate, when I had just arrived there. They were very different than me. They were lived men, loved to full around with women, they drank and they smoke cigarettes and pot. I was not like that. Yes, I was a father, but I had not know another woman but my wife. I was not like them. That was an unknown world for me, since I had never been exposed to it.

Even though I was married, I had not learned to fool around with women. I had not had any other woman around me, not even to forget my wife. I had not looked for anyone, not even in this long journey. For them it was so normal to go to the bar or the pub and look for a woman that was ready to go with any of them. There was always one or two that was an easy trap and willing to go to bed with an unknown person.

That was freaky to me. I could not understand in my innocent mind how they could get a girlfriend so fast. I mean, in my mind, there was no possible way that a man could have sex with someone they just met without any relationship. That was only for the brothel ladies, I thought, as a job. So I could not understand they paid nothing to them, but a drink or two, maybe something to eat, and they were ready to go.

Later I understood they were no girlfriends, they were only one night stands and no compromise in between them. It was an easy way to have sex without going to a whorehouse. Cheaper and cleaner too, and less risky to get a venereal disease, or so they thought. My sexual mind was so healthy that I had no eyes for anyone else but my wife, Maria Elena.

My brother had many problems with his mate, all because of her lazy sons. They answered back to my brother, they were lazy, they did not respect him as the authority of the house. The area where he lived was not the best place either. It was a place full of Latinos and black people of low incomes and illegal aliens. That made it full of lazy, bums, drug addicts, dangerous people, with all types of bad habits. I could see knife fights once in a while and any type of fights for nothing important.

Estela educated me well. She showed me how to eat correctly with my fork and knife, and not my hands. She taught me to be a responsible young man, to work honestly and to dress in an appropriate way. She taught me to iron my cloth and to respect what was not mine. She taught me to respect the elderly and to say good morning and good afternoon or good night, thank you and you are welcome. She did those good things with me even though I was still mad at her for all the bad she did to me. She had so many good things, but with such a wicked heart that she was also a very bad person. Maybe Hector fought the same way Estela fought with Ali, except Ali had his own respect for women and very clear that he did not pretend to divorce her.

I could see no respect in my bother's house. These were ordinary people with no education whatsoever.

One day we were at the porch talking, trying to get along with them, drinking a beer when suddenly a woman was chased by a man and every time he could come get her, he would hit her, he yelled at her and then she got away and continued running away, and the same thing happened again when the guy got to her, yelled, hit and she ran around and around. She kind of not ran away for good, as I could observe. This grabbed my attention since I had never seen anyone hitting a woman, so I told the other guys to go with me to help the woman and they told me to leave them alone.

"Calm down, Eduardo. Nothing is going on. Calm down," they said and that made me furious.

I stood up and yelled at them, "Can't you see the man is mistreating that woman? Let's help her!"

They answered calmly, "Don't get involved. Calm down. Leave them alone."

But I couldn't leave them alone, so I went after them and separated the man from the woman and told him to leave her alone. To my surprise, the woman turned around and shouted at me, "You asshole, go away. Leave us alone!"

"Go away, you fool! Leave us alone!" said the man too.

Ufff! What a backward world! I thought. I was shocked. I could not understand how a woman can be happy to be hit by a man as a love demonstration, if that was what they were doing.

Everything was new to me: the sons of my brother's mate yelling at each other and to their mother and to my brother. They smoked and drank, they slept around with all types of women, they did all this things that was not part of my way of life. My heart was not wicked at all and even though I had fought with Maria Elena because she didn't want to follow me, I did not have the courage to go after another woman, and less for just one night stand. I had only felt that great true love with Maria Elena. That type of love that I could skip eating just to be next to her. I was afraid to come close to any other woman. Maybe it was for all the things I saw and heard in the brothel I lived in when I was really small, how those women were so mistreated and were trapped in that "job" to feed their children.

I remember that when I was a child I promised myself to respect all the women and to never, never go to a whorehouse for pleasure. I saw them cry too many times after each job done. I felt sorry for them and I promised to respect women. It was a personal type of fear and respect toward them. Even though it seemed different as I was a father already, I truly respected too much my wife and I loved her too much to just go fooling around with anybody. I had not learned the contrary and in my mind, only one woman existed in my life.

I started to think that this was not a place I wanted to stay for too long. I did not feel comfortable with all those crazy people fighting with each other. I did not like all that disrespect around the house. I could not find the peace I needed. I was so happy to find my brother, and our long talks were the best that could have happened to me, but I was not happy there. I felt sorry for him. I wish I could have said to him to just go both of us alone somewhere else, but I never had the courage to tell him.

They were so nice when I first got there, but very soon the fights started as always. It was an environment I did not want. I could understand my niece Xenia for running away. If Estela and Ali were like Hector and his mate, I was also getting ready to leave. Every day I liked it less to be around them. I observed my brother, and I definitely did not want to stay forever there, nor bring my wife and child to this environment.

So one day, when I least expected it, I got mad with Hector too. I do not remember the episode how it happened, I just remember I got out all my frustration that I was carrying around since my childhood and forgot all the nice moments we had shared. We shouted at each other, we got really mad at each other, and I even remember throwing a hammer toward him. I had the hammer because I was trying to put a nail on the wall, and suddenly I threw it toward him, to his head without thinking about it. It was just a second and I made a hole on the wall. Thankfully, he avoided the hammer, and did not hit him. I had been thinking I was going to leave soon, but everything happened so fast, and the environment contributed to get hot, that I left that night in the worst way I could possibly go away: Mad, upset, in a fight and without a good-bye.

In that moment, I forgot for all the love he had shown me, in all the times he looked for me, in all the letters he had written to me, in all the good moments we shared. I just wanted to go away, to run away, as usual. I forgot really fast all those good times. I forgot about the letters that had hit my heart so deeply. I couldn't manage all the situation. I just felt hurt, frustrated with Maria Elena, frustrated with Estela's mistreat, frustrated for all the abuse that my brother lives, frustrated for his lazy stepsons, frustrated with my life. In a second, I ruined everything we had accomplished as brothers. I totally forgot the four months we had shared great memories. That night, we had a very horrible fight. My American dream was only frustration after frustration. *What am I doing here?*

After fighting so horribly with Hector, I remember the last words I told him: "I am sick of you, your family, the disorder of the life you live in. I am sick and tired of all the disrespect you receive and that you do not put a limit on them. I am sick of everything around you!"

"Go away from here son of a b——, you are such an ungrateful, asshole. I should have never gone for you. You are such a brat, go to hell men. Don't you ever come back here, you have died to me as my parents did!"

"You will see. Hector. I go away to look for my dream and the next time I see you, you will see me with money, speaking perfect English and I will come to pay every penny you spent on me, and if I can, I will come to rescue you from that miserable life you have!" I shouted in madness, took my things and left his apartment.

I left with no plan. I had no real plans when leaving my brother's house, so I don't know what was I thinking. I knew no body but my brother's friends and musicians. I had no family and again, I was alone. In an dead end situation. My life was a whirlwind of emotions and situations, it was a rollercoaster of different emotions to be exact. Happiness lasted too short and frustrations lasted too long. When I finally found someone who could rescue me and help me find a way in life, I messed it up. My mom and dad left me completely alone in this world. No plan, no friends, no family, no job, no wife, no child. I have nothing and no one in this world. I am truly alone. How stupid.

I left without knowing or understanding the world I was going to find outside. When I am alone, it finally hit on me that I am really, really alone and I do not know how I will make it through this loneliness. I have no legal papers, even though the court said that Hector could file them for me as a brother so I can get a residency, but Hector got afraid to be located and get obligated to pay all the child support he had skipped for too many years, so he never filed anything for me; besides, since we fought, even if he did, nothing will come to me. So I had no plan. Everything happened in a very bad moment.

In those days, I could not see the protecting hand of God in my life. God rescued me from a bad environment. God protected me from becoming a man who hits or abuses women. God had protected me from Estela and her wicked plans, and up to this point, I hadn't stopped eating. I had nothing, but I didn't even think of fighting with God because I did not know He existed. It was me with myself. I could not recognize that Supreme Being who formed me in the womb of my mother. I could not see that God was with me. I was mad at life, at Estela, at Hector, at the United States, which had not given me anything good so far. I was mad with the world itself.

16

In the Street

I grabbed the few things I had and left totally upset.

When I realized I was in the streets without any plan, I panicked. I had some money from the jobs I had done, so I could go and rent a room for the night while I thought what to do. I decided to explore all around the place and somewhat further away. With my backpack I started walking around. We had had dinner already so I didn't have to spend to eat that night. I was full actually. I decided to just walk around while I was thinking about what to do next. I probably had my mind in blank, just walking around trying to know my surroundings better.

I walked around without any direction for about three or four hours. My mind was in blank with absolutely no plan. All the jobs I had had with my brother and with his recommendations, were gone with the fight. Me and my big ego and foolishness threw everything away to the trash. I had no papers, legal papers, so I had no clue where will I get a job. Up to that point I never thought about the lack of legality I was in. That night I slept on a bench in a park. It was not a cold night, so I just hugged my backpack and took the bench as my first bed in the streets. It was probably going to be my "house" for a while.

While I was walking around toward nowhere, I started to notice that there were other people like me, without any destiny, just going around in the streets. I met a couple of guys who were drug addicts and members of a gang. I felt sorry for them, but they became my first friends. They talked some Spanish because they had ascendants from Puerto Rico. Probably their grandparents had taught them Spanish. They had ran away from home and lived on the streets. It did not take me too long to learn their way of living. I started to drink and smoke pot very fast.

What I had rejected and criticized of my brother's stepsons, I was doing it and learned to do so in the streets. I needed to be part of the group, to belong somewhere, to belong with someone. I do not know if it was like an internal revenge or a personal revenge against my brother. Actually it was against myself because I was not doing anything good. Pretty soon, my ravage person, the violent child inside me, came out to survive in the streets. I remember how much I used to fight against everyone while I was growing up, but now, I was stronger and bigger, so all the violence came out of off me.

My violent personality helped me to get involved with the gangs since that was a requisite. We were all violent and, needless to say, had no fear of dying. We couldn't care less about our lives. The gang members we carried knives, chains, bats, and things that could hit hard to anyone against us. In this gangs, though, no guns where part of us. At least not all the time.

If I see myself in the mirror, all I could see was myself aimlessly with no future and as a failed man. I continued with no plan, no aim, no will, no future at all. I was completely upset with myself and I would try not to see myself in the mirror too often. I did not like what I saw. I lived a full crazy life on those days.

I was part of the gang called Daily City Devils in a city near Brooklyn. They were my family and my life moved around robberies, drug, alcohol and wasting myself out. We drank until we had no money left, and then, we would go out to rob some more to get more money to start all over again to get wasted. We became expert burglars, and sometimes we robed car stereos, or we would go into a house to rob VHSs, TVs, and sometimes the whole car, depending of how much money we needed to continue wasting ourselves. When I was wasted and started thinking of my good days, inevitably my thoughts always went back to the best times I spent with Maria Elena. Then, I felt so worthless, so aimless that I got to hate being alive and hated myself too much.

Sometimes, when I got myself to be sober, I would sigh and told myself that someday things would change in my life. In those short times of being sober, I would try to imagine myself getting out of that crazy world to be a well being, to be a focused guy to become successful and bring my family some day to this place, but in a different situation. Life was worthless to me at that time. Then, when my 'friends' saw me too thoughtful and depressed, they came over with more beer and more drugs to start all over again. It was a merry-go-round situation and I didn't know how to change that in my life.

Most of the people I found in the streets where Hispanic people just like me. We had all gone after the American Dream of becoming a well being and become successful to support our families in our Latin Countries, but we had all found difficulties getting a job without legal papers. We were all under a great nightmare. A few of them where runaway Americans too, who had wasted their lives into drugs, women and rock and roll. We were all trying to survive the street life by being part of the gangs and robbing to get wasted. That was all we could think about. Our sight was blinded toward a better life out of drugs.

I met Mexican-Americans, Puerto Ricans, Nicaraguans, Salvadorans, Mexicans, and we all got involved more and more in that awful world. One thing took me to another and I did not know how to get out of it. I had no where to go, and they all became my family, as I had none any more. I loved the adrenaline and the feeling of running away every time we did something wrong. We learned to rob things to sell them easily in the black market and this gave us easy money to continue into this crazy life. It was a disastrous life, but it was an easy life. No job, easy money, adrenaline to the max and somehow, it was an easy life. A life to nowhere, but it was an easy life. I had formed myself the model of the street guy, fighter by nature, and I had gotten in problems more than once and didn't care about my future or my family.

The gangs were identified by colors and our color was red, another gang was blue, other green and so on. We were very well known as the gang of the devil park. I got a police record with the group. We laughed on the police faces as we knew we would just go into jail a few days and go back out very fast. We always got minor charges and usually I would go to jail on Friday and get out on Monday. I recognized that I was a problem maker. They would usually get me for drinking in public places, loud music, or for fighting with someone. Nothing serious as they never caught us robbing or getting into a house. The devil park was on the limits of Daily City, and it was our territory. And the police knew it.

I remember a day we had a sports car with the roof down that a friend had lend us a few days. I was drinking with a friend and we had bought a couple of six-packs and some pot. We were going around a tourist place with the music as loud as we could trying to find a place to park the car to continue drinking but with the car parked. We were bored and my friend wanted to pee. As we were used to live in the streets and peeing anywhere, he went into the park to find a tree to pee. I stayed in the car, with the music loud just looking him from there. I tried to tell him with signs to go away from the people to find a hidden place to pee.

It was a Saturday afternoon and in the park I could observe a group of Senior Citizens form the Italian and Greek clubs playing cricket. It was a nice group of people over sixty-five trying to have a nice afternoon out in the park. There was a lot of people as it was a beautiful day to go out. One of the elder of that club group, saw the intentions of my friend and while he was already peeing, the oldie came running toward my friend with a cane shouting at him: "Don't pee here you pig!"

Other elders came with that guy after my friend hitting him with the canes and shouting to him not to pee in a public place. From the car, I could see my friend running with a panic face and got into the car as fast as he could. My reaction was to immediately get out of the car, and in seconds, I went to the trunk and got out a gun we had just purchased and I shot into the air three times to frighten everyone to leave us alone.

I was not planning on killing anyone, just saving my friend. I got him into the back sit and I was the hero there with the gun in my hand shooting into the air. I don't know who was more scared, if the elderlies or myself, but in a second I thought I was 007 with the control in my hands over the avalanche of elderlies, and I was holding a gun. In less than five minutes, who know where from, a full set of police men and SWAT group surrounded us. Now I was the scared one.

There were snipers and policemen and police cars and the whole shebang surrounding us. They had surrounded us as if we were too dangerous for the people around us. We were just drinking and the big crime was to pee on a park tree. I felt like a real offender or a kidnapper. I didn't know what to think. I was wrong by shooting to the air, as that alerted the police. I felt like the worst guy on earth and since by that time I was one of the leaders of the gang, they had an eye on me, trying to catch me in the wrong situation to put me into prison. But our fights were not to kill our enemies, but to defend our territories. The guns were not used between us, we only used instruments of attack.

We all carried bats, chains, razors, and stuff like that just to hurt people but not to kill. I don't even remember why I had a gun, but I wanted to use it. Wrong day, wrong time, wrong situation. But in that moment, I felt like James Bond. Adrenaline was to the max and I started to verbally fight with the policemen.

I had more than twenty cops with their arms pointing at me. I became a stubborn person trying to become a hero. I kept my arm up pointing at them. I had become fearless and did not care if I would die in that moment. The negotiator would tell me things like "Don't be silly. You haven't done anything serious. Put your gun down. Slooooowlyyyy…We have snipers around. One order, one shot, and you are gone, man."

I didn't understand fully what they said because I still did not know too much English (just some street words), so my friend who was Puerto Rican translated to me, "No seas tonto, no has hecho nada serio, pon tu pistola abajo. Despaciiiitooooo… Tenemos francotiradores alrededor. Una orden, un disparo y te vas, hombre."

Finally, after an hour, I gave up. I put the gun down to the street and from nowhere, around ten men went on top of me. Needless to say that we both got arrested that afternoon. They hit us for disturbing the public places and took us to prison.

Back to jail, I thought. *And now, who knows how long!*

"When will I stop to have this worthless life?" I asked myself. Every time I got caught I would ask myself, but I always went back to it. I just did not know what to do to start a decent life. I was trapped in this horrible world.

On our way to jail, in the van they put us in, a fat man, around 250 pounds, with a dark-brown complexion asked me in Spanish where was I from. Apparently he was Latin. When I told him I was from El Salvador, he had compassion of me and asked, "Your country is in war, right?"

"Yes," I answered as if nothing bothered me.

"Why you Latinos come to mess up our country and get into trouble?"

"I don't know," I answered pointlessly and suddenly I got into a total desperation thinking about the war I had forgotten and I started to cry out like a little boy as I had lost my objective of coming to this country. It just hit on me hard in that moment.

"So maybe it has not being easy for you to adapt and incorporate here, right?" I nodded no with my head.

"Tell me exactly what happened to see how I can help you because when the SWAT and snipers are in a scene, it is because something serious has happened or someone dangerous is involved."

I tell him exactly what had happened, how we had the two six-packs trying to have a nice time together but my friend needed to go to the bathroom and all that happened around with the elderlies chasing him. Of course, I do not say anything about the marijuana we had in the car. He said he was going to try to help us, just because we are in war in my home country, but advise us that it is totally against the law to shoot to the air for no reason and to never do it again.

As usual, I was caught on a weekend and on Monday I was in court. I hear my name and the judge tells me to go in front of her.

"You are accused of having an open beer and drinking in a public place. How do you plead?" I was in shock for that simple accusation.

"Guilty," I said immediately.

"You must pay a bail of six hundred dollars and start going to an AA group for six months."

God definitely already had a perfect plan for me in my life, but in that moment, I just thought it was pure luck and not the hand of God protecting me from going to jail. The judge did not mention anything about the snipers or the SWAT group that surrounded us, plus all the policemen in the capture and the gunshot in the air. It was really a miracle and God protecting me, but I was still blinded from my own concupiscence.

17

The Awakening

I stayed in that life of bad decisions for a while and the more I got involved, the more I would meet people we could do wrong things with. We did a robbery here, another one there, going into prison for a couple of days, sometimes three. It was only forty-eight to seventy-two hours to be sentenced to pay a bail and take some courses which I took them most of the times but left in halfway into them.

This became a game to me. It was like playing cat and mouse. It was fun to get caught. Same thing happened all the time: disturbance in the streets, public places, loud music, drinking in public, driving with an open can, speeding, a couple of marihuana cigarettes, but not enough to be dealers, just our consumption. We were more into beer than heavy drugs, same silly stuff. Nothing serious. It was a game not to get trapped. The good boys against the bad guys.

It was fun to get trapped because the gang would get the money fast to get me out, as that was the secret code we had. Sometimes I did the whole courses, but nothing got into my head. My brain was blocked but I learned some street English, but maybe that was one of the obstacles: I did not know a full English language, so I was kind of blocked to not learn anything from all those good people. I kept myself in the same stupid, worthless mode.

One bad day, between gang and gang, between robbery and robbery, there was a great fight with one of the other gangs. One day, while I was in that lifestyle, fighting with the opposite gangs, robbing here and there, there was a big fight with one member of the other gang. Our gangs were not as the ones we have now in El Salvador. Our gangs were of bats and sticks, as I mentioned before. It was never our intention to kill anyone to be accepted into the gang. We all wanted to live, and dying was not part of the game. But there was a day that the fight was so heavy that the other gang got my friend John and between several guys they started to hit him with the bats so badly, that they ended up killing him. Before I could do anything to defend him, he was dead. I wasn't close enough to get involved to defend him, and when I got to the place, there was nothing to do.

I got so mad with myself for not being there with him to defend him, that I wanted to die too. I was destroyed inside and I cried and cried out of anger, of feeling helpless and of the hurt of feeling alone again, since he had become my best friend, my brother. I cried until I couldn't any more. After a while of crying and everyone seeing me so bad, the rest of the gang took me to an empty building to drink until I lost myself. John and I were the two leaders. I was alone again.

At the end of the night, or should I say early in the morning, we went to the van that served us as house the three of us that had no home. We were so wasted that I have no idea how I got there. I have a memory lagoon of that moment. What I do have very clear is that next day, I had such a hangover, I couldn't bare myself. I had a physical and moral hangover for all that had happened.

When I woke up with the hangover and I could finally get out of the 'bed', I looked myself into a broken mirror we had there. I looked pathetic. My hair was long and messy, a long beard with no real cut, without any care. I had a crazy look on my face. I had something like diabolic eyes, or that is what I could see in myself. I was pale for not having eaten well and for just drinking and smoking pot more so than eating food. I was a disaster. I had ruined my life.

When looking at myself into the mirror, it was like an awakening call into me. I could see I was going no where. It dawn on me very well that morning. I felt clearly the need to do something for myself. I had that strong call in my heart saying that He had not called me into this type of life. I couldn't recognize that was the call of God in my life, but I could feel inside me a big pain for wasting my life. It was not a life full of women and crazy sex. No. It was a messy life—full of beer, marijuana, and minor robberies.

I was going back and forth to jail, going to rehab programs, and learning nothing. Even though that mirror just reflected how lost I was, I felt inside me that a supreme being, someone bigger than me was telling me that this was not the life He had chosen for me. That day, after meditating and thinking in everything that had happened to my friend John, I suddenly wanted to continue living, to do something different with my life. I could not continue in that life or I was going to end like John: dead.

Around two years had gone by since I left my brother Hector's home. Maybe I was around twenty-one by then. I could not stand myself any longer. With the little money I had left from all the robberies we had made, I rented a room to get a good shower and clean myself. I went to buy clean second hand cloth. I bought a shaver, soap, shaving cream and shampoo. I didn't remember when was the last time I had showered well enough to feel clean.

I got into the shower first to shampoo myself and cleaned myself well enough to stay later in the tub with bubbles for a looooong time trying to think what to do with myself. I started thinking about my dead parents and how ashamed they would be of me if they were alive. I thought about Maria Elena and

Guadalupe again. I had buried them in my mind to live my crazy life.

"What are they doing? Would they think I am dead?" I asked myself.

Every time I got into trouble, inevitably I thought of them and how foolish I was of leaving them behind. Surely, Maria Elena had forgotten me and probably she had found someone else to love. I am not worthy for her to think about me. I am not even worth of being the father of Guadalupe. Simply, I am not worthy of them. So, the idea of going back to look for them, was not a possibility. I had nothing, so going back to bring them to this pervert world, was not something I could even consider. I think for the first time that it was good that she did not want to follow me here. I couldn't have her in the streets with me in this life. Or maybe if she would have accepted to come when I was at my brother's apartment, we would not be in the streets...I don't know.

I still have nothing to offer them, so I needed to do something good with my life if I still want to follow my dream to bring them here with me. So, in the analysis and meditation I did, I decided to move to New Jersey, south of New York to start again. I thought it was good to move out from were I had a police record, so this was far away enough to start a new life in another State. I knew nobody there, but I was alone anyway, so going south to New Jersey, or going north to Connecticut or Massachusetts didn't matter. It was just going away from all the gang friends to another state and start all over again, and toward the south, it was going to be less cold in my mind.

When I got to New Jersey, I knew no one, but asking and asking in the streets, I learned of a place where some small companies would send an employee to go pick up illegal people for hard labor jobs. I would be selected to do all types of jobs. I work helping to clean gardens, in carpentry, as a welder, as a driver, cleaning offices, cleaning windows, anything they could offer me, I would take. Anything that could give me clean money made me very happy. I felt worthy earning good money with my hard work. My inner self was happy with any kind of job because I was doing good things; clean money was coming to my hands, and I was away from all those bad people in the streets with whom I was involved. I was away from the drunks, the drugs addicts, the gangs, danger in general. It wasn't any easy money anymore, and it was not well paid, but it was honest money, and that made me happy.

I started to have self-love, and started to appreciate myself as a person. I started to love life and started to see things differently. It was like going from darkness to light. I felt so relieved that I felt alive once again! My self-esteem started to recuperate in my inner self coming out from the hole I had been in the past two years. One job took me to another one until I got to a place where they had a huge vegetable and fruit warehouse. I started to learn how to move the pallets into the truck. I loved to see how it was possible to move thousands of pounds of vegetables and fruits that were in a box, with a tractor that got out a pallet and moved it into the right place for the truck to be loaded.

I got to love that job and I was well behaved all the time. I got in early and left last all the time. I had no where to go or no one to visit anyway, so I stayed at work the longest hours I could to earn extra money to save. I had nothing else to do but work. I wanted to save as much money as I could to do something good with that money. Because of my dedication, the administration noticed me pretty soon. I had totally forgotten to drink and drug myself as I had no one to share that with.

Early one morning, after six months of working there, the manager came early to talk with me in his office.

The warehouse head was sixty-four and was about to retire. He had worked in that place for over thirty-five years and no one was trying to replace him. He got into the company very young and enthusiastic as I was, so they noticed me to replace him. Everyone knew he was going to retire and they needed someone very dedicated to replace him. He was going to leave the company in less than a year, when I started working there. There was people that had many years working in the company, but no one wanted the full responsibility of being the head of the warehouse. So the manager saw my willingness to work hard and that I was there early and left last every day, not knowing I had no family responsibilities, and the rest of the people did have.

So when I went into his office, really nervous, with my broken English, I understood he was offering me the position of assistant of the head master of the warehouse to learn real well all the dimension of the position. I felt so enlightened by that proposition, I decided to be an excellent assistant. For the first time in my life I felt worthy, and not only to myself, but by others. I felt such a sense of internal satisfaction in my inner self, I could not stop smiling. I had never felt so good before in my life in a job. That night I could not stop smiling and feeling so good. I had came forward out of the hole I was in, and for the first time I was doing things right all by myself. People appreciated me, and I appreciated the opportunity.

Working hard to go up in the company ladder, working hard to train all the people that came and go as helpers, I was totally delighted with my brilliant future. That night, after having the offer of being the assistant of my immediate boss, made me feel the happiest man on earth. Just to think about that less than a year ago I was thinking in killing myself, this was true luck.

Getting together with people of my same age that were also wasting their lives did not help me to make good decisions. Actually, all my decisions up to this point have been bad decisions, except leaving them behind. I started to think of all the people I had drugged myself with—Chinese, black, white, Hispanic. Race, color, or background didn't matter; we were all failures trying to lower our pain by smoking pot and drinking beer.

The problem was that marijuana got into cocaine and the cocaine into crack. Those were years of darkness with no will of living. I was totally depressed and fearless of death. And because I was fearless of death, I would go deeper and deeper into that crazy life. I got into a very bad addiction that I do not know how I got out of it overnight when I saw my friend John dead. I was crazy and fearless and what I liked to play the most was the Russian roulette. I saw more than one explode their brain right in front of my eyes. I didn't care. I was dumb and numb toward life. I thought any day would be my turn and all my suffering would end, but luck was on my side, because I am telling my story.

At the time, I thought it was luck but most definitely, it was God's hand taking care of me every time. I could not see him, plus no one talked to me about Him or His love for me. But most definitely, He had rescued my life by learning about my friend's death. God was the one talking to me in the mirror of that van, but I did not recognize Him.

When I felt appreciated and worthy by the company for the first time since I got to the United States, I thought that finally my life was going to change for good. I started to connect myself with different people, honest people, working people. I met people that gave me ideas of how to come forward and ways of escalating in the corporate ladder. These were moments of clarity in my mind. And when I had those clean and clear moments in my life, inevitably I would go back to the beginning...

"Where is Maria Elena? What is she doing? Would she have a boyfriend? Or has she gotten married? How old is my daughter by now? Is it worth it, for me, to stay in this country? Is this what I really want?"

I don't have the courage to call her again, but I don't have space in my heart for anyone else, either. I just do not feel I can conquer anyone else in my life. She was so special to me and I blew it. I had not learned to fool around with women. I just can't have one night stands and use them and forget about them. That is something I just couldn't understand about all the guys that did it. I couldn't understand how women would let themselves be used either. I simply cannot see myself with anyone else in my life. I am not ready to go on with my life to find someone else, neither I am ready to call her again. I am only starting to think of me of how to become successful here to propose her again to come with me, if she is still single, of course. I am afraid of knowing if she is single or not, so I prefer not to find out.

Even though I had met new people, like me, trying to work honestly, I really do not consider myself friends with anyone. So I feel alone, but not so alone to swallow my ego to call Maria Elena and ask her to receive me back in my home country, or to propose her again to come over to live with me here.

"When I become the head master warehouse man, I will earn much more and I will be able to save more and faster to be able to bring them with me," I thought, "but that is only my dream, and it has to be hers too."

I have learned that in different places in the United States, they are having demonstrations for the United States not to get involved in the war of El Salvador, as they have just finishing the war with Vietnam and they are tired of war. I also heard news of the war getting worse and worse, and they compared both wars: Vietnam's and El Salvador's. The people, not the soldiers, are asking to not get involved since the Vietnam war brought to them too many deaths and hurt already to their American families. I wished they would get involved because then the war would end faster. The guerrilla is getting support from Russia and the army is getting some weapons and advisors from USA, but no soldiers. We were at a disadvantage.

With all this news going around, plus my ego and my pride, it did not let me think clearly to go back to look for my love. I still felt ashamed of what I had done and felt a failed person, since I was just starting to do things right. I was angry with myself for wasting all this time in the streets and waking up to do the right things up until the death of the only friend I had found. I do not understand why I did not start to do things right when I went away from my brother's house. Maybe it was because I decided to stay in the streets; and I was so vulnerable at that point that anyone who came into my life, I accepted immediately, and it was good for me since I was alone.

During this time of brightness in my mind, body and person, I saved as much as I could to go back to school to learn English formally. When I felt I had enough money saved I decided to go back to Brooklyn, but to go to school to learn English. My brother had offered that to me as soon as we met, and I had rejects stupidly, but now I was ready to learn the good English instead of only the street English. I was ready to do it on my own. Instead of sending the money to my wife and daughter, or buying something, I simply quit to learn English. I do not know what I was thinking, but I did it.

Even though I did not go back to the streets and I was not a drug addict, or at least that is what I used to think, I find myself liking to use cocaine once in a while specially on weekends. I thought I was a casual user and that was okay. I still liked to drink beer, but my favorite game was to get everyone drunk to see themselves make a full of them, plus they paid the bill. This way I spent nothing when I went out.

I consumed drug and alcohol socially. I thought I had control over it, but I could not go without it for more than a week. Cocaine is an expensive drug, so I started to mix myself with drug dealers to get a few ounces in exchange of some favors or easy jobs. There was one I had more affinity with and he was known as The Mexican who loved to give out coke. Since the money I had saved to study was getting less and less because of the cocaine usage, I got closer and closer to the Mexican to make different jobs around his house. I would paint his house, cut the grass of his huge garden, I did errands, anything he needed for a few bucks plus a few free ounces.

One day, he offered me to become his children's bodyguard, and practically their babysitter in exchange for unlimited coke and well-paid job. The only restriction was that I had to use the coke at night when I was off duty and never in front of the kids. I was delighted with the great offer since I could continue studying in the mornings while the kids were in school and since I was going to have access to the cocaine, I did not think it twice. He was a drug dealer, and I was just his employee and a user. Becoming a drug dealer was not an option, really. I did not even consider it, since I really thought of myself as a good, honest man.

I worked honestly, but I got drug from a dishonest world. I was not interested in getting involved with any of those people because somehow, I had very clear I wanted to be an honest man. Have an honest job to earn money to live honestly. Drug dealing job was not in my view of life to become successful. I could see the Mexican had a very nice house, a great car, and a great life style, but I did not ask anything. The less involved I was, the better. I was quiet, and since I was a little crazy, I had no fear of dying. I put my body in front of his children if it was necessary. I worked for more than a year with him until I got sick of being their baby sitter more so than bodyguard.

They were a couple of spoiled brats that treated me as if they owed me, so one day I got tired of them and I quit. I broke all ties with him and all compromise to be around that weird environment. I was going to miss the access to the coke, but I did not like that environment anymore. I thought it was a dangerous place to be, and I did not want to be exposed to jail anymore.

I had met other types of people, and I had learned English and somehow I learned of a job in a theatre near there. They were looking for someone to give maintenance in the theatre and provided a place to live inside the theatre. I was in charge of fixing anything that failed or got broken. Everything to do with carpentry, electricity, plumbing, anything, I had to fix it. I earned a little bit more than minimum wage, but I had a place to live so

I save paying rent. All I had to spend money in was food. They knew I was illegal and they still gave me the job since they saw my need and will to work honestly.

One day, going out to eat, I met an old friend that we called Chino (Chinese). This Chino was not the same Chino I had found in Mexico, it was another Salvadoran who was also trying to survive in the Land of Opportunity. That night, he invited me to a Halloween party the next weekend. I was bored since I did not go out with anyone so I liked the invitation. The next weekend I dressed up as a burglar and we drank and talked happily till late at night. I had months of not having such a great time. That night, we agreed to meet the next free day I had, which was Thursday.

Maria Elena was not part of my life anymore since I had years of not knowing anything about her life, but every time I felt lonely, somehow, my thoughts went back to her. I missed her and wished I had her next to me. I couldn't stop thinking about her and every time a girl came close to me it became impossible to get into a relationship. I felt attached to Maria Elena even though we had not talked all this years and the last time was a big fight.

Thursday I met with Chino to drink some beers. After a few beers, Chino got the courage to tell me, "Eddy, I am planning to do something very serious, and I would like you to be my partner."

He was very serious and continued, "You know, I always dreamed of coming to this country, but it has not being easy to live here for me. I had not found a good job, and I have no legal papers to get a good one. In El Salvador, I was in the guerrilla before running away, but with them, I planned and executed several war crimes I hated to do. I was also involved in kidnaps which was a way to finance the war. I did things I wished I would have not done. I went over the limits of my own family humble beginning after I got convinced to participate with them.

"One day, I woke up thinking that the war we were fighting had no sense for me and that was not the life I wanted for me and my family. This is why I came after the American dream. It was the only way to get away from them. I thought life was going to be different here, but here we have to go into another type of battle every day. I am desperate and I am planning a robbery that will give me enough money to share it with you and to go back home with some money for my family. This robbery is my last option to get money to go back and see what I can do honestly back home. It is not my intention to do bad things or become an expert burglar. I just want to do one. And I need someone I can trust with me, and I thought about you."

I heard everything closely and could relate to his intentions, knowing they were not completely bad since he had good reason after all. He proceeded to tell me about the whole logistics and plan around it. I was not interested because I had found a job, an honest job and did not want to go back doing wrong things. I thanked him for thinking of me, but I said no because I did not want to go back to jail. Besides, it was too risky as it involved a bank and that was way out of my type of robberies I had been involved! So I wished him luck!

"I really can't get involved Chino, I am sorry. I just assure you I will not tell any one and wish you luck and hope that you do not get trapped!"

Chino was sad (I could see it in his face); but after that, I said good-bye and never saw him again.

That night, I meditated on everything we shared with Chino and felt sorry for him. Going after a big robbery was not part of my survival plan. I continued happily working in the theatre grateful I had a decent job and a place to sleep without extra pay.

I learned all the theatre routine and the dates when they had more sales and the dates were they had bad sales. I learned when each of the employees would come over to work and where they were located at each time of the function, before, during and after the function.

I had nothing to think about, so I observed and had fun timing them and checking if they came at the same time every day. It was always the same routine. I opened and closed the place every function day. I repaired the broken chairs, ripped carpets and any problems with the toilets or sinks. I felt safe and tried to give my best to keep my job for good. Inevitably, though, Chino's conversation came up to my mind every night when everything was dark and when I was ready to go to sleep: one robbery to get enough money to go back home.

Suddenly, after several months of going back to the same thoughts, I got an intense feeling and need to know about Maria Elena and Lupita and wanted to see them again. Chino had planted a seed in my heart and mind about the idea of going back home, but with some money. I had saved some, but it was not a lot. So, one day, without thinking it further, I started to see and observe the place to start planning my own robbery in the place I worked. Low risk. I fantasized about it, but I did not want to really do it as I had everything there. I would be too foolish to do so, but in case Chino came back, I could tell him all about it so he could go ahead and do it. I observed every detailed more closely.

I just fantasized about all the possibilities and observed more so the best functions and the worst. Of course, the best were on Fridays and Saturdays. I observed other small but important details I had not seen before. I noticed that the cashier was an elderly woman who was around her seventies. It was an easy part-time job for someone who cannot get a nine-to-five job. She only came to the theatre at the times of the functions and when there was a function, otherwise she would not come.

Every day, the actors and actresses would appear during the day to practice, if needed, specially when a new function was going to be set up. The carpenters and set design people also came during the day, but the cashier, only at function dates. She was new and I had no relationship with her. I didn't want her to see me too well, just in case. I planned it for around two months, but I never got the guts to do it.

My mind was not prepared to move on to another place. I would lose everything: I would lose my job, my place to live, and a secure job, which was the most important one. I would do it if I was sure I wanted to go back home but I wasn't ready to leave this country. Everything stayed in theory and dropped the idea. I had too much to loose and wasn't ready to go back. It was not worth it.

One day, though, the manager called me to his office, which was not a usual situation. Apparently, the immigration services had been investigating in that area to detect illegal aliens and they thought it was not worth their business to get into trouble having me there. So, that day, I lost my job for no reason at all, but for not having papers to work legally. They said they were really sorry because I was a good, hard worker, but they wanted no risk. They thanked me and gave me my month salary plus two more months so I could find a place to stay. As easy as that I had no job that day. I was on the streets again.

18

The Extreme

As I lost my job in the theatre, I found myself back to the streets without a plan of what to do if I ever lost my job or planned the robbery to loose it. I got three months pay but pretty soon I had close to none. I tried to get a job, but everyone was scared of immigration and very soon I was depressed. The thought of the robbery came alive in my mind every day.

The weekend after I got fired, I had bought everything I needed in case I would have the guts someday to do it. I did not tell anyone about it. I was not willing to risk anyone, plus the money was not too much to split it! So, after reviewing all the steps and movements in my head the whole week, on Halloween weekend, a year later of that weekend I found Chino, a Saturday, face cap on, gun in my right hand, black boots and a black jacket on, I waited patiently for the right time outside the theatre. I had parked my car around the corner of the place, in an alley with an escape street. I knew exactly when all the employees would go into the theatre to be available for the audience or any detail needed inside. The cashier would stay by herself counting all the money. There was a lot of movement on the streets as people were dressed up with costumes all over the place. Inside the theatre, the attendees were also dressed up in costumes, as there was a prize for the best one. I could come in and out without been noticed.

When all the employees and attendees were inside the theatre, the cashier was left alone, she would put the money inside a security bag, and the bag into a wood box I had constructed myself. Monday was the day to take the money to the bank. She just locked it with a very weak lock. It was just symbolic, as the bag was the real security item.

As everyone was busy inside, and the cashier alone, I came in with my face covered, showed her the gun and did not talk. She was really nervous and I could see her shaking, so she just gave me the whole box because she could not find the lock key. I told her in signs not to scream or I would kill her. She gave it to me without hesitation and I left. In less than five minutes, I left the same way I entered. I went running with the box in my hand toward my car around the corner, which I had left started. The owner of a business close to the aisle, saw me running with the box and he thought that that was not normal, but never got the time to see how I left as I entered the car and accelerated really fast on the opposite side. He went for a gun and shot to the air and the cashier had pushed the emergency button, which I forgot that existed. The police was there in ten minutes or less, but by then I was next to an artificial lake where I threw out my cap and I went into another place where I threw the gun, which I never used. I used gloves so there was no way they could connect me with the robbery. This was a clue Chino gave me. Ha!

I drove south for about two hours with my heart beating to the max. I did not know what to do after this, but finally I stopped in a very empty lot. No one was chasing me. I opened the box and the bag and I counted the money. I had more than $7,000! That was a great catch! But after smiling, when I saw all the money, it hit me and I started to cry! I cried as a child analyzing what I had done. I had been capable of ignoring Chino's offer, but I had done exactly the same: a major robbery! Now I am really a burglar, a dangerous person, a very cynical person with no feelings. I couldn't believe I had crossed the line of doing something very bad. I had ignored the minor robberies as bad, since those were my drug years and I was like in a comma. But this action had no name. I thought I was a good person, with a correct heart, but obviously I wasn't.

I deserve to go to hell, I thought for the first time. I felt bad but I couldn't change what I had done. Robbing car stereos and those things were one thing, minor stuff, while I was drugged, but this… This had no name. I had done the extreme and I was not willing to go to the police to turn me in. I regret it, but not too much! I had been crazy, but not stupid!

The following day, I went back to Manhattan and rented a motel for a week. Of course, I went to look for my alcoholic and drug addict friends of the streets and joined them again drinking and smoking pot. I had to drug myself to forget what I had done. We were drinking in the car of a friend when a patrol car pulled over.

"What's your name?" they asked.

As cool as I could be, I said, "Tony."

"That is not the name of the suspect, but your description is," said the policeman. My heart accelerated, but tried to keep myself cool.

"Suspect of what?" I asked trying to look innocent.

"The theatre was robbed last Saturday," he said seriously, and in a cynic way I answered.

"I had no idea it had been robbed." And I continued drinking my beer.

"We will continue investigating, so if you are the right person, believe me, we will come after you, so watch out."

As there was no other suspect, two days later, I got caught and took me to the interrogation room. They had me there for about six hours trying to find a connection, but they could get nothing out of me. I was never going to accept what I had done. They had not found anything to accuse me so they had nothing. They had to let me go, as they could not find anything to relate me for sure. No crime gun, no accusation. One more time I had fooled the system.

Seen myself free, without thinking about it twice, I decided to go back to El Salvador to see what was going on with my wife and daughter. That was the whole reason behind the robbery anyway, and I had waited too long. Some other people had the same destiny, so we formed a group to go back to the same destiny. Four years had gone by since I left. I crossed the border with no problem with my ID. When I was back in El Salvador, I looked for Maria Elena's cousin. Since I had arrived without telling anyone and it was a surprise for him. He got so happy we went to drink to a place called La Praviana. We were drinking until we were totally wasted, something I could do very well. Around 2:00 a.m., he took me to Maria Elena's home, my home, because he had a room in that place and thought it was going to be a great idea to surprise her. As I went in, my heart almost jumped out. Everything was as when I left. In the morning I was going to surprise Maria Elena since I had asked her cousin if she was remarried and he said she was still single. He assured to me she was not even dating anyone. I sighed and my heart got happy about those news. Maria Elena was alone with my daughter, no date, no boyfriend, no husband. I wished we could go back together, without being honest about my life in the north, of course.

Around 10:00 a.m., we woke up and the cousin was the one in charge to tell her the news.

"Cousin, I have a big surprise for you," he told her with a huge smile and a suspicious face.

"Surprise?" he questioned. "What do you mean?"

"Yep…Eddy, come out. Maria Elena is out here!" he screamed.

Maria Elena opened her eyes like sunny side up eggs. She had such a surprised face, mixed with anger and shocked, all at the same time. She immediately started yelling at me with all the anger she had hidden inside her. She had become a very tough girl, her heart was a rock heart. All her sweetness I was used to were all gone. She started treating me with anger shouting as a mad, crazy person.

Trying to calm her, I said calmly and slowly, "Look, Maria Elena, I had not come to fight with you, I have only come to see you and my daughter, My Love."

Hearing all her shouting, Lupita came out to see what was happening, and I could see her from afar, and her mother shouted, "Lupita! Go back to your room, now!" and she did as her mother said.

"And how in the world can you think I will be happy to see you if you abandoned us and cut all communication years ago? I am tired of you appearing in my life out of the blue! What do you think? That I will knee on your presence and embrace you happy that you finally decided to come back? No, Eduardo, you are three years too late. You are buried for me since we last talked."

And she continued, "So get the hell out of my sight now, and leave me alone once and for all," I could sense her upset and with no option of talking to fix things with her. I blew it and that was the end of it. My intentions to come back to her disappeared in that same minute.

In that same moment, my ego and internal rage came up immediately. I just got out of my pocket an envelope with two thousand dollars I had from the robbery which I threw to her and in a very rude tone I said, "Whatever you want! I don't want anything with you anyway! I just wanted to see my daughter and brought this for her expenses and whatever she needs. Since it is impossible to talk to you, fine, I am leaving tomorrow morning! This is the last opportunity I was giving you to come over with me to a better life. Obviously this is it! Stay, I don't care, I will take Lupita with me and you can stay. She is my daughter and she must come with me!" I shouted expecting and hoping she would not give her to me as I have nowhere to take her.

"You are out of you mind, Eduardo! Get out of my life," and she pushed me out and opened the door to kick me out. So with nothing else to do, and not really wanting to fight for Guadalupe, I left making the drama that I was really hurt. I was sad we couldn't talk, but totally relieved that I was not walking out with my daughter. What was I thinking? I just wanted to make believe I was a successful person in the US without being one. I was a drunk, drug addict and now also a thief. I just wanted to make myself present and know about her marital status. I still wished to be a family again, but obviously, I had blown it.

I left happy that she was still single. It was impossible to sit down to talk because she started shouting as soon as she saw me. Maybe it was too much to wake up in her house without her knowing about it. My ego and my pride were too big because I did not accept her rejection. Besides, I was not ready to accept that I was nobody, that I was just a sad thief with no future. I could never confess this to anyone. This was my own secret until I die.

19

The Bail

With nothing to do in my country, I go back to the United States without a 'coyote' since I learned my way the first time. I took a friend, Oscar, with me. He was my childhood friend. We crossed the border with no problem at all and we go back to New York and later to New Jersey. When I was back to New Jersey, I remember again the vegetable and fruit warehouse, so I thought about going to ask for a job, even if I was not the boss anymore. When they saw me, they were happy I was back, since this was a job I left to go to study English. They congratulate me because I had learned enough English to be able to do the paperwork needed for the job. I introduce them my friend Oscar but they didn't wanted to give him a job since he knew no English at all.

To protect him, I told them that they could hire both of us or none. I was going to teach him and I made myself responsible for him. Luckily, they agreed and both of us got a job. I am so happy they received me back, and then I start thinking that instead of going for the robbery when I was fired from the job at the theatre, I should have come back to this place. But, what I really love about getting the courage to go back home, was to see my beautiful daughter, at least for a couple of seconds and from afar. I also loved to see my single wife, and probably she still is, legally anyway. At least I am sure she has not remarried.

I stopped drugging myself, but the beer is part of my social routine in the weekends. A few months after working together with Oscar, we go out to a bar of the town. I was chilling there, drinking and talking happily with other friends, when suddenly some cops come over surrounding me. I didn't know what was happening and I thought it could not be related to the robbery as that didn't happen in New Jersey. Oscar got very scared because he thought they were after the illegal people, so he got up and went to the bathroom. Oscar panicked, and he didn't want to get out of the bathroom, but they are not after the illegal, the policeman tells me, "You are arrested for not assisting to a rehab court and not paying one thousand dollars for the bail you got more than two years ago, last April."

I had not paid that bail and I had stopped going to the rehab classes because I got bored. I totally forgot about them since that was long ago and never thought I would have any consequences, as I had never had one. I did not have a chance to give any explanations, they just took me to prison and then to court. It had been a while of not doing wrong things and not having any trouble, so I had lost practice on that, plus I had a very honest job, that's why I was surprised about all this. I did not understand what was going on, and I sincerely thought my record was straight since they could prove nothing about the theatre incident and I was in the right track, working honestly without consuming drugs.

The judge tells me clearly and without further explanation that I must pay the bail or she will give me six to nine months in jail, so I could receive the training I skipped in that occasion. I really panicked because I did not wanted to go back to jail for a long period. Going in and out of prison for the minor accusations was one thing, and even a game, but going there for a long time, was another thing. Besides, I was going to loose my best job ever, now that I was doing things right.

"Mr. Jimenez, no more opportunities for you. Either you pay the bail or you go into prison for six to nine months," said the judge more serious than ever.

One thing was playing with the system and being inside jail three to four days and one very different one to be nine months locked in. I really panicked and I sword I was going to pay her, but I needed time to do so. The judge had mercy as I proved to her that I had a decent, honest job. She gave me thirty days. If I didn't pay, I was going in. If I paid, I could go to my classes outside of prison. So the classes were still a must, in or out. The big problem here was that I had not saved anything in this time working honestly. I just spent everything drinking and inviting friends to drink because I felt secured in my job and there was no need to save since I had no wife anymore and I had nothing to save for. I regret that I couldn't think further up for the future. I couldn't go to the bank and get it out. That was impossible. All I had gotten from the robbery was gone too. How dumb I had been. No dreams, no future, no need to save. I just lived day by day…Wrong way to live!

I really felt anguished and in that situation, for the first time since I left, I think of my brother Hector. In my desperation, I come over to his place in NY to ring his bell. It was not to ask for his forgiveness, it was to get the money needed. I did not think of the rudeness of our last day and all the harm I did and did not appreciate from him. I just had in mind one thing, and that was to find one thousand bucks. When he opened the door, he yelled at me,

"Who are you? I do not know you! What the f—— are you doing here? You should be ashamed to show up! You and me have nothing to talk about, I do not know you, okay? Go to hell men!" and he threw the door on my face full of hatred toward me, and I do not blame him. I was the cause for all that reaction.

I provoked him and I had never gone back to thank him for having me there when he rescued me after my first time in prison.

I did not even had time to tell him about the reason of my visit. So that day I learned that our relationship was completely broken for good. As if I didn't know that already. I don't even know how in the world could I think of visiting him for help, since I had told him I was going to come back with money and been successfull. Yeah right! I never saw him again, but later on, I learned that he had finally left his mate and got together with a girlfriend he had in his teen years long time ago. He was with her for the end of his life, as he ended up dying from a heart attack. I never asked him to forgive me, nor thanked him for the time we spent together. I regretted that deeply when I knew he died.

Oscar was my only friend, but he couldn't help me with the money since he sent, monthly most of his money to his mother, so he had nothing saved either. I was always alone in life, no one to live for, and no one in my life, and I had panic to go back to prison for a long period. I tried to get a loan from many friends with the ones I would go out and relate in my job, but no one had the money. No one wanted to help me. No one. I did not want to tell my boss because I was ashamed of the reason of the bail, and he knew nothing about my past.

In the desperation, I went to look for the Mexican guy, the one I worked for as a bodyguard for his children. I did not know if he was going to receive me or throw the door on my face like my brother, but I was willing to take the risk. I had no other alternative I could think of. I knew he managed a lot of money in cash in his house. I had seen it, without asking any questions, as I never wanted to get involved.

It was a Friday when I went to his house. As I rang the bell, he came over to open the door. When he sees me, surprised he says, "Eddy! How good to see ya! What are you doing here?"

"I need a favor, Mex. I need a thousand bucks," I tell him without hesitating. "And sincerely, I have no idea who else can help me with this one," feeling my anguish face on me.

He opens his eyes, since I never asked for big money before, and asks, "What for, man?"

"I have a bail to pay, and the judge said that if I do not pay, I go in for six to nine months, and I do not want to be locked in!" I tell him with pain in my heart and somewhat ashamed.

"Wow, I see. Bail? What have you done?"

"Old problems, man. When I used to get into trouble before working with you. And it is a bail I need to pay," I tell him without giving details.

"Right now I do not have them. But come tomorrow Saturday at two, and we will talk about it to see how can you pay back," he said with a thoughtful face. There was only five more days left for the thirty days given by the judge, so I went back the following day.

"I had being thinking about your need, Eddy, and I will not lend you the money," my heart stopped, and he continues, "I will give them to you as a pay for some jobs you can do for me. I give you a package to deliver, and you earn a thousand bucks for it," he says without hesitating and hoping I was going to immediately be part of him and his business.

"No, Juan, I can't do it like that," I tell him. "I do not want more problems in my life, I cannot work for you like that. I can paint, do your garden, or even take care of your kids again, but working for you like that is not part of my plan. All I ask for is a loan, and I will pay every two weeks part of it until I finish," I tell him and then continued as I saw his face of disappointment. "I am sorry, I should have not come. I can't, sorry. Thanks, and sorry for bothering you." I turned around to leave.

Being a drug dealer is not in me, sorry, but no thank you. I rather go to prison for six months, than for the rest of my life! I think to myself. One thing is to use drugs, and another one totally different is to completely risk my life, I think rapidly. *Nope, not for me*, I think immediately.

He stares at me with a puzzled face, and I tell him before leaving, "I rather go to prison for nine months than for the rest of my life," I manage to tell him and I am about to go into my car when Juan calls me.

"Wait, Eddy! Calm down, man. No one is going to prison, come back tomorrow and we will talk. I will lend it to you. I see you are a good man. We will see how you can pay me back tomorrow. Okay?"

My ears cannot believe what they hear. I feel a relief smile on my face. Innocently I believe in his word and on Sunday I go back, happily to pick up the money. Wednesday is my due date, and I am in the time limit by now. I ring the doorbell with my heart pounding hard. I can hear voices inside the house and I could smell a barbecue going on in that moment. I am afraid to interrupt, but I still ring the bell.

"Hi, Eddy. We are waiting for you," he says with a huge smile.

I was shocked and I tell him, "I see you are busy, I can come back later."

"No, no, come in please, don't worry, we are waiting for you" he repeats. I do not understand his welcome words. "This is the guy I had talked to you about," he says to his barbecue friends. "He is a good kid, an honest guy and I think he is perfect for the job we need," continues Juan and I don't know what he's talking about. I just think they have a good job for me.

"Nice to meet you," said the three men at the same time, and they put out their hand to shake mine, one at a time.

"I am glad you came, Juan has talked to us about you" says one of them, and I turn to Juan and he says, "Remember what I offered to you yesterday? This men and I are in this and we need a good man like you."

"No, Juan, I told you this is not for me. I do not want to get involved," I tell him honestly.

"Calm down," says another of the men.

I have noticed those men were also Mexican, like Juan, because of their accent.

"Listen," says Juan, "do me a favor, while we talk here. Go get my white truck three blocks from here. I got drunk last night and I left it in the bar you already know." He threw the keys at me. Since I know his moves since I was his bodyguard long ago, I go walking toward the bar, and I bring back to the house the pick up truck, a Ford of long bed and a huge tool box in the bed. That was weird, I thought, because it is a tool box that it is used by constructors. A toolbox that is not too common, but I ask no questions. I get in, start the truck and came back to his place and I put it inside Juan's garage.

When I am back, Juan and his friends come out and start clapping and Juan says, "See how easy it is? You just moved three hundred kilos in this moment. You have earned your thousand bucks you need, plus twelve hundred more for doing this job," and he gets out all the cash in twenties with a huge smile.

I am scared and I throw the money at him and I go out running out of his site. I go back to my apartment running away from him and all that temptation. I get to my apartment with my heart out in my hand! What did I just do? I ask myself, furiously and totally upset for my innocence in this incident. I am upset with Juan for doing this to me and fooling me. And I am more upset with myself for not taking the money from him to pay the judge. I am so frustrated and I do not want to see more. I had seen too much already and I should go far away from them I meditate.

I stay there staring at the wall, thinking of all this, but I just can't become a mule for nobody. *It is easy money, but it is also too risky*, I analyzed.

20

The Partners

At seven the next morning, Billy comes over to my apartment. Billy was a guy that I already knew and was always around Juan. He worked for him.

"Here is your money. Take it, it's yours," he says and Billy continues. "Juan says to pay your bail and to go to buy decent clothes and come over to his place to talk," and then he left. No questions, no explanations.

One more time I felt like I was in a dead end. My mind got hypnotized and without further option in my life, obediently, I went to pay the bail and buy clothes. I went to the judge with the money and told her I got a loan from a friend. She gave me the address I had to go to take the course. I had to sign in twice a week for four months. I bought two slacks, a black and a khaki, six long sleeve shirts and a blazer. I also got some underwear, a couple of ties and two pairs of shoes. It was as I was numb, hypnotized or I don't know what happened, but I did as I was told.

When I was all well dressed up, I immediately changed my mind and evil came into me. Suddenly I said to myself, *I will go into this fully but my way. This can't be too bad. I have no option and he trapped me.* It was way too easy to earn $2,200! I can earn that same amount working hard for more than eight weeks! Mmmm,

I can earn money too easily to let this opportunity slip my hands. It is not like I am robbing anything, I am doing a job.

In this precise moment, I gave into the greatest temptation of all my life. This was a turning point, and everything was going to change drastically. I could feel something big was going to happen without comprehending totally what I was getting into. I was getting my way as a narcotics dealer, and precisely something big happened in my life. I was alone in this world anyway, and no one gave a damn about me.

I arrive very well dressed and I rang the bell. Juan greeted me with a great smile since he knows my moral is gone and he wins.

"You are going to work with me, right?"

"Yeah, Juan, but we will do it my way because I will be no mule for anyone," I said taking my risk and courage to put my own rules. "If I work with you, I am risking everything. So if I am risking my life, I want fifty-fifty, or I don't go through."

"What? No, Eddy, that cannot be done," he says.

"Look Juan, if you have thought about me and put an eye on me, is because I am a street man, I have contacts and I speak English. I can access many people you can't because you speak no English. Or am I wrong?" I tell him at once. "If I am risking myself, it has to be worth it, or I leave for good. We are even now. You owe me nothing and I owe you nothing at this point. My way or nothing."

"Well, Eddy, you are asking too much," he says cautiously.

"Yeah, Juan, but I am risking everything too. I didn't want to go to jail for nine months and what you offer me I know it's jail for the rest of my life if we get caught" I say.

"Exactly, you said it, IF we get caught, but no one is getting caught here. If we do everything right as we have so far, nothing is going to happen and you will have a great life," he says totally convinced of himself. And again I repeat, "Okay, okay, but we are doing things my way, I will send other people to do the risky stuff and I can make this business grow, really grow it. I assure you I can because of all the connections I have with the drug addicts' friends, but it is fifty-fifty or nothing."

"I have never done such a business with anyone, but I think it is going to be worth taking the risk with you. We will do a lot together, you will see. Your life is about to change for ever," he said and he extends his hand to shake and says, "Done. Let's start partner," and we started talking about the business. He goes immediately explaining the details of the business. He explains everything I need to know and how it works. Where the drug is imported from and how it crosses the border, but did not go into too much details. He did not explain any names or locations. That was his part of the business. I was going to become the distribution partner. I learn some logistics and simultaneously I am thinking of possible mules. My drug addict friends are perfect and more than happy to do so. Free drug in exchange of some dirty jobs. I start seeing a world of possibilities.

I see the perfect opportunity to make easy money, but I keep my 'honest' job to have a double life and an alibi. In a couple of months, I was driving a BMW, I had a great apartment and I also get a motorcycle. My circle of friends changed. There are two other friends of Juan's that are in business with him, but no one had the same type of partnership that I have. We managed an extraordinary amount of cash and to safe keep it without suspicion; we rented what we called ghost apartments. No one lived in them, just the cash. We got to be a twelve-man team working together to move the coke. What a coincidence! Jesus had twelve disciples and we were also twelve! I became so greedy, that I decided to stop consuming it because I preferred to sell more. I was not like that the first months, I would consume more, but then, as I learned about all the different qualities we sold, I got afraid to consume the bad quality one without knowing.

I started to move around with personalities of all type. Up to that moment, I thought the addicts were only the homeless, and street people. In this new world I learned that there were a lot of artists, actors, actresses and government people who consumed it. People from the government of different levels consumed it in high quantities. I was totally surprised about it, but I couldn't care what position they had, all I wanted to do was to sell. Most bought to consume part of it right there, and others will take home part of it or sometimes all of it. I didn't care who bought, all I wanted was to sell and to expand the business. I started to get invitations to very elegant parties and that was the favorite place to sell. I started to stay in five-star hotels of the best quality, to mix myself with the type of people that came over. The parties, were totally private and you could not get in unless you could show the invitation card. Very influential people would attend these parties. I enjoyed every minute of it. It was such an extravagant life like the one you could see in the movies, but I was living it! My life had turned around in a very radical way.

A guy that as a kid was an orphan and had to go to school barefoot was now dressed in nice suits of the finest material and meeting influential people of all the jet set and the government. It was a dream come true! I owned four or five cars of the actual year of the make. I wished and had a yacht and could go on trips everywhere around the US as many times as I wanted. I was living a dream and was enjoying every minute of it. I felt totally safe and thought this life was going to go forever.

In the organized crime you can find the way to buy and to do bad things that will do well to some people, but they are illegal. You get a way of doing wrong things without being caught, fooling the government, the police, the CIA and the DEA. All of them are after us: the drug dealers, but some play games inside with us too. We bought cars and houses with fake names or names of people who were unknown, so no one could suspect on us, and as a general rule, the luxury cars were not coming around with us in our daily life, just in the jet set parties, that everyone would go in a luxury car and ours would go in as one more. We would go around in a good car, but not a luxury one, so we would not bring attention toward us. I had a personal rule of not having in my apartment or the car I was driving any type of drug or money. Nothing was kept on me or with my things. I was careful about it. I kept myself in a low scale. No product, no money in excess, anyway. I always sent others to make the dirty jobs because I did not want to put my hands into it. I was not willing to risk myself. In my apartment I never kept big amounts of money, just enough to buy the daily necessities. The ghost apartments were for the big money. No need to keep it myself.

I always had two faces. I was in the mafia of the drug dealers, but I always kept my "honest" job. After leaving the vegetable warehouse after the arrest for the bail, I got a job in the International Airport of Brooklyn. I started driving the cars that took the luggage to the airplanes, and then I learned to be an aviation mechanic. I started to learn new job skills and the people in the company observed I was a hard worker. They started to trust me and I started to ascend getting a better-paying job with more responsibilities. They all knew nothing of my dark side. As I was ascending, the better paid I got, and that gave me more opportunity to buy more drug and alcohol, according to my coworkers. I did not think on saving any money or sending some for my daughter. All was about me and my pleasures. I did not think on saving to buy my own house, or one for my wife or daughter. No, it was about me, spending money with drugs, alcohol and friends enjoying this new life.

Billy was a young man who loved to be around rich people and get his good earnings doing our dirty jobs. He felt fearless and eternal. He was the guy that came over to look for me, bringing the money Juan sent to pay the bail. He loved to go around in motorcycles and his favorite ones were the BMW and Harley. I did not trusted him too much. I thought that because he was too young, he could do something very stupid and put us into problems. I kept telling Juan not to trust him too much and to have him near but with certain limits. Four or five years had gone by since I got involved in this exotic and extravagant life, so that made us be in the DEA and CIA list. The same cops would tell us to be careful because they were following our steps. They had us in the 'most wanted' list. We did not take that seriously, since Juan had many years in this business, and I was practically the new guy. But I was the one that expanded the business ten times more. The head masters of the whole organization were delighted with my entrance to their crew. We were not worried until one day when I came out of my apartment building by the back part of it and saw a car settled there with some men inside, totally polarized, and with the engine stopped.

Without fear to die, I got my arm out and knocked the window and shouted, "What are you looking for? Get the hell out of here or I will make a fuss right now with all the people who live in this place!"

Two men were inside with some radios, as I could observe. They just turned around to see me straight to my eyes and had a surprised face as I had caught them. They left with no further say.

21

The Elderly

Somehow, I was very popular with my coworkers of my "honest" job since once in a while I would give them some free soda or buy them lunch. Besides, I always had money on me since I had a good job and no one suspected I was a dealer. I tried to be around all type of workers and tried to be a good employee, so I could always have my alibi. I did not offer anything to them.

One day, my work friends told me, "Hey Eddy, treat us for dinner tonight!"

"Sure, let's go to the local fair," I said. For me it was a joke to get out some money. I didn't have a problem if I spent it all because I knew exactly were to go to get some more.

We went to the downtown of Brooklyn. The carrousel was there, plus the bumping cars and all this type of entertaining things around the fair. It was near Christmas and all my friends had no money because they had to buy all this presents for their families. I did not have a girlfriend, or a wife, or a kid, so I had no one to buy anything for and they knew it! It didn't ever occur to me to send for my daughter either. I had taken them out of my mind. I was dead to them and they were dead to me. So I had plenty to share with my friends.

There were all this fast food trucks around and we chose a place of pizza that was very famous because they served very fast, it was good and they had great service. Everyone wanted pepperoni pizza, but I wanted only cheese pizza (a three-cheese pizza was my favorite) because I had an upset stomach. It was a small place with no tables to sit, but it had some wooden boards that were to eat standing up without any chairs. This way, more people could come to eat to that place. The height of the wooden boards was a little more than three feet and they were set between column and column. It had very vivid colors for decoration and it was a very nice looking place.

I was very distracted thinking of our next move and the logistics of it. I had gone to that place with five other men. Pretty soon, we had the pepperoni pizza and a minute later, I got my cheese personal pizza. I took it to go to serve myself some more cheese, hot pepper and other spices. My friends had gotten a table for us to stand up to eat and started to eat as soon as they got it. My friends did not use extra cheese or any of the stuff I liked.

As I was serving myself, I feel that someone touches softly my back. I turn around really fast, thinking that it could be the cops, but instead, I see this elderly man with a white long beard with the softest looking eyes. I stare at him and he looks back at me, directly to my eyes. His eyes were so angelical and I had never seen that face or look before in my life. My whole body starts shaking with his presence and I do not know what to think or say. He just sees me and he says nothing, but I feel very intensively that he is telling me with his eyes and mind: "You are forgetting were you come from, Eddy."

Immediately my eyes get watered and I turn around to get a napkin to give him my pizza and when I turn back to him, the elderly had disappeared. I go out of the place running madly behind him to find him, but I do not see him. After twenty minutes of chasing him, all puzzled I go back were my friends were standing. I ask them if they had seen the elderly man go out. They all looked at me with a face that told me they thought I was crazy or getting crazy. Finally, one said, "What elderly?"

"The one that was with me in that corner!" I tell them loosing my temper. "I swear to you that I am not hallucinating or crazy, I just saw an elder man who touched my back and as I turned around to get a napkin to give him my pizza, he disappeared on me" But they saw nothing, just my frightened face chasing nobody.

I am totally convinced today that, that day, the elderly was the Ancient of Days of the Bible. It was God trying to get my attention, and once more, I did not get it. God chooses the worst in this world to do his works, and I was more than the worst. I was a total sinner, and I did not deserve any mercy from God, the Highest God.

I did not deserve the forgiveness of my sins either. What I deserved was to go to hell the day I get killed as part of the drug mafia of this place. That is what I thought in that moment. When I saw the elderly, I felt very strongly in my heart that He was giving me one more chance. But I didn't get it, or did not want to get it. I just did not think or believe there is a God.

I ate my pizza in total silence, and I walked back to my apartment thinking of this episode. I fell on my knees and started to see my life up to that moment. I did not know how to pray or repeat any prayers, and I did not believe in God but that was a supernatural moment in my life because I felt I couldn't get up. I was literally trapped on my knees. In that same moment all desire of consuming any drug was instantly gone. I could see right before me what my life had been like- my childhood, my orphan time, my girlfriend, my daughter, my marriage, my running away, prison as I crossed the border because of my sister's declaration, all the public drinking and all the times I had gone in and out of prison, and all the problems I had had since I decided to come to this country. All the honest and dishonest jobs I had

had, the robbery, the drugs, the alcohol, the bad friendships, etc. I don't know how, but in that ecstasy I felt inside my heart that God told me directly, "Either you grab my hand now or you loose yourself forever."

After the event of the elderly man, the company I worked for had to let go many people and I was one of them, except that I got the position of "layoff," which meant they would hire me in the first opportunity they had, but, it also meant that I had no job, so I had no more of my legal job income. I had no other choice but to continue my illegal business. The elderly man comes to my mind often in those few days, but I thought it was not the right time to go ahead with His opportunity of leaving that life. I just felt it was not the right moment. Period.

God is after the lost men, the wicked, and tries to rescue them; but naturally, man continuously escapes, trying to not show himself as the sinful being he is and trying not to accept His guidance because he thinks he can manage his life better than He can. Unfortunately, too many people understand that God is trying to rescue them only when they are in the deepest place on earth.

I was one of those people. I did not learn to follow Him by revelation as He appeared to me in the mirror of that van and sending the elderly man to the pizza place. Nope. I had to be in prison, alone, to pay for all my faults. This was the only way I could understand His greatness, His love, and His fidelity and mercy for me. I could have avoided prison if and only if I had followed Him after He sent the elderly man. He gave me the opportunity, and I am sure He gives it to all the wicked and not-so-wicked people too. It is a matter of obedience, something I greatly lacked in.

22

The Two Rolexes

The incident of the car checking on me was forgotten, but the incident with the elderly made me remember it and even doubt about continuing if I was exposing myself too much. Next day I told Juan, "We have to be careful, Juan, they are after us. One of these nights I found a couple of guys monitoring my moves outside my apartment building. I went to yell at them and they left, but now, I am feeling a little uneasy about it. We have to proceed with a lot more precaution than before. It is obvious they are after us, but have not found a way to accuse us." I skipped the part about the elderly meeting incident. He is the kind of person that would not believe in such an encounter.

I would not touch the drug, I would only give orders to people willing to do such a job, and they obeyed. The DEA was after us, but they could not see the connection I had with them since I moved around with different people all the time. Instinctively I was very cautious. A few days later, Juan calls me and he tells me: Billy needs to deliver two Rolexes, which meant, two kilograms of coke of the best quality. Two Timexes were of second-best quality, but Rolex was the most expensive, most pure and best quality cocaine we had.

"Don't send Billy," I said firmly, having a hunch about it. "Don't do it. Are they paying cash or credit card?"

"Credit card."

This was our codified communication to know the needs we needed to cover, the amount of product, and how the recipients were going to pay. Paying with credit card meant that we give the product and they pay later. When we delivered on credit card, we gave the product to a small or medium dealer, and they would sell it for a profit by ounces and then he or she would pay back. We never talked about kilograms, grams or anything that would put us in the spot. We talked about watches, shoes, slacks, shirts. We knew exactly what it meant. Two kilograms were two watches. Two grams were two pairs of shoes. Half a kilogram was a pair of slacks or a shirt. The quality was depending of the make of the things mentioned: Rolex watch, Pierre Cardin shirt or slacks, and Florsheim shoes were first class; Timex, Levis, and Payless were second quality. Pay cash or credit card was receiving the money instantly or waiting a week for the medium dealer to sell. The direct consumer would pay cash.

We were partners, but he did not do as I said. He went ahead and took the risk. He sent Billy to do the delivery in his motorcycle to a car shop out of the city in next town. It was a twenty-five–minute trip. After setting things with Billy, he called me to let me know what he had decided. I got pissed off because I felt that it was a set up. Billy was too young and too weak to keep huge secrets and with the minimum pressure, I was sure he was going to confess everything and everyone involved. Juan gave me the address and I jumped in my car and followed him furiously to observe from the distance. Since I was driving a car and he was going in a motorcycle, I got there just on time to observe the delivery. I was a block away, but could see clearly everything going on. I felt in a movie watching everything. Billy delivers the product in a backpack. Two young men receive it, but I do not recognize any of them as part of our small dealers. They are traveling in a car, but could not see the plate. They shake hands, get into the car, and each left opposite ways. They both leave the place and I stay observing if something suspicious happens. I was a nervous wreck and my heart was pounding real hard. I could just feel disaster coming up any minute. Nothing happened. I stayed forty-five minutes and nothing happened. Delivery was made around 10:00 a.m. I left near 11 and went home to prepare lunch and rest for a while. I had a party at 7:00 p.m.

Nothing happened, and I felt like a fool. I was the paranoid. At around 4:00 p.m., the phone rang, and the worst news came from the other end of the phone.

"They caught the two guys with two Rolexes," said Juan.

"You are so stupid, man! I told you! If you ever listen to me this wouldn't happen! I had the hunch and I could feel it!" I shouted.

We insulted each other and shouted things to each other for a while until I stop and told him, "You are such an idiot! Now I will have to do this for you! Listen to me carefully. Get the hell out of there you and your family, jump the gate of your neighbor, and leave. Go away now! Go to México, and I will go to your house. Surely they are on their way! I will be the bait but save your family. Go away. I am single and have no one, so I better go to jail and save you and your family. Your kids do not deserve seeing you in prison. Go! Go now! And if I do not get caught I will continue with the business, if not, you do it later! But go!"

I got into the shower to get a quick one since I was about to become the hero of the movie. I got my old car and went to the nice neighborhood to be the bait as I had said. I knew what I was exposing myself to, but I just had no fear of anything. I wanted to save my friend and his family. His wife and kids had nothing to pay for. I just thought I was immune because I had never touched any drug, or kept any of it in my apartment. They couldn't accuse me, I thought. The beautiful house that Juan had was in Redwood City, a private place and I just went around in a matter-of-fact face, in my old car. One of the men recognizes me and they follow me, block the road and catch me. They take me out of the car and hit me and start asking me questions later.

A group of cops go to check my car and open all compartments and doors and every corner of it, thinking I was stupid enough to carry some drug with me.

I laugh and tell them cynically, "I don't know what you are looking for, you are wrong with me. I have nothing, who do you think I am? I was just going through."

They hit me again because I was mocking them and I fall to the floor. After looking into the car, they find nothing, of course, and they pull me up and push me into the patrol car. They drive to the front of the beautiful house. They pull me out and push me to the front so I ring the bell. I did not want to ring the bell, but they hit my ribs. So I am forced to ring the bell. We had a secret sound we touched but I just ring it as a normal person. Silence. I ring the bell again. Total silence. I think, *I am glad Juan did as I said and left.*

"See?" I turn around to the cops. "There is no one home. What are we doing here anyway?"

"Ring again and if no one answers, we will put down the door ourselves," they pressured. So I ring again, and to my surprise, I hear a men's voice on the other side: "Who is it?" and Juan opens the door.

Oh no! I thought. *How stupid is this man!* Then they pushed me immediately inside the house. They proceed tying us both in the kitchen, on the floor face to face.

"Who is this guy?" they asked Juan pointing at me.

With my lips I say, "Don't say anything or I kill you!" as I had changed my mind of defending him for staying around.

"He is a guy who helps me with some jobs around the house" he says, knowing I was totally upset.

The cops had asked for a search warrant, but before it gets there, they start going around the house looking for some evidence to take us both. My heart is to the max. Juan tells me with his lips that he still has one million bucks and a kilogram in his room. He also has some automatic weapons upstairs. I told him never to keep anything in the house, but as always, he was too stubborn and always did what he wanted and thought he was never going to be caught. We could hear them turning around the beds, opening the closets' doors, the drawers, they opened and closed doors, we could hear all the movement that was going on upstairs. The search warrant was not there yet, so they were doing something illegal, but it was no moment to defend us. He was so stupid that he couldn't even hide well enough those things. They found everything, very fast.

"If you talk, I kill you and your family," I repeatedly told him with my lips in silence.

Three and a half hours later, after checking every corner of the house and having us sitting on the floor well tide, a detective comes over with the warrant, and as soon as he sees me he asks, "And who is this?" pointing at me. With that I knew they were not looking for me, and had no idea who I was. I was saved! Juan was going in, but I was saved (apparently).

"Don't know, he is just close to Juan, and he says he is a handyman for him doing some jobs around the house. We checked him and he has nothing in his car or apartment. He is clean," the DEA man tells the detective.

And he continues, "We checked on Juan too, and we did not find anything in the house. They are both clean. No illicit possessions."

"Apparently you are nobody, we checked on you, but we want to know what were you doing around here being a no body," says the DEA's guy. I kept silent. They let me go, and I went fast to the apartment to hide and think what to do. I didn't understand what happened there because they found everything and then they denied finding anything. They arrested him, because he was in the list of people they were looking for drug dealing. They arrested him and the DEA guys kept the kilogram, the million bucks and the weapons, as easy as that. The detective just believed them, and asked no further questions. He probably got a part of the findings. That is my conclusion because they denied it all.

Now I can see the supernatural protection I got from the Lord. It was a miracle that I wasn't caught that day. In that moment, I thought it was pure luck because I was so smart by keeping myself clean, but it was God's hand protecting me. Up to that point, I had no idea of His power covering me to protect me. I did not even think of Him or His existence. He gave me free will, and I chose the wrong roads—the wide road for the lost.

I thought I was going to be punished and sent to jail, but I still got saved. Once more, I was free to correct my destiny. I didn't understand why I was still free and was confused as to what to do with my life. You can think that with this event, I would just render myself to God, but that didn't happen. My heart became harder, just like the Pharaoh with the plagues. I just got stronger to continue the business in my own force, doing the wrong day after day.

23

The Second Trip

As soon as I was free, I went to my apartment to think. I stayed inside for three full days, thinking, analyzing my possibilities, trying to figure out what was my next move. Surely, the detectives were outside and intercepting my phone calls, so I kept myself still. I slept, rested, and just kept myself entertained watching TV, the news and anything that could entertain me. I analyzed all the possible scenarios about what had happened. They could catch all thirteen of us: me and the twelve that worked for me. All of us at the same time.

The truth is that if one talks, we all go in, I thought. After three days there, I thought they were gone, so I came out. I got into a very old car that was there and went to a public phone to call Billy to know if he was fine, out and alive. Billy did not answered. I called and called until he picked up. He was afraid to answer, but he finally did. Real fast we agreed to meet in an abandoned building in the downtown. We talked about what happened and it was a whole plan to get Juan. They were not interested on Billy, because they were after the boss. Exactly what I had suspected.

At midnight, we went to an apartment on the other side of the city were we had two million dollars saved up. I took a million to take to the major boss in Mexico, as that was the money Juan was supposed to deliver the next day, and that is why he had that money in the house. I gave some to Billy and I took some more for myself and told him to disappear immediately from our staff. I never heard of Billy again. What I did learn was that at the same time they got Juan, they also got a black guy and a Chinese guy, who I did not know their names but were also in the business indirectly with us. As for now, I was clean and needed to keep myself as such.

I did not want to stay in New York, so I left for Mexico looking for the major bosses, the ones that deliver us the drug. Asking around, I finally found them. They had never seen me because Juan was the connection for Mexico and I was the distributor in U.S.A. Juan was in charge to pass the product from Mexico to the U.S.A. Juan travelled often to México to meet with them and he was very reserved about the subject. It was his part and no one else needed to be involved. I knew very little about them, but I knew that they were in Ciudad Juarez, the same city that saw me living for several months before crossing the border for the first time.

So since I had lived there, I knew a few dark places around so I started my journey exactly in those places. When I finally found them, one of them came out to meet me and see our mutual faces and asked, "And who are you men?"

"I'm Eddy, Juan's partner."

"You have guts to come here to look for us men. You know our business is with Juan and no one else."

"Well, yeah, but they caught Juan, so I came to pay everything he owed you from the last shipment. Here is your money. Take it, it belongs to you." I answered coldly, trying to keep myself cool, but I was dying inside.

"Well, well, it seems you are a very 'honest' drug dealer! Hahahaha!" And he laughed out loud.

"Thanks for your honesty. That makes you part of our trusted team."

"Thanks, but this is it for me," I said.

"Stop, stop, stop right there, man. You just can't get out just like that. You've seen my face and I had seen yours. You belong to us. The most stupid thing you had done in your life is to come look for us face to face. I want you to know we will be looking after you, we will know where to look for you and how to find you. You belong to us, you are simply ours and we will know exactly where to look for you. You are our contact for the north now. We will know where to find you if you try to escape. So don't ever think you can get out of this life," he said seriously.

I got afraid. I thought that giving their money back I was free to leave, but I was wrong. The one that goes into the drug Mob goes out dead or by getting caught and going to prison. That is the risk and I wasn't really sure, or maybe didn't want to accept it.

I was already in Mexico and had some money—more than a couple of thousands—on me, so I decided to go back to El Salvador. As I always did, when I saw myself into problems, I thought about my wife and daughter, and I still had no normal life yet, and with that, nothing to offer them. I continued being a malefactor good for nothing man But they need not to know. It was 1991 and I was thirty years old. War was still going on, and nobody could see an end to it. The president was Alfredo Cristiani who had won in 1989 after Napoleon Duarte. Cristiani was a businessman and the first president for the new party ARENA.

On my way back to El Salvador, I thought to come over to my wife's house in a different way. I am hoping that she is still single and we can talk this time to go back together, start all over again so I can run away from the Mob, without her knowing about it, of course. If that didn't work out, I will have to ask for the divorce so I can let her free and I get the freedom to find someone else. I had to define my personal life. I needed to be free or back with her. Either way was fine with me, but I needed to know were I was standing. As of this point, I really do not know if I am married or a divorced man, since the last time we shouted at each other, so it is going to be good to find out.

If I am not mistaken, Guadalupe is about to turn sixteen, and I felt a deep need to see her again. I had missed all her growing-up years and I wanted to give her, her sweet sixteenth present since I did not know if I was staying or leaving. I was in a confusion stage. I was just going back home as a robot. I was lost in the world without a plan for my life, as usual. I wanted my "wife" to define it. Selfish but true.

This encounter was much better. We had the opportunity to talk instead of yelling at each other. I hoped with all my heart that she would forgive me and beg me to stay next to her. This was the perfect way to get away from the compromise with the head of the drug dealing organization. Nevertheless, the words of the Mexican were in my mind all day long and couldn't forget them. So I just knew in my mind, that I had come to say good-bye for good because it was not right that I expose them and make the mobs come after me. This was going to be the last time that I would come to look for them and I just knew it was a good-bye meeting. Even if I had the least possibility to stay, it was not right to do so.

I can't fool myself and her at the same time. They did not deserve having me around. Still, I needed to tell her I still loved her and to forgive me the abandonment I put her through, but nothing about it came out of my mouth. To honor Juan and my "clean" reputation in the organization, I had to go back and become the leader to continue the business. I was the clean guy for the distribution chain. So my heart wanted to stay with her and run away from trouble, but my head told me I had the moral responsibility to continue as the head of everyone in our side of the country.

In conclusion, I just saw her one day, and it was only after the night before I went out to get wasted to find the courage to go to her house. I gave her some money for Guadalupe's birthday or graduation, whatever she decided. When I was in front of Maria Elena, I did not even have the courage of asking for Guadalupe to get a hug and kiss from her for the last time. I just felt in my heart that I was saying good-bye to this world. Becoming the Leader, the head of the organization, made me become the most wanted head for the DEA and I knew exactly what it meant. I was going to fight for my life as long as I didn't go to jail. I rather die than going in.

This is why I felt I was saying good-bye. I did not have the courage to ask for her forgiveness. We chatted about everything and nothing. I could tell in her words and facial expression that she was resented with me. Maybe she wished too that I would come back for good inside her heart, but she was resented and would never admit it, or tell me about it. I didn't have the courage to ask if we were already divorced either. I was so stupid. I just love her too much and know she does not deserve my troubles. So I managed to tell her, "I just came to do any paperwork you need to get the divorce and let you free once and for all. I also wanted to give you the money for our daughter's sixteenth birthday or her graduation, whatever you need."

"I have not asked for anything, Eddy, so you can keep your money," she answered in a strangled voice and said nothing more. She did not mentioned anything about the divorce, so I assumed it was done.

"Whatever you want, but this is not for you. It's for Guadalupe. Please do me a favor and give it to her on my name."

"Get the hell out of my life! I buried you long time ago!" she said and with that she got the envelop, turned around and left. I made her believe I was sad, and hurt and my ego thought I had left behind a success image so she could regret it some day. I was well dressed with a very fine suit just to make believe what I was not. She rejected me anyway, and I didn't blame her. I had left and of course she was resented.

Maria Elena had changed. She was another person, she had a heart made of stone. We had both changed. I couldn't judge her for that. I was wicked and her...I don't know, but I perceived her very different from what I remembered before leaving. Even though we did not yell at each other this time, we had stopped being the great couple of our teen years.

Deep inside I wished she would beg me to stay, but I knew that was just a wishful thinking and was never going to happen. We were different, and we didn't know each other any more. We didn't belong to each other anymore.

I knew I was a dead man, but for no reason I had to tell her what my business was about. She just saw me well dressed and looked like a very successful man, but she did not ask, and I did not say anything either. I had no obligation of telling her anything. I was ready to go back.

I went back in an airplane, because, even though I was in wrong steps, I knew about a program in which the U.S.A. had approved amnesty to all Salvadorans who lived in the United Stated in 1983 and I filled in a formed and I became a resident. So I went back as if this was part of my daily life. Not impressed by a plane any more, but enjoying the flight back. I came back with my legal and right name, who was not looked for by the police. I came back through Houston. My Mob name was looked for, but my real name was not. I used for the mob my dead brother's name, Guillermo.

Juan is in prison, and I have no other option but to continue the business, I thought. *I will continue the business, but this time, I will not use any drug. I will only distribute it.*

I called Juan's cousin, whom I had not spoken to in several months.

"We are in a very bad shape. They got five more, so now there are six in, counting Juan. Billy is still running away, but you are in the black list, man." He continued, "so get the hell out of this place," so I went to New Jersey, close to the border with New York.

I thought I was far away enough from Manhattan, and I went out to look for a job again. I had a green card for being resident, so it was easy to get a job. I got hired in a company who serviced airplanes. I gave my real name for this job, and I became a mechanic again. I had experience and they appreciated that immediately. I was happy that no one knew me in that place, so I thought it was time to settle down once and for all. Since Juan's cousin had sent me away from the business, it was time to do things right this time. I thought of working hard for six months, save as much as possible, and then get a credit to buy a car or an apartment of my own. I wanted to do things right for the first time because if I did them right, maybe Maria Elena could send my daughter to study English and the university in this country, since she was about to graduate from High School. I perceived Maria Elena as a very tough person, but Guadalupe was about to turn eighteen in less than a year and she could decide for herself. I needed to be a decent person and a successful one.

So exactly after six months, I decided to go to an office who helped put together all the paperwork to go to the bank to get a loan. The first thing I wanted to buy was a car since all the good cars I had, stayed in Manhattan after Juan's arrest.

It was a glass office building, typically full of offices. It had many cubicles and a visit chair in every cubicle. I had grown my mustard and beard, I had promised I was not going to shave until I got a new opportunity to start all over again with my "new identity." It was not really new, it was my real identity, simply the legal one. A beautiful thin lady was the one looking after my papers. She had brown eyes and light skin, and she reminded me of my wife as they had the same build.

She asked what was the loan for and I said that it was to buy a used car. She asks my full name, my SSN, my job site, phone numbers, all the things that normally are asked for a loan.

Suddenly, I hear a guy that laughed out loud in the cubicle that was on our back. We could not see each other, but my heart jumps out. I just have the hunch that I know that laughter. It put me in alert while I was trying to fill in the paper with all my real data. I become a little distracted from the process and all my happiness, went away. I stood up cautiously to see who was the laughing man, and I spot the face of the same guy that Billy had given the two kilos. He saw me, but I am hoping that with my beard and mustache he does not recognize me. I cannot believe what I just saw. I finish filling in the papers as fast as I could and without looking back, I leave the place, but with his face in my mind. *Is it possible that he is an undercover agent?*

I went directly to my apartment and started thinking that I was looking more than I had to. I was imagining that the guy was looking for me, when I was really working very nicely in this new job away from all the bad people of the Mob. No one knows me in New Jersey, and I had not offered any drug, neither consumed it, so I conclude it is my imagination. I have a new life with a purpose set in my mind and that is to bring my daughter to this country so she can have better opportunities than I had. I am doing everything legally now, and I have nothing to worry about. So I went to sleep setting the alarm for 4:00 a.m. as my entry time was 5:00 a.m.

I could hardly sleep so I got up and got ready early in the morning arriving at the job site at 4:30 a.m. to set up the coffee for everyone. I loved to serve them like that and everyone liked to come in to work with the coffee ready.

When the coffee was ready and I was serving my first mug of coffee, I see a whole squad of the DEA people coming toward our working area. They all surrounded me to get me. The same guy that long ago told me to get a good lawyer because they will be looking for me, was the one that headed the people.

"You are wrong with me, man. You have nothing. What are you accusing me of?," I tell him coldly. My coworkers were coming in at the same time the squad was there, and they were looking at me astonished. They saw the whole show, and one of them says, "What are you accusing him of? He is a great fella!"

"You have the right to keep silent and everything you say can be used against you," says the cop, just like in the movies.

"You have nothing, what are you accusing me of?" I repeated, turning my face toward my mates. They had a surprised face I had never seen before. They were scared thinking they did not know who they had been working with.

I wanted to look innocent, but when I said, "You have nothing," I was basically admitting that they were looking for something I knew about. *Shoot!*

They take me into the police car immediately with no further explanation and took me to the police office where they had an interrogation room. I know there is a glass where they are observing me and all my body language. I had learned to be sarcastic, cold and to show no fear. They tell me that Juan had talked already and had said I was his right hand. I know they push you putting words on the other part to make believe they had talked. I just don't think he has said anything because his family is in danger if he does. They push when they are suspicious about something, but it is not necessarily true. I know all the tricks, I have been in and out of prison. I have seen movies. They are never sure when they push like this. I deny all relationship with Juan. I keep saying that all I did is maintenance for his house. What I used to do the first time I worked for him, so I knew exactly what to say. I deny everything they try to link me with. I try to keep myself serious and firm on my words. I did not want to be locked in.

"You will have twenty years because we have the two kilos of proof!" they tell me, to pressure me. "Your time can be less if you collaborate with us and help us around" they added.

Right there and then I knew they had nothing concrete in this case and could not link me with Juan for sure. If the others had talked about me, I did not know, but I was there to deny everything. I was not getting locked in if there were no proofs against me. The two kilos were given by Billy, I was not involved and they knew it. I was in Juan's house when they stole one kilo, and a million dollars, so I had that against them.

"You have nothing!" I said laughing at them. "Here the criminals are you guys. You guys are first class thieves. You stole everything that Juan had in his house, you cannot deny that or do you want me to specify what you stole? I know they are behind that mirror and I can talk away." I said. "You have nothing to accuse me about. So let me go I have a decent job and have things to do. You cannot find anything because I was just a simple employee."

Since they kept silent, I continued and talked about their crime: "You have nothing, and I know that you know that you stole a million bucks, a kilo of coke and all that armament you took. I was there, I knew what he had because Juan confessed it to me when we were at the kitchen tied and seated on the floor. You got Juan and I was free, as I was innocent then as I am now." They knew I was saying the truth and now that was my best card as I knew someone was recording everything behind the window. Their bosses will ask about it and now they were in trouble. This are the same guys that let me go from Juan's house.

"You've got what you have. Nothing! You are trying to guess to accuse me for being in the wrong place at the wrong time." I said.

They could not get anything else from me and I could see their frustration faces.

"I don't know why you have me here. I need to go back to work, so let me go," I insisted one more time.

Six to seven hours lasted the session. I was decided to win and to play with the authority, as they had too.

They locked me in anyway, even though they did not have any proofs against me. Between trial and trial, interrogation and interrogation, six to seven months went by and we had no sentence, no final verdict. Five out of the twelve where still running away without being caught, and apparently, Billy was one of them.

If Billy was caught, surely he would cry out everything, but his name was never mentioned. He was the weakest of all and I still had no clue where he was. Hopefully he left toward Mexico, but I never knew.

In those six or seven months, they put all seven of us front to front to break up our psychology and they would say something like "He says you did so and so," and they did that backward too. We only looked at each other without speaking up. With our eyes, we would affirm our honor pact of not talking about each other. This pact is very important and is part of the honor code of the mob. You cannot trust anybody, but at the same time, we all need each other. The code says that if one is caught, he goes alone to prison. No testifying against anyone else. If you talk against someone else, I could get killed for talking against one of us. It is a matter of life in jail—death out of it or get killed anyway if you talk more than you should. Period.

24

The Verdict

We all went to court simultaneously. Hudge, Mike, Lee, Juan, another Salvadoran, two more and me. Juan was the first one to be judged, and when I hear his verdict, I know he has negotiated in exchange of giving information. He is the only one that can involve me as no one else has seen me before. Every accusation he accepts and gives info about, gets in exchange less years. The maximum is twenty years and he gets ten. After his verdict, he is taken away. In that very moment, I interrupt the Judge and I say, "Judge, I have something to say to Mister Juan."

And without waiting for his consent, I yelled at him, "Si abrís la boca Juan te mataré a vos y a tu familia! Te lo juro por mi vida! te voy a matar donde te encuentre! Ya no me importa la vida!" (If you open your mouth, Juan, I will kill you and all your family! I swear it on my life! I will kill you, wherever I find you! I can care less about my life!)

I never thought about any consequences saying that in front of everyone. Since I yelled in Spanish, I do not know if someone else understood or if someone translated to the Judge, but I could feel my face hot of anger. Everyone was disturb by my screaming and a fuss was made inside court. They took him out and he saw me with a panicked face and then he put his face down to go out without any resistance. For his body language I knew he had involved me without any proofs other than his word. And I knew I was going in, but didn't know how long. When everyone calmed down, the judge continued with the sentence of the rest. Some were given five years, others three, depending on the involvement, what they had admitted, and negotiated while in captivity before the trial. Most were only mules and had spoken out. Juan and I were something else, the leaders, the owners of the business but I didn't know how much anyone else had talked about me.

I could see everyone had given names, addresses and places we used to deliver and that is how they caught seven of us. No one wanted to go in by themselves. The Mob code had being broken. It was just a matter of time when the Mob was going to come after us when we finish our sentence.

I insisted they had no proof against me. I knew they had non, only what others had spoken about me and against me.

"Tell me what you have against me. Give me the evidence, real evidence of what you are accusing me of," I would tell them, "because I don't know why I am here."

I was always playing low key without having too much money on me, and never a gram of coke in my car, but everyone else, they consumed all the time and carried the product around in the cars and held an amount in their houses, without fear, until they got caught.

"Everyone have accepted what they had done and your are the only one that does not accept the bad that you have done," said the lawyers to me. It was a word game on the table. No evidence, just words. They always told me I deserved twenty years for denying all involvement and not declaring myself guilty. I was fearless and was not willing to admit anything.

I saw that they condemn Juan to ten years and he was sent to a State prison. I had been in a state prison many times when I would spend the weekend for drinking in public places and when I went to prison because of the kidnapping accusation. I had seen in that place many crimes, assassinations, rape, and a lot of horrible things, so I pitied him and knew I was not going there. The other Salvadoran got eight years and the rest five and three.

When they got to my verdict, it said: "Eduardo Antonio Jimenez Case # 29-5460 has being found guilty of conspiracy and intent of possession and distribution of cocaine. Offense level: 29. Level of imprisonment is of 121 months".

With that said, I got ten years because they had no physical proof, but because of the level of the offense, the sentence was for a federal prison, which are very different than the State prisons. The federal prison are of maximum security. They believe me dangerous because I deny giving any info and never accepted anything. Besides, I was rude and cynical and yelled at Juan, which gave them evidence. My days on the street as a child was brought out and my rage and internal anger flourished in this process. My anger toward Juan, my loneliness, my foolishness and my ego did not let me show any sensitivity toward the whole process. I didn't care and I felt I had won since they could not put me in for twenty years. I felt superman. I didn't know what was waiting for me in that prison, as I had never visited them before. I was ready for my new adventure. Up to this point, I did not know they were of maximum security.

Afterward, I learned that in the federal prisons, there is no room for lowering the sentence for behaving well. We have to finish all the time given in the Verdict. I already had a sentence given, and there was no going back. I had no choice but to accept, without further do. I had no choice but to accept, and I could not accuse anyone for my decisions. As I thought I was very macho, and that I had ethic in this illegal business, which its nonsense, but that is how I felt. I felt with much bitterness and hatred and anger in my heart against the seven sentenced before I was, but more so toward Juan who did not talked me out of this. I saved his family on time before they discovered the million bucks and the kilo in his house, but he didn't want to go in by himself. He wanted revenge. That rage I had since my childhood years became stronger and well set in my heart. I even felt inside I was shaking with all the hatred inside. I was furious with everyone, with Juan, with the world, with life, with God, and with myself.

I am taken back to the county jail temporarily, where I had been in the whole process of the questioning before the judgment. They had to prepare my transfer to the Federal prison.

To be able to transfer me, there is a lot of paperwork and protocols to follow specially for the prison assigned. Besides, the nearest prison is located in New Jersey and the Verdict was in Brooklyn. Since the arrest up to the transfer to the Federal prison, nine months had gone by. How ironic, nine months I did not want to go to prison instead of the bail that put me into all this mess. It has felt like a never ending process. I thought nine months was too long, and just to transfer me to the place I will live my next nine years is the time that I refused to complete. How dumb. I have been so stupid! This is the worst thing I will have to do for the next decade! My best decision ever. Yeah right!

"If I hadn't paid the bail, I would have suffered nine months inside prison and back to the streets free, to find a decent job. I wouldn't be waiting my transfer to the federal prison, I would be waiting for my daughter to come over by my side!" I would, I think, but, ' I would' does not exist. Playing to go in and out of prison for light accusations have finished in a loooong sentence, a one that I cannot visualize the end of. I can't imagine what will I do all that time in the same place without freedom to go around.

On my transfer day, I got to thinking, *If I had made better decisions, I would not be here. But I became greedy, loved being rich, the fast richness I never could dream about. I loved the high-class life, the new "friends," the nice cars, the beautiful ladies, the power I felt. I just thought I was invincible and that I was never going to be caught,* I kept thinking to myself. I do not even know why I am thinking all this if there is nothing I can do to bring back time. Nothing to do, but to be locked in for ten years, and this is just the beginning.

I wake up of my thoughts and I am finally arriving at the New Jersey federal prison. I have chains around my waist, my feet and my handcuffs with chains in my hands. I get into the procedure of all prisons. They unlocked the chains, take off my clothes for the checkup. They take me to shower to check me up and to see if I have a tattoo or any special natural sign on my body, or something hidden. No shyness is welcomed. They touch me and see me. I have no choice. First time I am checked this way. They give me orange cloth with the emblem of the new prison. They put back all chains and handcuffs to take me to the pictures session. Front picture, right side, left side, handprints, the whole process. I have all the chains as if I am an assassin, someone to be careful about. I feel bad they treat me like such. I had never killed anyone. More than nine hours had gone by since I left Manhattan.

After that process of the pictures and handprints, they take me to a small room. It is an isolation cell. They call it the adaptation cell. I do not know why they call it like that, but I don't fight anymore. There is nothing to do, I just obey like a robot. The custodies do not know anything about me. They do not know if I am violent, dangerous, a rapist, an assassin, nothing so far. Since I am in the maximum security place, they do not know what to expect from me, but I am calm and humble in a way. I was so aggressive in the court, even threatening Juan, that I couldn't believe my calmness. I guess I just gave up. Because they had nothing in concrete about me, they just couldn't define my behavior, so just in case, they sent me there. Or that is what I thought anyway. They had the order to send me to the adaptation cell for thirty days.

I later learned that they cannot imprison two of the same band in the same place, they have to go to different prisons even if that means going to a different state or different cities. We were seven, so they had to find seven different locations. We could not get in touch with each other. I do not know if they chose this one for me because they ran out of options or because they really thought I was dangerous. Of course, I did not believe I was dangerous, since I was only the leader, never killed anyone.

I discovered that is it also prohibited writing letters between interns, and we did not have to know where anyone of the group was. We are permitted to receive letters from outside, though, and also I could write to anyone that was outside prison. Of course, they check everything before turning in the letters. There is no privacy. That is finished, gone. I realize in that moment that I was never going to receive a letter since there was no one that wanted to keep in touch with me. I had no girlfriend. My ex-wife had no idea about me. My brothers are both dead to me since I fought with the only one I had left. My parents are gone. My half sister is a devil. My street friends will never write. No family, no friends, no kids, no one. Again, it hit me how lonely my life is. Again and again I find myself alone. The only true loves of my life have being Maria Elena and Guadalupe and they had absolutely no clue about me. I had never written to them, neither had ever sent any money to them, not even when I had lots of it while working with the Mob. This was no time to write to them for the first time either. *What a loser!*

I am a loser and they shall never find out. It is better they know nothing of me. They won't suffer for me, and I don't suffer for them. If I die here, so be it! They give me my ID, a pair of shoes, a T-shirt, underwear, an orange jumpsuit, typical of prison, and they take me to the isolation cell assigned. There is a stainless Steel bed without sheets. That is the first thing I observe. I am in prison and there is nothing I can do any more but to render myself to my new life, so I do not resist myself to nothing. There is nothing I can do anyway, but to learn and follow the system.

My life has ended and I will die here, I think.

I do not realize what is happening and what will I go through in the next thirty days until the door is closed. The cell is dark. There is a sixty-watt lightbulb and a little closed window at the top. There is an air conditioner and is very cold, and I have nothing to cover myself with. An armored door is my company, with a small hole in the bottom to let me in the food, I assume. The room is small, around 2 meters by 2.50 meters. (around 6 and a half feet by 8 feet) To get to this point, ten hours had gone by since my process began. I am really hungry and thirsty and very tired, but I got nothing offered to lower my hunger. I fall asleep on an empty stomach. I assume that letting me hungry is part of the process. I have no right to ask for any food, and I didn't ask for anything either. I kept silence.

25

The Isolation Cell

When they closed the door, I start to observe in detail what I have inside the cell. There is a toilet, a shower with no curtain, a stainless steal bed, and that is it. I am isolated with no privilege to talk to anyone but myself. Not even to the guard outside. I am with my self and no more. This isolation time is a method to break psychologically and emotionally any evil person to soften his heart and interior being. I have gotten there with the handcuffs and the chains around my waist, feet and hands. They take them off as I enter the little room. An absolute silence is my company.

As I observed and realized my situation after the door is closed I yelled at myself, "Congratulations, Eddy! This is how a criminal graduates, and you graduated with honors!" I threw myself on the floor to cry. My spirit finally breaks. I cried and cried and wiped of internal hurt. I had gotten to the lowest anyone can be. I just can't hold myself anymore. While I was agonizing and crying, my mind brings me back through all my life. All the nice things of my childhood and youth. I thought about my mother, that I knew for such a short time and I thought about my dad and how ashamed he would be of his youngest son. I thought of the day that my brother died and when my dad died. I thought of all that I had to go through to survive my childhood years and all the not so nice things I did while growing up. I remembered the day

I stole the chickens. That episode had taught me to be honest, and I had really repented of doing what I had done. *How did I get here?*

I thought about my sister rescuing me when I was left alone as an orphan and how good she used to be, and how evil she was at the same time. I thought about Maria Elena and her beauty and noble heart.

"My princess, Guadalupe! How could I leave them? What was the point? To end up like this?" (I am talking to myself here.) "She doesn't deserve a father like me!"

I do not want her to know how bad I have being. She would never be able to love me, forgive me, or even like me in any way. The relationship with Maria Elena and her birth was the only good thoughts I could ever have in my mind.

"How did I end up here after I left her? When did my mind got hypnotized with the idea of a better future? I was so happy with a family of my own! I lost the only best thing I ever had! How stupid I have been. All started to go after the American dream and to be a successful man, which I never was. What a waste I am!"

The only good thing I have ever done was to fall in love with Maria Elena. That was such a pure and innocent love that we lived together and has been the best that ever happened to me, I thought. *My only dream was to have a successful life in this country, to give a better future to them. And now, I find myself isolated, alone, and with nothing in my hands*, I thought while crying out loud whipping and meditating to myself. I yelled at myself and cried. I couldn't stop crying. No one could listen to me anyway. This was the lowest I could be and I was getting out all my hurt, all my anger from within. Going in and out of prison for drinking in public was just a big joke and a game to break the system. But this is another story. This is totally serious and there was no way back or any forgiving time either. I understand up to that point that I had lost all privileges as a man, as a father, as a brother, as a citizen, as a person. I am full of garbage.

I cried out of anger for making so many bad decisions. I cried of hurt for all the wrong I had done, for how stupid I had being in each decision. It was a bad one after another bad one. *How awful!* I thought about my brothers: the death of the first one, the encounter with the second one. The lost friendships with him. I had found myself alone so many times in my life and this was not the exception of the rule. The only big difference is that now I am alone, really alone in the middle of nowhere to go, with no one to visit me ever!

I am alone in that room and I continue crying in my loneliness. It is a heavy loneliness what I feel. I think I cried for hours and hours. I could not stop blaming myself between sob and sob. And is then, between sob and sob that I finally think of God, that distant God I saw in the churches hanging. I remember of that Christmas when I sold firecrackers that I saw complete families going into a church and I envied those kids who had parents when I didn't.

I remember the awakening I had in front of that mirror in the van after the death of my only friend and after drinking until getting all wasted! I remember the Ancient man that touched my shoulder in the pizza place and he saw me with those celestial eyes I can not take out of my mind. This encounters were signs of Heaven, God looking for me, and I had ignored it every time. After hours of wiping and crying and remembering my life, for the first time, I cried out to reach God in a truthful way.

When I calmed down and stopped crying, I started to fight with God as if He was the one to blame for all that had happened to me. The elderly comes to my mind again.

"I have heard people saying you are real, God, but I cannot see you! I have *never* seen you in my life! If you were real, you wouldn't have abandoned me!" I said, discharging my anger again. "Help me find you, to know you because if you really exist, you wouldn't let me be an orphan. You wouldn't let me be sent to prison!" I shouted at God as if He was responsible of my decisions.

"God, if you exist, you have to prove me that you do. I do not know how you will do it, but if you really exist," I told him, crying. "*Change me* if you are real, or *kill* me to stop suffering."

"Inside prison, I only have two options. I kill someone, or someone kills me if I am weak. But I want You to change me please! I can't live like this anymore!" I repeated again and again, whipping at Him, sobbing in between. "*Change* me if you are real."

I don't know how long I was in that sobbing, whipping and crying out loud and claimed and challenged God until I finally fell asleep exhausted of the whole process of the day and of crying my guts out. I had never cried so much in my life. That night I took out all the hurt and anger I had stuck inside since my childhood years. I fell asleep exhausted and without any food in my stomach since breakfast. It was probably midnight by then.

Asleep, in my profound sleep, in my dreams something happened that had never ever happened before and never has 'til now. Deeply asleep, I could continue seeing all the good and bad things I had done in my life. It was as if I was seeing the movie of my life. I continued seen my good and bad decisions. The hurt I had lived after every bad decision and the loneliness subsequently. I also saw happy moments, like when I would go out with my father for breakfast to the market and he would buy some times plastic cars to play around. The happiness of learning a job since I was so small, and the happy moments in night school where I met Maria Elena. How happy and how hard it was the pregnancy and all the difficulties we went through to be able to get married.

"We were so happy together!" and I could feel a smile on my face.

The incredible part of this experience is that it was like in three dimension. I could see myself lying down, and it was as if my spirit had left the body. Suddenly I can see myself outside the little room I am locked in. I see myself seated over a huge rock that is over a hill and from there I could see the horizon, the sky and the ocean. Or maybe it's a lake. I could feel the breeze from the ocean, I could even feel the smell of the beach. I am seated there all in black and I have a very long beard and I am worried for the things of life and the future. I can see Maria Elena from far away looking for me, really trying to see me and wishing me well, waiting for the moment we can encounter ourselves again. I even smile when I see her because I continue loving her and no one else has filled in her place in my heart.

I see Guadalupe growing up without a father, alone, lonely, away from everyone, like shy, for the first time I get an extreme desire of seeing her again, see both of them again. I am thinking of them when suddenly, I feel something behind me. I feel it so strongly behind me the presence that I feel fear. I don't have the courage to turn around to see who it was and I don't want to open my eyes either to see the infinitive of the sky and the huge ocean. A bright light from which I felt the heat was behind me and it was so powerful that it covers me completely. I feel it so strongly that I squeeze my eyes and I fall on the floor, like in shock in fetal position, in total shock. But I feel a huge peace in my heart. I feel so peaceful that as I am opening my eyes I say, "Forgive me, forgive me, forgive me, don't abandon me, I need you Lord. I really need you in my life. Show me your path, forgive me please. Please forgive me for not believing in you."

I start crying again, but this time, I am crying of contentment. I feel relieved. Then I feel someone touching my shoulder, and I hear out loud, "I have never abandoned you, nor let you alone. I have been next to you and with you since your mother's womb. All your sins are forgiven," and in that same moment I felt that peace that goes beyond all understanding. I could not believe it. I had never heard or read those words in my life. It was unexplainable.

The fear I had felt at the beginning had totally disappeared. I close my eyes again and whipping I was afraid to open them. I don't know how many hours had gone by, but it was the most beautiful moment of my life. I felt a type of peace that has never been my company. I did not want that peace in my heart to disappear. I couldn't understand all that was happening to me that night, but I didn't want it to end.

When I finally open my eyes, I am still in the same room, on the floor, in fetal position, lonely as always, but something inside had changed in me. God had visited me. I was a different man. I was a new man, with interior peace. A peace that was exchanged by the hatred, the resentment. I could not explain it, but it had happened inside my soul, my own self. A miracle had happened that first night.

I saw around me and I felt so happy I wanted to share it with someone else. I started to knock the door to the guard outside. I shouted and shouted I wanted to share something extremely wonderful that had happened to me. I knocked and knocked and jumped and shouted, "God visited me! God touched me!" I shouted many times as happy as I can be.

It was happiness yelling out and knocking the door, I was so happy, and just wanted to share my happiness. No one answered. I do not know if no one heard me, or they just ignored me, the point is that no one answered back. After shouting and jumping and knocking the door for fifteen or twenty minutes, I came back to realize my situation. No one could talk to me, or see me for thirty days. It was only the first night and it was still dark outside and I had twenty-nine days more to go. So I went back to my sheetless bed to fall down asleep in fetal position with a big smile that only I could understand.

Early in the morning, like around seven, they put inside a plate of food. I was in such ecstasy with what I had seen that night, that I was not hungry at all. I forgot how tired and hungry I was from the day before and I had no other thought in my mind that to review everything I had lived and seen again and again. It had been so beautiful and so real, that I could not do anything else but to be grateful in my inner self for such a beautiful experience. I didn't know how to express myself, as I did not know how to pray, so I just meditated in the experience, smiling at the experience on the rock over the hill. The infinitive ocean and sky, that for me were a sign of the beautiful future that awaited me outside that cell. I was full of positive possibilities when I get out in ten years. I will have a second chance to do things the right way. That was the explanation for that view of the ocean and the sky. God was with me and He had visited me. It was so clear that all the doubts I had about His existence, were gone that same night.

"He visited *me*. Me who had hated Him, doubt Him and done many bad things in life. I didn't deserve to be visited, but I was. Me, the worst sinner, a thief, a liar, an authority trickster, a drug dealer, a member of a mob, a drunk, a drug addict, a nobody. Me. He visited *me*!" I was so grateful.

"Who am I to have such a privilege? Literally the worst of the world, but He decided to answer my doubts about His existence," I kept reminding myself.

I was in ecstasy for about three days. I hardly touched the food. I was miraculously not hungry at all. The Lord sustained me. I think they got worried that I hardly touched the food the whole three days because they had no idea what was happening to me. They didn't know if I was sick or why I was giving back almost the whole plate of food back. They could not ask me or talk to me, so they didn't know, but I was fine. For the first time in my life I was fine. Really good, actually. Something had changed inside me. I definitely felt different.

The fourth day, with the plate of food, they put in a book.

26

The Book

I looked at the book and was grateful they had sent a book for me to be entertained with something all this time left. I was locked in to talk to no one for thirty days and I still had twenty-six days to go. On the top it said The Bible. I had never opened a Bible in all my life. I had only seen it once that day that I crossed the border and got together with the people who took me to the airport. I didn't think it was important so I left it behind.

There was no one who took the time to introduce me to this book. Now that I think about it, the pastor with whom we cross the border should have talked to me about it, but he didn't. Maybe he didn't carry one.

The closest I have been to God and religion was going to catholic churches when I was a child selling firecrackers and in the youth before getting married to Maria Elena. We did not get married by the church since we were living together already, so I never went to a priest. I was also present in the big confusion made with the assassination of Monsignor Romero in front of the downtown cathedral. I had been close to them, but had never gone into a church. I was not interested, and no one had told me to go, not even my wife. In the United States I had never been close to any type of church at all. And a Bible...I had absolutely no idea what could have written inside it. I had no clue it was important to read it and since I did not know what it was, or what it was for, I did not imagine it was important. I was hungry by now, so I concentrated in eating all my plate.

After four days, I ate it all and I guess everyone got surprised. I even enjoyed every bit of it. I missed my beans and tortillas for the first time, but this food was not bad. I was happy even though I was in the lowest point of my life, physically speaking, but in the highest point spiritually speaking. It was unexplainable. Then, I felt that that book was going to mean a lot to me, so after eating and having nothing else to do, I started reading out loud, "In the beginning God created the heaven and the earth. And the earth was without form, and void; and darkness *was* upon the face of the deep. And the Spirit of God moved upon the face of the waters'" (Gen. 1:1–2, KJV).

Immediately I could tell that God was trying to tell me something. He was describing my life: I had felt without form, and void; and darkness and those words hit my head: *without form and void*. It called my attention to see that it said that God had created the heaven and the earth.

"How can that be?"

Inside I felt as a different man and I asked, "God, if you created heaven and earth, can you recreate my life too? Or not?" and I took the Bible to read it all day long. I couldn't stop reading it.

The light was not too bright, but miraculously my eyes did not get tired and I read page after page without wasting time. I felt that I did not have enough time to finish reading it and I felt a huge need and urge to read everything that was written in it. It got to a point where I only ate once a day because I did not want to waste my time. I had a never ending thirst. I read even the parts I did not understand. I read day and night. I was curious for everything written in that Holy Book.

I read it start to finish again and again. I didn't understand most of it, but I kept reading. All I knew is that I was without form, and void and wanted to change that, as the creation changed to a beautiful place. I read about the miracles and marvels that had happened throughout history. The problem was that every time I read it, I had more questions and no one to ask. Everything was new information to my head and I was like a baby trying to walk and with the need to understand and learn everything. I needed answers, and I wanted to go out to get them answered. For the first time, I found that answer written in that precious book in Hebrews 13:5 (KJV). The words were "*Let your* conversation *be* without covetousness; *and be* content with such things as ye have: for he hath said, I will never leave thee, nor forsake thee." *I will never leave thee, nor forsake thee…* The words He told me before I read the Bible. I was impressed. And then I read verse 6.

"So that we may boldly say, The Lord *is* my helper, and I will not fear what man shall do unto me." *The Lord is my helper? Wow! Nothing can be done to me if He does not need it in my life.* These were the exact words I heard the first night I was locked in. Those words made a deep impression in my soul.

Before I knew it, the thirty days had gone by. I did not remember how fast time went by and I was so thankful to have all this time alone to read and meditate what I read. I could analyze and read all the book, alone and without interruptions (except for the food).

The day was here when I was going out of that cell. I was going to be assigned to a normal cell were I would have a roommate or roommates, I didn't know. Somehow I felt attached to those lonely days were I was in silence and in direct communication with God, reading His Word all day long, but at the same time I was impressed that time had gone by and I didn't even noticed it. I didn't have time to count the hours days or weeks I was in that cell. I was grateful about this and I bless the man that put that book inside my cell. The best book ever: the Bible. I never knew who put it inside, but I bless him and wish the best for him.

I couldn't believe how beautiful I saw everything around me as I went out. The natural light looked so nice, even my new cell looked wonderful. It had a mattress and sheets! Wow, I felt in a five-star hotel! And the luxury of having a roommate to talk to, was the best part of it. I felt privileged and loved by my Father. I was seeing everything wonderful inside prison.

The first thing I asked for after getting installed in my new cell, was spiritual orientation. I needed answers for all my questions. They asked me what was my religion. Religion? I don't know, but since I didn't know what else to answer, I said I was Catholic. I was nothing, but that is what I saw most. I had never practiced any religion, but catholic sounded good to me. I asked if there was someone I could talk to and they told me that there was a Priest that came over every two weeks.

They perceived me so calmed, passive and maybe I looked peaceful because they couldn't believe it was me, the same mad, person they put under a loneliness treatment thirty days ago. The haughty, arrogant, aggressive man that had gone into the cell, was left inside. It was buried there. My face had changed to a softer one. When they saw me so transformed, they started to give me jobs and assignments inside the prison. The assignments called privileges are given to the prisoners with more than a year inside in this type of prisons, and I got them just about immediately after getting out of my thirty days.

To this day, I can assure to anyone that those thirty days are the best thing that had ever happened to me. They were days in which I could recognize for sure that all my life I have been in the wrong places with the wrong people and taking the wrong decisions. I could also recognize that Jesus had forgiven my sins, my wrongs, my mistakes. Everything is going to be different. I am different. I wanted to be like Joseph, the dreamer of the prison in the Bible.

My first job was in the kitchen washing dishes. This was new for me. I was so surprised that I enjoyed so much doing this job. I had never been a dish washer and all I had washed before was my own dishes. I had never been locked in so long either nor had I ever hold a job inside prison. This is because my stays were short and all I did was sleep and go to eat free for the weekends.

I had to adapt myself to a new routine in my life. There was a schedule for everything. There was an hour to wake up and shower, a set hour to go help in the kitchen, a time to walk around and chill, a time for cleaning duties, a time for more kitchen duties and a time to get locked in. In other words, there was a structure to follow and a schedule that has to be followed by all the long term interns so we don't get bored. I had never been exposed to follow a strict schedule, except in classroom when I was a child. I liked the order and discipline given in that place. I needed the discipline in my own life.

The days went by like this: I got up at 4:00 a.m. and at 4:30 a.m. I had to be in the kitchen, I did my duties inside and we served at 6:30 a.m. At 8:00 a.m., it was the workers' breakfast time. Then I would rest a while, went out to walk around or exercise and then again, I had to go back at 11:00 a.m. for my duties in the kitchen. I had lunch at 2:00 p.m., and then again, rested, exercised or walked around to meditate up to 4:00 p.m. We served at 5:00 p.m. and I ate at 6:30 p.m. Then we prepared everything for breakfast next day. We got locked in at 8:00 p.m. sharp.

We would chat for a while with my roommate, I would read the Bible for another while and then went to sleep around 9:30 p.m. or 10:00 p.m. And next day started exactly the same way at 4:00 a.m. Day after day the same routine. Luckily, I was busy and had something to look forward to. Working was a blessing, because I was busy all day and had little time to just sit around and wait for time to go by. Days went by fast for me, faster than those who had no privileges. Even getting out the garbage was a privilege, because you got busy somehow in your mind. I was privileged and I could see myself as Joseph, God was with me. I started as a dishwasher, then as cook helper and as they started to trust me, I would have more privileges. Sometimes, I would only pick up the dirty dishes and put them for the dishwasher to wash them, sometimes I would prepare the vegetables cleaning and cutting for the next meal. I felt so useful that I felt happy doing this things.

It is so contradictory because when I was free, it never occur to me to go to a restaurant to ask for a job, since I thought I was too smart to do something like washing dishes since I already had a career as a welder. Now, it was such an awesome privilege, that the job didn't matter. I would do anything and everything: dishwashing, peeling vegetables, cutting them, picking up dishes, taking out the garbage, clean around, serve the food, anything was good. Feeling useful in a bad situation was the best that can happen in this place. My self esteem was growing inside me as I progressed with those privileges. I could see other interns that had such a boring face because they had nothing to do but see time go by. I felt the days so short, I couldn't be more grateful. When I least expect it, a week had gone by, then two weeks, then two months and before I knew it a year had gone by. God is good to me.

About a week after, I was out of my initial isolation, the day I was to get a meeting with the priest was there. I tell him all my experience since day one and all I had seen and felt in my heart, the supernatural experience was what I most vividly exposed to him. I was so full of joy telling him and when I finished, he answered coldly to that:

"You have gone through a very emotional moment since you have no more liberty. Your experience is nothing new to most of the people who are in this place. They all go through a similar experience. Nothing is supernatural. That doesn't exist, it is only in your mind. Cool down my brother and the first thing we will do is to confess you and then I will give some prayers for you to repeat as penance. You will say three The Lord's Prayer and three Hail Marys three times a day. You know those prayers, right?" he asks me and I look at him with a puzzled face.

I am full of questions and I just don't get an opportunity to ask anything to have all the answers. Maybe because it is our first encounter. He does not give me the opportunity to ask anything so I ask, "What is the Hail Mary? And what is a penance? And what do you mean you will confess me?" innocently I asked as I had no idea and the conversation was almost over.

"Oh my God! And what do you know about religion, boy?"

"Not much, really, this is why I had told you my encounter with God. This is the only closeness to whatever you want to call it. I have read the Bible, though and I have many questions about it, can you answer them now?" I tell him rapidly.

"You have to fulfill the penance by praying the Hail Mary at least three times a day and The Lord's Prayer five times a day as a penance," he says. "Do this everyday until my next visit."

"But you have not answered any of my questions, Father and I have read the Bible and it talks about Jesus, sin and repentance, and I do not know how that is. What is sin? How can I repent? Is that when I confess?" I ask. "I haven't read anything that talks about having to make a penance or about Hail Mary prayer. So I don't know what to do. Please give them to me written because I have no idea what are you talking about, or better yet, show them to me where are they in the Bible."

"Don't get into all that, man. Don't worry too much about life. You repent when you confess, so that is the first step we will do. Confessing is telling me all the wrongs you have done and you will come to mass every time I come every two weeks. Meanwhile, you will pray the Hail Mary and The Lord's Prayer as I said," he said without any more instructions.

Then he asked me to confess all the wrongs I remember at that time, which I feel God has already forgiven because of all the peace I can feel inside, but I am obedient to him and told them without entering into much details.

I still do not understand everything, but even though I am full of questions and I am not satisfied with the solution after reading the Bible so many times, I obey repeating the Hail Mary and praying the Lord's Prayer as he said as a sign of obedience to the only religious man I have ever talked to.

I was happy that the Lord's Prayer was found in the Bible in Mathew 6:9–13:

> **9** After this manner therefore pray ye: Our Father which art in heaven, Hallowed be thy name.
>
> **10** Thy kingdom come. Thy will be done in earth, as *it is* in heaven.
>
> **11** Give us this day our daily bread.
>
> **12** And forgive us our debts, as we forgive our debtors.
>
> **13** And lead us not into temptation, but deliver us from evil: For thine is the kingdom, and the power, and the glory, for ever. Amen.

and even though it is not exactly the same as the one the priest gave me, I repeat the one in the Bible, I also found something similar to the Hail Mary in the Bible when Maria went to visit Elizabeth, Maria's cousin, when Elizabeth was pregnant with John the Baptist and Mary had already conceived Jesus, in Luke 1:46–55:

> And Mary said, My soul doth magnify the Lord,
>
> **47** And my spirit hath rejoiced in God my Saviour.
>
> **48** For he hath regarded the low estate of his handmaiden: for, behold, from henceforth all generations shall call me blessed.
>
> **49** For he that is mighty hath done to me great things; and holy *is* his name.

50 And his mercy *is* on them that fear him from generation to generation.

51 He hath shewed strength with his arm; he hath scattered the proud in the imagination of their hearts.

52 He hath put down the mighty from *their* seats, and exalted them of low degree.

53 He hath filled the hungry with good things; and the rich he hath sent empty away.

54 He hath holpen his servant Israel, in remembrance of *his* mercy;

55 As he spake to our fathers, to Abraham, and to his seed for ever.

It is not the same, but at least I found a place where Maria is exalted by her cousin being recognized as the mother of the Lord Jesus.

Every two weeks, I would go to mass and I would come close to the priest at the end to ask more questions, but he always changed the conversation and did not get involved with me. He always went back to telling me to assist to mass, confess my sins, pray Hail Mary, and the Lord's Prayer. That was his only solution. I didn't know if I had more sins, since I had told him everything I remember that first encounter. So I kept going to mass obediently. I was not satisfied, but I obeyed. I felt I was lacking important information. There has to be something more than this and no one wants to tell me about it. I am just thirsty and I want more.

I started to read the Bible again from Genesis to Revelation trying to find my own answers. I asked God but He never, ever again appeared to me as in that first night.

A little more than a year went by of well behavior and questions without answers. No one in this prison could answer them. No one else had the same spiritual thirst I had. No one could clear my doubts. I couldn't believe I was the only one with all this questions and no one else wanted to know more about God or the Bible.

Could it be possible that God has only visited me? Am I chosen for a special job as Peter was? Or as Paul was? Me? I thought without sharing my thoughts to anyone.

One day, I got a notebook to write down all my questions and thoughts and I was grateful for that. It was my best present after *the book*. I asked God to introduce me to someone who could answer all my questions, since I had them written one by one.

As they observed me focused, hard worker, helping other interns not to fight, asking questions about God and His existence, I was earning trust with everyone in the prison. Because I was all the above, I was transferred to a new place with less security, as this one was high security. They could tell I was no danger to anyone since my first encounter with God in the isolation cell. They didn't know what had happened to me, but I could feel peaceful and apparently they noticed it too. With this transfer, maybe God had something prepared for me since I didn't understand why they were moving me from where I had a job that entertained me, plus I was really used to this life. Besides I had not asked for a transfer.

Now I realize that it was God's plan to take care of me.

27

Howard

When transferred to another prison, I discover there were other jobs I could entertain myself with, but the one that popped out immediately was a welding shop that was unused. I asked why it was unattended, and they told me that no one knew how to weld. I offered myself to be the teacher in that place as I was an expert since childhood. They had all type of machinery, and some I knew exactly how to use and others I was to discover. This equipment was there for a long time and no one used it, as there was no expert. Welding was natural for me since I started learning at age nine. I became an expert at twelve and I got a paying job at thirteen. It was wonderful not to have to wash dishes, and to go back to my expertise.

Since at welding there is a spark, and we can initiate a fire in no time, there were guards surrounding me and they were watching me constantly. Also, there were fire extinguishers at hand. Every move I made, they followed me with his eyes or physically walked behind me. It was as if I had my own bodyguards. I was in no position to break the rules, so I followed each and every one of them. I was determined to obey and that gave me more respect each week that went by. I was a new man and was not willing to go back in any way to the bad decisions in my life. Even though I was a new man, deep inside I was still selfish and greedy and I felt superior because I was the expert. Who ever I liked, I taught them how to work as a welder, but if for some reason I did not like the person, I did not made things easy for him. I would only let him observe to learn, watching me work.

I felt interior peace but I was still somewhat greedy and loved to show off all my knowledge, as I felt important and superior to the rest of the prisoners because most to them in this prison had no careers or expertise in anything. I knew it was not right, but it felt good to be admired and respected. I must admit that a little of my old me was still alive.

In this new prison, since it was not of extreme danger, there was more space for relaxation, sports, and entertainment. Some prisoners would just walk around, others played soccer, others basketball and some others just sat down to read or chill. The point was that if we did not play any of those sports, we could just walk around or sit and chill and chat. It was just more spacious and I would only sit down alone to read my Bible. I had a never-ending thirst of the Word.

Howard, an American man, one day came over to the welding shop. He was sentenced to twenty-five years in jail and he had two years to go. He was punished because he had a place where he processed amphetamines in an illegal way. So he had already paid twenty-three years locked in and he had gone through many different workshops in all the different prisons he had been in that long period of time, but welding, he had never learned. No one had appeared there that could weld since Howard was in that place, so when he saw the shop in use, he asked to be transferred to it. He was a born again Christian and had decided to be a good man when he goes out after finishing his sentence.

When he got his transfer to "my shop," he came over to learn to weld. Howard was a nice man, soft and pleasant to talk to.

He felt different from the rest, but since I was still in my "I am superior" stage, I was somewhat rude to him.

"Hi, my name is Howard. What's yours?"

"What do you want?" I rudely spoke.

"Nothing, calm down, I just want to learn to weld. I have more than twenty years locked in prison and I have learned many things, but welding I know nothing. So I want to learn before I go out in a couple of years," he said softly and calmly, but I didn't listen too closely.

"The machine is there. Watch me and learn" I said coldly, as I had told many other people before.

Howard had had his portion of mistreat in life, and he had had his own encounter with God, but I didn't know it in that moment. I hadn't realized the soft way of being either. What I did notice was that in the free time to relax, he would go apart, got out a Little blue book and he read out of it. I just thought that in such a long period of time, he had become self-centered to prepare himself to go out to the real world. He was always alone reading that little book. It did not look like my Bible, so I didn't know what he read.

After two weeks, I got too curious and I had to ask him, "What do you read?"

"The New Testament. Is the Word of God," he said without hesitation.

"You read the Word of God? Howard, I can't believe it! I have to tell you my story. Can I?" I asked forgetting how rude I had been with him. My ego wall fell immediately and I felt so good to find someone to talk about God.

"Can you answer all my questions?" I asked him at once. I immediately felt I had found the right person to talk to. I had felt weird being the only one that was really looking for God and His purpose in my life. I couldn't understand why he read only half of the Bible, but I was joyful that I had found someone that read it anyway.

Instantly, the barrier was broken.

"Howard, I had been reading the Bible since I had an encounter with God in my isolation cell," I started.

"Isolation cell?" he asked. "You go to isolation cells only in the federal prison."

"Yeap. That is where I was before coming here."

"Have you killed someone?"

"No, not at all!" I laughed and continued. "I have been reading the Bible since I had my encounter with God in the isolation cell…"

Then I shared my whole experience, and how supernatural it was. Howard was surprised of all the details I shared and how incredible it had been. His experience was totally different.

"I have not stopped reading it since I got it in the isolation cell. I see that mine is longer that yours and has more sections. What is the difference?" I asked.

"What I have is the New Testament, which begins with Jesus' Life, The Gospels are called, which is nothing more than the story of Jesus on earth from four different perspectives: Mathew, Marcus, Luke and John." He explains with a great smile. In this moment, we both forgot how rude I was and I apologized, for it. We became best friends immediately.

"There are two specific things that come out to my mind when I read the Gospels. Jesus and what he talks about sin," I tell him, "and I have a notebook filled with a lot of questions. Can you answer them for me? The thing is that in the federal prison, I used to meet with a priest, and all he told me was to pray the Hail Mary plus a few rounds of The Lord's Prayer. I repeat them as he said, but I still feel there is something else out there for me. I want more information and all my questions answered," I told him."I need more information about Jesus because the Rosary and Hail Mary does not talk about him and I do not understand fully why I need to repeat those prayers. I pray to Mary and I do not understand why I have to pray to her. If I am not mistaken,

I read that she was a chosen woman because she was obedient to God, and He chose her from thousands of other woman, to get pregnant of Jesus because she was virgin and special."

"That is correct, Eddy, she is a special woman, and the chosen one, but she does not save us since she did not die for us. She was only the chosen vessel to bring Jesus to earth." he confirmed and continued. "Eddy, have you received Jesus Christ in your heart as your personal savior?"

"What do you mean 'receive Jesus Christ in my heart'? What in the world is that?" I asked, puzzled and more confused than ever.

"Okay, so if you don't know what that is, then you have not received Him. Do you want to receive him?"

"What does that mean?" I asked again.

"It means that when you die, you go directly to heaven if you receive Jesus in your heart."

"But I have been a bad person and I have done many bad things in my life, how can I go directly to heaven just as easy as that, just praying? Don't I have to do many good things in my life to deserve going to heaven?"

"The Word of God says in Ephesians 2:8–10 [KJV], 'For by grace are ye saved through faith; and that not of yourselves: *it is* the gift of God: Not of works, lest any man should boast. For we are his workmanship, created in Christ Jesus unto good works, which God hath before ordained that we should walk in them.' Have you read it?"

"Yes, I have read it but I do not understand how is that by grace I can be saved through faith, what faith? How is that?"

"What this means Eddy is that you have to put your faith in Jesus who died for your sins in the cross of Calvary, and He died for my sins too and receive Him in your heart to be saved, because there is no works that can be enough to earn the right to go to heaven when you die. There is no grays here, is either white or black. Either you have him in your heart or you don't. Period. And with that, either you go to Heaven or you go to Hell. Now, do you want to receive Christ as your personal savior to be saved and go to heaven when you die?

"But what type of question is that? Of course I want to receive Him!"

"Okay, then let's pray, repeat after me: My Lord Jesus, I recognize I have sinned against You and men. I am a sinner and I had done too many bad things I deserve to be here in prison because I took very bad decisions in my life trying to manage it myself without knowing You. But now, I ask you to show me your way, to save me, to heal me from all the bad things I have in my heart. I plead you to be the owner of my heart and to write my name in The Book of Life so that when I die, I can go to Heaven with you. Please show me your way and govern me in all ways. In Jesus's name, Amen." I was repeating after Howard and then I continue telling him all my questions. Luckily (not to say as a blessing to me as I didn't understand it too well) he answers many of them and as he sees the thirst of knowledge that I have to know more about that Jesus that was crucified in the cross and that I had found in the Bible. And now He just saved me. Wow! He was able to read about the Old Testament in my Bible too. We really got to have great times together and suddenly, he tells me he is going to do something special for me.

"I will take you to the chaplain," he told me very seriously.

"What is a chaplain?" I asked him more seriously, as I thought it was something wrong. "It sounds bad my friend."

"You worry too much, my friend. On Sunday Look for me after breakfast, and I will take you."

It was the best thing Howard could do for me. I will never forget that love gesture he had for me and my salvation.

So that very special Sunday…"Eddy, this is Steve Wilson. He is the chaplain in prison," he said when introducing us. With the greatest smile I have ever seen, he puts out his hand to shake mine and then pulls it to hug me.

"God bless you, my brother, and welcome to our chapel." Up to that point I had no idea that there was a Chapel in the prison and up until then, I understand why I didn't see Howard around on Sunday mornings after breakfast. A chaplain is a spiritual guide, and in this case, he was a pastor who taught the Word of God. I only knew that the priests existed, but a pastor? Now I think about the guy we crossed the border with that said he was a pastor. I wonder if he was this type of pastor. I wondered what type of teachings he taught. Steve was a military guy who worked in the base next to our prison. It was about eight minutes away, so he worked there as a Chaplain to them during the week, and for us on Sundays. Howard had been my tutor, up to that day and I had learned so much with him. He became my first and only good friend in prison. Someone I could trust and open myself to. We talked so many hours about our understanding about Jesus, the Bible and the New Testament, that I cannot even count them. I have a real friend with whom I can share everything. I felt happy about that divine encounter and I never missed out a service from that day on.

One day, when I least expected it, Howard told me, "Eddy, I have some news for you."

"What's wrong, Howy?" I ask. (That was how I called Howard)

"In two weeks, I am going out. I have finished my time here," he says. I freeze since I had not realized that two years had gone by since I first met him. I felt I was going to feel lost when he left and will have no one to talk to. I was being selfish in that moment, as I still had a lot of time to go. But then, he continued, "Pastor Steve Wilson wonders if you would like to work in the chapel with him instead of the welding shop."

"And what am I supposed to do there?" I ask puzzled. "What I know how to do very well is welding...I have seen the chaplain only on Sundays and I have talked to him a couple of times, so I do not know him too well. He looks peaceful, though and I like that. You know I periodically go every Sunday to his services, which they are very different than the mass, and I do not feel too comfortable with your proposition. I do not feel I am ready to work next to him. I need to know him better. Besides, I do not know how I will be useful for him. Do you think it is the best place to be? I have no clue of how to be a chaplain's helper."

"Of course, Eddy, don't be afraid. Steve will answer anything I have not been able to. He will guide you better with a better understanding of the Word. You will see how well you will be with him and what a privilege you will have to be chosen to be his helper. Steve is very dedicated and he will pay attention to you and your doubts. All you have to do is to help Steve prepare the services, that means, cleaning the place, cleaning the chairs, put the chairs in order, prepare the music, all the things he usually uses in each service," he tells me, assuring me it is great to be next to him. "You have trained many people already in the welding shop, so that will continue without you."

"But how come you are leaving in two weeks and you haven't mentioned anything?" I ask with my heart being stressed out with that notification, and my voice is somewhat shaky not wanting to know for sure.

"I didn't want you to start worrying before time. Besides, I needed to be sure about the date when I get my written notification. I just got it this morning after breakfast."

I have a deception face because all this time I hadn't find anyone to talk to from the bottom of my heart, and now he is about to leave. I have mix feelings, as I am happy for him because he is finally going out free, but I am sad because I will feel alone again! I am a bit selfish, but that is how I feel. Upon seeing the disappointment on my face, he says, "Eddy, I have other good news for you. I am in a four-man cell, and they are all Christians, people who are born again. And they asked me to propose you to take my place to keep the four of you together in Christ's name.

They don't want to have who knows who as roommate. They want you instead of me."

"I am very grateful with you, Howy, so if you think this is the best for me, then please introduce me to your cell friends," I tell him somewhat more relieved about it.

It was a great opportunity to room with people who talk my same spiritual language. I was going to miss so much my friend Howy, but he deserved a good life out there in the free world. All his youth and young adult years were spent locked in and he was a different man, a renewed person by the Holy Spirit and he deserved a second chance in the real world. Howard has a piece of my heart and all my gratitude for helping me and spending all that time together talking and discussing about the Bible that I didn't understand. I will never forget this person and I really wish I could see him again some day face to face to thank him again.

"My blessings to you, Howard. You blessed my life."

28

Steve Wilson

After my encounter with God, since it was so extraordinary between Him and I, and a bit incredible, the truth is that I was a little ashamed to carry my Bible around, so I had not identified as a Christian with anyone, but Howard. This is why I did not know other people who had my same faith in Jesus and God. I would see them in the services but have not made any friendships with anyone else, but Howard. And this is why I was a little shy about going into a cell with three other people who I had not identify before. When attending the service, we had limited time to talk and we hardly made any friendships. Inmediately finishing the service, we had to go to the dining tables to have lunch, as always. Nobody really talked openly about Jesus or whatever we learned in the services.

"If God is given you this opportunity to live with other Godly men, take it and don't worry about the rest. I am sure you will get along fine. I know them and I had talked to them about you and your supernatural encounter with God and they are anxious to know all about it first hand. I will help you with the guards to have you moved there when I leave."

"Thank you, my brother. You are a very special person," I said, grateful for his proposition.

So on an afternoon a week before Howard was leaving, he introduced us together to say good by and for us to meet. For the first time, the five of us, and without worrying what was going on around us, we held together to pray for Howard's life in audible voice, so we could hear each other. We all cried of mix feelings between happiness for his freedom and at the same time for leaving us behind. We did not care who was around us, and we prayed and talked without any fear. We cried and laughed because someone very important in our lives was leaving for good. That day we promised to each other that we will help each other to keep our faith alive and to help each other in any problem we find in the way. We were together because of our faith. Howard gave us that inheritance and he put us together.

My first and greatest tutor in my life disappeared like that from my life. From that day on, the four of us never again were ashamed of carrying our Bibles around and we would get together in the free time to meditate, read and pray. There was like a spiritual seal between us, thanks to our common friend Howard.

Howard had been the Chaplain's helper, so I was honored to take his place, and not one of the other three friends. Maybe I was more thirsty of learning, or maybe he felt the guidance of God to propose me, I do not know, but certainly that was one more miracle in my life.

The day before he left, I was moved from the welding shop to the Chapel to work with the Chaplain. Chaplain is the person in charge of the spiritual guidance, in this case, Born Again Christian guidance, the pastor. Steve Wilson welcomed me happily because of all the recommendations Howard had given about me.

"And what is my job here?" I ask after been greeted and welcomed.

"The first thing that will happen here is that you will become my disciple" he said.

"Disciple?" I ask puzzled. "Like Jesus had twelve?"

"Exactly, but there are not twelve, just you for now" he said with a huge smile on his face. I will never forget that angelical smile on his face welcoming that day. This was the great opportunity that God was giving me to learn about Him from his servant Steve.

"So you will answer all my questions?" I ask anxiously.

"Well, well, one step at a time. First I will show you how to read the Bible. I will explain the composition of it, who is who in the Bible, who are the writers, who is the writer talking about, some books are historical, others are poetic, others are prophetic, and this way you will understand it better. There are thirty-nine books in the Old Testament and twenty-seven in the New Testament. Have you read the Bible before?"

"Yes, of course. Like twenty times. And every time I read it, I get more questions and some others are clarified by themselves. I have a whole notebook filled with my questions, and some had been cleared by Howard, but some are still there waiting to find the right person to answer them, and I think I found him," I said happily.

"You surprise me with your answers, I had never found anyone that had read the Bible twenty times! Not even myself!" he said surprised.

I became his disciple from that day on. My other three cellmates were the first ones to come over to the service to help me arrange everything for the service. We cleaned and put up the chairs ready for the service. I was in charge of the sound, logistics, I took track of the library for the interns, and I had to keep record of the assistance, conversions, disciple groups, etc. Since I couldn't do it all, my three friends were part of my team. I was the right hand of the pastor, and the closest to him and they were my closest team members. Those first six months pastor dedicated a lot of time teaching me and answering all the questions that I had. One by one, the doubts I had were clarified and I understood more and more the great sacrifice Jesus had done for me and how sinful I was. I did not deserved to be forgiven or saved, but Jesus was the sheep that died for my sins and thanks to His sacrifice, I could be saved from hell and if I die today, I go to Heaven. It couldn't be for my works since I had done too many bad things, and I had taken one bad decision after another. God had forgiven me through the sacrifice Jesus did for me in the cross. For the first time I felt free even though I was freeless physically. The Holy Spirit was my company and I felt complete in Him.

"When I found in the Bible in Psalm 27:10, which says, 'When my father and my mother forsake me, then the LORD will take me up,' I could see that this was exactly what had happened in my life. Those words were real in me, He had rescued me and for the first time I could let go the resentment toward God for the death of my parents and brother. "God let me live all that suffering and let me do all the bad things I did, to end up prisoner to give me freedom, a freedom I could only find locked up." I analyzed, talking with pastor Wilson.

"That's right, Eddy. God is love, and He has forgiven all your sins and now you are a free man, spiritually speaking. I think you are ready to get baptized, my brother."

"Baptized? Like Jesus got baptized?"

"Do you want to?"

"Of course I would like to get baptized! But where can we do that?" I ask puzzled.

"Don't worry about that, I will resolve how and when. I will see who else is ready for this step of making public his faith for Jesus. You know that baptizing does not save you, only receiving Jesus in your heart, repenting of your sins, saves, but getting baptized is a public act to verify in public that you have given yourself to Jesus, as He did it publicly too. When you take this step there is no going back, you are sealed with the Holy Spirit to do the works Jesus gives you in this world. You have been chosen to save many and I am sure your life will change in the years to come," he said fully convinced and I believed him.

I could hardly wait for the day I was going to be baptized, but more so, the day I was going to go out to share my faith with all those people with whom I did all the bad things in my life. Those people with whom I did drugs and drank, even to those I sent the drug to when I was a distributor. I was making a list in my head and I could see a lot of work I had outside. Even my brother, I had to go find again to ask for his forgiveness.

"Ufff! I have a very important mission with all those people. They need to know about a lively God, about Christ the savior and show them how to repent to turn their lives around before they end up in jail like me," I thought almost in an audible voice. Then I prayed, "My Father in heaven, please give me the opportunity to go back to those people and introduce them to your Son. You know it was not my intention to do bad things, but I didn't know any better. All I knew was to do bad to myself and others. Lord, use my life for others to meet you before it's too late. Please prepare me so that I can be ready to share your Word out in the world."

I prayed innocently out loud with Steve, and I still had seven more years to go locked in.

"Start with the ones around you," I felt God was telling me in my heart.

"Start with the ones around you," pastor Wilson told me, confirming what I just felt in my heart. So that same day I promised God I was never going to be ashamed to share His Word to anyone the rest of my life. I had the mission to share my experience, my life, the good and the bad to bring more and more people to Jesus. He was going to train me inside to be able to work for Him outside. I had all the time of the world the next seven years to practice and to meet all those men who were also in prison with me.

That night, I shared my feeling to the other three cellmates and they told me they had the same feeling, but had not started yet. So that night we agreed to start fishing people for Christ. We fished them, we showed them how to do the repenting prayer, and we invited them to assist to our Sunday service. That year, the assistance increased threefold and we felt so happy to finally be doing the job that the Apostles did almost two thousand years ago: share the Gospel to everyone, Jews and non-Jews. We talked freely about Jesus' love toward everyone who accepts Him. My life had turned around 180 degrees and I couldn't believe it! The four of us became the disciple's teachers, guided by the pastor. I felt so happy, truly happy for the first time in my life. I felt full of Jesus' love toward me, and His mercies had come in me. My happiness was not filled by a person or a situation, not even by money, as I hardly had any of it, I had no one to love and I wasn't free. It was Jesus who filled me up with His words in the Holy Bible and the Holy Spirit guiding me each step I gave in my new life. The four of us prayed every night for every person we had fished during the day, and asked God to put us more people in front of us the following day. We were like the four musketeers working together. A sense of purpose was governing my life now, and that was the most awesome thing that could have happened. Each day was a new opportunity to reach out to more people. I was so blessed!

Without noticing the "long" days, time went by really fast, as we were busy fishing people and we felt so useful that God gave us the grace every day. It was one after another that will repent and come to Jesus and that gave us so much hope. There is nothing else that makes you feel more fulfilled, than working in God's purpose to show the way to Jesus to all the lost people out there, and for us, inside a prison. Everyone could notice our interior peace and they all wanted the same. With each man repenting, we were also rescuing them from going to hell when they die. We were men spiritually free and saved, even though we were physically locked in.

Some weeks after promising to evangelize inside prison, the day of our baptism came up.

"Eddy, I want to let you know that I will baptize you in a beautiful place so that you never forget it," he said with a huge smile. "You and your three cellmates are the first chosen...We will go to the Hudson River in New York."

"We are going to a river out side of this place?" I asked really touched with the tears in my eyes. I couldn't be happier. It was an undeserved gift I was receiving from God. I do not know how he had managed to get a permission to go out, but I guess pastor had given them the security that everything was going to be fine, for sure no one was going to attempt to escape, he assured to them as he told me. We were the first group, and the experimental group. The four of us were the fortunate ones as it was the first time they were authorizing such permission.

It was the most beautiful day in all my intern life, well, after my encounter with God. At the same time, I was so ashamed for being a prisoner. We went to a small town next to a part of the Hudson river which was famous that when the summer came, they had many tourist that went out for picnics every weekend and sometimes during the week. Needless to say, it was summer. There was a place where there was a beautiful park that was the people's favorite and since it was a nice, sunny day, lots of people were there barbecuing and having fun with their families. It was past noon on a Saturday.

Interrupting their family day, here comes a bulletproof van from which four prisoners dressed up in an orange jumpsuit, with chains around their waist, feet and handcuffs come out from it, with our faces showing up. With us, came the pastor plus five guards: one for each of us, plus an extra one who was in charged to unchain and chain us back, plus the driver. The guards carry their fire-guns ready to shoot one of us if we decide to run away. Non of us was willing to do so, so we were of no danger. Still, the deal was that they had to follow all the security rules, which they did and we had no resistance at all. We followed their instructions.

I am the first to go out of the van with my face down, looking at my feet because I didn't want them to see me, as if I knew anyone, but I just felt ashamed of myself in a way. It was ashamed that I had to know Jesus in this condition. The visitors stopped everything that they were doing to turn around and watch what was going to happen in front of their eyes. This was a very unusual situation. As we go down, one guard for each of us points us with his machine guns. I suppose it looked like if they were going to assassinate us in front of everyone, but it was far from that happening.

The breeze starts flowing around us, and I forgot all the show we were putting on for the visitors, and I lift my face to see around me. I instantly forgot the chains and my situation. It was so nice to see the nature, outside. Feel the freedom sun. "Ahhh, nice."

We started to walk toward the river in a row, one behind the other. The guards pointing at us, as I said, one per prisoner. The extra one started to unchain my chains. I was the first one to go in. To get into the water, the pastor got something like a White tunic that we put on top of the orange jumpsuit which we put right in front of the river. As I went in… It was a glorious moment! I felt the heavens were opening and I could even feel that God was telling me, "This is my chosen son, born to do my works."

It was an indescribable moment of relief, peace, throwing down the river my old man, and welcoming the new man inside me: a completely renovated man. I just can't describe this moment, it was just so special in all forms. The most supernatural moment after my encounter with God was what I was experimenting. I do not have words to express them.

While I waited for the other three to get baptized and experience the same wonderful experience I had, I went to the side to sit on a rock to receive sun and get dry. I could feel my happy face looking around. The public, with their mouth open of unbelief, they would applaud as we were going into the river to get baptized. For each of us, was a success type of sensation, we had won over the darkness we found ourselves before. We felt extreme emotional liberty, spiritual, and personal too. The public gave cheers and celebrated with us in this extraordinary event they had not expect to watch that afternoon.

As my cellmates were going in, I started to observe around and I could see a sunny day with hardly any clouds around. The sky was a beautiful blue, with very little white clouds around. I looked around to the river and it looked like an infinitive "ocean." It was a very long river and I thought it was the largest I have ever seen. I was seated on a rock and then it dawn on me: It is the same image I saw that first night in the isolation cell! I couldn't believe it! God had shown me this moment that first night and I felt the same peace I am experimenting in that very moment. I remember the peace I felt with that vision and it was the same. I couldn't hold it anymore and I started crying, but it was out of being grateful for everything he had let me go through to get to this moment. I cried of happiness, not of sorrow, and I felt so blessed with this exact moment that was going to stay in my life forever.

I observe that I am sitting on a rock and the bright light I saw in the vision is the exact light I can feel in that moment. I felt God was next to me. God had given me the vision long time ago, but of course I hadn't understood it till that precise moment. The only thing that was not present from that vision was Maria Elena, so in that moment I decided I was going to pray for her, her soul, her salvation her encounter with God. I feel the need to intervene for her soul to find peace and happiness, as I had found it. I remember I saw her looking for me, but maybe is backward and God is putting in me to intercede for her spiritually for Him to rescue her. I do not think I will ever see her again, and I cannot think that she will even give me the opportunity to come over to talk to her and ask for her forgiveness. I do not deserve it, she will never understand and I don't think she will give me the opportunity for that, but I feel the urge to intercede for her. The only two times I have seen her since I left her were only fights, we shouted at each other, I asked for the divorce, so most likely I am divorced anyway, and she has continued with her life, remarried and had other kids.

But in this moment of happiness, there is no space to think about what she has done in her personal life. All I am worried about is her soul and I feel a big sorrow for her. My heart is filled with love toward her again, for her lost soul and I ask God to save her. Married or not, in San Salvador or in another place, I ask for her salvation. I love her deeply in God's love and I only want the best for her and my child.

"Father Lord, I urge you to rescue Maria Elena's soul and Guadalupe's too, in the name of Jesus, Amen," I prayed while looking at the blue sky.

Pastor brought us together after he is finished with the four of us and we all hugged together. We prayed thanking the Lord for this special moment in our lives. The guards are pointing at us, but I could see a huge smile in their faces as they had seen a miracle in front of them. They put back the chains because that is the protocol, even though they know we do not need them. They just follow the rules, and we accept it because we do not plan to escape.

We go back into the van and we are all silent meditating in the beauty of the experience. Suddenly, one of the guards turns to the pastor and says: "Pastor Wilson, this day I had seen with my own eyes how these four men—even though they are in chains and they are without freedom—are actually in peace and have happiness in their hearts as I can see it in their faces. I do not have that peace or happiness and I am free and without chains. How can I have the same?"

"Do you know Jesus? I mean, have you received Jesus in your heart as your savior?" he asks without hesitation.

"How do you do that?" he asks with a puzzled face somewhat ashamed for not knowing what he is talking about.

"Repeat after me to receive him. Lord Jesus, I recognize I am a sinner and I repent from all my sins. Please forgive me and clean my soul. I beg you to come into my heart and save my soul today. I want to have peace, the same peace I see in these men that are freeless. Save my life and I ask you to guide me the rest of my life. I recognize you as my only and sufficient personal savior and I ask you to write my name in the Book of Life, so when I die, I can go to heaven. In the name of Jesus, Amen."

"Amen," finished the five of them.

To our surprise, the five guards that were sitting with us in the van, repeated at the same time the prayer in their heads in silence. When they finished, after saying Amen, they all smiled.

"Now what?" asked another guard.

"When you are off duty, look for a church to go on Sundays, to learn more about the Bible and Jesus. Buy a Bible and read it, and whenever you want, if you are in duty on Sundays, you can come to my meetings inside prison. Share what you have seen today: this miracle with your family and friends and everything you have just experimented. All of you do the same, and we will make the reign of God larger and larger.

We were all surprised with that gift God gave us. That experience was more glorious than we had expected. Even the guards received Christ! They will have to talk to the driver, as he did not hear anything. So the four of us got baptized and the five guards saved! Awesome!

When we got back to the prison building, we happily went to dinner and then to rest in peace. We irradiated more peace than we had before. I do not know how to explain it, but something beautiful happened inside me. I feel so complete, so happy, so nice, I just feel filled by the Holy Spirit.

Next day, since it was Sunday, I woke up early to go to arrange all the things around the Sunday service. The four of us gave our testimony and what we lived and felt that glorious day. Then the pastor asked who wanted to get discipled with him to get prepared to get baptized. Many raised their hand and the instruction was that they had to look for me at the end of the service. When I showed Pastor Wilson the list, he couldn't believe all the fruit that those testimonies brought up that day. He couldn't be happier with the result.

"I think the time has come: the most desired time in my life since I started working here," he said to me.

"What do you mean? Are you leaving?" I asked puzzled.

"Leaving? No. Of course not. Let me explain. There is a university-level theological program, that I had dreamed about for years but there are two requisites that I have never been able to fulfill. This program gives a scholarship through the Nazareno University to all interns interested, but we have to fulfill those requisites."

"What are they?"

"We have to have at least sixty signatures of prisoners who want to receive this degree. I see forty-two people singed up to get baptized, plus you four, and about fifteen more, we can fill that one. It is a three-year program, it is a very serious compromise and who signs up, has to agree to stay in the university the full three years."

"Piece of cake, Pastor. What is the second one?"

"The second one is that they must be high school graduates. They have to say where they graduated from and the university looks for the transfer papers. They do all the paperwork."

"Let's do it!" I said enthused. "I will get the other signatures in no time together with my mates. Don't worry about that one." I tell him enthused about it. "You should start doing the arrangements."

In two days I had all the signatures needed, and more. I got eighty and Pastor Wilson was surprised! So in the fall, we started classes. We studied three years and when I was about to graduate as a student of Theology, Family, Angels and other things, I get a letter from the federal court.

You have to understand that I had not received any letter from anyone all this time, since I had no one to receive it from and the only letter I receive is one from Federal Court... My heart jumped out of my chest.

When we receive a letter from the Federal Court is most likely for bad news: transfer, another hearing, or more years inside prison.

"My God, what happened? What did I do wrong?" I asked God, worried.

I did not have the courage to open the letter by myself, so I go to pastor Wilson to find the courage.

"Pastor, I have received a letter from the Federal Court and I know there are only two reasons to get one. One, because they found evidence against me and they will extend my time here. Two, because they found a guy named Billy and he confessed my relationship with Juan and they will extend my time. So any way I see it, I am getting more time inside!" I tell him in anguish! "I don't know what to think." All the peace I have had and the joy experienced instantly went away, and my heart hurt from anguish."

"I am afraid to open it, so please you do it."

"Let us pray first for you to accept whatever comes in here," he said, and with my head, I approved of his suggestion.

"Father Lord, You that know it all, and that have my destiny in Your hands and have Eddy's destiny in Your hands too, I beg you to give peace to Eddy to accept what it is inside this letter. Let him have faith over his future which you have already recognized.

We bless your name and the future you have for him. In the name of Jesus, we pray, Amen."

Pastor Wilson opens the letter and reads it in silence. For a minute or two, which felt like an hour, I am waiting for him to tell me what it is about. I just can't see it, but I observe his facial expression and it has a surprised face. As he is reading it, his eyes open wide and starts smiling slightly. I do not understand his reaction. Then, after that minute or two waiting, he smiles with a huge smile and says, "In all my career as chaplain in prison, the last fifteen years I have seen this happening only twice," he said cautiously. I opened my eyes wildly as I do not understand.

"What do you mean, pastor?" I ask with anguish in my heart, keeping my breath while I had asked, with fear, as I don't know if I want to know.

"You are the third one. Calm down, Kiddo. Are you willing to accept what it says? There is good news," he said to calm me down. I breath deeply. "I know this is God's working in you already. Read it yourself." And he hands it down to me.

I read it and I can't believe it myself. God is giving me the biggest blessing He can give me and I couldn't imagine. I did not expected it. I haven't asked for it either, but God was already working in my life without even asking for it.

Generally speaking, the Federal letters are bad news, but for me, it was a gift from God. The letter said that I had to go back to the court in New York because they had sent from the Federal Court a forgiveness manifest, with external supervision for my good behavior.

"What does this mean? I don't really understand it. Why do I have to go to Federal Court again?"

"Have you noticed that more or less every six months they have given you psychological, physical and mental tests? The most important is the psychological test. In those tests they evaluate you as a person, a human being with emotions and good or bad conduct, without you even noticing they had been observing you all this time. In which programs have you been before each evaluation?

"I have been in the kitchen, in anti-drug programs, violence program, welding making park benches, social work, with you as your helper and in the Nazareno University," I answered.

"Exactly, in each and every one of them you have shown to be exceedingly diligent, and good at what you have done. You have been obedient, well behaved and nice to everyone. You have never been mean, rebellious, stubborn, and selfish…Or have you?"

"Really? Nope, I do not think so. Since I had my encounter with God in the adaptation cell, I decided I was already locked in and I could do nothing to change it, so adapting and collaborating was going to be my new life style. This way I will do something productive and I was going to keep myself busy to not feel the looooong ten years I had to be incarcerated. One thing took me to another until I came here to work with you."

"God is giving you a great gift, my son. God is taking you out of this prison before time, and you haven't even asked for this. He knows what is best for you. I am the one that looses here, because we had worked so good together, and now God is opening a door for you outside and I will not be the one who stops them. I am sure He has a big ministry for you prepared out there somewhere. Are you ready to go out to the world, my son?"

"Are you sure that is the interpretation of this letter?"

"Maybe you are not sure about this, but God has given his sentence. You have **a verdict changed by God** that no man can change back."

"But here it says that they are forgiving five years of prison, how can that be? I learned that from Federal Courts, not even a day is pardoned and I am getting five years? Without asking for them? This is all too weird for me!"

"I don't know, Bro. God's paths are different than ours. You should only praise Him and thank Him for this privilege because He is an Almighty God and an awesome God. There is nothing hard for Him to do, and we are in front of a miracle. He gave a son to Sara and that was impossible for men, but not for Him. Why would it be hard for him to lower your sentence? You are ready and He needs you out there and only good things can happen to you Eddy. You have a mission to tell everyone there is something good out there if they only repent. There is hope, there is a new life if they let God act in them."

I listened carefully and he continued, "Only God can make extraordinary things with ordinary people that let Him guide them. Ever since you came to work with me, I knew that God was preparing you for something big. Is the hand of God in your life. Imagine everything you have accomplished during these five years. First of all, He changed your life by touching you personally, even before anyone would talk to you about Him. You have been chosen since your mother's womb. Even though your life has not been too easy, leaving you as an orphan, God let you develop yourself in free will so that all your errors could be used to bring many to Him. The one that has been forgiven much, loves much.

"Remember Magdalene crying on Christ's feet? Her sins were forgiven. And the adulteress woman that was taken in the middle of everyone to accuse her? She had an encounter with Jesus and He forgave her. And the woman who had had five men in her life and was getting water from the well in the middle of the day when no one else did because she was ashamed of herself? She was also forgiven. And Paul, the prosecutor of the followers of Jesus, the one that agreed on Stephen's death? He was also chosen. You have been forgiven and your story has to be known to everyone who is without hope, abandoned, or in trouble. You have to write it and take it to the world and impact many lives. You are the chosen vessel to rescue thousands of people out there and you have already started in here. Have you realized how many disciples you are leaving behind in prison?

"The university started because you put your mind into it. The disciple groups started because of your work. You are about to graduate with a degree in theological studies and as a pastor from a university in the USA, and you are locked in. Imagine all that you will accomplish in the outside world? Only good things can happen to you," he paused and continued thinking out loud with a meditative voice: "I will miss you very much Eddy. You have changed me, and many more. I bless your life and I will never forget you. Be sure I will continue praying for your life, your destiny, and I want you to always look back and remember where God has taken you out from, only to be grateful that you were rescued and you had rescued many more because you were obedient. I bless you my brother. God has great plans for you, never forget that."

I cried with Steve Wilson, my second tutor and mentor, and a great friend I had in my imprisonment. Steve influenced my life for ever and I will always be grateful to him and he has a part of my grateful heart. I am so grateful for you Steve and will never forget you. I bless your life too.

I cried of joy that night as I told my cell mates, but I was also afraid of going out so soon. I had been in a "safe" place all this time and I didn't know how the outside world would be for me and what the future was going to be like. After all, inside prison, I had a place to sleep and "free" food.

29

The Verdict Changed by God

The letter said that they forgave me five years of my time in prison for my good conduct, but the rest of the sentence, the five forgiven, I was going to be under Federal supervision. This means that I was going to have to report myself every day to the Federal office: let them know where I worked and lived. Also if I had no job, I had to tell them. I could go out and look for a job again to start my new life as a new person. God was giving me a second opportunity, but this time, taken by His hand.

I couldn't stop smiling after the good news and unexpected blessing. I started to think of all the people I wanted to contact to tell them my story and the good news of Jesus in my life. I couldn't wait to look for all those people I met on the streets, that lived in the streets and survived in the streets. I wanted to find them to ask for their forgiveness for being part of the bad things out there, but also to present Jesus and a new life vision with Jesus in their heart. I was marveled, since I was about to graduate from the university with a degree in theology, a great accomplishment I had not done while I was free. My brother Hector offered higher level education to me, and I refused it. I wonder how my life would have been different if my ego was not in the way all the time and I would have learned English early in my days in the US and then go to the University.

Five years had gone by since I got imprisoned and I kneeled for the first time that first night I was in the isolation cell for those thirty days. Since I saw that light that gave me peace, I did not see life the same way. I kneel myself very often to ask God for His guidance and everything has changed in my life. I see everything so differently. I observed the flowers and the trees around me, they are so beautiful, where before I took them for granted. God's creation is beautiful.

That night, after praying and breaking down with pastor, crying of fear, of happiness and of joy, I finally went to my cell. I shared everything that had happened to my cell mates and they had never heard of anyone getting five years off the sentence forgiven. They were joyful with me because it was a miracle that we were experiencing. No one, before going to court to prove innocence, has gone out before time. A full miracle had happened.

After all of them went to sleep, of course I couldn't sleep. I was too excited with all this going on. So I start searching for God with all my heart thanking Him for His mercy over my life. The letter said I was to go out when I finished the first sixty months of my sentence and that meant I had two more months to go before going out. Soon this will take place.

It was the end of October and I was to go out in early January 1997. I was graduating in December. So, taking advantage that everyone was sleeping I start searching for God with all my heart.

I started thanking Him for letting me out soon, thanking Him that I was going to be in front of the judge soon. I also thank Him for giving me the opportunity to go back to Brooklyn and Manhattan to preach to my lost friends. I thanked Him for letting me met them and started to mention name by name of all my alcoholic friends, my drug addict friends, my burglar friends, with whom we stole to survive, and all those people that had no future in their life.

I asked Him also to confirm me where I had to start since I hadn't seen them in all this time and I didn't know if I was going to find them in the same place. I prayed intensively and almost in ecstasy. I stayed quiet and I could see clearly in my mind the map of El Salvador drawn in my mind, and I came out of it like fighting with the vision and I would tell God my plans of going out to those people I had met in my lost years in New York. I even wanted to preach to the Federals that got me locked in and thank them for doing so. I continued praying and thanking Him for the great gift He had given me to go out before the time was up, and to have time to go out to preach the gospel to every creature as the Bible says in Matthew 28:18–20.

> And Jesus came and spoke unto them, saying, All power is given unto me in heaven and in earth. Go ye therefore, and teach all nations, baptizing them in the name of the Father, and of the Son, and of the Holy Ghost: Teaching them to observe all things whatsoever I have commanded you: and, lo, I am with you always, *even* unto the end of the world. Amen. (Matt. 28:18–20, KJV)

And this was the scripture that was guiding me to do my evangelization plan for my friends, and I would say, "Lord, please confirm my plans so that my path is blessed by you. Bless my path toward El Salvador. Sorry, Lord. I am going crazy here. Please bless my path going out of here, I meant to say."

I continued praying and I couldn't stop thinking of El Salvador, and I stayed silent for a few moments. I couldn't talk but in my heart I felt the great need to go back to my home country and I thought I was going crazy. I constantly saw the map in my mind and I have a spiritual fight in my heart and with God. I was like in a tridimensional stage in my mind because I wanted to go to Brooklyn and Manhattan, and God would show me the map of El Salvador, and not New York.

"I do not want to go back to El Salvador," I told God. "I have nobody there, and I have too many years away. I know no one and I do not want to go there" I hear myself telling the Lord.

I am astonished at myself for what I just said. I breath deeply and I close my eyes again. I see again the map of El Salvador in my mind and I find myself telling God I have no one to go to in my country. All my family is dead.

"You have your wife and your daughter out there," I feel the Holy Spirit is telling me in my heart.

"My wife? She must be married already and probably have a new family. Why should I go there? I can't change that," I tell Him in my heart.

I didn't know what was happening. Three times I said the same thing arguing I had no one in El Salvador and three times the Holy Spirit told me to pray for my wife and my daughter whom I had practically forgotten. I could see my life restored away from the Mob, the drug dealing, I could see how He had preserved my life even in the worst moments of it, and I could see the miracle of getting me out of prison before time, but going back to El Salvador to look for Maria Elena? That was crazy and too far away in my mind and my wildest wishes.

I had a spiritual fight with God for a long time discussing with Him and telling Him that there was no reason for me to go back when I had too much to do here in New York. And He kept reminding me I had Maria Elena and Guadalupe waiting for me there. Fighting with God, I fell asleep and dreamed of the beautiful volcanoes and mountains we have in my country.

I dreamed of the beach and all the nice places I knew before coming to this country. I didn't understand. I frankly thought He put them back into my mind to pray for their souls and to send angels to protect them. Maria Elena has most likely remarried and probably has more kids. She deserves to have a faithful husband and a man next to her—someone who protects her, not someone who abandoned her. Everything she deserved and that I was not capable of giving.

"Bless Maria Elena, Father, and rescue her soul. I beg you to do so. Please bless my daughter too."

30

The New Letter

Right before, the day comes in January to be in court to go out five years before time, I received another letter. A federal official gives it to me and says, "Mr. Jiménez, your are officially receiving a deportation order for breaking the laws of the United States of America." This letter comes from immigration officials.

"Deportation? What? But I am a resident. Why will you deport me?"

I couldn't understand what was going on in my life. On one side they condone five years for behaving well and on the other side they are giving me a deportation letter from immigration?

"Could it be possible that God was preparing me because He knew I was going back to El Salvador?" I ask myself. "He knew about this letter way before I did! I will lose my residence status for sure!"

Inside prison, there are other careers that we can get prepared on and there are prisoners that help other prisoners with the laws and the sentences because they have studies in law school inside prison if they had been college graduates before getting locked. There was one who had specialized in immigration and deportation laws. I went to look for him after I got that letter.

"They will take you to court and they are going to declare to you there and then why you have a deportation order. But you have on your favor the good conduct shown all this years, plus the condonation received before even asking for it, by the Federal Prison. You can fight over that. What happened is that four years ago, Senator Janet Reno pushed a law saying that if any resident or illegal alien broke the law, with a violent crime, including drug dealing, stealing, murder, and the like, they must be deported to their home country. Only US born citizens shall be able to stay here, like me, as I have no other nationality and no country to get deported to."

"This law has only been approved in New York and a couple more States, and since you were sentenced in New York, even though you are in another State now, it applies to you directly," he explained. "So when you are in the deportation trial, you will be able to defend yourself with the good you had done in the Federal Courts.

I go to court when my time of federal prison finishes after five years, according to the Federal Court, and in that same court, the people from Immigration services take me and transfer me to a new prison in Oklahoma. They send me in an airplane with two guards. This is a prison where the ones to be deported go temporarily. They had everything planned and coordinated that same day.

God is starting to impress my destiny from here in a way I could not expect. Nothing I had planned goes with God's plan. To begin with, they transfer me in a nice airplane, an Airbus. Even though I had handcuffs, I did not feel so worthless as before, because I had no chains. When I got to Oklahoma, they took me to a closed building without gardens or courts or patios outside to walk or exercise. It was all air-conditioned/heated building. It was a fifteen-story building and all the cells where for two people, but for some reason, they put me alone. I was impressed that He was taking care of me even though I was fighting with my deportation as I couldn't understand it.

All the prisoners that come to this building for the first time, they are assigned to the first three floors and the most dangerous ones in the top floors, is what I learned of how we were distributed. The prisoners that where there temporarily while waiting for the deportation sentence, they put us in the central floors, between the fifth and the eighth floor, and we were supposed to be there for only three days. As if this was a three-day hotel stay, but with prisoners. The guard, when I registered, assured me that I was going to be there for only three days too, while they arrange my deportation. I had no other choice but to surrender to God's will, even though I still fought inside myself with that idea of going back to my home country.

Every floor had everything we needed: The cells, of course, plus a hall, chairs, a TV room, a dining room place which was also the place to sit and talk. The TV room was the largest place, and it was surrounded by thick glass where they could observe us from outside, plus they could observe us from the cameras all over the place. The capacity was a maximum of eighty prisoners per floor.

Since I was the first one to get there that day, I was assigned immediately to the kitchen to wash dishes and help in the kitchen. Back to step one. I fought with God in my heart because I didn't understand why He was bringing me back to step one. I was going back in my life, instead of forward, I would meditate.

Again, I would start my job at 4:00 a.m. till 9:00 a.m. Then they would let me go rest a while until 11:00 a.m. Then I went back to the kitchen from 11:00 a.m. to 3:00 p.m. and from 5:00 p.m. to 7:00 p.m. I was in the serving meals place for noon and night. I would take a big spoon to serve the meals to all the prisoners, the same way I did in my first Federal prison. Those few days I wanted to testify about Jesus and the forgiveness of all sins to as many people as I could. It was going to be a short stay, so I had to use my time wisely. My free time was used for that. I met a boy that was there because he killed an elderly woman who after doing that horrible act, tried to suicide himself but never got the courage. He accepted Christ as his savior. If I was there for only that boy, I was happy about it even though I couldn't understand God's path.

I evangelized and at the same time I would fight in my heart on the idea of going back to El Salvador. I was decided to fight for my right to stay in the United States, since I had no desire to go back to my country.

Every floor had its television place, but there is no orientation to anything when you get to that prison. Everyone survives the best way they can. Some are murdered inside, and others are raped. Those guys that go into prison for raping a woman, they are raped by other men in an accepted revenge to the right the woman had lost and for the rapist to learn his lesson for not being sent to the electric chair. The murderers kill out of love, or hate, but hardly after raping a woman. We, the drug dealers, had never seen anyone that had raped a woman, since that was out of the code. We could fall in love with them, buy them expensive presents to buy their heart, but never rape a lady. They were sacred to play with, maybe, fall in love, or have a good time with them, but never ever rape them.

The third day came and went and I wasn't called out. So, the fourth day I go back to the kitchen but started wondering what was going on. In the first break of the morning, I go to the official and asked him what has happened with my hearing.

"Why am I still here? I am supposed to be free already and they told me I was going to stay here only three days. Today is the fourth day and I do not know what is going on."

"I have no idea why they haven't called you. Probably there is something they have to clear out in immigration that is not defined yet. You are a strange case to court, I guess, but don't worry. You are fine here."

Again, I started to pray intensively and God started to work in my heart and to treat it to soften and do as He wished. I thought that maybe God wanted me to be close to Him, praying all this extra time and to pray for Maria Elena and Guadalupe seriously. Without knowing her marital status, I had to pray for her salvation. I prayed for their hearts so that when they see me, they can have a soften heart to have the opportunity to talk to them, listen the gospel, and if He had mercy, get their forgiveness. I wanted to have the opportunity to let them see me as a renewed man, and not that greedy, grouchy, neurotic man they had seen the last time. Even though I hadn't accepted to go back to El Salvador, IF I did, I wanted that opportunity, and I prayed for their hearts.

The fifths day, I still did not know what was happening. Time went by slowly and even though I had some things to still do in the kitchen, I had more time off and that was driving me crazy. These five days felt too long. I couldn't understand what was going on.

"What do you want with me Lord? Why do you still have me here?" I would ask again and again.

Analyzing myself in those long days, I still had a huge resentment against Juan and I asked God to take it out of me. All hatred that I could feel against all of the others who talked against me, I asked him to take it away from me. I still praised Him and thanked Him for letting me in the bad things because that was the only way I had met Him.

"God, if You are taking me out of here, I ask you to change my heart completely. All men that I had mistreated, the ones I had hurt, the ones I did wrong to, forgive me for it. Please make me free of all those wrong things in my life. Your Word says that I have to love my enemies, but I do not know if I am capable of doing so, but you know it. Try my heart and make me free—totally free. I beg Your forgiveness for abandoning my wife and daughter. I ask for Your forgiveness for all the bad things I have done."

I prayed that again and again. It was desperation what I was feeling. I was there without knowing what was going on—almost out but was still in. I still did not understand God's plan. I couldn't see it. By now, all I would do in the kitchen was serve food, and I had a lot of free time. It was driving me nuts.

31

The Miracle

I was in the TV room lying down, watching TV with other people when I heard the electric doors next to the common area opening. It has a loud noise when they close as if someone is hammering. They open for two reasons: when new prisoners come in and when prisoners go to court or out. Otherwise, there is no reason to open because the guards use the elevators which have a code and a key to be used for them to come in and out of each floor.

Curious, I turn around to see who was coming in, as if I was going to know someone. I never know anybody because two prisoners that know each other must never be in the same prison, as I had said before. To my surprise, the last person I could ever think I was going to see again, comes in. I never know anyone, but this time, God was taking me to the extreme heart test I could ever have. Juan comes in. To the same floor, out of the fifteen. Juan is there.

The same Juan that introduced me to the drug dealing. The same I had shouted out of my lungs in court that if I found him I was going to kill. That same one, whom I had resented for my punishment of ten years. That same Juan I had prayed about yesterday and today, is the one coming into my floor. I had just prayed to God to prove my heart. I had a long beard, but when he recognized me, he panicked, because we were the same guys, but I was a different person and he didn't know it. To my surprise I did not feel resentment, I felt compassion for him. We had not seen each other since that horrible day in court where I shouted at him. It was literally impossible that we be together according to the internal laws of prison. But again, God was showing me He is the expert of the impossible.

Juan knew nothing of me, and I knew nothing of him, but I had asked God to change my heart completely and to prove it. I feel compassionate toward him and a fraternal love instead of hatred or resentment. I shake inside because God is working my inner self. I am confused and for a short moment I feel afraid of him and myself, because I do not know how will I react if he attacks me. I do not want to know. I can forget all the things I have learned and experimented so far.

"God, please, take control, and guide me please. Guide my words, give me wisdom, please, please," I would repeat to myself. "Guide my words to him, wisdom words, take control over me and this encounter please," I kept praying in silence, maybe for a minute or less, but it felt like an hour.

One of the reasons why prisoners that are on their way to court can't stay more than three days is precisely because they can encounter other people of the same crime. They can make contact for good or for bad. They never know. And besides, the others don't know if they are working as undercover or as a protected witness to get more evidence. It is too risky and they try not to have this happen ever. I rapidly think that maybe he is getting deported too and I was not supposed to be there any more, but they didn't check.

The miracle happened in my heart first. I was there, in front of the person whom I had shouted I was going to kill in court, the one who put me in all this trouble. Juan went to a corner to sit on the floor as if he was a scolded cat. He was silently observing me. I could see him with his panicked facial expression. I sat down in front, on the opposite side, to observe him and observe my heart.

I wanted to be cautious when coming close to him. I was silently praying to have the right words to him. He was the first person I had to ask for forgiveness and this way I have to prove my heart to God.

Finally I get up and start walking toward him and he gets so scared that he starts shouting out, "Auxilio, auxilio! Me quiere matar! Auxilio!" (Help, help! He wants to kill me! help!)

"Cálmate, Juan. Solo quiero hablar contigo." (Calm down, Juan. I only want to talk to you.)

"Auxilio, auxilio! Me quiere matar! Auxilio!" (Help, help! He wants to kill me! Help!)

"Cálmate, Juan. Cálmate, Juan." (Calm down, Juan. Calm down, Juan.)

"Fight, fight, fight!" chanted the other prisoners, and a big mess is made right there.

"Auxilio, auxilio! Me quiere matar. Auxilio!" (Help, help! He wants to kill me. Help!)

" Cálmate!" (Calm down!) I say firmly and I throw myself to the floor to hug him to hold him and calm him down. He was shaking and I said softly to calm him down, "Solo quiero hablar contigo, te lo juro." (I only want to talk to you, I swear).

"What's going on here?" asked a guard with a fully loaded weapon.

"Nothing. He doesn't know English and wants to go to the bathroom. I am trying to help him, but he got afraid," I said calmly.

Juan gets puzzled with my reaction. I am not the same man he saw the last time. Finally he calms down and sees I really want to talk to him. When I was just going to start to talk to him, the bell rings and that is the sign to lock us up.

So I go to my room and start praying. I thank God for the reencounter and I start seeing the magnitude of that miracle. What it really means. God, in His infinite mercy, in the perfection of His will, He made up this Godly appointment. This is a Divine date and this is the reason I am still in that prison. I am not free,

I am not deported, I am in a prison that it is impossible to cross with other prisoners of the same case. Wow! I am here to serve my enemy, whom I can love. The saying "Love your enemies" came alive in this encounter. A friend, a partner who became my enemy, is now someone I can love and show it to him. My heart is hit with emotion, primarily happiness and joy. God has taken me to this moment to present the gospel to my 'enemy'. To get saved my worst enemy? Yeah! That is the purpose. God reminded me that it was His plan to meet Him. He let me get into the bad paths to meet Him otherwise I wouldn't have looked for God otherwise.

This is my opportunity to talk to Juan about Jesus, it is the perfect moment that God had created to ask for forgiveness and forgive at the same time. It was another miracle that can only be created by the Lord. Perfect time to learn that I don't hate him anymore.

Early the sixth day in that prison, I went to the kitchen to help around and then served the food to the prisoners. Juan looks at me busy. I see him too and when he comes around, I give him the biggest portion I could give out and the best food I could give him. I gave him extra things, like extra fruit. Every meal that day I did the same thing. I see his puzzled face, but we did not talk that day. At the end of the day, I take a big apple and go to look for him.

"Mirá, Eddy, honestamente desconfío de vos." (Look, Eddy. Honestly, I do not trust you.)

He looked into my eyes in fear.

"Yo sé Juan, pero mira, han pasado cosas extraordinarias en mi vida y quiero compartirlas contigo. Dios ha cambiado mi corazón, y soy otro." (I know, Juan. But look, extraordinary things have happened in my life, and I want to share them with you. God has changed my heart, and I am not the same—)

"No me hables de Dios, estoy peleado con él, no sirve, no existe para mí. Además, ni religioso que soy, para que me estés hablando de Dios." (Don't talk to me about God. I don't want to know anything of Him. He is nonexistent to me. Besides, I am not religious for you to talk to me about God.)

He continued.

"Si de verdad me querés ayudar, mejor ayúdame con otra cosa. He tenido problemas con el negro que tengo en mi celda y quiero cambiarme porque temo por mi vida." (If you really want to help me, help me in another way. I have had problems with the black guy I have in my cell, and I want to change cell because I am afraid he will kill me.)

"Veré lo que puedo hacer." (I will see what I can do.)

That same afternoon, I went to the official and explained the problem that Juan has and that he is afraid to die. The official looks into the booking records and sees that the only cell that has space is mine. I am still alone, so I go back to Juan and tell him, "Dice el oficial que te va a mover a mi celda, pues es la única que tiene una cama vacía." (The official says that he will move you to my cell because it is the only one that has space.)

"No, a tu celda no. Me vas a matar buey. Me quiero salvar de ese negro para que me mates vos, no buey, ni que estuviera loco." (No, not your cell. You will kill me, man. I want to get saved from that black guy, and now you will kill me? No way! I am not crazy man.)

So I go back to the official to tell him that Juan does not want to move to my cell.

"Tell that him that this is not a hotel. Either he changes with you tonight or he stays with the black. He has no say on these things."

That night, he moved to my cell and all lights went off almost immediately he moved in.

Yes, it was not a hotel, but every three days they gave us shampoo, toilet paper, soap, shavers, a comb everything we needed for our daily cleaning needs. They changes sheets and towels every three days too. Every three days we were supposed to be out of there, that is why every three days they gave everything new. It was my second three days in it and it was my sixth day, and tomorrow it will be my seventh day and I was going to receive everything new again since I had no news about my case.

That night, we talked about his wife and kids and what had happened to them. I asked him if his wife would visit him but he said that to save his kids from this tragedy, he had asked her not to come close or communicate in the best interest of the children. So he knew nothing of them anymore. His time in prison had been very different than mine. His heart was still hard and had anger for getting caught.

He hated himself and was still in internal dilemma with the system. He was so confident that he was never going to get trapped that he had never imagined himself locked in. Of course, all the ones who make the bad, think that they will never be caught. I was one of them. But God's word says that there is nothing hidden from God that will not be discovered. One day sin catches up with us, and God always finds a way to find us. We are the ones that fight with Him to try to control our lives. We are the ones that deny God's love for us and continually fight over His mercy. Oh, we are so stubborn! At least I was!

I totally forgot that time went on and I was still in that place. We spent three days together with Juan, just like Jonah in the womb of the big fish. Three glorious days in which I could testify of all the miracles I had had. All the great experiences I had with God, since the first day. I told him my first miraculous encounter in the isolation cell, the jobs I have had, the encounter with Howard when I was moved to another prison, and then my tie with Steve Wilson. I told him about my Theological studies and that I graduated from college, and then I told him about how they had forgiven five years of my sentence—which is half of my sentence—and that I was free, but now I was there to be deported, or maybe stay if I convince the judge. I didn't know about that part yet. I was going to fight in court to stay, but God had the last word. He listened to me cautiously and in disbelief. His stay was different as he hadn't learned any new skills so far since they still don't trust him. He was there temporarily to be moved to another prison.

My heart was moved in an impressive way those three days. A new cycle was given to us. I had no resentment toward Juan, I only felt compassion, fraternal love and felt pity for him. I wanted him to receive Christ in his heart, but even though he listened to me, he was still in disbelief. These were three days for my heart to be restored from an enemy, who was really my friend. Three days to preach the gospel and God's love toward His children. I preached intensively about God's love and forgiveness until the fourth day, my tenth day inside that prison. At 3:00 a.m., they came to my cell. It was not a weird time, in the middle of the night, since I started to work at 4:00 a.m., I would get up around that time. But they came to tell me, "Eduardo Antonio Jimenez, pack your things. They are coming for you in half an hour."

When I was waken up, I understood the greatest miracle that Jesus had done in my heart. He had restored me in all senses. I had peace, restoration, unconditional love, and I hadn't understand it yet.

I hugged Juan very emotional and I could feel his sorrow and us crying from a very sad good-bye I had ever experienced. I felt so much love for him in the right sense, Godly love to be more clear. I felt as if I was leaving my brother behind. I wanted him to know God, and I couldn't do it, so I hurt inside for it.

When he hugged me, he told me in my ear, "Eddy, verdaderamente tuve miedo cuando te vi la primera vez. Y cuando entré a tu celda también. Cuando dormías, me apresuré a agarrar el peine y la rasuradora para hacer un arma mortal contra ti. Pensaba cómo iba a matarte, porque prefería matarte a ti primero antes que tú me mataras. Pero a medida que iban pasando las horas, y te escuchaba atento he podido ver que realmente eres un hombre cambiado. Casi no dormía pensando a qué horas te mataría, pero veía esa cara de paz en tu rostro, que no podía hacerlo. He visto que Dios sí existe al escucharte y deseo que algún día pueda conocerlo como tú lo has conocido. No es mi tiempo todavía. Solo espero que Dios no llegue demasiado tarde a mi vida,"

(Eddy, I was really afraid of you the first time I saw you. Also, when we were alone in this cell, when you fell asleep, I would go to get the comb and the razor to make a weapon to kill you first if you attack me. I planned how to kill you first so that you wouldn't kill me. But as the time went on, and as you talked to me, as I listened, I could see you are really a changed man. I hardly slept thinking when I was going to do it. But I couldn't do it. I have seen that God exists while listening to your miracles, and I wish one day I can meet Him too. I just hope God does not come to me when it is too late. It is not my time yet.)

He showed me the comb with the razors in it ready to kill me and finishes, "Veo un hombre diferente al que conocí en las calles." (I can see a different man from the one I met in the streets.)

He finishes and let me go.

"Quiero conocer a ese Dios, amigo." (I want to meet that God, my friend.)

He said that with a smile.

"Dios te bendiga Juan. Realmente quiero que conozcas a Dios. Ese Dios verdadero que me ha salvado y me ha cambiado. No siento ningún rencor hacia ti, todo lo contrario, pues si no fuera por todo lo que vivimos juntos, jamás hubiese sido rescatado por el Rey de reyes. Te amo en el amor del Señor, Juan. Búscalo y lo encontrarás," (God bless you, Juan. I really want you to know God. The God who is real and has saved me and changed me. I feel no resentment toward you. It is the contrary because if it hadn't been for all we lived through together, I wouldn't know the King of Kings, who rescued me and will rescue you too. I love you in the name of Jesus, Juan. Look for Him and you will find Him.)

With that, we said good-bye. I felt bad that I couldn't get to the salvation prayer with Juan, but at least I testified to him and planted the seed. I pray for his encounter with the Lord.

32

The Verdict Changed by God continues

They moved me to another Federal Prison. This one was for only deportation people. I learned fast that it was huge. It had a capacity of around five thousand people. Every day there were deportations. This was the very last stop before deportation to the home country. I heard of deportations of people sent to Russia, Germany, Israel, France, México, Guatemala, Nicaragua, El Salvador and many other places.

We were all illegal aliens or prisoners with residency that had broken the laws and had a deportation order. A year had gone by since I left the prison where I served with Steve Wilson and all this year, God had treated my heart. I had asked Him for peace to accept His will, whatever the sentence was.

We were ten prisoners that passed at the same time with the same Judge. First we went to a small room where we got a lawyer assigned. I prayed to accept God's will in my destiny. In my group we were of all nationalities. There were a couple of Jews, gotten for armament traffic, a guy from Nicaragua, a Guatemalan, both for drug traffic, but since they were illegal, instead of going to prison here, they were simply deported to their countries of origin. There was a German that had raped a girl, so a little of everything. All illegals, except me. All deported to the country of origin.

I heard the story of the German man. He has an anguish face and my heart jumps out and I cannot stay there without talking about Jesus.

"Buddies, as the Apostle Paul I talk to you today. We all come from different countries but we are all in the hands of one judge. For some is a loss to be here and for others it is to find death further ahead. We do not know if we will find forgiveness or deportation with the judge. But what I see here is a common thing. We have all committed errors, otherwise we would not be here. We have sinned. We have all violated the human laws, the laws of the United States, and we have all been trapped, braking the laws. This reminds me that does not matter our personal condition, our past or our sins and errors, God gives us a second chance to be in front of a Judge some other time, but this time it is the Supreme Judge, who died for our sins around two thousand years ago and He was sent to the cross without sin, to pay for our sins.

"We are here to pay for our errors, but Jesus paid for our sins already. If you repent today and receive Him in your heart, He can start changing your lives and your destiny. He changed mine and I feel peace. We need to accept Him in our hearts to start changing. We are here all the same, with our orange jumpsuit with chains around us. We are here to pay for our errors, but Jesus paid for them already. We need to repent to change our lives. The Judge will take away our physical chains, but the internal chains, the chains of the bad that we carry on ourselves when we go back to our countries, only Jesus can break them. If you want to give your heart to Jesus and ask him to change your life, and you want to go one day to the Eternal Judge, repeat after me...

"Jesus, please come into my heart. I beg you to forgive my sins and to make me a new creature. A new man for a new path that You will guide me to. Help me please to take better decisions. I beg You to become my personal savior in the name of Jesus, Amen."

It was a quick prayer as we had no time to waste. To my surprise, everyone prayed with me: the Italian, the German, the Guatemalan, the Mexican even the Jews. I was glad I could be used for this crucial moment in our lives. Right after I finished praying, God's sovereignty was showed to me. I was the first one to go into the court.

"Thank you Lord for the short time I had to show Your mercy to these people. Please help them in their paths. Please help me with the judge I am about to go. You are my Supreme Judge and You have the last word for my destiny," I prayed in silence.

The female judge hears my hearing and the declaration of the sentence of why I am about to be deported.

"Mr. Jiménez, the Judge is there, next to you, but if you have something to tell the court in this moment, it is your time to speak or be quiet for ever," said the lawyer.

"Honorable member of this court, with all the respect that you deserve from the State of New York, the Supreme Court, and the same law that has brought me to you in this place, and like it says in the dollar bills, God bless America! God has blessed my life and God has been real in my life. He has transformed it, He transformed my heart and my being while I have been imprisoned. And the same way you believe that God blesses America, God has blessed my life. You see, I did not ask to have my sentence shortened from the Federal prison, but God made it happen, and now I am in the mist of a deportation sentence of a law that came out one year after I was sent to prison."

"Mr. Jiménez, are you a born again Christian?" she interrupts.

"Yes, Your Honor, and the sentence that you have in your hands is what I did before I came to know Jesus as my Personal Savior. I met him in my Isolation Cell the very first day I was sent to the Federal Prison, and my transformation began that very first night. So this morning I am pleading you to let me go back to the streets of New York to do things right and try to rescue all my lost friends. My country was in war for more than twelve years and it is probably all destroyed and I really do not want to go back there," I finished and kept silence.

The judge looks at me and kept silence for about two minutes, thinking about her decision.

"Do you have $1,000 to go back to New York and start again?"

"No, of course I do not have them, but I can see how I can get them," I answered promptly, not knowing how to get them. I did not think about that possibility. How naive, of course I need money to stay or to go. Either way I need money and I had received two cents an hour for all this years. I have a little, but not close to $1,000. Maybe 10 percent!

"Mr. Jiménez because of your good conduct in the federal prisons, and because your country had been in war, I give you your freedom to stay in the United Stated of America without loosing your Residence so you can start again a new life and make a new story of it. You will still have to present yourself daily to a federal office for the rest of your original sentence as it is stipulated of now, that is…mmmm… for the next forty-five months."

Another miracle! I thought. *Thank you, Jesus.* I prayed in silence as I close my eyes, thanking the judge and my Lord.

I was the only one not deported. Many things came up to my mind. I had a whirlwind of emotions inside. I felt successful and my desire of staying here was given to me. They took me immediately to another cell in the same prison, but in another floor while they did all the paperwork to get out and I get somehow from who-knows-who $1,000 bucks needed to go back to New York. I had no idea who to ask for this money, but I knew that God was not going to let me alone in this procedure and He must have a plan. The rest of the guys were sent to their embassies to get them a temporary passport and then to the nearest airport to go back to their countries.

In that cell, I was alone again and I started to have my second spiritual fight with God. First I started by thanking Him the opportunity to leave me here in the U.S. and start again doing things right. I thanked Him and broke down crying of joy. While I was praying thanking Him for this outcome, my mind went back to thinking about El Salvador.

"Eddy, you want to stay here but I have other plans for you. Better plans for your life, your future," I felt God talking to me.

That was it. I stopped praying and started meditating. Those words echoed my mind and I couldn't get them out. I started to fight in my heart and my mind because I really, really did not wanted to go back. The country is getting rebuilt after war and I had nothing else to do there, but to look for Maria Elena to ask her forgiveness. Nothing more. I could not even imagine the possibility that she was still single after all these years of silence. So I started thinking that maybe God wanted me to go to El Salvador to do exactly that: Look for Maria Elena, talk to her, and ask her forgiveness and then go on to South America as a missionary talking to the people in the streets, or at least that is what I can imagine myself doing IF I go back home . I still fought with the idea to go back. It had no sense to me. I could call her to ask for her forgiveness by phone. Why expose myself to lose my residency? It didn't make sense.

I was free to go, but I stayed in prison. I didn't have the money to go out and I was fighting with God. For a full week, I stayed in my cell and I hardly went out to eat. Even though the cell door was opened, I stayed inside praying and praying. I fasted most of the time fighting with God. I repeated to him again and again, "I have no one in El Salvador. I do not want to go there, please God, take that out of my mind. Let me work for You in this great country."

But He insisted and everyday I felt more and more conviction in my heart that He was calling me to go back. He wanted me back to El Salvador and I couldn't understand His plan and the dimension of it. I continued fasting and fighting in my heart.

Finally, I asked for a paper and told God, "Okay, Lord, if you really want me to go to El Salvador, I need peace in my heart and that You confirm it to me physically because I still want to stay here."

Like Gideon proved God, I proved Him too. I asked for something that was impossible to be resolved, even though He had shown me He was the master of the impossible, I pushed it the farthest I could.

To prove God, I asked for His confirmation by writing to Pastor Steve Wilson.

Dear Pastor Wilson,

It has been more than a year since I left your side, and believe it or not, I am still in a prison, in Oklahoma. I have been treated by God in a very hard way. He is cleaning my heart to the max, giving me unexpected trials where I had gone through successfully learning that my heart has really changed. I am stronger spiritually but right now I have a serious fight in my heart. I finally went to court to be sentenced to be deported but the judge gave me the opportunity to stay in the United States because of the war that we had in my country. All I need is $1,000 to go back to New York. You know I would give them back to you as soon as I can.

But the truth is, that my fight with my internal self is that my heart says I should go back to El Salvador. I feel God is telling me to go back but I really do not want to go back. I am afraid to go back because I have nothing there, and the opportunities to work are smaller. God insists I should go back but I resist myself. I am in panic to go back as I do not know what will I find. I feel more secure in this country and I know God can use me here as well.

Because I know you are a man of God and you will pray to God for the answer I need, I am sending this letter, not knowing if you will ever receive it. Whatever God tells you in your heart, I will accept and obey without fighting anymore.

I know I am asking the impossible, but God is the master of the impossible. We have seeing it too many times.

In the love of the Lord,

Your servant,
Eduardo Antonio Jimenez

I folded the letter, asked for an envelope and I put in the envelope and wrote on it: Chaplain Steve Wilson, the name of the prison and the name of the State where he was. In the top left corner I put my name, my prisoner number, and the name of the prison I was in that moment. I was still in Oklahoma. For six years, I had not received any letters. The Federal laws prohibit correspondence between prisoners and also from prisoners to officials. No correspondence is permitted at all of that type. We could only receive official letters, or letters from people outside the prison, like from friends and family. I had none of them. So since the system prohibited such correspondence, and the Chaplain was also considered "official," I did not know if he would ever receive it and if I was going to receive an answer back if he did. I sent it anyway. It was my way to prove God to confirm His decision to send me to my country.

The mail takes three to five days to get to a destination inside the United States and other three to five days to get back if answered in that same day. So I was not expecting anything for a week. But five days later…

"Eduardo Antonio Jimenez you have mail!" they shout.

My heart pounding hard, as I wasn't expecting anything for a few more days. This was too soon, it is probably another official letter, I thought. In that week, the officials had asked me if my plane ticket and the money is in the way to go out and I just told them I was waiting for it.

My hands were shaking when I received it. Sender: at the left top corner said: Reverend Steve Wilson. I had pushed my faith to the maximum intensity and the miracle maker, and He had answered. Another miracle.

I held my breath when I opened the envelope, Steve Wilson has sent me a card with a picture of the world on it. It also had animals: elephants, monkeys, lions, giraffes, and many more. Animals from all over the world. Just as if it was Noah's ark's animals but without the ark.

Written in it was Philippians 4:6–7 and a note which says, "If God is taking you to El Salvador, He will use you there. Whatever happens with your wife, that is secondary. Do not fight with God. He knows what is best for you. Go in peace."

I look into the Bible and search for Philippians 4:6–7 to confirm what it says.

> Be anxious for nothing; but in every thing by prayer and supplication with thanksgiving let your requests be made known unto God. And the peace of God, which passeth all understanding, shall keep your hearts and minds through Christ Jesus.

I stay silent in shock. I didn't want to hear those words, but I knew they came from God.

As soon as I finish reading those verses, I kneeled to God thanking Him for his mercy, His answer and His patience with my spiritual fight against His will. Again I break down crying out my fear and thanking Him for understanding the dimension of His will in my life. I didn't know what was waiting for me out there, but His presence is so strong in my heart, that I have no more doubts of His will. I do not know what is waiting for me out there, but what I know is that I have to obey. He wants me to go back to my starting point: my home country.

It was Saturday, and even though it was a weekend, I asked for a phone to call my lawyer.

"Joe, I am Eddy Jiménez, and I need you to represent me in court please."

"I did that already Eddy, and you are free to go to New York, why are you still in prison?"

"That is exactly what I need to talk to you about, I need you to represent me again."

"You don't have the thousand bucks don't you? You want me to lend them to you?"

"No, no it is not that Joe, I need to talk to you urgently and personally to explain myself."

"I will be there Monday morning, early in the morning. I hear you nervous. Is it something wrong? What did you do?"

"Well, something has happened, but it is nothing wrong. Maybe you will not even understand it, but I have to talk to you in person. I will be waiting for you first thing on Monday morning."

Joe arrived at nine on Monday, and he was surprised that I was still there. He did not understand why I was still there and what the urgency was about.

"Joe, I need your to represent me again to get out, but not to go to New York, I need to be deported to my country," I tell him at once.

"What? You are crazy, man! How in the world can you think of that? If you ask for deportation, say good by to your residency, you loose it for ever, did you know that?"

"Nope, I didn't know it, but I suspected it."

"Why do you want to go?" he asked puzzled.

"Tell me something, what happens if I go to New York for a while, I work for a few months to save some money and then I go to El Salvador?"

"That is not possible. You have to report yourself for the next forty-five or forty-eight months to the feds. If you don't, that puts you in the category of 'escaped from the law'. You become a fugitive, in other words. They will look for you and they will bring you back to a prison to finish the full term inside. So no, you can't do it because that is illegal. You can only go after finishing your time without a problem nor losing your residency."

"Then, the only way I can leave legally is by being deported?" I told him, analyzing the situation. "This sounds illogical." And I continued.

"You will probably don't understand it, but God is urging me to go back to El Salvador. Believe me, I have fought against that idea for the past month and I got to a point where I tried God to give me an impossible sign, and he did it against all odds. He has confirmed in my heart that I belong back home and I need to go to look for my ex-wife and my daughter to ask for their forgiveness for all that I made them suffer."

"What did you do to try God?" he asked me a little curious as he didn't understand my petition and didn't care much about God either.

"I wrote to Chaplain Steve Wilson of my former prison and he answered back," I said very seriously.

"You did what? Oh man, you are definitely crazy. How could that letter go out? Your God is awesome. Maybe I should meet Him too."

"I don't know, but it did."

I also told him that an official came over to me over the weekend and asked, "Well, are you leaving or not? Why are you still here if you are already free to go? You have not received your ticket yet?"

"I am waiting for a person on Monday since I still haven't gotten my ticket to leave," I had said to the official. He stayed puzzled, but said no more. "I continued praying and fighting with God, trying to find my peace about this decision," I told Joe.

"Eddy, are you understanding very well what you are asking me? If we go to court, there is no going back. If I ask for your deportation, which has been pardoned, and they deport you, you will not be able to come back to this country again. Never again. Are you clear about it?"

I looked down and, with a timid voice, said, "Yes, I understand. That has been my point when arguing with God, but even though it is not what I want, I am following what God wants for me. I understand that I leave behind any opportunity of doing things right in this country, and sincerely, I have no idea why is God taking me back home. After fighting all this time against this decision, I have surrendered to His will and I have to trust Him that He knows better what to do with me, even if I do not understand right now. Will you help me?"

With a continued puzzled face, the lawyer did not understand my decision, but he understood my conviction and he had mercy on me. He saw I was desperate to define my situation to change the judge's decision.

For me it was very clear. I had analyzed all the scenes possible: if I stayed, I would have to work for a few years until finishing the ten years given reporting myself daily, having enough time to save and then go to El Salvador without loosing my residency, but God was not taking any risks with me, and closed all opportunity to the Devil to work into me tempting me with something that would make me go back to my old man. I knew exactly where I had money hidden in New York and I could play with temptation. When getting deported, from that place, they send you immediately to the embassy and then to a plane to fly you back. As a deported person, I could fly back for free and leave behind everything: my past, my friends, everything. My plan was not God's plan so I had no other choice but to follow His plan. In that instant, I remembered Isaiah 55:8 (kjv), which says, "For my thoughts *are* not your thoughts, neither *are* your ways my ways, saith the Lord."

When I go back to the judge, she was more than puzzled with my decision and she explained to me that if I leave the country I was loosing all legality in this country.

"We have no time for games, Mr. Jiménez. You said that you have no one in your country, and eighteen years have gone by.

What are you going to do over there?" told me the judge trying to change my mind.

I just looked at her, tempted to decline my petition, but my heart explodes with a certainty I had never felt before. It was as if the Holy Spirit was filling me up with courage when I opened my mouth. "I understand, Your Honor. It is really not an easy decision, and it is not my decision, but God's decision. I do not understand it myself."

"Are you sure you want to go back to your country?" she asked again interrupting me.

"Yes, Your Honor. I am sorry for all the trouble I have caused, but as I told you, now that I am Christian, I am more than sure that it is God the one sending me back. I do not understand why, but I need to obey. That is my last petition to your court, Your Honor."

"Without further do, and to go on with the next case," the judge says (after explaining to me that I was going to be banned from entering the United States for the next five years, not forever which I thought it was great because I did not expect it), "Prisoner number 5122 has been granted his voluntary deportation as soon as possible. Next case please."

I was sentenced to be deported to El Salvador on July 14, 1997, eighteen years after I left my family behind. I was thirty-six years old by now.

Two days after God's changed verdict, I was in a plane flying toward San Salvador in obedience to the Lord and against my will. I did not know what will I find after the war, or how was God going to use me, but as Abraham left his family behind to go to a new destiny he had no clue where it was, I was kind of doing the same, but the difference was that I was going back to my home town with no plan sketched out. Even though I had grew up there, I had no idea what was waiting for me.

33

Returning Home

After I received the sentence to go voluntarily deported in the court, I go back to the prison to prepare my transfer. I am in Oakdale, Oklahoma, in the Immigration Detention Center and I have to be transferred to Louisiana to the El Salvador's consulate, the closest to Oklahoma.

So when I get to the cell, I kneeled myself again to thank God for His decision and to have given me the courage of doing so. I break in tears while thanking him what I do not understand and I literally feel in my heart that God says, "I did it so you know that for Me there is nothing impossible and even though your plan was to preach to your lost friends, my plan is another. In El Salvador I will show you my plan, the plan of your life. Go like Abraham went and I will show you great things."

So now I am totally convinced in my head and my heart that God wants me back. I still think that my relationship with Maria Elena is definitely broken, but she deserves an explanation and deserves to find peace in her heart as I had. Reconciliation is out of the possibilities, but forgiveness is my goal. And it is exactly now that I feel totally in peace with my decision. I feel congruency in my heart and mind and I stop fighting internally. There is no going back, as the lawyer says, and I feel peace. A supernatural peace. I start interceding for Maria Elena's soul and my daughter's and pray for the opportunity to be able to sit down and talk like two adults. *She probably has a wonderful husband and more kids, and she deserves it*, I thought without being worried about that. All I was interested is in her soul and her salvation.

The following day, early in the morning, even before breakfast, they take me in a road trip from Oklahoma to Louisiana, where my Consulate is. The protocol dictated that to transfer a prisoner, chains have to surround him or her. I was chained as the protocol said, knowing I was getting free anyway. Two federal officials accompany the trip. When we got to the Consulate, the person in the front desk stopped the officials and told them that I could not enter with chains because that was Salvadoran territory. They were not afraid of me and they treated me as a human, as a citizen and not as a criminal as I looked with the chains. I thank God for His mercy in my mind.

They asked me who I am and what have I done. I summarize where I come from, and why I am there. They asked my parents' names and I told them but clarified that they were dead.

"Both of them?"

"Yes, both of them. Mom died when I was about four, and Dad when I was about six."

Surprised, they continued asking me questions and I continued answering them all. They were asking questions for about an hour. Seeing that I answered all without hesitation, and honestly, the good and the bad. Then, they took pictures, get my fingerprints and they put my data in a cardboard type document that was given to me as a temporary passport. They just believed all the data I gave them since I had no documents with me. I cannot prove my name, birth date or the names of my parents, so they just believed me. The only document I have, is the court's deportation papers and my number of prisoner.

"Do you have any open case or crime in El Salvador?"

"No, I don't."

"Did you started drug trafficking since you were in El Salvador?"

"No, in Nueva York about ten years ago."

"Do you plan to continue with the drug trafficking in El Salvador?"

"No way! I have left that behind because I am a new man, transformed by God. I just want to obey Him and do things right. I really regret all the bad things I did in this country, well in the United States, and I have asked for my voluntary deportation even though I had the choice of staying in the United States, God has pressured me to go back to my country and start again doing things good and honestly," I answered honestly.

After ninety minutes of questions and answers, I was given my provisional passport to be able to travel back that same afternoon. The Federal officers take me to a flight that goes direct to El Salvador.

They take me to the airport handcuffed, but not chained. The officers have to be next to me until they sit me down in my assigned seat. I was to go into the plane last. When they finally called me and with all the passengers seated, the officials start walking by my side, and they are stopped at the entrance of the boarding stand. The flight attendant tells them I cannot walk into the plane with handcuffs, so they have to take them off before entering the plane. They can go with me, but with no handcuffs. Surprised, they obey. I felt dignified again.

So they take them off and they walk with me in the hall up to the back of the plane, where my seat was. It was in the last row next to the bathroom. I am in the middle seat, on the left. In the hall seat is a young man around twenty-five, no more. The other window seat is empty.

When I sit next to the young man, I feel so strange. The Federal officers leave the plane. When I entered I was a prisoner and in two minutes I am a free man. Instantly I am free! I forgot what it felt to be free! I can't believe I am in a plane again, going away from the American nightmare. It was everything, but a dream, that's for sure.

The guy looked at me and said, "You got into trouble, huh?"

"Yeah, for a while I did, but I am a new person now," I told him eagerly to start preaching the gospel with no fear or shame. We did not introduce ourselves, because we start talking immediately. So I didn't learn his name. The environment felt so weird when I walked into the plane, as everyone looked at me and I could see their faces with fearful expressions upon seeing the Federal official following me. I just walked seriously and sat on my seat. It was nice that the young guy did not get scared of me, all the contrary, he was so nice, I was surprised. Everything happened so fast, and as the federals leave the plane, they give us instructions to buckle up.

In my own thoughts, I start remembering that the first time I got into a plane was to go to Mexico to come to the US as a wetback through Mexico. Eighteen years have gone by since that day. I cannot believe it!

"It feels weird to finally be free, but thank God all is over! He has changed my life forever," I tell him to start sharing the gospel with him. But then he interrupts, "You are a Christian now. I can see."

"Yes, I am. And you? Do you know Jesus?"

"Of course I do! I am Christian too," I looked at him with a huge smile.

So we started talking happily about our lives and our present situation. And suddenly, he interrupts and says, "Let's see. Tell me your story."

So still without knowing his name, but feeling both of us safe talking to each other, I start telling him how hard it was to cross the border illegally, just to go to prison for the first time with the trap that my half sister put on me. I knew no English and I got into her trap. And right there I start my story and every fifteen or twenty minutes, he interrupted and said, "God has a great plan for you. Actually, God sent me to keep your company and to assure you that God is the one acting on you so you have more faith, things will be okay. Just have faith."

"Yeah, right," I said and without taking him seriously, I continued with my story. I told him about my encounter with my brother and how I lost his friendship and all relationship with him. How I started to live in the streets starting to loose myself little by little as I entered the sub-world in the streets.

All the flight we talked, it was like five hours we talked, or shall I say, I talked; but he always interrupted me every fifteen or twenty minutes, saying the same things.

"God has great things prepared for you, and actually, I have been sent to you. God has sent me to you so you know that this trip is God's plan and to make sure you will be fine. All you have to do is have faith." Similar words, or the same, every twenty minutes during the whole five hours.

When I was about to finish telling my story, when I got into that plane, he asks, "And what have you planned to do? Are you going to look for your family? Your wife? Your daughter?"

"My ex-wife," I said. "Not today. I have no idea where they are."

"Your parents?" he asked.

"Well, I skipped all my youth, and I have had no parents since I was six." He frowned.

"Where do you plan to spend the night? I know God has a plan for you and I am here to keep your company."

"I really have no plan. All I know is that I have in my mind to look for a childhood friend's house, whom I helped to cross the border with me, but he did the right things and I am sure he has prospered. I lost track of him, but God is directing me to his house."

"And how are your going to look for your friend who is not here?"

"No, man, I will look for his family, his mother. I am hoping his mother is still in this country. That is what I feel in my heart I should do. But I am not sure where they live. Remember I have eighteen years of not coming back and I skipped the war, so I do not know if she moved during the war.

"Continue with that faith, my brother, that I will keep your company. If you do not find her tonight, you can come over to my place," he says very excited by the adventure that is about to start.

"How are you going to San Salvador?"

"By bus, I suppose."

Honestly, it was very strange to have an invitation to go to his house that night since I just met him and I still have no idea what his name is. I was thankful, though for his offering, as that became my plan B.

Everyone got out of the plane, but the instructions were that I had to go out last. The last one to board and the last to get off. My luggage was a little box with my Bible, some underwear, a pair of T-shirts, some devotionals, and stop counting, that's it! That is all my luggage. I also had a few dollars because I had worked in prison for two cents an hour for many hours. That added up.

"At the exit, we continue talking," said the guy and left. "I will be there to see all that God is going to do tonight."

When I got out of the plane, the airport officials—or shall I say the immigration officials—were waiting for me.

The immigration official went next to me, and a couple of policemen followed us to the basement where I see some offices and the airline luggage storage rooms. He sat me on a bench, and they handcuffed me.

"They are going to be right with you," said the official and left.

We landed around 6:30 p.m. and after thirty minutes, a policeman appears again and asked, "Have they taken your fingerprints?"

"No, Official, not yet."

"Someone is coming then," and he disappeared.

Forty more minutes go by, fifty minutes, an hour and finally, another official comes over.

"Have they taken your fingerprints?"

"No official, not yet."

"Someone is coming soon," and he disappeared.

I start worrying since it is getting darker and darker by the minute. I start to pray, finally, since I cannot get up to ask for assistance. I start praying for a miracle to happen in my life again. I am hopeless there, with no rights. Or do I have rights?

Finally, after waiting for approximately an hour and a half, a third policeman comes over and asks exactly the same about my fingerprints. He takes off my handcuffs and takes my fingerprints.

"What do you have in that box?"

"My Bible, devotionals, and underwear. Do you want to see it?"

"Are you Christian?" he asks with wide eyes.

"Yes, I am, I found Christ in prison," I tell him to testify.

"I am too and I go to the Taber," he says with a smile. At that point I have no idea what the Taber was, but I am happy that a Christian has come to take my prints. Another miracle.

"When you settle down, I invite you to my church. I will give you my number so you can call me," he said nicely and he wrote his home phone in a piece of paper.

I just can't understand how everyone is so nice to me. The guy in the plane, and now this guy.

"Do you have any charges in El Salvador?" he asks.

"No, I don't."

Why were you deported?"

"I asked to be deported voluntarily. The thing is that first, I was accused for drug trafficking, and was given ten years in prison, but after I served five years in prison they let me go out on good behavior. I just got involved with the wrong people which I have repented already. Then, I was free to go, but immigration gave me a deportation sentence, even though I was a resident because of a new law in New York. So I was given the choice to stay or come back. I had chosen to stay at first, and it was granted, but God put in my heart to ask for a voluntary deportation, and here I am," I said sincerely.

"You are not doing the same here, are you?"

"Nope, that is finished in my life. That was the old me. I am a new man in Christ. I plan to share my story with other people without hope, so that they can meet Jesus too, like I did."

"The procedure is that you have to go to Mariona Prison for seventy-two hours while we investigate that you have no charges here." Mariona is the most populated prison in San Salvador, the capital city.

"But I have done nothing here"

"You have never had any problems here?"

"No. Never."

"Do you have family?"

"Nope. My parents died when I was a kid and I used to have a wife and a daughter before I left to the United States. They are the ones I come to look for so that they forgive my abandonment eighteen years ago.

"You left when the war started?"

"Yes, and my daughter was three."

"Are you still married to her?"

"I don't know, but I doubt it. I have no idea. The last time I talked to her we fought and I asked for the divorce. That was long time ago and I haven't communicated by phone or letter ever since. So I do not know my marital status."

"But you are coming to ask for forgiveness even if you are not married?"

"Yes, that is what the Lord put in my spirit."

"Look, I really should keep you seventy-two hours while the investigation of your precedence goes on, but I feel you are sincere and you are no trouble at all. I will let you go tonight and I will do the paperwork for the details of your deportation. Don't worry. Just call me when you can to go to church with me."

And again, *another* miracle. God sent another angel to rescue me and to skip all the protocols. He gives me his phone number and tells me the way out. It is extremely dark by now as it is late.

I go walking down the external aisle of the airport, in front of the glass doors of the counters, all the way down to find a bus or a taxi. When I am walking down, out of a taxi comes out a male voice shouting, "Eddy, come on in!" I turned puzzled. Who in the world knows me here? I asked myself.

When I come close, I see that it was the guy from the airplane, that I never knew his name. He learned mine, because in my narrative I would mention my name.

"I will be your witness of what God will do in your life tonight. Come in, I will take you to San Salvador."

"No, don't worry. I will take a bus home."

"You are crazy, Brother! The buses stop coming at five thirty, and it is almost nine! Just come in. Don't fight with God."

And without a better option and recognizing that this guy was another angel sent by God, I come into the taxi offering to pay half of the ride.

"Come in," said the taxi driver. "He has told me about your life, and I am Christian too. I also want to see with my eyes what God will do in your life. I have a lot of expectations tonight, and God has put in my heart not to charge anything so I can witness the miracle in your life."

Every step I take is a miracle itself. I am surprised of everything happening since I decided to follow God's command to come home. Every detail is a confirmation that God has a perfect plan for me.

"Where are we going?" asks the taxi driver.

"I don't know. All I know is that the family of my friend Oscar lived near the general cemetery by Santa Anita."

"That place has changed a bit because now there is a four-street road: two going south and two going north, and an overpass. They turned down many houses, but we will go to see what we find. Do you have faith?"

"Sure… I have faith?"

"Continue like that, with a lot of faith because God has sent me to witness all the great things that He will do in your life," the young man said again.

We got to the General Cemetery around 10:00 p.m. it was a place not too familiar to me. We stopped in front of some houses to start searching for my friend's house.

"We want to see your faith and we will be waiting until they open the door," they encouraged me.

I started ringing the door bells looking for the Arana Family. One after the other, it was not and they did not know them. I rang door bells up until around 10:30 p.m. Then I go back to the cab.

"No one knows the Arana family," I told them very disappointed, frowning.

"Can you recall another detail of the house or anything that was near? Something else that might guide us?" asked the taxi driver.

"Well, all I remember is that their house was near a cafeteria where people from different companies would go to eat breakfast and lunch. People who worked in Yamaha went there very often," I told them trying to remember more details.

"Continue ringing bells. One more and give that new detail. You have faith, don't you? Search until you find," said the guy.

"But look at the time. It is almost 11:00 p.m.!" They look at me and make signs to go out and continue my search.

I ring a bell in a house that has a dim light and a lady, who appears to be in her seventies, comes out the window to see out. She sees me, and puts on a bright light and opens the door. I excuse myself. "Madam, I am sorry for interrupting at this late time. I just arrived into the country and I am looking for a family of last name Arana, the family of my childhood friend Oscar Arana."

"I am sorry," she said in a sweet voice. "I do not know any Arana family."

"They had cafeteria where the employees from the Yamaha would come to eat," I insist, "I have not been here during the war as I left in 1980 and I have no other contact but them and I do not really remember where they are located," I can feel my anguished face by this time of the night. I am starting to desperate.

"I do not recall the last name, but the only cafeteria that has been in these zone is two blocks going down the street, near an orange house. Go that way," she said, pointing to our left.

"Thank you so much for opening the door at this time of the night, and thank you for giving me a clue. I am so sorry to bother so late."

"It's alright! Go in peace".

I go running back to the cab and told them the new clue I got and the taxi driver says, "Oh, yes, I remember exactly where it is, now that she mentions the way and the orange house, I know where it is."

With a big smile on my face, around 11:20 p.m. we get to the place. God makes such incredible and impossible things to happen, when we are in His path and we search Him with all our heart. Even though I am worried about the time, my new friends keep encouraging me to continue with the search.

We all got down of the cab when we got to the place: the taxi driver, the Young man and me. The light is on. They observed me as I went to the door to ring the bell at that late time of the night. Trembling, I do it. My heart is pounding so fast. A girl about thirteen opens the door and gets scared to see a man standing there and she shuts the door on my face before I can even start talking. I hear her running inside calling her Mom.

I turned around to see my new friends and they make me signs to ring the bell again or knock the door. I rang the bell, again. Total silence. My heart pounding like a thousand times a minute. I hold my breath as I hear some steps coming toward the door. I feel I am about to receive my new miracle. A woman about my age opened the door, stared at me for a few seconds, and with tears in her eyes, shouted happily, "Eduardo Antonio Jiménez!"

I jump back from her reaction and I am impressed she calls me by my full name and I step back.

"Honey, run to where Mom is, and tell her that Eddy is back!" turning around to her daughter. The girl goes out running and the woman steps up to hug me and says, "Eddy, you came back! Don't you remember me? I am Ana, Oscar's sister!" I am paralyzed by this welcome.

As we are hugging, the girl didn't understand, but obeyed her mother. I look at my friends with a huge smile in their faces, observing the miracle we were hoping to find. The young guy comes over to bring my box and to say good-bye. I hugged him and thanked them for keeping my company in this search. And he says, "Today, I have seen God create a miracle of love in front of my eyes. Continue with that faith! Remember God sent me to be by your side to see this miracle. See ya soon!" the taxi driver waved good by with a huge smile. I could see some tears on the young man's eyes, as he was as excited as I was.

And he disappeared from my life. Never knew his name, never saw him again. Up to this day, I think he was an angel with a mission to keep my company as he said. There is no other explanation.

"Come in, come in Eddy, my mother is coming soon. She is in a vigil and she will be so happy to see you." But I insisted of staying outside until her mother came. It was not a good time to go into a house without a mother present. After all I am a decent man.

Oscar and Ana's mother came in running not believing the miracle of me standing there in the front of their house almost at midnight. She came in crying of happiness and came in running jumping to hug me tightly, as if she was hugging her own son Oscar. She is crying as if I am a lost son. I don't understand why so much commotion. All I know is that I helped Oscar to go with me to the United States without charging anything and he has grown in his success over there. I lost track of him since I got arrested in front of him. Oscar stayed in the right track working hard, learning English and getting better jobs every time from what I learned from them later. He sends money for his mother and sister every month. They are grateful for what I did, I can understand, but crying and hugging me like that? I didn't understand.

When the mother calms down and stops crying from the happiness of seeing me she starts explaining. "I was in a vigil, and we were exactly praying for your salvation and for you to come back home. You have no idea how much we have been praying for you, for your life, your salvation, your wellbeing. We have years of praying for you!"

She hugs me again and now, I am the one crying as I hear her words since I didn't know God had people that I do not know praying for me. I fell on my knees and understood that God was definitely in all this process. The taxi driver and the young man, were both angels in my life. They saw with surprised eyes, how Ana received me: Ana's happiness and her mother's tears, were all too much to be just a coincidence. This was the closest to another miracle in my life. I couldn't understand the presence of God in all this. I just couldn't digest all that I had lived in the last twenty-four hours since I asked for my deportation. It was too much to handle without shaking of all the wonders around me.

We all kneeled—Miss Isabel, Ana and I—thanking God for all His mercies upon my life, for all the miracles in my life and for helping me find them that night. We prayed I don't know for how long, but we did not feel our knees hurting at all. Our spiritual connection was so strong, we just prayed and prayed and prayed thanking Him for everything.

Finally, we finished crying and praying, and we sat to talk. By now it was past 1:00 a.m.

"You have no idea how much we have been praying for you, Eduardo. I was in a vigil, as every month, interceding for your life. We did not know anything about you, except that you were arrested long time ago and assumed you were in prison," she started.

I never imagined that my friendship with Oscar since we were children, was the one that God was going to use to find a place where to stay that night. My heart was so grateful for that welcoming and I still could not understand all of God's mercy over me.

Without having to ask anything, she said promptly, "Don't worry about anything. You can stay here all the time you need."

"Miss Isabel, thank you so much, I really appreciate your offering, but as soon as I can go to find a place for myself, I will go. I do not want to be a burden for you."

"No, my son. I am so grateful with you for taking my son Oscar to work in the north and showing him the way to have a way of living, that he always talks about you and prays for you too. Oscar always say how good you were to him so he will be so happy to know that you are free and fine back home! So you have nothing to worry about. You stay here for good if you want."

"Thank you, Miss Isabel. I really did not know what I was supposed to do when I came back, but God put in my heart to look for you and I see He was not mistaken. I am only sorry about the time I appeared."

"Don't worry. God has everything planned because we were all up to welcome you."

We talked for a couple of hours some of my bad adventures and my good ones too. I shared with them my miraculous encounter with God that first day in the "transformation" cell. Then I tell them in a summary all the good things that happened inside prison and how I fought with God about coming back and how I had to choose to obey Him and what happened this twenty-four hours until I found them. They were impressed of all the journey since my conversion and happy for me.

"You have to rest, honey, we will continue talking tomorrow, so you tell me more about it. I am tired too," she said looking at the watch and it was past 3:00 a.m.

"Excuse me, Miss Isabel. Just one question."

"You want to know about Maria Elena, right?"

I blushed. "Yes, I wanted to know—"

"I won't tell you anything about her, you will have to learn about her by your own means. All I can tell you is that she is in the same place you left her. It is not my duty to tell you any more."

"Thanks, Miss Isabel." I sighed.

"Are you going to look for her soon?"

"Yes, that is the first mission that God put in my heart. I want to look for her with the only intention to ask for her forgiveness for abandoning her, whatever her marital status is. I do not need to know or meet her family. It is her and my daughter I owe an apology to."

"Go to sleep, tomorrow will be another day" she said with a smile. She gave me a pad to sleep on the floor and a sheet to cover myself.

Miss Isabel was a sweet lady in her seventies, with a lot of energy for her age, but she continued to be a part of a poor family. They did not have a room for me, or a couch, so I had to sleep on the floor. There was no man in that house because Ana was not married, she was a single mother so it was only her (Miss Isabel), Ana's daughter, and Ana. I went back to my childhood years sleeping on the floor. A flashback came to my mind, but this time, I am so thankful for sleeping on the floor. It feels great, actually.

Even though I slept on the floor and this was a poor family, I could feel the most important feeling in my life: familial love and the presence of God in that place. I went to sleep thanking God for all His wonders and blessings since I entered the Consulate, the plane, out of the plane, immigration, out of the airport and in the search for this house. I thanked Him for all the people He put in my way, the angels that kept my company till I found Ana, the happy welcoming I got, all the good things I had experienced since I asked to be deported, following God's direction. Definitely, God had set all these surprises, and they confirmed I had done good obeying God's voice. I can't wait to see Maria Elena again. I am so excited about that moment! I am praying she is also ready to see me and accepts my apology to close that cycle in our lives.

God is good. When we obey Him and follow His path, all the doors that would be closed under other circumstances, He opens them wide and clear. I couldn't imagine all the good things He had prepared for me. I repent from fighting against His will and blessed the moment I got conviction in my heart to obey.

34

The Search

It was Monday, July 8th, the "following day." The day I went to sleep…I woke up at 7:00 a.m. waiting to be surprised by God again this day. Even though I had slept only about three and a half hours, I couldn't continue sleeping. I had a big job to do today. I showered, I changed my white T-shirt, ironed my only pair of pants, and took my Bible ready to go out to look for Maria Elena. I asked Ana for instructions of how to get there from their house, but they did not let me go till we ate breakfast together.

We happily ate breakfast in a familiar environment. The four of us: Mrs Isabel, Ana, her daughter and I. We ate the best fried beans I had eaten in all my life with newly made tortillas. I had forgotten my childhood most eaten food. Immediately I remembered mom serving us beans every morning and every night.

I couldn't believe I had these nice ladies in front of me as my guardian angels while I do God's work. I hadn't had such a lovely environment in such a long time. The only real time I had it was before my mom's death and while I was married with Maria Elena for a few months. Between and after those times, all I had was me with myself until I found God and started to experiment His love. Around ten, I finally started my trip toward the bakery to go ask for forgiveness.

I started to walk from Cucumacayan Street up to the Third of May Street, remembering those childhood places, having some flashbacks here and there. I was walking slowly, praying for her heart to be ready to see me. I was getting nervous the closer I got, and even though I wanted to see her, I was panicking with the encounter and for her reaction when she sees me. I do not know if she will reject me, or have the patience to at least listen to me. I am nervous. Very nervous.

Before going to court the last time to ask for my deportation, I had shaved and had asked to have a hair cut. While in prison, I had grown my beard and hair. My beard was long and not well taken care of, and my hair was so long it touched my waist. I thought about doing something good for me and for someone else, before leaving, so I donated my long hair to the wig companies that make wigs for children with cancer. I had shaved all the beard too, because I thought it was going to be better to appear in a nicely shaved way, than in a hippie look. I had two days without shaving, so I stopped in a Barber shop to shave clean again.

In the barber shop I saw in my way, I shaved to look as clean as possible. Since all I had was dollar bills, I paid with a dollar my shaving job. The barber was grateful because it was more than twice his fee. Our Salvadoran currency by then was colones and the change rate was 8.75 colones for a dollar. He charged 3 colones for the job and got 8.75 in a form of a dollar bill. The barber gave me more specific directions of how to get to the bakery.

I kept walking and praying, and since I was walking slowly because I was afraid to get there, noon time came up. I found a cafeteria and stopped to eat and to meditate some more. I didn't know what will I say, but I asked the Holy Spirit to illuminate me with the right words when I see her. I hadn't had time to think what to say, or write down like a sketch of all the things I wanted to tell her. Everything had happened so fast, my mind was going in a whirl.

Since I stopped fighting with God and decided to follow His will, things had changed so fast, I just had no time to really think what was I suppose to say or do. I had found an angel here, an angel there, but always someone unknown by me, although known by God to keep my company in this adventure. I could recognize all the nice people who treated me as a human being, as a good citizen since I got to the Consulate of El Salvador. No one has treated me as a criminal, all the contrary, I have been received and treated like a king! I have been dignified. Having the young man next to me in the plane, plus him not letting me give up until I found Ana, and her mother, plus the Christian policeman in the airport who goes to the "Taber," and let me go instead of sending me to a national prison, is a miracle after another. I had had much more than I deserve. Now I am the son of the King; and He is treating me as such and not as a criminal, which is all the enemy knows how to do well with the lost.. I was living in a dream! I have been transformed!

Finally, around 2:00 p.m., I find the courage to continue my path toward the Third of May Street. I get there just about 3:00 p.m. and rang the bell. The first thing I see is that five kids run out of the house, playing, when they open the door.

Good Lord! Maria Elena didn't waste her time. She is full of kids! I thought. *But I do not blame her. She had the right to do so.*

I sigh and my mother in law comes over to the door opened by the children.

"Good afternoon! Is Maria Elena in?"

"Who is looking for her?"

She asked, looking at me with a puzzled expression.

"Jiménez," I said as she always called me by my last name.

"Jiménez, Jiménez died in this house."

"No, Jiménez died but he has resurrected."

"Jiménez?"

"Yes, Mama Tita. It is me."

"Jiménez! What are you doing here?"

She finally asked in a welcoming voice.

"Visiting. And I want to know if Maria Elena is here because I want to talk to her."

"Maria Elena is not here. She is at the supermarket."

"Can I come in to wait for her?"

"No, you wait for her outside. She will be here any minute now."

With a smile on my face, I went to the other side of the bus stop to wait for her. In a few minutes a bus stops and my heart starts pounding fast but she does not come down from it. When I start calming down, a few more minutes later, another bus arrived and from it, she comes down carrying some bags in both hands. I cross the street as fast as I could and I see she stops at the little store next to the bus stop. She still had not seen me, and that stop gave me time to cross the street and go to her. She had to wait because there were other people in front of her.

"Can I have a Coke please?"

"Make it two."

Recognizing my voice, she dropped her bags to the floor and turned around. Then she looked at me with a scared face.

"What are you doing here?"

She asked without hatred in her voice; it was also not with rejection but with genuine question and fear. This calmed my nerves.

"I just want to talk to you, if you will let me."

I told her as sweetly as I could, looking into her eyes directly. My heart was full of love all over again.

"What do you want to talk about?"

"That's the point. I need to talk to you to tell you all the things that had happened, and I want nothing more. I just come to talk to you. I am not asking you for anything."

I waited patiently for her answer as she stared at me without a word.

Maria Elena

I looked at him in silence, observing his newly shaven face. He looks so different than the last time I saw him and my heart is exploiting of happiness, but I do not want to show him that. My long time prayer has been answered and he is back! I am excited to see him and I am extremely happy to hear his voice. I do not understand myself, I hated him so much the last time I saw him, but today, I feel so blessed to see him again and I had been waiting for this moment for too long. Of course, I want to talk to him, but I need to be cautious. I wanted to hug him and kiss him all at once, but I didn't. I needed to know his intentions.

"Help me with the bags then."

I told him as coldly as I could after a couple of minutes. He had gotten the Cokes and paid for them too.

Eduardo

I take the sodas and pay for them as she observes me for the longest two minutes of my life. I grab the bags and followed her in silence.

When we get to the house, she tells the kids to go out to play because she has a visitor, and she tells me to come in. We sat down in the same sofa we used to sit when we were together. The old sofa of our life together was still there, as if time has not gone by, but I do not mention anything about it. Maria Elena looked at the wall clock. It was 3:30 p.m. when she said, "You have thirty minutes."

With that sharp tone of voice, I thought that her husband would arrive after 4:00 p.m. and she did not want to have him find me inside the house. It was too complicated to explain that I had appeared after eighteen years of abandonment. And she was right. I do not blame her and understand her petition.

"Thanks for the opportunity, Maria Elena."

"I just want to let you know why I am back and I want to tell you my testimony."

I start telling her my story since I left and how Estela had tricked me and then I continued into when I found my brother, we fought and then I started to take too many bad decisions, decisions that took me to prison. I do not enter into details of the bad decisions, or the drug distribution, I just keep it as bad decisions because that is not the point of my visit, but my encounter with God is. I want to start from my first day in that isolation cell because that was when my transformation time began.

"I want to tell you what I experienced since I got to the isolation cell and I met God Himself."

I started telling her the extraordinary experience I had that night and how I could see in a vision how she was searching for me but she was far away.

That same night, I started to pray for you and asked God to have you in good health and started to pray for your soul. Three days later, I got a Bible. This one [and I show it to her], and I started to have an inexplicable thirst for reading it, and I had not stopped reading it up to this date.

Maria Elena

I heard him listening carefully and I was so surprised for his transformation. I could see his face was different and he was so happily telling me his story, I just sat there and listened without interruption. I had to keep myself serious and give no signs that I had been praying for him too. I could not put my feelings in between, because I have to put him in trial to see if he is really transformed for good because God had sent a prophecy to my life that he was going to come back transformed. It was hard to believe and even though I could see it in front of my eyes, I had to prove his real transformation. I have to put it to test.

When he says he starts praying for me and my soul, I looked at the wall and coldly said, "Your thirty minutes is up. Sorry."

"Can I come tomorrow?"

"Come back tomorrow at the same time and I will give you another thirty minutes."

He gets up politely and leaves attending my instructions without saying a word. When he goes, I go directly to my room and I kneel myself to thank God for his return and for his encounter with the King. I break down in tears and I know I am ready to throw myself to him and hug him and kiss him all over again forgiving him his absence, but I need to be calm and try him out. I am ready to forgive, but I am still resented in many ways. Mix feelings are inside and I just can't play around anymore. Either he is transformed and I will forgive or he is a fake and he will disappear for good from my life. This is a decisive moment for my life after all this years waiting for this miracle, but I am ready to let him go if he is not the transformed person I have been promised by God.

I can't wait for him to come back tomorrow. I count the hours but say nothing to Guadalupe.

Eduardo

I didn't want her to just listen to my story, my intention is for her to learn about the love of Christ in my life and hers, and everything He has done in my life. Everything that He has forgiven so that she comes to His feet too. I wanted to close this circle and reconcile my own life looking for her forgiveness, and then I could go on with my life, and she will go on with hers, happier than ever together with her husband and her children.

I respected her limits and left without arguing. I did not want her to get into trouble with her husband. I went away happy that she received me and that we had been able to sit down to talk for the first time since I left. I cannot know what is going through her mind, as she was serious, just listening, all the time.

With her permission, I came back the following day at 3:30 sharp.

She had me coming five days in a row for thirty minutes a day, Monday through Friday I would tell her as many details as I could remember of my transformation. I testified about Howard, about Steve Wilson, about the university studies and all the work we did inside prison, trying to get to the point where I was going to ask her to receive Christ in her heart and then ask for her forgiveness.

She listened to me carefully, but was attentive to the watch and exactly in thirty minutes, she asked me to leave. She was saving her husband's heart, and she was right. I admired her for that. She was as nice as I remembered her. Too bad she is not in my life any more. I messed up, I was so dumb!

Up to this point, I have not asked for my daughter Guadalupe. I figured it was one step at a time. First, it was her heart I needed to relieve, and then it was my daughter's.

Finally on Friday, I start closing my testimony telling her about my deportation time, and all the rustling I had with God about coming back. How I finally surrender with the only purpose to come to have this conversation with her. So I end up telling her,

"Maria Elena, I know I cannot change anything that happened in the past. We had lost a life together because of my fault. I cannot change anything, and I do not expect anything from you or my daughter. All I want is to ask you to forgive me for leaving you alone. I look for your forgiveness from the bottom of my heart. I really repented for all the suffering I made you go through. As you see, God has forgiven all my sins, and I do not know if you can forgive me too after all I did to you. After this, you can go on with your life and your husband, and I will disappear from yours and will bother you no more."

Maria Elena

I looked at him, into his eyes as he was speaking, and I could not hold myself back anymore.

When I started crying, he said, "I know I have given you too much hurt and trouble, and I ask you to forgive me from the bottom of my heart, and I want to know if you want to receive Christ in your heart as you forgive me too so He can change your heart too. I am sorry, I am sorry."

I couldn't stop crying and as he said those words, I cried more! I cried because I was removing all the hardness of my heart and breaking all walls I had created between us. I had been wishing to hear those words for the past four years and finally my stone heart breaks down when I hear him saying that he is sorry for everything. After a few minutes broken, I raised my face and looked at his compassionate eyes. From the bottom of my heart, I hear myself, still crying, say, "Yes, Eddy, I forgive you."

He takes my face with his hand and asks again, "Do you understand what you are saying? It is forgiving and not remembering anything, not bringing out all the hurt again. Forgive me as God has forgiven me."

"Yes, I understand perfectly. And after listening to you for five days, I can see you have truly repented, and if God has forgiven you, who am I to not forgive you too?"

Eduardo

I worried when she started crying because I did not know why she was crying. I didn't know if it was of all the anger she had inside or if she was crying and then she was going to get up and send me out for being so selfish expecting her to forgive me after all the suffering. She continued crying when I finally tell her with a broken voice, "Thank you."

Tears start flowing down my face. "Thank you, My Love."

I said that without thinking and without knowing if her husband was going to show up any moment as it was past four by now. She didn't stop me after thirty minutes this time.

Maria Elena

When I finally calmed down from crying out all those hidden feelings, I finally managed to tell him, "Lupita and I have been born again Christians for four years, and we have been praying for you all this time, day and night."

I break down again.

Eduardo

I cannot believe what I am hearing and with my eyes wide open, I remember that around four years ago, God put in my heart to really start praying for their heart and their salvation.

Surprised by her words, I finally get the guts to ask, "And Lupita? Where is she?"

"Every time I had told you to go, it is because she comes back from work around this time, and I didn't want you to see her until I knew your real intentions. She knows nothing of our encounters, but she is about to come in. Wait for her to see her."

I did not expect that surprise, so I finally get up and hug her not knowing her marital status and at this point, I could care less, because I do it innocently and with a fraternal hug, a hug that meant all the forgiveness between us from heart to heart. She hugs me back and it feels so good. My heart blows out of happiness, wishing her back in my life! An impossible dream!

A few minutes later, Guadalupe happily comes in, as she does every time. We are standing there with Maria Elena and as she sees a man there, she stops, looks at me and says between exclamation and question.

"Daaaaad?"

As I shook my head yes, she ran down to hug me tightly. It was a hug I had dreamed of for too many years.

"How do you know I am your father? You have not seen me in years!"

I asked her, too excited for the situation. I cried and hugged my grown-up girl, who I had not kissed or hugged since she was three.

Guadalupe looked at her mother, and she gave her a look of affirmation.

Crying, Guadalupe said, "Because when I was growing up, and I started to ask for my father, mom would always tell me that you were away in a long trip, but that one day you will come back. She repeated to me constantly that when a man comes into the house, it was going to be my father, so it has to be you!"

I could not believe what I was hearing. Now I was the one crying as a child. I had received double blessing that afternoon: Maria Elena's forgiveness and I have a daughter back into my life! My heart stretched out with so many good news. I don't understand. I am puzzled.

As I understand what Lupita is telling me, I turn around to Maria Elena and I ask, "And all those kids? They are not yours?"

"No, you fool. They are my sister's kids, my nieces and nephews."

She said and laughed. Now I was confused. I thought I was coming to ask for her forgiveness and leave to the rest of my destiny to South America as a missionary, but God had another plan for me. He had this huge surprise I could have never imagined in all my life. I had all this mixed feelings with so many emotions in one day.

"Don't go away again, Daddy," I heard Lupita saying. My heart shrank of a pain a father can feel for failing his family, abandoning my daughter when she was a child.

"No, Darling. God has brought me back as a new man to stay with you."

She hugs me again and cries with happiness and joy of having me back home. In that moment I learn that they go to church at the Tabernáculo Bíblico Bautista Amigos de Israel to congregate on Sundays, which is also called the "Taber," the same place the police man in the airport goes to. Now I understand that God created that divine appointment with that policeman. She tells me that she has never been married again or lived with anyone else all this time.

When Lupita goes to the kitchen to wash the dishes and we are alone I finally asked, a little frightened, "Maria Elena, I do not pretend to have dominion over you or my daughter, and I am not here to tell you what to do since I myself do not know what is what I am going to do. But tell me something are we still married?"

"Yes, Eduardo, we are still married. I never had the courage to file in the divorce papers because deep inside I had the hope that you would come back."

Now I hugged her in disbelief more confused than ever. God knew what was waiting for me here, but I had no clue. I could have never ever imagine my wife waiting for me until I came back, not even in my wildest dreams I could think that God had prepared a reconciliation with my wife, and He wanted us together again.

"I do not want you to do anything that you do not want. I am really not prepared to come back together. To tell you the truth, I thought God was bringing me to my country just to ask for your forgiveness and then go on with my missionary call toward South America. But God has surprised me beyond my wildest thoughts with your true forgiveness and this great gift of us being still married."

"Yes, I agree we have to pray and start knowing each other again, since too many things have happened in both of us since we were together."

She said the sweetest words I could have ever heard from her. In disbelief, I said, "Yes, let's pray if it is His will to come back together as a couple. If it is His will, it will be so. It is in His hands."

What am I thinking? "If it is His will?" Can't I see it? It is all planned by Him for us to become a family again, and I am still doubting of His power! What a fool I am!

She looked at me and hugged me. I've had so many years of not feeling a loving hug from a woman that I didn't remember how good it felt.

"Would you let me go with you to church on Sunday?"

"Of course, I would love to go as a family."

I couldn't believe the great blessing God had prepared for me sending me back home. How stupid I was by wrestling with God. I just never thought this could be a possibility, not until this day. It caught me off guard.

During that week that we met in the afternoon, I had gone to look for a church to go, as I had no idea of this surprise. I had found one in the Flor Blanca Colony, but of course, I rather go with her. So she took me to the Tabernáculo Bíblico Bautista Amigos de Israel Central, to hear brother Tobi. I was impressed of how big it was and how many services they have. I expected to find the policeman of the airport, to thank his nice procedure, and introduce him to my wife, but it was hard to find him between all those people and all those services. They had one at seven, next at nine, and eleven in the morning, and three and five in the afternoon.

Now that I knew I was staying here, I decided to start looking for a job. I had many skills and I thought I could get a job very soon. I started my search, but the country had started to get up after the peace treaty and I was not willing to lie in my interviews, so when asked where I had worked in the past five years, I had to answer that I worked inside prison in the US. I guess people got scared and I was never given the opportunity to get a job.

Desperate of the situation, I proposed to my wife to move to a smaller church, so that we could have a more familiar type of setting and maybe there we could get some marriage orientation.

We moved to the church I had seen before in La Flor Blanca. I felt God was moving us there to find new opportunities.

A year went by dating, visiting, talking, going to church, and I was still living in Mrs. Isabel's home looking for a job diligently every day trying to move out. She assured me not to worry, but time was going fast and I was feeling bad I was not giving any money into the household.

I got involved in all the ministries I could of that new church, preaching in the Mariona prison which is the largest prison of the country and it was where I was supposed to go for seventy-two hours to investigate my deportation. I would testify all the miracles I had experienced testifying of God's love. I would preach in the buses, in the street, everywhere God sent me, I worked continuously in His works, and sometimes I would get an offering, but a normal eight-to-five job, I could not find.

I was used to going back to Miss Isabel's house walking since I had no bus money and was not going to ask Maria Elena for any. She knew I had non, but this was part of my process, and I was the man, so I never asked for any and she never offered to give me. I was ashamed to ask or to receive it from her anyway. It was an hour walking distance trip and I walked back joyfully every day we met. I was just happy to know her again and to enjoy her sweetness in my life.

One afternoon, after a year of going back and forth from Mrs Isabel's house to Maria Elena's home, going to church together, and dating again to know each other, it was around 6:00 p.m. when she said, "Stay for dinner."

"Thank you, darling, but no. It is late now, and I do not want to go back through those streets too late in the dark into the night. Maybe another day. Let's plan a lunch or a breakfast, don't you think?"

I said as softly as I could not to offend her for the offering.

"You are not understanding, Eddy."

She looked at my daughter as she continued. "Lupita and I want you to come back home."

"I have seen enough evidence of the change that God has done in your life, and I had asked God to help us adapt ourselves into our new life together."

I was shocked as I am caught off guard, again. God has everything arranged! I guess she was ready even though I wasn't. All this time, we had dated as if we were a new couple and had never even insinuated to have any intimacy relationship. We were like new boyfriend/girlfriend relationship.

I didn't know anymore what it felt to have a woman next to me, as I had had no intimacy with no woman since I left her. It sounds weird, but it is true. I was too timid to approach anyone, and she was the only person that I had felt free to be myself. I was really happy that she took the step for this, because I was scared to ask since I had no job. Besides, I had forgotten how it was to live as a family 24/7. I had daydreamed about it but had no courage to ask.

That night, I returned for good to the home I had abandoned. I came back to my home in an extraordinary way, miraculously, may I say. And in that extraordinary event, after searching for a job for more than a year, that same week, as if God himself sent the signs, He opened the door to serve in a ministry full time with my wife, as a family. God was waiting for us to be a real couple to send us to His works, paid by the ministry. This time, Maria Elena was ready to leave the bakery to follow me wherever God sent us. So we moved to Usulutan, about two and a half hours from home. It was a dream. Except that Lupita couldn't follow us because of her job and university studies. In a way, it was good, because it was time for us alone to become closer again as a real couple.

I now understand that my redemption started since I was conceived in my mother's womb. God, in His mercy, had it all planned out, so I could experiment everything, suffered as I did, to let me get up to the point of being in the bottom of my life to start working on me. I had to go down, to get up, be hurt, to later feel peace, for Him to transform my life, inside out. He took me out from the dark to the light. He got up to the redemption of my soul rescuing me in all possible ways a man (woman) can be rescued. It has made my family an example of restoration in the impossibilities of the circumstances. God changed my Verdict for sure.

You do not have to be in the bad paths to meet Him, but know Him to do His Will. He restores everything. I have seen it, and I have lived it. I am a walking miracle that can give testimony of it and of Him.

35

Conclusion

If you have had a hard, hopeless life—filled with abandonment, rejection, depression, bad decisions—and you have lost all hope to fix yourself, please give Jesus an opportunity to work in your life. If the main character in this story was restored against all odds and had overcome all obstacles, you can too. With Jesus in your heart, there is nothing that can stop you from turning your life around and doing things better. In Jeremiah 33:3 (KJV), it says, "Call unto me, and I will answer thee, and show thee great and mighty things, which thou knowest not."

If you feel like you're at a dead end, like nothing is going right in your life—say, your relationships are broken, your finances are dismal, you feel lonely and misunderstood—look for Jesus. Maybe God has sent you signals, but you have not heard them or you chose not to and tried to fix things yourself. And now you are at a point where you are ready to accept help. The Lord's help.

Maybe you already know Him, and you are like Job when he said in Job 42:5 (KJV), "I have heard of thee by the hearing of the ear: but now mine eye seeth thee." But you have not experienced the last part where you really get to *know* him. Don't give up. Look for Him; and He will rescue you, heal you, and show you the way. Say this prayer:

Lord, I recognize I am a sinner because I had done bad. I need you to show me your way in my life as I had not been able to do a good job. I repent from all the bad I had done. Forgive me please from all my sins. Come into my heart and save me. I want you to be my Lord and Master of my life. Show me your path, and help me become what you created me to be.

I do not know what my destiny is, but you do, so please show me. Write my name in the Book of Life so that if I die today, I go into Your presence. Please surprise me and guide me with Your hand to help me do things right. I entirely give myself unto You, in the name of Jesus, Amen.

Now ask God to show you a church wherein you can learn more of His Word. Read the Bible and congregate in the church where the Holy Spirit leads you to. The denomination does not matter, but the important thing here is your relationship with Jesus. God has a path already paved for you and has chosen you before you were born, since you were in your mother's womb. He is only waiting for you to surrender yourself to Him.

Do it today. Don't waste more time fighting with your own efforts. It doesn't matter what you have done or where you are when you read this book. You might be in prison too or in the comfort of your home. It doesn't matter. God is a god of second opportunities. God is awesome and can turn around any situation around. God makes you a new creature in Jesus's name. Congratulations for Surrendering to Him.

If you do not know what type of church to go to, if you consider yourself a person who is not religious but wants to *know* Jesus, or if you are not sure what religion you are or want to be in, I invite you to search for a chapter of the Full Gospel Business Men's Fellowship International (www.fgbmfi.org) near you. These are a group of businessmen of all religions who'll teach you about the love of Jesus through their transformational testimonies (just like what's contained in this novel). When you listen to those powerful testimonies, the Holy Spirit will help you find a place that is right for you. There are chapters for men, women, and youth chapters. It is not a church and will never be one, but it is a safe place to start knowing more about Jesus and to learn how to have a relationship with Him.

Author's Note

God says, "Call unto me, and I will answer thee, and show thee great and mighty things, which thou knowest not" (Jer. 33:3, KJV).

I made bad decisions in my adolescent years. They were because of the loneliness I felt from certain familial circumstances then. We are the product of our decisions and that of the circumstances that got us to make those decisions. But more than that, we are the constructors of our future, so we do not have to continue living miserable lives the rest of our lives.

I am sure God has a wonderful plan for your life, but *you are 100 percent responsible* to seek it and find it. *What is your purpose? What makes you happy?* What is your dream? Happiness, believe it or not, must be part of your purpose. I am sure God has let you come to this point in your life to let you find yourself and Him in your life. You are not an accident. You have a purpose. Find it, do it, and be happy. You have a mission to accomplish for Him. The sooner you find it, the happier you will be.

It has taken me more than fifty years to find my passion to write. Don't delay yourself that much. Look for God's purpose in your life, and let Him guide you. If you are older than me and you feel incomplete, there must be a reason. And that reason is that God still has a mission for you. Look for Him and obey his will.

I don't know about you, but I do not want to look back on my life when I turn seventy or eighty or ninety and have the following conversation with my grandchildren:

"Granny, is it true that when you were around fifty, you had a dream of writing best-selling novels for them to be made into movies? What happened that you never did it?

"I got afraid no one would like my novels. I also never took the time to start writing because I dedicated myself to serve your parents, my husband, my other children and my parents. Time went by, and now it is too late."

I figured that should not be the answer. It would be too sad. My golden years would be empty and unfulfilled, and I could never motivate anyone to pursue their dreams. I want you to dream big dreams and lift them up to Jesus.

I want my grandchildren to be proud that I followed my dream to write novels and in the process, show them that they can always pursue their dreams if they really take the time to plan them. I want them to ask me, "Granny, can you tell us how you started to write so many good novels? I want to read them all and be like you and go after my dreams, Granny!" That will definitely fill my heart.

Now that you've accepted Jesus in your heart, dream big dreams, and look for God to help you in your path to pursue them. It is never too late to start again. Eduardo did it, and God gave him far more than he could have ever dreamed of.

Yes, this is a novel, but the life described in it can reflect anyone else's in so many ways, circumstances, and situations. Surely you were able to relate with Eduardo or Maria Elena in more than one instance.

I say it again. Look for help and search for your happiness in the mission God has for you. The point is to follow the dreams that God puts in your heart. If you have them, it's because He gave them to you.

Contact Us

You may contact us for any of the following:

1. Personalized counseling
2. Conference with the writer or other leaders
3. The Spanish version of this novel
4. Sharing with us your experience upon reading this novel to give us feedback of the impact in your life

Please recommend this novel. Help us to turn it into a movie by recommending it. You may get your copy at the following websites:

- www.amazon.com
- www.barnesandnoble.com
- www.corteingles.es
- www.apple.com/itunes

With every book you buy, you are making a contribution of 20 (twenty) percent toward Misiones para Cristo (FUNDA-MICRISTO). In El Salvador, Central América.

Send in your name, and phone number so that we can help you the best way possible and get back to you soon. Just drop us a line to tell us your testimony and how this novel helped you. Whatever you share will be treated with utter confidentiality. We wish you a great life full of success here on earth and in heaven and that you get the courage to go after your dreams!

Write to us to at averdictchanged@gmail.com